RESCUED

Where had she seen him before? Those slanted grey eyes and those high cheekbones looked familiar. She licked her dry lips. Metallic-tasting blood trickled from one corner of her mouth.

He lifted her head onto his lap against the white embroidered front of his blue silk coat. With clean fingernails he untied the cruel knots in the stretched leather thong. Raw stripes encircled her delicate wrists.

Her jaw smarted and her cheek still stung from the attack. With gentle fingers, her rescuer bathed her face and hands in the cold water brought by one of the servants. Then he lifted her onto the back of the wooden saddle.

As soon as he settled himself in front of her, she slumped against his back, her head on his shoulder, arms loosely encircling his waist.

She breathed in the clean man-sweat. Who was he? Why had he helped her? The heat of his body soothed her. The horse stepped forward.

Megan's spine stiffened. She remembered! She knew where she'd seen him before. His was the face from her dream. . . .

HIGHLAND JADE

Stephanie Bartlett

BANTAM BOOKS
TORONTO · NEW YORK · LONDON · SYDNEY · AUCKLAND

HIGHLAND JADE

A Bantam Book / September 1988

ISBN 0-553-27208-X

Published simultaneously in the United States and Canada

Bantam Books are published by Bantam Books, a division of Bantam
Doubleday Dell Publishing Group, Inc. Its trademark, consisting of
the words "Bantam Books" and the portrayal of a rooster, is
Registered in U.S. Patent and Trademark Office and in other
countries. Marca Registrada. Bantam Books, 666 Fifth Avenue, New
York, New York 10103

PRINTED IN THE UNITED STATES OF AMERICA

KR   0 9 8 7 6 5 4 3 2 1

To my children,
Joshua Bartlett Kaine
and
Ariel Jennie Stultz,
I lovingly dedicate this book.

Special thanks to:
Penny Lee Colvin, Con Sellers and the class, Meg Ruley, Barbara Alpert, Mr. Ray Kell, The International Cultural Society of Korea, Mr. Moon Toe Sang, Mr. Oh Young June, Mr. Kang Jung Sub, and
my mother,
Sidney Charmaine Morrison,
who all helped make *Highland Jade* a reality.

Characters

FROM SCOTLAND

Anthony Devlin, friend of Jemmie Carlisle, entrepreneur
and rogue
James (Jemmie) Carlisle, young husband of Megan, now
deceased
Megan Scott Carlisle
Anne Bruce Scott, wife of Robert Scott and mother of
Megan, now deceased
Robert Scott, father of Megan, now in the New World
Robbie Scott, brother of Megan, now in the New World

THE HOUSE OF KOH

Koh, patriarch and husband of several women divers
Sonyŏ, youngest wife of Koh
Grandmother, oldest wife of Koh
Jung's Mother and *Kwang's Mother*, two of Koh's other wives
Tai's Mother, next-to-the-youngest wife

THE HOUSE OF YI

Yi Jongwhan
Yi Jongsun, Jongwhan's younger brother
Yi Dong Chul, father of Jongwhan and Jongsun
Munja, Jongwhan's wife
Yang and *Pu*, Jongwhan's grooms

KISAENG

Madame Lee Insung, mistress of the *kisaeng* house
Lee Soonhee, Madame's daughter
Sin Pilsu, foster daughter of Madame
Ok's Mother, an old cook
Hanyo, a serving girl

THE HOUSE OF CHANG

Grandfather Chang, an old, blind fortune-teller
Chang Kwangin, his five-year-old grandson
Chang Youngsook, his fifteen-year-old granddaughter
Auntie Soh, Chang's housekeeper and neighborhood mid-
    wife
Im Young June, Youngsook's husband

THE ROYAL FAMILY

King Injo
Crown Prince Sohyon
Prince Pongnim

THE MANCHUS

Yongolda and *Mabuda*, Korean turncoats, now Manchu
    generals
Kong Yuduk, a Manchu general
Emperor Chung Te, originator of the Ching dynasty
Captain Obuto, misogynist and animal lover

THE KOREAN COURTIERS

Chi Yoha
General Choe Myongil, emissary to the Manchus
Chong On
General Im
Kim In, savior of the crown prince's two-year-old son
Kim Kyung-jeung, in charge of the fortress at Kangwha
    Island, son of Kim Nyu

Kim Nyu, prime minister, father of Kim Kyung-jeung
Kim On Yun, Jongwhan's enemy, Korean coward and traitor
Kim Sanghon
Kim Singuk
Nam Angap, conservator of supplies at Namhan Fortress
Neung Pongsu
Oh Talche
Sim Chip
Sim Kwangsu
General Yi
Yun Chip
Yun Pang, preserver of the royal ancestral tablets

Glossary of Korean and Scottish Words and Phrases

Aigo—an exclamation, like "Hey!"

Ajŏssi—uncle

Anbang—inner room, women's quarters

Angma—demon

Arirang—Korean folk song, unofficial national anthem during Japanese occupation

Bairn—baby

Bulgogi (pulgogi)—braised beef

Cash—Korean coins with a hole in the center for stringing on wire

Cathay—China

Celadon—renowned Korean ceramics of a rare blue-green color

Chaddae—a legless chair

Changdan—city in northern Korea

Changga—a whore, or whorehouse

Changok—merchant's wife's cape; traditional public attire

Changpu—wild iris, the roots of which Korean women boil to use as shampoo

Chatchuk—pine-nut porridge

Chesa—spirit offering consisting of food and wine

Chiggi—A-frame backpack

Chilsŏk—new moon, seventh month, lovers' holiday

Chima—a long Korean skirt or jumper with arm straps, tied in the back

Chinju—pearl
Choban—breakfast
Chogori—a short jacket with long sleeves, tied to one side
Chorongbak—hollow gourd used for storing water
Chubang—kitchen
Chugŭn—dead
Chungchong—province of Korea
Chungmun—name papers symbolizing ancestors' spirits
Chunmin—the lowest class
Chusŏk—full moon, tenth month—harvest celebration

Dai han—senior cold, the coldest time of the year
Doxy—whore

Gaol—jail
Gilly—tiny pink flower
Ginseng—highly prized mandrake root, used for medicinal
     purposes and as an aphrodisiac

Haenyo—woman diver
Haepari—blue jellyfish
Hallasan—a mountain in the center of Cheju Island
Halmŏni—grandmother
Ham—a wooden chest or trunk containing gifts of cloth
     from the groom's family for the bride's family
Han—river running through Seoul
Hanbok—traditional Korean clothing
Hangŭl—the Korean alphabet
Han-jan-man—just one drink
Hansik—Cold Food (Memorial) Day
Hanyang—ancient name of Seoul
Hanyo—maidservant
Harabŏji—grandfather
Hardtack—hard bread or biscuit eaten by sailors
Hideyoshi—a Japanese general who united the Island
     Empire at the end of the sixteenth century
Hung—spirit, enthusiasm, grace in dance
Hwangap—sixtieth birthday; with the first, the only two
     celebrated
Hyŏpmu—white-clad singer

Ibul—patchwork quilt

Imjin—river in North Korea, also name of Korean-Japanese war of 1592

Kalbi—beef

Kamnida—go

Kamok—jail

Kamsa hamnida—thank you

Kanghwa—island in the mouth of the Han River

Kashio—get out!

Kat—a sheer, black top hat made of horsehair

Kayagum—stringed instrument similar to a dulcimer

Kichim—a polite cough or soft scratching to get one's attention (knocking on a door is considered rude in Korea)

Kimchi or kimchee—fermented cabbage with red pepper and other vegetables

Kisaeng—professional female entertainer, similar to geisha of Japan

Korae—shark

Kudu—shoe

Kul—oyster

Kumgi—taboo

Kut—séance, spirit ceremony

Kwabu—a widowed woman

Kyŏngju—a province of Korea

Li—Korean unit of distance, one third of a mile

Magutkan—stable, barn

Makkŏlli—sweet rice wine of a milky-white color

Makkŏlli-jip—a shop serving makkŏlli

Manchan—time period between 8 P.M. and midnight, when men leave the streets so that women can come out of the house to shop and visit

Manchus—a tribe of nomads who conquered China in 1644 to form the Ching (clear) dynasty

Mangkun—a tight black skullcap worn by Korean men

Mashimnida—eat

Michin—crazy

Mŏt—spirit, charisma
Mudang—female shaman
Munŏ—octopus
Muu—white icicle radish

Namdaemun—South Gate of Seoul
Namu—tree
Nanun piji opsumnida—we are even
Neh—yes
Nipponese—Japanese
Norigae—jeweled accessories hung from the *chima* by
    ornamental knotted cord
Nye—yes

Ocher—a dark yellow earth tone
Oegugŭi—foreigner
Ojum nuda—urinate
Ŏmŏni—mother
Ondol—a floor of clay, heated by ducts connected to the
    kitchen fire, covered with oiled, yellow mulberry
    paper
Oshio—come
Ottŏssŭmnikka?—Are you well?

Pabo—idiot
Paenchu—pants
Paji—pants
Pansu—a fortune-teller; always male, often blind
Pindaetok—sweet-potato pancake
Piwŏn—secret
Pogurak—ballgame dance
Pok—days of rest during the summer
Prefecture—area of local government
Pulgogi or bulgogi—braised beef
Pulta—Korean for Buddha
Punchŏng—a type of rust-colored or black Korean pottery,
    less valuable than celadon
Punyang—province in northern Korea
Pyogae—hard bolster pillow
Pyong chin—the year of the dragon (1616)

Ruff—wide, pleated collar, starched to stand out

Salpuri—a solo dance to rid oneself of grief

Samgyet'ang—ginseng chicken soup, eaten as a restorative

Samsŏnghyŏl—the site of three deep holes in the earth of unexplained origin on Cheju Island

Sanjŏk—Korean-style shish kebab

Saranbang—the front room of a Korean house where visitors, usually men, are entertained

Shijanghada—(You're) hungry

Shogun—ruler of Japan

Sienna—rust color

Singbyŏng—spirit sickness suffered by women before they become *mudang*

Sonyŏ—girl

Soron—South Party, a political faction

Surrim—Korean wrestling

Tabal—paper package; also the name of the manhood ceremony in which a boy's hair was cut and tied in a topknot

Taepung—typhoon

Tano—Spring celebration, fifth full moon

Tao—log raft

Tartar—a derogatory term for Manchus

Toduri—dance rhythm, drumbeat

Tol—First birthday celebration; with the sixtieth, the only two celebrated

Tol-harubang—smiling grandfathers, huge statues of smiling men carved from volcanic rock, found only on Cheju Island

Tongsin—husband

Totan pae—sailing ship or junk

Vermilion—a bright orange-red color

Wee—small

Wŏnmu—drummer-dancer

Yalu—river in northern Korea

Yangbaechu—oriental cabbage

Yangban—aristocrat, member of ruling or highest class

Yangmal—padded stockings of woven cotton

Yin and yang—a circle divided by a curved line, in Korea red and blue, symbolizing air and earth, man and woman, good and evil—part of the Korean flag

Yo—mattress or pallet

Yobo—a term of endearment between spouses or lovers

Yobosayo—an exclamation to get one's attention, like "Hey!"; also a greeting

Yŏja—woman

Yokwhan or Yogwhan—a Korean inn

Yomnio mashio—never mind

Yŏnggam—Honored Sir, a polite term of address to *yangban*

Yoolmu cha—buckwheat tea

Yoot (or yut)—a game played on holidays, especially New Year's, similar to dice

Yot—toffee-type candy made by boiling barley, often flavored with mint—a New Year's favorite

Yut (or yoot)—a game of chance, similar to dice

Yurt—a domed hide tent used by the Manchus

Pronunciation Key for Korean Words and Phrases

Vowels

a	as	*a*	in	father
ae	as	*a*	in	hat
ai	as	*i*	in	mine
e	as	*e*	in	met
i	as	*ee*	in	meet
ŏ	as	*u*	in	hut
o	as	*o*	in	home
u	as	*oo*	in	moon
ŭ	as	*e*	in	taken
y	as	*y*	in	yes

Consonants

no distinction between *b, p, f,* or *v*
no distinction between *r* and *l*
no distinction between *d* and *t*
no distinction between *j* and *ch*
no distinction between *s* and *sh*
other consonants equivalent to English pronunciation

HIGHLAND JADE

MANCHURIA

Mukden

Yalu River

K

O

R

E

A

EAST
SEA

Han River

Kanghwa
Fortress

Seoul

Nam Han
Fortress

Imjin River

YELLOW
SEA

Pusan

Kado Island

Cheju City

Cheju Island

Mt. Hallasan

Taejŏng

Sŏgwipó

1

September, 1635. The Yellow Sea

The storm's power was as beautiful as it was terrifying. Saint Elmo's fire danced in the schooner's rigging, silhouetting the bodies of the men aloft, like spiders in a giant web. Sunset changed the solid canopy of clouds beyond the three masts from luminous green to glowering purple. Deafening wind tore the orders from the boatswain's throat and drowned his shouts in its roar.

Megan Scott Carlisle clung to the hatchway, driven above deck by the stench of fear in the cramped hold below. She gulped clean air and clenched her fingers on the slick wet wood, swaying as the storm batted the ship between towering waves.

Fear knotted her belly. She took a deep breath. What now? Go below again and listen to the other women sob and curse?

There were nine—no, ten after Shanghai, each with different coloring and features. No two dressed alike or even spoke the same language. All had been collected along the way, some bought outright, some tricked into slavery as she had been. The others might not even know their destination. She'd been aboard the longest, since Scotland. A succession of ports flickered through her memory, the odors of sweat and decay mingling with the rich scent of spices.

She should try to comfort the others. But how? They wouldn't understand if she tried to talk to them. No, she knew she would go mad if she had to listen to the frightened jumble of their voices any longer.

Maybe she could find a place to hide on deck until the storm ended. Her mouth twisted. If Devlin caught her, there was no telling what he would do. He wanted all his "cargo" safely stowed away until they reached Nagasaki. Two more days he'd said. She shuddered, then turned back toward the open hatch. The smell of tar and woodsmoke coming from below decks mixed with human smells of excrement and vomit. She covered her nose with her free hand. Maybe he wouldn't catch her. It was a risk she was willing to take.

Fear gripped her, but she forced herself to step out on deck. She cowered under the storm's onslaught, suddenly aware of the vastness of the ocean and her own vulnerability. She plastered herself against the outside of the captain's cabin and wondered at the madness that made men build tiny ships and venture far from land.

She avoided the ragged crew scurrying to obey the master's orders and inched toward the wooden rail at the ship's side, balancing herself against the chopping heave and roll of the slippery deck. The sharp tang of lightning reached her nostrils after a clap of thunder. Cold spray misted her red hair and white skin, forming shiny drops that quickly soaked into her heavy wool gown. With one hand she pulled the tartan shawl closer, then tied it securely at her waist.

She gripped the railing hard. Above the roaring wind, the ship's timbers groaned and screamed. Megan's stomach churned as the deck bucked even more furiously. Since the storm had begun earlier that day, they had eaten only cold food—greasy salt beef and moldy bread, washed down with brackish water. After nearly two years at sea, Megan had long since gotten over being seasick, but now her belly emptied itself over the railing, leaving her shaking but relieved. The sour aftertaste of bile clung to her tongue.

Blast the stinking ship! She'd be glad to stand on dry land again. But it would be better to stay at sea forever than to reach their destination. She shivered at the thought of the Shogun's palace. How long since she last lay in Jemmie's arms? She closed her eyes, trying to blot out the storm and the ship, striving to remember the taste of his kisses, the man-scent of his sweat, the gentle touch of his hands.

Some women remarried right away, eager to have a man again. No matter how sweet the memories, even after two years the thought of another man's touch disgusted her, especially a slant-eyed heathen. Her belly chilled at the thought of yellow hands fondling her breasts, stroking her thighs.

A pox on Devlin! That cowardly fop, so sure his "bouquet of lovelies" would open the ports of the Island Empire. Although European priests and traders had frequented the Japans for decades, only men made such long voyages. Foreign women were unheard of, a rare prize, according to Devlin. As if she cared tuppence for his filthy profit!

Why was she so weak-willed? If only she could do something. But what? She sighed. She'd tried for two years but could never come up with a plan for escape.

Mother would've known what to do. She'd been so strong, even on her deathbed. Her blue eyes had burned bright, like bachelor's buttons in her waxy face. Dark curls cascaded over the white lace nightgown. Her elegant, transparent fingers closed over Megan's tiny stained hand, crushing the little bones together. "Always face your fears and they will fade to nothing, my daughter."

Hot tears slid from her eyes as she nodded. "Yes, Mother, I want to be strong like you."

This won a radiant smile from the pinched face. The vise grip on her tiny hand had loosened and the eyelids fluttered down.

Born a Bruce, with the same strength of will that carried Robert the Bruce to victory over the English, Anne Scott's spirit had burned bright through the long years of the wasting sickness. Her death plunged her only daughter into a world of men. Helpless to prevent her mother's death, Megan tasted the same hopelessness now.

The waves darkened from purple to charcoal then black as night descended. Men hurried to light lanterns. Megan's thoughts turned to home. Did Father know about

Devlin's betrayal? She sighed. Even if he did know, he would never find her here, in the farthest corner of Asia.

If only Jemmie hadn't ridden out on that last border raid. No, she couldn't blame him. He'd been a good husband to her. Resplendent in red battle tartan and trews, he'd smiled down at her from the saddle that last morning.

"James Carlisle, promise me you'll have a care. Come back to me a whole man, promise!" The sweet smell of heather rose from the trampled flowers at her feet. She bent and plucked a sprig, then pinned it to his bonnet.

She stood on tiptoe to meet his lips and hid her face against his wool jacket. The warmth and safety of his love enclosed her for a moment.

"Don't worry, Meggie." He released her, gently pushing down on her shoulders until she stood level again. His voice was rich and quiet. "I'll be back, and if not, you can trust Devlin. He'll take care of you." Those had been his last words to her.

Oh, Jemmie! Sweet, trusting Jemmie! Devlin had brought him back at sunset across the saddle, his scarlet plaids stained dark crimson with his life's blood.

He'd been a fierce fighter, but such a gentle lover, like a child at play. She smiled as she thought of him in the bedchamber on their wedding night, laughing and drinking wine, teaching her the sword dance, then teasing her for her brazenness—to dance a man's dance, his own wife!

The smile froze on her lips. What would he think of his wife now? And his friend? It had never occurred to him to doubt the honor of another gentleman, especially one carrying letters of introduction from the Highland lairds. Devlin had fooled them both with his fine clothes and courtly airs.

She turned her face into the wind to stop the tears before they fell and pushed Jemmie's face from her thoughts. In its place she formed a picture of Father in the New World, carving out a rich plantation in the wilderness with charters from King Charles. It comforted her to think of Robert Scott building an empire for his sons, watching his grandchildren grow.

She grabbed the railing as the ship turned across the

wind and the bow slipped into a deep trough between walls of waves. The deck leveled, the shouts of the sailors echoing in the relative quiet. Megan let go of the rail and scuttled toward the open hatch. She'd had enough fresh air and freedom for the moment. Even the hell below-decks seemed preferable—at least there she could stay warm.

Just as she reached out her hand to grab the hatchway, something clamped her upper arm like an iron band and spun her around. Ice edged Devlin's thin voice. "So, Pretty. Decide to take a stroll on deck?" His pale blue eyes looked white as he held the lantern near her face. "Stupid bitch!"

Rage twisted his handsome features. He looked like a weasel, small but vicious. Rain stained his velvet cloak and doublet, and the plume in his Cavalier's hat hung limp like his grayed lace ruff. His breath stank of sour rum.

He loosed her arm so suddenly she almost fell, and she cringed from the blow she knew would follow. At that moment the ship vibrated. An inhuman shriek obliterated all other sound. The deck that had been level beneath her feet a moment before became a cliff, rising above her as she slipped down its steep side, trying desperately to grab hold of something, anything. Horror contorted Devlin's face as he slid past her and over the side.

Men scrambled over the rigging, shouting. The boatswain's voice rang out above the others. "The mast! Cast her free!"

The rail stopped Megan's fall, then jerked upward out of her hand. With the mast suddenly cut free, its weight no longer heeling it over, the ship righted itself. Megan sailed through the dark air and plunged into the raging water.

As cold as the wind and spray had been, the sea was colder, so cold that her body shrieked with pain as she struggled toward the surface. Darkness surrounded her, pressing into her eyes, her nose, her ears. Slimy brine filled her mouth when she tried to breathe.

The wool gown stuck tightly to her legs, dragging her deeper. She flailed her arms, pushing against the leaden water. Then numbness replaced the sharp cold. Her struggles slowed. Panic gripped her belly, and her chest began to burn with unexpelled air. She couldn't just give up, she couldn't die like this. She wanted to live, even a life of shame and suffering if need be. As long as she stayed alive, she could hope. Somehow she must find her way back to her own world. But first she must live! Terror churned through her. She flailed her aching legs with renewed strength.

Sudden agony exploded in her head. Nausea overrode everything. Something had hit her, something big. Blindly she reached out, twisting and thrashing the water with deadened arms. Her hand grazed a hard surface. Frantically she struggled toward it, embraced it, twined her arms and legs about its girth. The broken mast carried her aching head above the surface, salt water streaming from her mouth and nostrils. She gulped air, then retched violently again and again.

Waves crested over her as the spasms diminished. She pillowed her head against the tarry surface and lay panting, gripped by terror and cold.

Without loosening her grasp on the rough wood, she raised her head to peer into the darkness. She was alive, but what happened to the ship? Lanterns glimmered in the distance. The storm drove the schooner before it, farther away from her with each passing moment. Even if she could muster a voice to hail them, they'd never hear her above the storm.

Now what? A bitter taste filled her mouth. Tears of fear, of sorrow and frustration welled up in her eyes. She'd fought too well. She'd saved herself, but for what? To die a lingering death, clinging to a scrap of wood, without fresh water, without any hope of rescue.

A moment of rage burned in her. It wasn't fair! None of this was her fault. And she knew whom to blame.

A curse on you, Devlin! May you rot on the bottom of this ocean. A bitter smile twisted her lips. At least he'd washed overboard, too.

She sighed, then lay her head on the mast again, inhaling the stinging reek of tar and salt, and waited for death.

2

Pain beat down upon her, twirled giddily up and down her body, and settled throbbing in her head. Megan's hand shaded her eyes from the glaring blue of the sky. Why was she lying in the open instead of her room? No wonder she felt cold, without any bedclothes or drapes, without even a bed. She took a deep breath and willed herself to sit up. The horizon tilted and whirled. Seabirds shrieked curses in her ears.

Bits of memory swirled inside her head. She'd survived after all! Wet sand ground into her palms as she pushed her aching body upright and stood. Drenched tartan wool slapped against her legs, and the wind whipped her eyes with a lock of hair. She smoothed it back across her temple. The pain in her head intensified, closing her eyes and turning her stomach inside out. She sat down again. Her hair felt sticky. She stared at her reddened palm. My God! Blood! Something had hit her as she'd struggled in the water. In the surf nearby lay the broken mast. Bits of its tarry wood still clung beneath her nails.

Worry nagged at her. She should do something. Her mind cleared a little. Danger! She was in danger! Fear chilled her—she might bleed to death if she didn't stanch the flow! What would Father have done? She'd never liked to watch him when he tended his wounds, or those of her brothers. The sight of blood made her faint. Why hadn't she paid more attention?

She knew the answer well. It wasn't the first time since she left Scotland that she'd asked herself that question. Her father and brothers had never made her do anything she didn't want to do. She learned to avoid anything she didn't like. Had they let her get away with so much because they

7

felt as guilty about Mother's death as she did? The thought intrigued her, but she couldn't pursue it. Now she must think, remember. Cold water. Clean bandages. Yes, that might work.

A crystal wave spread itself impossibly thin as it crept within inches of her foot, then drew in on itself and raced backward, carrying yellow sand in its claws. Plenty of cold water here, an ocean of it. She crawled into the surf, splashing icy handfuls over her head. Salt flamed in the wound, stealing her breath. She gritted her teeth until the pain ebbed—she couldn't bear any more of that.

She teetered to her feet again and stumbled up the beach away from the tide. Clean bandages. Peeling her soaking skirt away from her legs, she uncovered the tattered remains of her linen petticoat. Near the front a few ruffles remained from her monthly scavenging for absorbent rags. She picked the cleanest she could find, although all were gray with continual wear. She wadded one piece and pressed it against her temple, groaning aloud and biting her lip. With her other hand she wound another strip around her head. It took her three tries to get the bandage to stay, and then she suspected it stuck only because it absorbed fresh blood. She retied the band around her head as tightly as her numb fingers permitted.

What now? Think—what would Father do? *Calm down. Count your blessings.*

She was alive, she'd done her best to mend herself, she'd survived the shipwreck, and somehow she knew nothing would ever frighten her so much again. But what about the others—the crew and those whimpering, terrified women?

And what about Devlin? If she'd survived, perhaps he had, too. And if he was alive, he would find her. But what if he was dead? Joy shot through her. To be free of him at last! Free! But free to do what, to go where? Panic replaced her joy. How would she live with no one to take care of her? She'd never been alone. No, Devlin must be alive, maybe somewhere nearby. She must find him!

Megan jerked her head to look up the beach. The horizon tilted again for a moment. Piercing her eyes, pinpoints of light reflected from each grain of frozen yellow sand. Breath smoked white from her mouth and nostrils.

Dreading what she would find, yet hoping it was true, she stumbled toward a heap of wet maroon velvet. Anthony Devlin's blue eyes seemed to stare at the waves whipping spray over tall, golden-brown rocks. Crusty sand cupped his cheek and partly filled his open mouth. Bile rose in Megan's throat as memories erupted of that mouth crushing hers.

He'd left her alone through most of the voyage, preferring the company of the spaniel-eyed cabin boy who trailed after him day and night. Then the poor little wretch had sickened with fever, moaning and whining on the forecastle until she, for one, had prayed that he might die and his misery cease. After the crew sewed the boy's skinny corpse in sail canvas and slipped it over the side, Devlin took to prowling the women's quarters after dark, bestowing his attentions on first one, then another. Many nights she'd listened as he stumbled, swearing, through the hold until he fell to the deck. Sometimes his victims complied without a sound, but some protested. Then the hold would ring with the sounds of vicious slaps and sobs, followed by whimpers of pain and rutting grunts like a barnyard animal's. No, the bellows of a stallion or a bull sounded clean and pure beside Devlin's wheezing lust. Next morning, one of their party would sport a bruised lip or a swollen eye and would wince when she walked or sat.

Only once did he come to Megan's side where she lay on the cold planking atop a pile of rags. "On your belly, slut," he breathed, the stink of rum and decaying teeth gagging her for a moment while he fumbled to untie the strings of his codpiece. Sudden rage took her when she realized what he meant to do. This perverted animal had been her husband's best friend, had taken his trust and trampled it, but this, this was too much! She drew her knees up to her bosom. When he sprawled atop her, she planted her feet against his chest and pushed with all her strength. His cry ended in a hollow thump and a groan, then silence. He must have hit his head when he fell. What if she'd killed him? Her heart pounded. Why had she done it, why was she so stupid? If he lived, he would probably beat her near death, but if he died, she and all the others would be at the mercy of the crude, violent English sea dogs of the crew.

A quiet oath chilled her as he stood over her again. The sudden blow across her face made her ears ring and her stomach turn over, and blood trickled from her split lip. "I'll not bother myself with a strumpet like you," he wheezed, "but you'll rue the day you ever defied me." He'd tortured her daily with blows and curses, but on his nighttime forays, he'd kept far from her berth after that.

Filthy cur! How many times had she wished him dead? Now, even in death he'd betrayed her.

Devlin's grayed linen ruff clung to the front of his doublet. Her fingers touched only cloth when she knelt beside the body and peeled the wilted neckpiece up from his soggy chest. Beneath lay her engraved gold pendant, the Clan Scott emblem. It weighed as much as five gold sovereigns and was worth more. He'd told her so when he took it and placed it around his own neck "to keep it safe" for her. The braided chain was of a piece; no way to get it off save over his head.

She swallowed and took a shuddering breath, then laced the fingers of one hand through his coarse blond hair. Fury fired her veins and gave her strength to lift his inert head. Her other hand yanked the chain free, its thick links raking bloodless furrows in his pallid flesh.

Trembling, she pried open the secret catch of the locket. Blurred and faded with seawater, the miniature of her dead husband smiled up at her. Sobs filled her throat. He looked the same as the day he gave it to her, the day he asked her to be his wife. Now he lay dead and buried, and she was lost in an unknown land, half a world away.

The tears exhausted her. She willed herself to stop. She would carry Jemmie's memory with her always, no matter where fate took her. Someday she would find her family, maybe even marry again and have children. But now she must think of the present and put past and future away if she hoped to survive.

Megan's parched lips grazed the tiny portrait in her

hand. She closed the case and hung it about her neck, tucking the icy metal inside her bodice where it would not be seen by other greedy eyes. She'd not make that mistake again.

Her calf muscles twitched with a desire to kick the lifeless form with its gaping mouth and bulging eyes. The cause of so much misery, he'd dragged her around the world, away from her father and brothers, away from the new life they were building in Virginia. She'd only wanted another start in a place where men could earn an honest living from the land, not by raiding the English across the border. He'd taken all that from her, and now Devlin lay dead at her feet.

Now truly alone, she didn't even know where she was. Somewhere between Cathay and the Japans, Devlin had said before the storm. She turned to look at her surroundings—nothing but sand, rocks, and the everlasting ocean.

Far out at sea she glimpsed black specks bobbing with the swell. Seals, perhaps. They'd wallowed near shore and played in the waves near Shanghai. Over wind, surf, and seabirds, an occasional whistle pierced the air. A school of dolphins instead, such as the ones who had followed the schooner off Siam. Sailors said they were good luck. May they be so now!

Salt wind lanced through her. She'd freeze if she stayed here. Without another glance at the dead man, she trudged back past the broken mast toward a tall outcropping of dun-colored stone. It might protect her from the wind at least.

Near the rocks a dry scent of woodsmoke vied with the briny smell of the ocean. She staggered to a halt. Ahead, in a sheltered cove, a group of women warmed themselves around a small blaze. They stood naked, their bodies golden, their long hair slick and black. Could she be dreaming?

Some of the women drank from smoking cups. The smell of fish stew came from a cauldron squatting in the flames. A hollow ache in Megan's middle reminded her how long she'd gone without food. Somehow she must think of a way to get them to feed her before her remaining strength gave out.

Other women in long white robes knelt on the far side
of the fire, pulling shiny wide ribbons of green and black
from large wet baskets and spreading them on woven mats.
The stuff looked like leaves or weeds from the ocean.

The calls of the dolphins sounded much closer here.
She turned. A dark speck separated from the group on the
horizon and came straight toward the cove. When the dark
shape reached the breakers, a human face appeared above
the water. A woman stood and walked out of the waves,
wearing only a belt with a knife jutting from it. Megan
looked again at the horizon. Instead of a school of dolphins,
could it be women bobbing and whistling in the icy sea?

The swimmer carried a rough basket in her hand, a
bright yellow gourd dangling from it by a cord. She turned,
and her slanted eyes looked into Megan's. The woman
pulled the knife and pointed it. She shouted something that
sounded like *"Angma!"* The others backed away, pointing
and repeating the sound.

Terror filled her again—but wait! As strange as they
looked to her, she must look even stranger to them with her
dripping red gown and wild coppery hair. Perhaps they
wouldn't harm her if they thought her a witch or a demon.
Suddenly she felt very tired. What did it matter? To die
quickly by their knives or slowly by freezing or starving—it
made little difference.

With aching calves she pushed her body forward to the
fire. An empty bowl lay forgotten in the sand. Megan
retrieved it and scooped hot liquid out of the black iron
kettle, hardly caring that it burned her hands and lips. As
she sipped she looked over the rim of the bowl at the
whispering women. They seemed to be discussing what to
do with her. While they talked, she would eat.

She felt more than tasted the pungent salty brew as its
warmth radiated through her. Not fish, but broth, with
slimy green strings in it. Seaweed. Her empty stomach
started to rebel, but she swallowed hard. She'd learned to
pick the maggots off salt beef and knock the bugs out of her
hardtack on board ship. She would eat this, too, and
survive.

Megan glanced over her shoulder. Still the women huddled together, looking at her. She loosed the empty bowl. Ignoring her unwilling hosts, she sank to the hard sand, untying the ankle strings of her gillie shoes and pulling off the tongueless leather slippers. She'd thrown her ruined stockings overboard long since. Her numb feet prickled in the warmth from the fire. The scent of wet animal arose from her wool dress as it began to dry and stiffen with salt.

The sound of a footstep whispering in the sand brought her from her stupor. A white-haired woman with dangling breasts and withered thighs stared down at her.

Megan grimaced. Only a perverse feeling of stubbornness kept her from surrendering to her obvious fate. Well, at least she would die warm and with a full belly. Pulling her knees under her, she mustered whatever energy she owned for a weak defense.

Gnarled fingers grasped a handful of Megan's hair. The bloodied bandage slipped from her injured temple.

She grabbed for the old woman's bony wrist, but colored sparks exploded in her eyes. Powerless, she watched her own fingers loosen and fall from the crone's forearm. Slowly the fire dimmed to black.

3

Moon of Autumn Cool, Year of the Boar, Cheju Do

From his vantage point, Yi Jongwhan could see the road ahead, twisting in and out among rock outcroppings, always within sight and hearing of the sea. A low wall of volcanic rock edged the windward side of the narrow track, breaking the chill ocean breeze. A curious pattern of open spaces in the black stone barrier intrigued him as he sat beside it. The design slowed and diverted the persistent

invasion of sea air, without offering the total resistance that
might cause the wall to crumble and fall. Somewhat like the
history of the island itself, or indeed, of the entire Kingdom
of Korea.

One of the servants coughed and spat, then scuffed his
straw shoe in the sandy road. Jongwhan sighed, then
nodded. The man was right—they should continue on. He
hadn't traveled this road before as they had. They knew
how long it took to get from Cheju City to Taejong Village.
He hadn't seen the south side of the island until today. But
duty must come before the pleasure of the beauty around
him.

He settled in the tall saddle and motioned the men
forward, then resumed his interrupted stream of thought.
A man's homeland was like a wife, to be admired and
protected from the outside world, not to be soiled by
intruders. His lips twisted and he shook his head. Like
some men's wives, at any rate. He winced at the thought of
another man with his frail, pitiful wife. He wished she'd
conceive a son, for her sake as well as his duty to his
ancestors. Hadn't he tried? But they took no joy in the
union. He swallowed the bitter taste of failure.

For the hundredth time he stopped short of wondering
about his father's wisdom in picking such a wife for him. It
would be disrespectful to question his father's choice. He
owed his life to his parents and followed their wishes at all
times. Still, he could almost be jealous of his brother,
Jongsun, for his robust, tempestuous wife. She, at least,
would give the family sons. Perhaps when he returned to
the mainland, she'd be carrying a child. With the lineage
assured, his home would be calmer. Meanwhile, he'd enjoy
the respite of this far-flung outpost.

Cheju Do, aptly named "Island Over There," was as
beautiful as any corner of the kingdom Jongwhan had seen.
Today the sky glowed cerulean, the peaceful deep blue of
late summer, belying the early winter storm that had
slashed the island two days before. Although gentle, the
wind's icy edge made him glad of the padding in his official
blue jacket.

His hands on the high pommel ached for charcoal and

brush. At every turning the road presented him with fresh
vistas, each more vivid than the one before. He memorized
every rugged tropical scene, in his mind sketching sea-
scapes and landscapes, mentally poring over his pigments
to choose the clearest blue for the sky, green for the sea, or
yellow ocher for the sand.

His breath caught at the perfect composition of the
panorama before him. If only he could stop here and
capture this view forever. But even if he had time, it would
not be seemly for the new assistant to the Prefect of Cheju
Do to stop and play with watercolors in front of servants.
He coughed as the sweat of horses and men rose to him on
clouds of dust. Jongwhan glanced at the men who jogged on
either side gripping the long stirrups, as much to steady
themselves as to keep him from falling out of the tall
wooden saddle.

They were good men, but peasants, after all. One
could not expect them to understand the needs of a
yangban. So his father had told him many times. A
gentleman must be sensitive to appearances, particularly
one charged with redeeming the honor of his father and
family at court. The last two years passed through his
memory in a painful blur of shame and rage at the dishonor
done to his father and grief at the time lost from his art.

The King had exiled his honorable father without
explanation after years of loyal support and service. King
Injo continued to send back the exiled courtier's unopened
memorials, long heartfelt letters his father worked over and
over, making certain the calligraphy was perfect, the tone
conveying just the right feeling of humility and pride.

It must be a conspiracy. One of the other advisers must
have gotten King Injo's ear and filled it full of poisonous lies
about the elder Yi.

At first, Jongwhan could do nothing but watch his
father's spirit crumble. Then came the request that duty
prevented him denying—his parents asked him to enter
the civil service, to work his way into the King's good graces
using any and all the connections they still had. Only in this
way could they hope to find the source of the lies and
restore the family's honor and his father's position at court.

Although he wasn't much of a clerk, his hard work and eagerness to please had advanced him in a short time to the second-highest position in one of the kingdom's prefectures, albeit the smallest and poorest. But he couldn't rest there. Somehow he must get back to the mainland, to Seoul and the court.

Until then he must curry favor with King Injo's prefect, even if it meant going on absurd errands about the island.

He would not allow even this ridiculous story of a demon from the sea to ruin his pleasure in the fresh autumn day. Only peasants and women believed in demons. "A creature with copper hair and scarlet skin," the messenger had gasped. The wives of Peasant Koh had overpowered it and carried it to their cottage.

That was the trouble with this backward island—too many women, so many that even the poorest man had as many wives as he wished, all in the same house. And the men themselves were so spoiled and pampered by the women that each must always have his own way. They fought bitter duels over inexplicable island politics or drank and played chess, while their many wives dived for whatever living they could retrieve from the sea.

Not much of a living, judging by the hovels Jongwhan and the two servants trotted past. Walls of black island stone topped with wood and mud pressed ugly blank faces toward the sea. A network of ropes held the thatched rice-straw roofs in place in defiance of the constant winds. Rocks hung at intervals for weight—a sad parody of the baubles suspended from a *kisaeng* dancer's birdcage crown.

Finally, just as Jongwhan almost gave up the notion of ever using his legs again, the servants drew the trotting horse to a stop beside a large cottage on the outskirts of a small settlement.

"*Yŏnggam*, Honorable Sir," the servant said with bowed head, "this is the humble dwelling of Peasant Koh, where the demon is being held." The man's voice shook, but whether from the need to address his superior, or from the close proximity to an evil spirit, Jongwhan couldn't tell.

"Thank you, Pu." He smiled to reassure the man. "Please go and call forth Peasant Koh if he is within."

Jongwhan swung his stiffened leg over the pommel and sat for a moment atop the built-up saddle platform. He inhaled the salt tang of sea air. Reaching down a hand to the other manservant, he slid from his high perch to the ground and winced as his heels hit the sandy earth. He hadn't ridden much since he'd left his family's estate in Kyŏngju.

Koh emerged from a low doorway. His smooth, shiny clothing showed evidence of recent attention from his wives' sturdy arms and laundry paddles. Evidently he disciplined them well. A long gray pipe extended from his complacent mouth. Its horsehair stiff and shiny black, a new *kat* covered the man's black topknot.

Jongwhan nodded his approval. Fitting attire for meeting a government official. Koh looked clean, well-fed, and lazy.

The peasant bobbed his head an inch, then stared undaunted into Jongwhan's eyes, waiting for the young aristocrat to speak first.

The older man's insolent stare made Jongwhan flinch. To slight him was one thing, but he wore the batwing hat of the King's special messenger. An offense to him was an offense to the King. Ice edged his formal words. "*Ajŏssi*, Uncle, you sent word to the prefect of a captured demon. The prefect has sent me to investigate."

Koh smiled, showing strong teeth yellowed by smoke. He bobbed his head again. "Within." Holding the bowl of the pipe between finger and thumb, Koh gestured to the open doorway. Then he turned and sauntered toward the village, leaving Jongwhan to stare after him in amazement. Never had he encountered such lack of respect from a peasant.

His two servants didn't look surprised or embarrassed by the fellow's behavior. Perhaps this lack of deference to nobility passed for manners in this forsaken precinct. Jongwhan squared his shoulders. He would ignore the insult for now and get on with this odious task.

As Jongwhan stepped out of his leather riding boots and stooped to enter the low doorway, he noticed the thickness of the walls. It had taken many yearly coats of fresh clay to create this stout dwelling. The thick oiled-

paper floor glistened a shiny deep yellow in the dark
interior. Ducts running under the room to the kitchen fire
warmed the floor beneath his stockinged feet. Momentary
pride filled him. The Nipponese called his people garlic
eaters and barbarians, yet even the lowliest Korean cottage
had been warmed in this clever way for a thousand years.
Heat rose, intensifying the presence of dried seaweed on
the close air.

In the corner, an incredibly old woman squatted on a
rice-straw pillow, grinding seashells to a fine powder.
Beside her lay a white *yo.* A guttering wick floating in a
seashell filled with oil illuminated the thick cotton bedding
and its sentinel. "*Halmŏni,* Grandmother." Jongwhan
nodded a polite greeting. "I come to see your demon."

The old woman lowered her eyes and did not answer.
Stepping closer, Jongwhan looked down upon the still face
and hidden figure swathed in a white *ibul.* He bent closer.
The face looked entirely human except for the coloring.
Instead of a normal golden complexion, pure white skin
covered regular, almost flawless features. A flush of coral
spread across the cheekbones and full lips. Hair like beaten
copper framed the wide forehead. Only the blood-soaked
bandage on one temple spoiled the perfection of the face.

A memory tickled his consciousness. Somewhere he'd
seen coloring like this before. It would come to him. He
wished he could see the eyes behind the sienna lashes. *All
scarlet and copper.* What monstrous form lay beneath the
quilt? He lifted a corner of the *ibul.*

Jongwhan reacted as an artist and a man. The sym-
metry of the figure he saw intensified his longing for paint
and brushes. Smooth skin glowed in the flickering light
with the translucence of white jade. In perfect proportion,
small domed breasts rose, coral tipped, above a smooth
torso and slender waist. A triangle of burnt sienna down
nestled between gently flared hips. The curly mat, much
thicker than a normal woman's, pointed down the length of
her slender legs. Bruises and scrapes marred the radiant
surface but could not hide the beauty of the woman before
him.

The form stirred, moaned. Chestnut lashes lifted, and

Jongwhan stared into jade-green eyes. The face quickened into a smile so radiant he gasped. A whiff of woman-musk sent a sudden longing through him that was no longer artistic but all male. He dropped the corner of the quilt. The sleeper's eyes closed again, and the smile faded.

Jongwhan darted a quick look at the old woman. She met his gaze for a moment before she averted her eyes. Was that hatred or disgust he saw? "Your demon, Grandmother, seems to be but a woman."

She nodded but made no reply.

"I see the copper hair, but where is the scarlet skin?"

The old woman pushed herself upright and shuffled to a chest in the corner, its lacquered finish, like her face, spiderwebbed with cracks of age. Returning, she thrust a bundle of stiff red cloth into his hands. "It came off."

Straight green lines crossed one another on the red woven background. The stuff smelled of animal, like the sheepskins of the Manchus.

That was it! He remembered where he'd seen skin and hair like this before. Years ago, before he had married, the Manchus marched into Seoul, only to find the King safe and invulnerable at Kanghwa Do, surrounded by Korea's best troops and weapons. As frightening as the invasion had been, those were good times. His father was in favor then, and Jongwhan was himself the favorite playmate of Prince Pongnim. The King had taken them to visit the master armorer, a man from the far south, with a flaming beard and milky skin. What name had the man taken? Pak Yon? Yes. A foreigner, but the King allowed him to stay, even marry within the artisan class, because of the brass cannons only he could forge.

This was another foreigner, a woman. If the King wished the creature brought to court, this could be a way home, a way to advance his cause. He must hasten back to the prefecture and send word to the King. But first he must make sure Koh and his wives treated the woman well—she must not die before he could make use of her.

"Take care of your woman-demon, *Halmŏni*. She belongs to the King now."

Bobbing her head, the ancient woman resumed her seat on the pillow.

As Jongwhan stooped to clear the low doorway, an image of the body beneath the quilt came unbidden to his mind. He fought a desire to go back, to look again, to test the taut softness of the smooth white skin. Shocked at his own reaction, Jongwhan shouted for the servants. He must find Koh and make sure his orders were carried out.

4

Jongwhan surveyed the quaint scene around him. Oil lamps gave a ruddy glow to the score of faces in the small wineshop. Men sat in twos and threes at low tables, eating and passing cups of wine as they talked. Outside, the purple-black ocean reflected the darkening sky. Two old women closed the latticed doors against the sharp evening wind.

"Young Sir, another cup?" Koh bowed politely as he placed his own cup in Jongwhan's hands.

How could he have thought the man rude? To think he'd almost refused when the islander asked him to have *han-jan-man,* just one cup. That was hours ago, but it seemed like no time at all. A warm glow surged through him as he thought of all he'd come to understand about this place in such a short time. Too bad he'd be leaving soon. It might be backward, but the island did have a certain charm.

And he'd thought this man such an ignorant peasant. Why, he was just about the most entertaining drinking companion he'd ever known. Their conversation had ranged from island weather to women, art, philosophy, and back to women again. On each topic Koh spoke his own opinion with authority, unlike the diplomatic meanderings of the King's courtiers.

Jongwhan drank quickly, emptying the cup as Koh watched. The creamy liquor slipped down his throat, leaving only a slight sour aftertaste. With both hands he handed Koh the cup and lifted the wine vessel to return the courtesy. Custom required drinkers to pour for each other, never themselves. It was a fine idea, drinking with a dear friend. Why didn't he spend more time enjoying life? Perhaps he took himself too seriously.

As Koh downed his drink, Jongwhan congratulated himself on his good fortune in discovering such a friend and the foreign woman, all in the same day. How could they have ever argued?

"But surely, Young Sir, you have experiences enough of your own with women?"

Jongwhan leaned his elbow on the table. "To be sure, Uncle. But there are women and there are women. I have dallied with *kisaeng*, but that means nothing more to me than momentary satisfaction of the flesh. I have never met one I would care to have for a mistress."

His mouth twisted in a bitter smile. "My venerable father chose my wife for me when I was a child. She is older, and not healthy." He paused. "An obedient and virtuous lady, but she does not warm my soul."

Koh cleared his throat. "Consider yourself lucky. I have five wives, all strong-minded." The older man shook his head. "You have heard, no doubt, that on Cheju Do the women rule the home. In my home, it is true." He swept his arm outward. "I freely admit it. They do the work, and I do as I please."

Poor fellow! What a life for a man. "Thank you, Uncle, for confiding in me."

"Think nothing of it." Koh lowered his voice and leaned forward. "But it is not only here that men obey their wives. On the mainland, too." He pursed his lips. "Have I told you yet the story of the old magistrate of Kyŏngju?"

Jongwhan smiled. "I confess, I have not heard it. Please, I would be grateful for the telling."

"If you insist." The peasant straightened his back and rested a hand on each knee. "The old magistrate had a young, strong-willed wife. As the years went on, the poor man became more and more convinced he was henpecked." Koh swayed a little, then continued. "He wondered if other husbands had the same problem, so he called together all the men of the prefecture. He asked all those whose wives ruled the home to stand on his right." The storyteller gestured with his right hand, then held up a forefinger. "Only one moved to his left. He thought, 'Well, of all these husbands, only one can control his woman. Perhaps he can help us all if he will tell his secret.' So he praised the man and asked how he got his wife to obey."

Koh hunched himself down and sucked in his cheeks, his voice a squeaky imitation of meekness. "The little man blushed and stammered, but finally he said, 'Your Excellency, I do not understand all this. All I know is that my dear wife warned me to stay away from crowds, so when all these men moved to your right, I naturally obeyed her orders and moved to the left.'" The peasant sat back and slapped his knee. "So you see, I am not alone in my plight."

Jongwhan's hearty laughter seemed to please the older man. He recognized the story, but Koh's version struck him as the funniest he'd ever heard.

He watched as his new friend lit his pipe, then sat with him in companionable silence. For the hundredth time Jongwhan pondered the problem of duplicating in paint the blue-green of celadon glaze, like the pot that held their wine. Emerald green and white, with a touch of cobalt blue. Yes, he'd try that next time. In spite of its chipped spout and cracked glaze, the urn might have been lovely when it was new.

The rest of the shop's furnishings also showed age and neglect. Straw nudged out of the frayed seams of the ragged pillows, and scratches and stains covered the rough wooden tables. Only the raw sienna of the *punchŏng*ware cups added a new note in the shop's song of disrepair. Still, the floors seemed clean and he hadn't felt the sting or itch of lice. Nothing disturbed his comfort. Camaraderie and the smell of fermented rice filled the air.

He closed his eyes. In his mind his hands cupped smooth white breasts, teasing the coral nipples, traveling over the smooth belly to the precious triangle of chestnut hair.

He started, opening his eyes. It must be the wine, or

being without a woman so long. How could he want a foreigner? Why, she was hardly human! Even so, her beauty tormented him.

Koh's steady gaze brought his mind back to the business at hand. Jongwhan's voice sounded fuzzy to his own ears. "So, speaking of women, what shall we do with this strangely colored demon your wives have dragged from the sea?"

Drink glazed Koh's eyes and his lips curved into a beatific smile as he sat cross-legged, looking like an effigy of Buddha. After a time he answered, "I shall keep it safe for you, out of friendship." He placed a pudgy hand atop the table. "I will order my wives to see that it is fed and clothed until you return, although what you, or the King in Seoul, want with it, I cannot understand." He blinked. "But it shall have to work when it is able. Agreed?"

"Uncle, I am most grateful." He tried to bow but had to catch himself on the table. "Another cup of *Makkŏlli.* I insist." His fingertips felt numb as he picked up the cup with both hands and pushed it into Koh's limp grasp. When Jongwhan leaned across to fill the rough earthenware cup, the rickety wooden table tilted. Milky-white rice wine gushed out of the ceramic spout, splashing onto Koh's clean white sleeve. Jongwhan stared at the soggy cloth, stupefied. Koh chuckled, then roared with laughter.

Jongwhan joined him. A profound satisfaction in just being alive filled him. With his fingernail he traced a design on the stained tabletop, drawing the wine into smooth crescents and arcs. He belched contentedly. Never could he remember such good side dishes in a *makkŏlli-jip:* fresh oysters, dried squid, and soft brown acorn gelatine. No wonder customers filled the place, even without *kisaeng* to entertain the men. The sketch completed, he compared it to the image of supple white flesh in his mind, then wiped at the sticky surface in disgust, obliterating his first attempt. Not even close.

Koh's voice drew his attention from his failure. "Now, Young Friend, since our business is concluded, we can discuss something of real importance." The peasant stroked his chin. "What think you of the convention of painting only the Gentlemen?"

Jongwhan concentrated. Although he did not agree with those conservative court artists who painted only the four Confucian symbols, he had no desire to undo the last hours of negotiating and drinking. He visualized the dead, stiff still-life watercolors of the Academy, each like every other, trying to find some complimentary or diplomatic comment. He rubbed his eyes, but a clever answer evaded him. "In truth, I see more in the world to paint than only these four."

"Just so, just so." The older man leaned forward, smiling. "If you would see paintings of another sort, come back with me to the cottage." The man's mirth had disappeared along with his earlier languor. Intensity shone from his small black eyes.

Relief warred with distaste in Jongwhan's mind. He dared not refuse and chance bringing insult, but he feared he couldn't manage to pretend admiration for some crude, untutored paintings. Koh was a jolly fellow, not a bit uncouth, but certainly not a master of watercolor. At last, unable to see an alternative, he smiled broadly. "With pleasure." He pushed himself to a swaying stance. "Lead on." He gestured grandly.

Koh caught him as he lost his balance, wrapping both arms around him and pounding his back. "Come, Young Friend, we will walk in the night air and sing old songs of love and sadness."

Ducking out the low door and into the night, Jongwhan appreciated his stout companion's support. A huge full moon lit the sandy road as they reeled toward the cottage at the edge of the village.

Recovering a little, Jongwhan raised his voice to accompany Koh's strong, clear singing. The ballad told of a young wife who killed herself rather than bring dishonor to her husband's family. Their harmony filled the quiet street.

Koh stopped abruptly at the edge of a cliff where the road turned. Before them an expanse of silver-tipped waves spread to the edges of the starry night. A path of light pointed the way across the water to the round belly of the moon. Jongwhan stood beside Koh, swaying in silence.

The breeze shifted, carrying with it the pungency of the small bay. Again the image of a white-skinned body possessed Jongwhan's mind. He licked his dry lips, tasting her taut flesh.

He shook himself, then turned to his companion.

Tears glistened on Koh's full cheeks. Jongwhan had to strain to hear the gruff whisper. "When the soul is empty, one has only to look." The older man stepped onto a narrow side path.

Wiping sweat from his face, Jongwhan followed a few paces behind, amazed at the fellow's sensitivity. It had never occurred to him before that a peasant might feel things as deeply as an aristocrat.

The odor of damp earth and exotic blossoms mingled on the night air. They walked between stunted pines until they reached a small clearing. Jongwhan came abreast of his companion and stumbled into something hard and cold. He drew back. "Excuse me," he mumbled to the darkly human form. As he turned, moonlight glinted off a huge black nose and bulging eyes. Fear gripped him and he leaped backward, knife in hand, into a fighting crouch.

Koh's shrieks of laughter brought him to his senses. "Two demons in one day, Young Sir?"

Jongwhan flushed, his relieved laughter rising to join Koh's. The giant statue of black stone stared benignly back at him. He sheathed his knife and stepped toward the smiling image to caress its pitted surface. "But what is it?"

Koh knocked the long-dead ash from his pipe. "Grandfather stone. Some say they were here even before the first three found the island." The peasant squatted in the clearing. "On the other side of Hallasan, near Cheju City, is a place we call Samsŏnghyŏl. There you will find three holes." His grin flashed in the moonlight. "It is said that the first Koh emerged from one of those holes, with his companions Yang and Pu. They hunted and fished and lived well." Koh fussed with his pipe, refilling it from a pouch at his belt. "One day they met three princesses who brought them gifts of grain and livestock. Later they married. We are their descendants." He stood and rested a hand against the dark stone surface. "Yet it is said even they worshiped the *tol-harubang*, the smiling grandfathers."

The older man stooped and picked up a small stone, setting it on top of the low pile of rocks at the idol's feet. Then he sat, legs crossed, and bowed, lifting his arms to the god of the stone, whispering a prayer.

Jongwhan chewed his lip. The man obviously believed in the spirit world. How could he reconcile these contradictions? One moment Koh appeared as clever and human as any *yangban*, the next a superstitious peasant again.

Rising, the peasant brushed his white leggings and cleared his throat. "Come, Young Sir, another song, a bawdy one this time."

The older man didn't stop singing until they approached his home. Jongwhan warbled a note or two on his own, then quieted when he passed his servants, sleeping on the steps. One of them embraced the heavy wooden saddle, the other clenched the horse's reins in his fist as he snored. Like a child playing thief, he stifled a giggle and tiptoed toward the door to the men's quarters.

He marveled at the honor Koh showed by taking him into his private world. He could hear the fellow cursing as he tripped and banged inside, but finally a yellow glow shone from the doorway. He must have succeeded in lighting the oil lamp.

Half falling, Jongwhan sat on the top step. There, across the courtyard, just behind that door, lay the magical creature who haunted his thoughts. If only he could see her one more time, drink in her beauty, kiss her awake. He clenched his fists. No, he couldn't insult his host by entering the women's rooms without permission, or even by asking to see her again. He had no wish to explain his longing to Koh or anyone, not even to himself.

Why hadn't he thought up an excuse to avoid looking at the man's scribblings? He struggled out of his riding boots before ducking inside. The room was small, separated from the main house by a rough bamboo-mat curtain. Bedding filled one corner, an old chest another. Yellow ocher clay outlined the plain dark stone of the walls.

On a low table lay a partly finished scene of men drinking at a wineshop. Even by the fluttering lamplight, the jeweled colors and sweeping lines drew him into the tableau. Vermilion, azure, and cadmium shimmered from its surface. Jongwhan could almost hear the din of the men's voices as they laughed and boasted, swore and argued. Bending closer, he realized his mouth hung open and he closed it. The beauty of what he saw sobered him. "You did this, yourself?"

The older man's face brightened, and he nodded. Jongwhan's eyes were drawn again to the painting. This was what he'd been trying to do, to paint life as it was, the everyday scenes. The attempts he'd been so pleased with now seemed like nothing compared with this masterpiece. He, a *yangban*, with years of the finest tutoring, couldn't come close to the work of a self-taught peasant.

He reached out his hand to the glowing surface, then stopped. Looking into Koh's eyes, he said, "Uncle, I am honored you have shown this to me."

The peasant cleared his throat. "Go ahead. It is dry."

Life seemed to vibrate from the painting into his fingertips. He shook his head in wonder. Around the walls stood neatly tied rolls of silk, each a completed work. If only he could spend his life here, studying with this man. "Uncle, will you show me the others?"

5

Jemmie looked down at her as she lay uncovered in their marriage bed. His hand shook with passion as he held up the corner of the quilt. When she smiled to reassure him, he lay down beside her and covered them both. His cold hands chilled her and she tried to warm him with her body, but her Jemmie was dead, a hole in his side where his life had drained away. Then his face changed, became Devlin's gaping death mask.

She screamed and raced toward the water to wash the

smell of death from her hands. The sea reached up its foamy arms and swept her in. She moved with the waves, farther and farther away from shore. She must try to get back, she must try. Darkness pressed around her.

She opened her eyes. Blackness surrounded her. The blow on the head, had it left her blind? Or was she dead, buried but awake, left to lie alone in darkness for eternity? For long moments the thought paralyzed her. She turned her head an inch at a time. There, in the wall, thin stripes of shadow cut across a square of faint silver light. Prison bars? Well, at least she could see. It must be night, perhaps moonlight.

Her hand found cool air as she slipped it out of the bedding; then she recoiled as it touched something warm and hard. She held her breath. Had she touched a living creature? She listened until her ears rang with the silence, then stretched out her hand again. The floor—the mattress lay directly on the floor, and somehow it was warm.

She stared into the darkness, white spots dancing in her eyes. There seemed to be no guard. Now would be the time to escape. Making as little noise as possible, she pulled the thick cover off her body. Cool air made her shiver and draw her arms around her chest. She was naked! Someone had taken her clothes. Not just her gown and petticoat, but her linen singlet. She couldn't remember being without her singlet before, except at Easter when she had her yearly bath and sewed on a new one. Everyone wore singlets, men and women. She knew because she'd made them for her father and brothers every year after her mother died. What kind of people would take a person's underclothing? Worse than that, someone had seen her without any clothes, maybe more than one person!

She reached for the locket. Anger flared through her. Before she left, she'd get her mother's locket back or know the reason why. She sat up, clutching the bedclothes to her unprotected body.

Her anger cooled. How could she hope to escape into the darkness with nothing to wear? Her head began to throb. How could she escape anyway? She didn't even know where she was. She couldn't even ask—she hadn't understood a word the women divers had said to each other. Her heart sank. Would they tell her even if she knew how to ask? Perhaps they would make her a slave, perhaps . . . A dozen possibilities crowded her fevered brain. The pain in her head pushed her back down into the soft mattress. Tears rose to her eyes, but she fought them back. There was no one here to wipe them away for her now. She knew what she must do—she was alive, she would get strong. She would learn to understand this place and these people. When the chance came, she'd be ready. Until then, she would wait, and survive.

The clucking of chickens and the singing of a young woman came to Megan through the open door. She smiled at her own imagination. The cozy room, its walls bare, lay empty of furniture except for a lacquered chest in one corner and the bedroll in which she lay. Nothing evil lurked in the corners, not even dirt. The clean floor shone in the late morning light and a fresh sea breeze blew in from the bright outdoors.

The bars she'd seen the night before were slats of wood over paper, sort of combination door-shutters. They stood open, revealing a view of a rocky shore. That explained part of the nightmare, the waves sweeping her out to sea. Not too surprising, considering the shipwreck. She shuddered in spite of the warm room. And seeing Devlin dead on the beach explained the part about him. But she hadn't dreamed of Jemmie for months.

She wrinkled her brow. The face in the dream differed somehow from Jemmie's. She realized the expression of longing had made her think of him, but the eyes in the dream had been gray and slanted, and Jemmie's cheek-bones weren't that high. A chill ran through her. What if it wasn't a dream, but real? What if some heathen man had looked at her, obviously wanted her? She fought down her panic. Her fear of the natives conjured up that face—it was a dream, just a dream—it had to be. She forced herself to relax and enjoy the warmth and safety, at least for the moment, letting the soothing notes of the woman's song lull her.

She wondered what the singer looked like and renewed her resolve to learn all she could. With gentle fingers she explored her body for wounds. She winced as she touched her temple, but at least she could look about her without the terrible headache of the night before. She actually felt good, and happy to be alive. For now she'd lie still and wait.

The singing stopped. Another voice spoke. The words sounded like muffled English, not like the singsong of the Mandarins she'd heard in Cathay. The new speaker sounded like a man, and out of sorts by his tone. Megan's contentment oozed away. Questions nagged at her. What did these people want from her? Could she cope with whatever happened? Again she pushed down her panic. Whatever happened, she'd find a way to manage.

As the volume of the scolding rose, the woman answered each peevish demand with one quiet syllable, *"Nye."* Megan thought she heard tears in the woman's replies. Finally, sobs filled the air. The man's voice now changed to a soothing mutter, and little by little the wailing decreased to sniffling.

Gradually the soothing tone became bantering, punctuated by giggles from the girl. The sudden drumming of running feet receded, then approached again as the man chased the now squealing girl right toward the room where Megan lay. She just had time to close her eyes and feign sleep as they thundered through. The odor of damp earth and tobacco smoke hung in the air after they passed.

From an inner room came the thud of bodies falling. Evidently the hunter had caught his quarry. After a period of quiet, she heard the unmistakable sounds of two people making love and both enjoying it very much.

She gasped in shock. Animals, to do it in the daylight! She had seen and heard much aboard Devlin's ship, and before that she'd come to enjoy nights in her husband's arms, but she'd certainly never heard anyone make noises like that! And with another person so close by! Disgusting! The moans peaked, and then only the muttering of the hens could be heard in the yard.

Gradually, her shock receded. Was it really so awful,

what they had done? After all, they owned the house. And in all fairness, they thought her unconscious. Perhaps they were married, or whatever served as marriage here.

Still, the experience left her feeling uneasy, as though she ought to do something. What if he took a fancy to her next? Just as she decided to try to get up, the man's heavy tread approached. She lowered her lashes so that she'd look asleep, but left them open a slit so she could see this beast as it passed.

He was dressed all in spotless white, some kind of long pantaloons, like loose trousers tied at the ankles, covered by a long white jacket. He stood tying the strings of his broad-brimmed sheer black hat under his square chin. Relief washed through her—he looked nothing like the face in her dream.

He hummed to himself as he passed her, not even glancing in her direction. He stopped in the low doorway and bowed, muttering and bobbing his head toward a dark shape on the casement. Megan strained to see what it was. It looked like a rotting fish head.

A new wave of shock hit Megan. The filthy heathen! Praying to that grotesque idol. She did not think of herself as a religious person, having only attended Easter service each year. But at least she was a Christian. Or had been. She'd thought of Job and his trials many times on her trip. She tasted resentment anew. If God was testing her, she failed.

She grimaced as a new thought struck her. A fine job she'd done of learning to understand these people. Everything she'd seen and heard, she'd judged by her own standards. "Judge not," said the Scripture, not that many lived by it. Most mouthed the words, then went ahead and did as they pleased.

Hadn't she learned anything from her years with Devlin? If nothing else, she should know that things were not always as they appeared. Before she judged these people, she must understand much, much more.

The man finished his prayer. A very long-stemmed white clay pipe trailed blue smoke from his mouth as he ducked out the low doorway.

He stopped on the second step to take a pull of tobacco, then rocked back on his heels. From the back he looked very pleased with himself. Straightening his jacket, he continued down the steps and out of Megan's sight.

After a few moments she hauled herself to a sitting position, leaning against the clay wall and pulling the white cotton quilt up to her chin. Why did her body feel so weak? She must have been unconscious some time. Her stomach growled. Should she try to get something to eat? Should she call out, or just wait until someone came?

Stockinged feet whispered across the paper floor. The young girl bustled into the room tying her jacket and smoothing her hair. She sang softly under her breath. When Megan cleared her throat, the girl stopped, put her hand to her mouth, and turned to face Megan with wide eyes. *"Ottŏssŭmnikka?"*

Megan tried to think of a gesture to show that she didn't understand the question. Finally she shrugged. The girl nodded. A tiny smile lit the young face. She pointed at her temple, then closed her eyes, pain contorting her features. Then she pointed at Megan. *"Ottŏssŭmnikka?"*

Megan touched her bandaged head and smiled. "Much better, thank you." Her stomach growled again. Megan pointed to her belly and frowned, then pointed into her open mouth.

The girl cocked her head, then her smile widened. *"Shijanghada!"* She scurried off.

Like the man, the girl was dressed all in white. A full skirt fell to her ankles, and over this she'd tied a short jacket. Her dark hair formed a smooth knot at the nape of her neck. She looked about Megan's age, eighteen, or a little younger. Her husband, if that was who he was, looked much older.

The young woman returned, carrying a steaming basin. She'd understood! With both hands she held the bowl to Megan's lips. *"Mashimnida. Samgyet'ang."*

Megan cupped her hands around the dish. A faint odor of tilled earth mixed with the savory smell of chicken. Poison? She hesitated, then shrugged. Why save her life to poison her now?

"*Mashimnida!*" The girl nodded and smiled.

Megan sipped. She couldn't remember when food had tasted so good. She emptied the bowl, urged on by her hostess each time she paused. She hesitated, then plunged her fingers into the bowl and scooped up the pieces of meat from the bottom of the dish. The girl nodded and smiled again.

With her belly full, Megan sank back. She still needed to learn so much. She frowned. How could she begin to understand these garbled words? Or get them to understand King Charles's English?

On impulse, she pointed to her chest and said, "Megan," then pointed to the girl. The girl frowned, so she repeated it. The round tan face lit with understanding.

"May-khan," she repeated, pointing. Then pointing at her own chest, the girl said, "Sonyŏ."

Megan tried to imitate the sounds. After a few tries, Sonyŏ clapped her hands and squealed. The girl danced around the room, pointing at objects and saying the names, until Megan's head spun with the words.

Soon she realized she had another pressing need. How could she ask for a privy? She couldn't walk that far anyway. Would these people have chamber pots? Her full bladder throbbed. She had to try, or wet herself.

Placing her hand low on her belly and frowning, she tried to imitate the sound of a hissing stream of urine. She repeated it until her breath ran out.

Sonyŏ frowned, then left the room for a moment and returned with a large clay bowl.

With the girl's help Megan managed to climb onto the makeshift chamber pot. She relieved herself at length, then the girl took the bowl and hurried out the door. Water splashed outside and Sonyŏ returned, drying her hands.

Shivering, Megan pulled the quilt around herself as the breeze freshened.

The girl cocked her head, then went to the chest in the corner and drew out some bundles of white cloth. Nodding and smiling, she approached the bed and pulled off the quilt.

Megan resisted, but the young woman kept cooing

"*Nye, nye,*" until she got her way. Holding up some pantaloons, she said, "*Paenchu,*" then helped Megan to pull them on and tie them in place. The material felt like soft white cotton. Next came a long full skirt like her own, which she called *chima,* and a short jacket tied to one side that she called *chogori,* both of the same cloth as the first.

Standing back, the girl laughed and clapped her hands, then flitted off, coming back a moment later with a comb and a shiny copper circle. Sonyŏ showed her how to hold it to catch her own reflection. Then the girl began combing the tangles out of Megan's matted copper curls, gently avoiding the bandaged temple.

Just as she finished knotting the reddish curls at the nape of Megan's neck, a shadow fell across the doorway. The old crone who had attacked Megan on the beach stood staring down at her. "*Kashio!*" The old woman's face contorted into a mask of rage.

6

Moon of Chrysanthemum Autumn

Winter edged the chill dawn breeze on her sweat-covered face. Megan paused and shifted the round clay water jug higher on her back. She wiped her brow on a forearm, avoiding the bruise on her temple. How many weeks had she been here? It must be October or November by now. She curled her aching fists for a moment in the long sleeves of her padded *chogori.*

Grandmother had pulled two pairs of quilted pants and matching heavy jackets from the chest a few weeks before when the weather turned chill. The old woman donned one set and gave Megan the others with a grunt.

The old woman puzzled her. She seemed protective one moment and distant the next. What did Grandmother

really want of her? What an old dragon she'd seemed that
first day, storming in and tearing off Megan's white jacket
and skirt.

She fumed the whole time she dressed Megan in
baggy trousers and a loose jacket like her own. The
other women wore skirts—only Megan and Grandmother
dressed like men. And in place of the knot Sonyŏ had made
at the nape of her neck, the old woman had braided one
long queue. All the rest of that day Grandmother had
waited by the low bed, for all the world like a bitch
protecting her pups.

No wonder her captors confused her. They took pains
to nurse her back to health, yet they worked her like a
slave. She shrugged. The women all worked hard here,
especially the *haenyo*—even in winter they dived in the
ocean for food and pearls. At least they hadn't forced her to
do that—yet!

But why did the women work so hard when the men
didn't seem to work at all? She shrugged. This wasn't
Scotland. She pushed her hands against the front of the
cloth straps and arched the bunched muscles in her lower
back, then dug her straw shoes into the sandy path and
moved on.

Sonyŏ's slender figure disappeared around a boulder
ahead. Twice since the first cock crowed they had trudged
from the cottage to the clear-water spring near the shore, at
least a mile each way. Why couldn't the island have a river
or stream? It rained enough, but the water seemed to seep
into the ground and disappear.

She sighed. A few more minutes and she'd be back
inside the warm kitchen, boiling rice and stirring the soup
for breakfast. Her stomach growled.

The cottage came into view on the other side of a stand
of scrubby pines. The black courtyard wall stood shoulder-
high, chunks of rough stone stacked without mortar. She
wondered again why it stood at all. It was neither tall
enough nor strong enough to protect the inhabitants.
Perhaps it simply marked off Koh's property. In any event,
it was as good a place as any to keep the never-ending
supply of stones the women pulled from the fields.

Beyond the wall, crisscrossed ropes held the thatched roof of the cottage in place against the strong island winds. Dried fruits and vegetables hung from the rafters, bright colors contrasting with the black stone and gold clay mortar of the walls.

Three slender logs suspended between stone uprights formed the house-yard gate. The top two crossbars rested on the bottom bar, the ends pulled from the posts to indicate the residents would return in a few minutes.

Megan stepped through and stopped to slip the bars back into their holes. Visitors seeing the gate would know someone was home now, ready to receive callers.

She quickened her pace inside the house wall and stopped in the courtyard. On one side of the kitchen door stood a black ceramic water vat, as high as her waist. She dropped the cloth strap off her right shoulder and bent to pour the contents of her burden into the waiting receptacle, then shrugged the jug and harness onto a nearby table and hurried into the cooking room.

Sonyŏ squatted before one of six tiny stone hearths, her white skirts clenched between her knees to keep them away from the clay floor. She fed barley straw into a small blaze beneath a pot of bubbling soup. Cast-iron pans of different sizes and shapes nestled permanently in each of the hearths.

Smoke hung in the rafters of the small cookhouse, blackening the roof supports and the inside of the straw thatch. She had tried to ask why they didn't use a chimney, or at least a smokehole, but Sonyŏ had just shrugged and mumbled about the smoke's signaling an attack by the yellow dwarves from the south.

Did she mean men from the Japans? Megan's pulse quickened. There were white men in Nagasaki. Maybe they would come and take her back home to Scotland. Her mouth twisted. And maybe there were fairies in the glade and cherubs in the sky. Well, she'd seen neither. She'd waited for men from the south, but she'd seen nothing of them, either.

Megan bent to add straw to the fire beneath the pot of mixed grains. Savory steam rose from the barley, rice, and millet. Tiny bubbles popped on the surface. It was almost done. Cramps gripped her belly. She gritted her teeth. Would she never get used to the food? After all these weeks her bowels still turned to water some mornings. She stirred one last time, then rose and scurried to the outhouse.

Not even a roof protected the stone platform at the back of the compound. The pig in the adjoining pen snorted and came running when her straw sandals scraped on the stone step. She untied the waist string of her pants and bit her lip at the cold of the stone seat.

At first the thought of the pig waiting below to gobble up whatever fell through the hole had disgusted her. After the distaste ebbed, the mental picture of him poised beneath her, snout up, amused her. But today he failed to catch his morning meal and it hit his head, splattering her buttocks. Irritated, she wiped at her cold, wet backside with barley straw. The pig snorted and rooted in the foul-smelling pit. "Idiot," she muttered, pulling up her *paji* and lapping and tying the front.

At the cookhouse door she used a dried half-gourd to dip water into a waiting clay basin. The cock crowed again. The other wives would rouse from their warm beds soon. She re-entered the kitchen and closed the paper-and-lath door against the wind.

Squatting before the cookfire, Megan loosed the strings of her worn jacket. She dipped a clean rag into the cold water and washed beneath her arms and under her breasts. At first the islanders' insistence on washing had seemed unreasonable, but now her daily wash refreshed her. Besides, if she didn't wash, Grandmother would wrinkle her nose and hand her a bowl and a cloth.

Snores erupted from the sleeping room beyond the paper wall. The wooden-slab floor thudded when Koh turned over in his sleep. Sonyŏ raised her face from the steaming food and smiled. Her expression reminded Megan of the adoring looks her sainted mother had turned on her father.

A hollow loneliness gripped her belly at the memory, but she pushed the ache aside and returned the young bride's smile, rolling her eyes and shaking her head in mock

horror. Sonyŏ laughed silently, covering her mouth with
her hand.

How could the woman love Koh? To share him with
four other wives, and the way they all fawned on him and
pampered him. And why? He never worked, but spent his
days drinking, playing chess with his friends, reading, and
painting, while his wives, and Megan, worked from dawn
to dark or later.

And the household couldn't help hearing when he
made love to Sonyŏ. Grandmother just covered her head
with an *ibul*, but Tai's Mother sobbed and drew her small
son's wicker cradle closer. Megan tried not to listen, but the
sounds stirred something wild in her belly. Would she ever
have a man again? She shuddered. Not a fat sluggard like
Koh. She shook her head and retied the jacket and pants,
then emptied the washbasin out the door.

She rinsed the bowl with another dipper of water,
swirling it and tossing it after the first. She filled it again
with soup and lifted her wooden spoon from the holder,
then squatted in a corner and spooned hot liquid into her
mouth. Sonyŏ joined her, sharing the one privilege of rising
early—eating first instead of waiting for the elders to finish.

Megan sighed. She liked this part of the day best, and
it was almost over. In spite of the heavy water jug, she liked
hiking to the beach and back. After the others left to go
diving, the real work would begin.

She spooned the last of the soup into her mouth and
filled the bowl again with mixed grains. The heat of the food
made Megan's palms ache for a moment.

For the past week she and Sonyŏ had spent hours each
morning with their hands in ice-cold water, rinsing and
cutting *yangbaechu* for *kimchi*. The egg-shaped heads of
cabbage had frilly leaves and a milder flavor than the tight-
leaved variety in Scotland.

They also cut the tough roots of *muu*, like large white
carrots, but with a flavor more like turnip. Worst of all, they
ground hot red peppers into a fine powder. It burned each
nick and cut in Megan's hands when they layered all the
foods in a black crock with salt and water.

Megan and Sonyŏ together dug holes in the rocky soil

to bury the filled jars. Then they bound straw into small cone-shaped houses to set over the covered pots. Sonyŏ told her this would keep the food from spoiling or freezing.

After a long morning, the wives would return from the sea and spread their catch to dry on the roof. Megan and Sonyŏ fixed the noon meal—more soup, grain, and *kimchi*.

Then she accompanied the wives to the fields to harvest and plow. Megan's job was to gather the black rocks that daily worked their way to the surface and add them to the nearest wall, something she'd done time and again in Scotland.

At dusk they returned to the cottage for another meal, this time with pork or fish added. Sometimes Sonyŏ would boil sweet yellow roots, then mash and fry them in grease like scones. Megan savored the taste of this favorite food called *pindaetok*.

She and Sonyŏ made their evening meal in the cookhouse from whatever the older wives and Koh left in the communal dishes. Then Megan crept gratefully beneath an *ibul* and slept until the first cock crowed.

The sun rose and set, rose and set, but she was no nearer to escaping. Rest, food, and hard work had restored her health.

She saw small boats beached in the sand, but she could never steer one herself. Women were forbidden on the boats. For that reason they built small log rafts called *tao*, or swam close to shore. Sonyŏ told her that many men had died at sea in *taepung*, like the storm that had swept Megan to their shore.

Whenever she asked about the Japans, Sonyŏ pressed her fingers against Megan's lips and shook her head. Yellow dwarves had come from the south when Grandmother was a girl, killing all the men and raping the women. And generations before, evil-smelling warriors from the north had swept across the island and many men died. Now only a few survived. Perhaps that explained how one man could afford many wives.

Well, she had no intention of becoming part of a harem. She must form a plan. Until she could get away, she'd eat and work and be glad to stay on land. She

shivered. Nightmares of thrashing about beneath black
waves still plagued her sleep.

Sonyŏ jostled her elbow. The dish in Megan's hand had
grown cold during her reverie. The young wife's eyes
twinkled. She dipped her chopsticks into the *kimchi* and
dropped a chunk into Megan's cereal bowl.

Powdered red pepper covered the fermented cabbage.
Megan wrinkled her nose at the smell. She scooped cereal
into her mouth, then followed with the *kimchi*. It did add
flavor to the bland mess of grain. Her mouth burned, but
she nodded at Sonyŏ and wiped the water that dripped
from her eyes and nose.

Sonyŏ giggled. Then her face sobered and she lowered
her eyes. The paper doors to the inside swung open like
shutters and Tai's Mother entered the kitchen, her small
son on her hip. The young matron's brows furrowed. Her
eyes raked Megan's face and rested for a moment on Sonyŏ's
bent head before she filled her bowl and retreated to the
warm inner room.

Kwang's Mother and Jung's Mother followed, muttering about the early hour and the poor quality of the food
before they also disappeared inside. Finally Grandmother
entered.

The old woman stopped at Sonyŏ's feet. "Youngest
Wife, how many heads of cabbage have you prepared for
the winter?"

Sonyŏ answered without raising her face. "Two hundred, Grandmother."

The old woman grunted. "Then you can finish the task
by yourself." The hooded black eyes turned on Megan.
"You will come with me, Sea Demon. You are strong
enough now to dive with us, to become a *haenyo*."

The cold wind cut through the thick cloth of Megan's
jacket. She shivered. Koh's wives chattered and shrugged
off their clothes as if they were dressing for a party. They
stowed the folded garments in niches in the rock, with
weights to keep the wind from carrying the things into the
tide pools below.

Nearby the children shrieked and gamboled in the wet

sand. A boy of eight fed driftwood into the small fire. A girl of six rocked baby Tai ~in~ his round-bottomed wicker cradle.

Golden bodies gleamed in the gray winter light. Muscles rippled in Grandmother's withered arms and legs. She frowned. "Disrobe." It was an order.

Megan shook her head. She wouldn't—couldn't get into the water. There must be some way out. Four faces watched her. She turned to run, but Tai's Mother caught her wrist. Jung's Mother untied the jacket and Kwang's Mother undid the pants. Megan stood shivering, as naked as the rest.

Grandmother pointed at the dark blue waves. "*Kamni-da*." Megan fought and twisted, but the wives easily pulled her into the salt water up to her chin. As soon as they let go, she scrambled back toward the shore.

The old woman shot toward her, grabbed her around the waist, and threw her over one gnarled shoulder.

Megan pummeled the bent back and kicked the waves with all her might. The old woman waded back to the deep water and heaved her into the cold brine.

The copper taste of fear mixed with the brackish water filling her mouth. She thrashed her arms and legs, trying to get her head above water. Why were they trying to drown her? Why had they saved her life just to kill her now? The water darkened around her. All strength left her and she sank, ears ringing in the silence beneath the waves. The nightmares had come true.

Hands grasped her body and hauled her to the surface. She coughed and spat, wiping her streaming eyes and nostrils. The hands dumped her roughly onto the hard-packed brown sand. Her vision cleared.

Grandmother stood over her, wrinkled brows knotted. Her voice sounded puzzled. "May-khan, you are a sea demon. You come from the sea. Why do you not swim?"

"No demon, Grandmother. Only a woman, a *yŏja*, like all of you." She ground her teeth. She didn't know enough of their language to explain the shipwreck. "I rode here on a . . . " What the devil was the word for mast? "*Namu*." That was tree. Would they understand?

The old woman sucked in her breath and raised her

eyebrows, then shook her head. "*Yŏmniŏ mashio*, I will teach you."

Grandmother picked her up like a child and carried her again into the waves. "Your body is fat, fatter than a man's, and your lungs are much stronger. Only a woman can be a *haenyo*, a diver. The fat will keep you warm and help you float."

Megan clung to the knobby shoulder. She noticed for the first time that the water made her warmer, not colder, than the chill winds above. Her knotted muscles relaxed a little.

"First you must learn to swim on top of the water, to become mistress of the sea, instead of being at its mercy." Strong fingers pried Megan's hands loose. "Then I will teach you to dive and pluck the sea's treasures for your own."

She spoke slowly in soothing tones, showing Megan how to lie on her side in the water and push one palm forward and the other one back and demonstrating with her hands the scissor action of the legs. Finally, with a shove, Grandmother sent her free and alone into the water.

Megan floated for a moment, then sank, flailing and sputtering. Gnarled fingers closed around her shoulders and the old woman yanked her to the surface again. The wrinkled face pushed up against hers.

The old woman punctuated each word with a shake. "Listen, and do as I show you."

Once more Grandmother flung Megan into the waves. This time she managed to stay afloat and paddle around. The fear drained from her, leaving a relief that almost amounted to joy. She wasn't going to drown after all! Strength surged through her arms and legs. She could swim!

All too soon Grandmother towed her to shore. "Dress and keep the fire going. Watch the children. Tomorrow you will try again." Her withered lips twitched up on each side. The old woman bobbed her head, then shouldered the orange gourd buoy and waist-high wicker basket and followed the other *haenyo* into the waves.

Megan trudged toward her dry clothes. If she actually

learned to swim and to dive, maybe the others would see her as a person instead of a freak. Maybe she could find a way to escape. And somewhere deep inside, for reasons she didn't understand herself, she wanted very much to learn to swim.

7

Moon of Bitter Cold

Jongwhan drummed impatient fingers on his right foot where it rested atop his left knee. Usually this posture, reserved for *yangban* only, brought him satisfaction on his weekly visits to the magistrate's office at Songup. In his presence all the officers, except the magistrate himself, had to kneel. It served the exclusive bastards right, after they had rebuffed his overtures of friendship.

But today the formalities of representing the prefect at this backward village plagued him almost beyond endurance. The constable dragged forward the last two prisoners. Only the night before they had disturbed the kingdom's peace by fighting with knives in a local tavern. The magistrate bowed, offering him the privilege of passing judgment. Jongwhan shook his head.

"The law is clear on this point. So is the punishment." The official's voice carried through the door and down the broad steps to the courtyard where the accused knelt in chains.

Tears streamed down the face of one combatant and trickled into the jagged cut on his cheek, a memento of the previous night's excitement. The other man glowered his defiance. His chin jutted forward and his lips pressed together into a thin line. His attitude would change when he heard the sentence.

The magistrate paused, then cleared his throat. Jongwhan glared. The man was insufferably dramatic. He should have passed judgment himself. Anything to be done and away to Cheju City again.

"You will be flogged in public immediately, eight lashes each. You will then spend the next moon in the *kamok*."

Sobs broke from the first prisoner. The other's eyes widened and he groaned.

The magistrate nodded to the constable. "Begin."

Two men dragged the first prisoner to the flogging platform and laid him face first on the crossed beams, tying his ankles and wrists. The screams of the prisoners filled the air, punctuated by the smacking sound of the wooden paddle.

Jongwhan stayed seated with his back to the scene of justice fulfilled, pretending disinterest. In truth, the sight of cruelty sickened him. Intellectually he believed in punishment. One couldn't sanction knife fights in taverns and keep the peace, but the sight of one man inflicting pain on another disgusted him, even in the name of the King's law.

He closed his eyes and willed his mind to other matters. The words of his honored father's most recent letter still burned in his mind. "Your mother and I find no fault with you, our son, for our enemies are strong. It is our fondest hope to see our family's honor restored before we join our ancestors. Continue to do your best and justify our pride in you."

He had deliberately omitted any mention of the foreign woman from his letters. He wanted to spare them the disappointment if the plan failed. Almost three moons had passed since he had dispatched a carefully worded memorial to the King in Hanyang, the ancient city most people called Seoul, or "capital city," but still no answer had come.

And what of the foreign woman? Only his full schedule of trivial duties had prevented him from seeing her, drinking in her beauty. Her supple white limbs and curling copper hair filled his dreams. True to his word, Koh had sent a message saying that the creature's health had mended. But what if some islander took a fancy to her and carried her away? He pushed the images from his mind. No sense torturing himself.

The sound of the lashes ceased and the screams diminished into the distance. The two fighters had tasted the King's justice. If they lived through a month in the stinking jail, they'd be free to cut each other to pieces once more.

He opened his eyes again. The magistrate bowed to him, signifying the close of formalities for the day. He returned the courtesy and rose. When he emerged from the tall carved doors, Yang and Pu jumped to their feet and hurried to ready his mount for the trip home.

Jongwhan strode across the compound, stretching his cramped legs after hours of sitting. A runner puffed through the gate, handed a message to the gatekeeper, and collapsed against the wall. The old servant squinted at the paper and the seal, then turned and called out, "A message for the Honorable Yi Jongwhan from His Excellency, the King."

The leather soles of Jongwhan's black boots crunched loud in the sudden quiet of the courtyard. He held his head high, knowing all eyes in the compound rested on him.

With shaking fingers he took the letter and broke the royal seal. His heart pounded and the words seemed to jump off the page. "We are pleased with your report of the foreign woman. Await our summons." He read the short message again, then folded the missive and slipped it into the pouch that hung from his belt.

Only the shaking of his hands showed the intensity of his excitement. He bowed farewell to the assembled officers and mounted his sturdy island pony for the long ride home. But inside he was screaming and dancing for joy. The plan had worked! He would be called to court!

Now he had only to wait. His pulse slowed. He longed to pull the message from his pouch, but he knew by heart the words it contained. "Await our summons." No word of how soon the summons might come. It could be days, or years. More waiting. How much longer?

Memories of the shipwreck beat at the edges of her mind, keeping her from concentrating and tightening her already tortured chest. The cut on her temple ached in the icy water. "The sea takes life as it gives life," Grandmother had warned.

Bubbles streamed upward as Megan pushed her body down toward the underwater jungle, beautiful and silent. Sea creatures stood out in vivid colors against the charcoal-gray waters. Yellow coral pointed gnarled fingers at her. Purple and orange starfish crept over pitted black boulders. The spiny fish would hide there in holes and overhangs, blending in with its surroundings, poison fins waiting for a fish or a diver to get close enough to strike. A school of yellow butterfly fish parted and flowed around her as she forced her body deeper.

Currents fondled her breasts and thighs with cool, slick fingers. Slimy black kelp pulled at her ankles. Far above her, Grandmother's legs moved apart and together, apart and together. The surface of the water flattened the rest of the old woman's body into a golden blob.

A soft-bodied *munŏ* the size of her fist streamed past her head, its eight arms rippling. The dim light kept her from seeing much beyond the kelp beds. At least no jellylike *haepari* floated on the currents nearby, dangling death from blue tendrils.

She pulled the knife from her teeth. Working against the pull of the water, she cut slimy blades of black kelp, trying to fill the basket tied to her side before her air ran out. She worked until the pressure of the air burned inside her chest. Memories of the shipwreck smothered her. Panic paralyzed her chest. She'd die unless she swam up to the air above. Strength surged through her legs as she kicked up from the gloomy depths. Breaking the surface, she pushed the air from her lungs in a high, piercing whistle, a shriek of fear and relief.

Across the chopping swells the lined face of Grandmother turned toward her. White hair fanned around hunched shoulders as the old woman bobbed up and down, treading water in the purple-gray brine. In spite of her many years, Grandmother remained a strong swimmer.

All the lines in her face pointed at the sea bottom, and

her chin swung from side to side. "No. You must take in more air, hold it longer. You are always in a hurry. You are young, but you will learn patience. Now, again."

Knowing from past lessons how little good it would do to argue, Megan stilled her panting and filled her lungs as she'd been taught. With a kick she pulled her bare buttocks over her head and pushed again for the kelp beds.

At first she'd been shocked by the family. The women all called Koh *tongsin*, husband. They all pretended to respect him when he was around, but the one they all obeyed was Grandmother. Even though the old woman had no children or grandchildren, Megan had never heard anyone call her by any other name.

The kelp shivered as she kicked along the bed, skimming close to the sandy bottom. Grandmother frightened her a little, not that the old woman ever harmed her. But she seemed so distant, almost as if she was testing her. What did she want?

And why did the old woman insist Megan learn to dive? The shipwreck still haunted her, even after she'd overcome her fear enough to stay afloat. She didn't mind swimming above the water; in fact, she sort of liked it. But diving brought back the darkness, the fear, the pain.

She stopped cutting kelp and rubbed her temple. The wound had healed, and except for an occasional twinge when she got cold, it didn't bother her. But the mast could have killed her. She could have died so many ways. Her chest tightened, and the cold, dark water pressed around her. Panic flooded her mind, and she kicked herself toward the sky.

This time the Grandmother didn't frown; she nodded once. "Better. Be married to the water. Forget your past fears and other lovers. Let the water take you. Once more."

Megan's impatience grew. She thought about refusing. What right had Grandmother to talk of lovers? What did she know of Megan's fear or pain or loss? The old woman's black eyes bored into her, commanding her. Hating herself for her weakness, Megan bit her lip and gave in. She took several deep breaths and pondered the meaning of the old woman's words.

Somehow she'd never thought of Grandmother as a woman, at least not one who would have a lover. She knew the old woman was Koh's oldest wife and the one who really ran the family. But did he ever bed her? From what the other wives said, he shared his bed with the youngest wife, Sonyŏ. It shocked Megan to think of Grandmother as a young woman in bed with a man. It reminded her of the feeling she got when she first realized her parents made love.

Thinking of her father in Virginia brought pain and guilt. She had done nothing to try to escape. She hadn't even thought of him much. There was so much to think about here.

How many months had she been on this godforsaken island? Would she never be free of this upside-down world she'd been cast into? Everywhere she went, children followed behind her, marveling aloud at the "beast from the sea" and how much like a human she looked. Adults who had never seen her would pull her red hair and pinch her white skin. It never seemed to occur to them that she might have feelings.

She did look very different among their dark heads and golden bodies. At first they looked to her like copies of one person in their identical white clothes. Then she saw little differences. Some were taller, some fatter, some cleaner. When she looked into their faces, she saw skin as light as an English peasant in the summer, and some as dark as a Malay. Hair color ranged from dark brown to coal black, and eyes were gray and hazel and deep brown. The tilted eyelids and high cheekbones rested in faces that were oval, round, square. But nowhere did she see the face that looked out at her from her dream.

Her cheeks grew hot against the chill of the water. Could one of the men in the village have looked at her as she slept? No, it must have been a dream. She smiled as she remembered her shock at lying in bed with no clothes that first day. Now she took pleasure in slipping her nude body beneath the *ibul* each night. She reveled in the freedom of the loose clothing as she dressed and worked each day. And even the cold couldn't mar the delight of pushing her bare skin through the waves.

Even so, she was glad only women dived. People pawed at her enough with her clothes on. She didn't like the thought of strangers, men, watching her swim.

A school of pollack darkened the sea above her. At least the family didn't stare. Except for Sonyŏ, they rarely spoke to her, and their slanted eyes seemed to look past instead of at her. Even the round-cheeked children stayed away, peeking around their mothers' skirts as they sucked chubby fingers. But they didn't poke and prod, or talk about her as if she weren't there. Sonyŏ tried to teach her the language after the others left to go diving, although it seemed more like a game, with Megan as a new toy.

She reached the kelp bed and turned slowly around, peering into the dark waters. Seeing no danger, she opened the basket and used the knife to cut green kelp. When her chest tightened, she blew small bubbles from her nose as she'd been taught and tried to imagine the water as a lover, holding her, caressing her. The ache in her temple subsided, and she began to enjoy the strange world under the waves. It couldn't be any stranger to her than the one above water.

Nothing made sense here. The women worked while the men minded the home, unless they had as many wives as Koh. Five wives were enough to keep food on the table, so one stayed home to clean and cook and take care of him. Megan had expected jealousy among the wives, but for the most part the household remained peaceful. If bickering started, Grandmother let it continue for a while, then stepped in and settled it quickly. The others feared the eldest's anger, yet they clung to her for comfort. She delivered their babies and kept them fed and clothed, Sonyŏ had told her.

The muscles in her throat ached, and her mouth went dry. "Let the water take you." She continued to work, not rushing, but moving as fast as the water would allow. Among the kelp she found sea creatures, rough-shelled gray *kul*. She knew they sometimes had *chinju*, creamy-white jewels inside, and they made tasty eating. She grabbed several slippery handfuls, prying them from the rocks with her knife, and pushed them into the basket on top of the weeds. Not until the container overflowed did she allow the water to carry her to the top.

The high whistle emptied her body of spent air and her mind of fear, for the moment at least. The cool salt air tasted sweet upon her tongue.

The old woman's voice held anger. "Either too little or too much. I thought you had been swallowed by a *korae*, a big fish, you stayed down so long. Enough. You did well." She turned her wrinkled face to shore, hidden power in her withered arms skimming her bent body along the gentle swells.

As she followed in the old woman's wake, the glow of work well done, of fear challenged and vanquished, warmed her. She had fought the ocean and won! She wanted to shout and jump up and down. She dived, seeking some way to express her joy. Ahead, just beneath the waves, Grandmother's stringy legs worked up and down. The steadiness of the rhythm, the strength of the knotted muscles, filled Megan with gratitude and tenderness.

Then her heart gave a jump and a chill ran through her body. Gliding close to the surface, a blue cloud drifted, pulsing, in Grandmother's path. Shaped like an upended teacup, the transparent creature dangled tendrils that stung whatever it brushed against. The poison of the *haepari* could kill an unsuspecting swimmer. At the least, its sting brought fever and madness. She must warn the old woman, but the menace loomed so close already. Megan couldn't swim that fast.

Air shrieked out of her lungs as she broke the surface. "Grandmother! Grandmother!" she shouted, but the old woman's rhythm never slowed. Megan had to reach her before the jellyfish did. She plunged under the waves again, tracing the current the sea creature rode. She could swim faster under the water than on top.

For a moment it looked like the two might pass without touching after all. Her heart filled her chest and her throat. Almost there—she must get there in time.

Then, as Megan veered to avoid the creature's path, Grandmother's arm brushed against the shimmering dome and her leg tangled in the tendrils. The old woman's body jerked, and she faltered.

8

Megan shivered as she stood and walked out of the waves, half-carrying, half-dragging the old woman across the frosty sand toward the small fire. If only they'd thought to leave soup bubbling in the iron pot. Bad enough the old one was hurt without both of them freezing.

She settled the injured woman on woven mats near the small blaze and covered her with a long padded jacket. Please let her be all right.

She knew some of the language now—enough to understand most of what the family said to her, but she still had trouble forming sentences. "Grandmother, I go to village for help."

Muscles worked in the corded throat. The old woman's voice came in a wheezing gasp. "No! May-khan, you must stay; you must help me now." Blue tinged the wrinkled lips with pain or cold. The glazed black eyes stared at her.

Warmth rushed through her at the woman's words. Grandmother needed her, wanted her to stay. The warmth faded and she bit her lip. What if she left and the old woman died? But what if she stayed and the old one died anyway? Icy fingers of fear clutched at her chest and belly. No, she couldn't leave her. "*Halmŏni*, Grandmother, tell me what to do."

"*Ojum nuda*, make water on the poison."

What new insanity was this? Some heathen ritual to appease a sea god? The old woman was seriously hurt but wouldn't even be sensible long enough to help herself. She would never understand these people, never! She shook her head. She would not take part in such nonsense.

The old woman's face puckered with more than pain. "Ingrate! How can you deny one who has given you your life? The sting of the *haepari* is nothing to the pain you give

51

me. If you will not help, be gone! I will heal myself."
Panting, she pushed herself up with one arm.

The old woman's angry words stung. "But Grandmother, how can making water stop your pain? I must get someone to help you!"

Sinking back on the rough mat, the old woman sighed and closed her eyes. "Urine takes the fire from the wounds. Please, May-khan, the pain is great."

Should she believe the words she heard? Grandmother believed what she said. Could it be that such a simple thing could cure this pain, or was it just island superstition? Maybe the poison had made the woman mad.

She must do something—she couldn't leave the old one writhing on the sand to go for help. She didn't even know where to find the other wives, and she doubted Koh and Sonyŏ would know how to help. Her mind swam with confusion and fear. Anything was better than standing here helpless. What could it hurt, other than her own pride, to do as Grandmother asked?

Megan positioned herself over the old woman's body, but her bladder would not empty. She took a deep breath and relaxed. Hot liquid left her cold body and spattered on the row of red welts on the shriveled yellow leg. A row of red circles surrounded white dots on the old woman's arm. She moved until they glistened as well. A yellow puddle formed on the mat, then trickled off the edge and sank into the frozen sand. The warm animal smell of urine filled her nostrils. Never would she have believed herself capable of such an act.

Lines softened in the wizened face, and a sigh escaped from pinched lips. Color returned to the wrinkled cheeks, and Grandmother opened her eyes. "Thank you, May-khan. Bring kelp from your basket to cover the wounds. This will draw the poison out."

With the poultices in place, the old woman closed her eyes again and lay silent a long time beside the fire. Megan pulled on her padded *paji,* tying the baggy trousers at the waist and ankles, and hurried into the heavy patched *chogori,* knotting the short ribbons over her right breast.

She felt hollow, as if she hadn't eaten for days.

Swimming in the icy ocean made her hungrier than she ever remembered. She found and ate her share of cold fried tuber cakes, flat and slightly sweet, and chewed dried wafers of green seaweed. It wasn't scones or even porridge, but it filled a clinging belly.

She checked the injured woman. Grandmother's breathing sounded deep and regular, and she seemed to be sleeping. Her color looked normal, although her sunburnt brown skin made it difficult to tell.

Megan gathered her baskets and moved away. The fishy odor of drying kelp hung in the crisp air. She added the contents of the baskets to the cache of seaweed ribbons curling black against the brown mats spread in the sun. The wide flat leaves clung to her fingers, to the basket, to each other, as she smoothed them into rows a single layer deep.

Megan put the oysters back in the basket, though the thought of cracking the shells and eating the slippery insides stirred her hunger again. She'd save them for the old woman.

When she returned to the fire, Grandmother opened her eyes. "Please, May-khan, is there food and fresh water?"

Megan fetched the *chorongbak*, the hollow gourd filled with water, and the *tabal*, and opened the paper package holding their cold food. Then she showed the old woman the shellfish. "I crack for you, Grandmother."

She offered up all the halved shellfish, but the old woman pushed some of them back to her. No pearls. Megan shrugged and swallowed them whole, the pungent taste of raw fish biting her tongue as the rich, smooth ovals slid down her throat.

"May-khan, until today, a debt lay between us—you owed me your life. Now, *nanun piji opsumnida*, we have no debts. I have long seen questions in your eyes. Ask."

Megan blinked. She had so many questions. She longed to know more about the old woman's relationship with Koh, but she looked into those black eyes and couldn't ask. Instead, she went back to that first day, when she'd wanted to know but didn't have the words. "Why I dress like man?"

Slanted eyes crinkled at the outer corners and a low chuckle tumbled from wrinkled lips. "I forget you are young, and to attract men is a natural desire. Is this your wish?"

Megan shuddered. To attract these men? "No!" She shook her head.

The lined face became still. "Good. It was my hope to protect your freedom and my household. Our *tongsin* is weak. Soon he will tire of Sonyŏ. To dress you like a woman would make him want you like a woman. And so for other men."

Then the face in the dream *was* just a nightmare. Why did sadness tinge her relief? Nonsense! It was only that she missed Jemmie. That must be it.

Now that the conversation had turned to men and women, maybe she could learn what she so wanted to know. "Grandmother, what was your life like when you were young like me?" Her cheeks flooded. What if the question broke *kumgi*? What if she offended the old dragon?

Grandmother stirred and sat up. Removing the poultices, she tied the white jacket over her withered breasts and stood to step into padded pantaloons. Although she pinched her lips tight, she favored the wounded limbs only a little. The woman sat again and turned her wrinkled face toward the ocean. Then she reached out a clawed hand to pick up a stick and drew lines and circles in the hard sand.

"I was past twenty, older than you, when I married. Koh was young, no more than twelve. There weren't many young men to marry. Many were lost at sea. Others fought duels or were killed in the Imjin War. But I was lucky—I was strong, a good diver, a good provider, and pretty, too." Her momentary smile showed strong white teeth. "We were happy. I petted him and made much of him, as his mother had done. He loved to paint, and I was a good enough diver so he didn't need to work. Soon, he came to understand more of manhood, and as he grew, he became a tender and powerful lover." She dropped the stick and laced her gnarled fingers together, drawing her knees up to her chest. The old woman sat in silence for a time, her eyes once again on the waves.

"But with each waning of the moon, our hope of a child dwindled, and his spirit drew away. One day he brought home another woman to share his bed. She gave him children, and he grew happy again, and I was happy for him, but sad for myself. I tried to love his children, tried to be a sister to his new wife, but inside I cried that they should take my place in his heart."

The black eyes looked once more straight into Megan's. "So I worked, and he brought home another, and another. I am proud of the way the family prospers. But still, in my heart, I cannot love his wives or his children. I carry a young woman's wish in an old woman's heart—I wish for a child of my own."

A tear slipped down Megan's cheek. She longed to throw her arms around the old one, to hold her, comfort her, but she had never seen these people embrace. Instead, she reached out her hand and touched the old woman's knee. What she knew of the language left her. She only hoped Grandmother could read her feelings from her face.

The black eyes bored into her again, then a knotted hand stroked hers, the skin of the old woman's palm like soft old leather.

"And now, May-khan, I have you."

It took a moment for the meaning to sink in. Did the old woman want her for a daughter, to take the place of the children she never had? How could Megan explain? She must leave, must get back to her own world.

Face the truth—she might never leave the island anyway. Wasn't it better to belong, to be loved, to make an old woman happy, and give up her dreams of escape? No, she couldn't let go of her home. But she could be Grandmother's child for now, until the time came to go.

Maybe it was cruel to accept the offer and still plan to get away, but the black eyes compelled her. She couldn't say no to the love the old woman offered, or the hope she read in Grandmother's face. She looked down at the corded hand that covered her own and nodded, then raised her eyes.

A smile lit the aged and sunburned face of her adopted mother. "And tomorrow, my little fish, you will take my place; you will dive with the other wives."

9

Moon of Snow and Ice

Megan spread the last black ribbon of kelp on the brown mat and pushed herself up, stretching her cramped back muscles. She brushed the gritty yellow sand from her palms and rubbed her face. The clean, ocean smell of the leaves clung to her fingers.

She was tired. Long shifts in the icy sea drained away her energy, even after three weeks of diving every day.

She pulled the straps of the *chiggi* over her shoulders. The sturdy bamboo frame allowed her to balance a large load on her back. She fell into step beside Grandmother, glad that the old one chose a slower pace than the two moving up the path ahead of them, glad of the old woman's silence instead of the chattering that echoed back.

The low rock walls along the sandy path looked like ones in Northumberland. When she blurred her eyes a little, she could imagine thatched cottages beyond, and peasants who spoke the King's English. They would be eating bread and butter and drinking tea. For a moment her chest ached so much she couldn't catch her breath, and tears filled her eyes. She missed her home. Would she ever see the Highlands again?

A rough hand clapped her on the shoulder, and a smooth, narrow face stared into hers. Then Tai's Mother smiled and turned, scurrying after the others, her plump son bobbing on one hip and a huge basket of dried kelp on the other.

After today, she had three friends, and if the others didn't like her, at least they respected her.

The contest had been the other woman's idea. Tai's Mother had been Koh's favorite before Sonyŏ. After the birth of her son, the family never used her own name again—instead, she was known only as her son's mother. The youngest diver, except for Megan, her strong young body allowed her to dive deeper and longer than the older wives.

From the day of the *haepari*, Megan's strength and skill increased. Today, Tai's Mother had begun each dive with her, going deeper and working longer in the kelp beds. Her smug smile as she shrieked the air from her lungs surprised and angered Megan.

After the second dive, Megan pushed herself deeper and worked beside the young woman until they both had to kick to the surface for air.

"You, Sea Demon!" The other woman's voice was shrill with challenge. "You think to mock me, but it is yourself you mock. We all know you came from the sea, and it is your real home. Why else would your skin be like a fish's belly and your hair like red algae?" The woman spat the words. "But I say to you, I am the better diver. Your gills have dried up with living on land, and you must breathe air like we do. You may fool the old and weak"—her gray eyes flicked at Grandmother treading water nearby—"but we know you for a demon still."

"Peace!" Grandmother's gruff command echoed over the waves. "We shall try your skill. A dozen times a man's height below us lies a bed of *kul* filled with pearls. You two shall dive together. She who stays down longest and brings back the most shellfish shall be known as the better diver."

Tai's Mother paled and opened her mouth to speak, then snapped it shut without a sound. Glaring at Megan, she drew air in, expanding her chest a little more with each breath.

Megan shivered in the icy wind as she filled her lungs. A faint buzzing in her ears and a tingling in her fingers and toes signaled her body's readiness for the dive.

"Now!" Grandmother barked. Megan plunged be-

neath the waves. The silky water warmed her face after the
icy breath of the wind. Silence rang in her ears. Her arms
pulled to her sides through the gray liquid. A stream of tiny
bubbles tickled their way between her breasts and past her
thighs. Her legs opened and closed, pushing her farther
and farther below the surface.

Beyond the kelp bed lay the edge of the reef. An
underwater cliff stair-stepped to the dark ocean floor. She
hesitated until a gold and black arrow swept past her and
over the lip. Tai's Mother raced ahead of her.

Megan arched her body and slipped over the side and
angled straight down into the darkness. Only dim light
reached these depths from the gray sky so far above. Sea
creatures glowed with an inner light, like the many-colored
paper lanterns she'd seen in Shanghai, too many shapes and
colors to take in all at once. She fought a desire to look
around. Instead, she searched the ledge for the other diver.
There, a yellow body hovered near an outcropping of rock,
prying handfuls of shellfish loose and stuffing them into a
basket, a yellow gourd floating above like a flag.

Megan powered herself to the nearest pile of shell-
encrusted rocks and pulled the knife from her teeth. She
levered clumps of oysters from their moorings with the
glass-sharp stone blade, loading her basket as quickly as
possible.

She yawned without opening her mouth to relieve the
pressure on her ears and blew bubbles to ease her straining
chest. The excitement of competition made her heart sing.
She'd never tried to be the best at anything. Her brothers
sometimes let her win footraces with them when she was
little, but only to silence her cries.

But now she really was good, a good diver—good
enough to race the best! And she might even win!

Megan turned toward the other diver. The woman
moved in slow jerks, air escaping from her lips in big
bubbles. Tai's Mother shook her head, then tipped her face
up toward the gray light. Putting her arms to her sides, Tai's
Mother pushed herself upward.

Megan had won! An underwater current played cool
fingers over her buttocks and belly. "Like a lover," Grand-

mother had said. Yes, like a lover. Would she ever have another? The dream face came to her again, but she pushed it away. What did it matter if she never had another lover? She had the sea, and she was good, finally the best at something!

The buzzing in her ears grew louder. With regret she loosed the sea's hold on her and followed her vanquished foe to the surface above. Had she miscalculated, stayed down too long?

Even as she whistled the last of the spent air from her lungs, Megan knew her life with the family had changed. Tai's Mother bit her lip and turned away from Megan's gaze. "You win," she muttered.

Without thinking, Megan pulled a handful of oysters from the basket and sent them to the seafloor. "We both win," she said, holding up the half-empty basket. "I stayed in the water longer, but you brought back more."

The other woman furrowed her brow, then flushed under her golden complexion. She smiled and nodded, then swam toward shore. The other wives nodded politely, acknowledging Megan for the first time, and followed Tai's Mother.

"I am proud of you, Little Fish—proud that you won, even prouder that you didn't shame one who tried to shame you." Grandmother's smile lit the cold gray air. "Now we must finish our work on shore. The winter days are short. The sun hangs high above the clouds."

Megan had followed the stream of white hair that floated out behind the old woman. Grandmother had indeed given her a new life. Strange she'd never known what joy it could be just to work.

Megan twisted her lip. Diving might be a joy, but carrying a *chiggi* full of dry kelp was somewhat less pleasant. She shifted the load a little higher. Only a short distance to the cottage now. A babble of voices rose beyond the next bend in the sandy trail. What could it be? Surely they wouldn't tell Koh and Sonyŏ of the contest. The divers rarely spoke of their work at home.

How strange it seemed even now for the man to stay home and the women to work. What would her Christian neighbors at home have said? They thought they lived as God intended, and that every other way spelled damnation. Before she came here, she'd have agreed. And yet, in a way she felt as much at home here, on this island, as she'd ever been in the all-male world where she grew up.

They rounded the bend, and Grandmother stopped. Two strange men stood near the cottage door, talking to the *tongsin*.

The old woman grabbed Megan's arm and took a step back, but then Koh hailed her. She let go of Megan's arm and trudged forward again.

"Grandmother, what is it? What does it mean?"

"My daughter," the old one said, then shook her head. The withered lips moved, but no more words came.

Something was wrong, terribly wrong, but what? Sonyŏ rushed down the steps, pushed past Koh, and ran straight toward them. "May-khan," she sobbed. "They come to take you away!"

10

Megan's body felt hollow, like a dried gourd. Her mouth filled with the taste of ashes, and tears of disbelief welled in her eyes. She shook her head and looked from one face to the other. Only Grandmother didn't turn away but looked steadily back into her eyes.

"No, Grandmother, tell me it isn't so. I don't want to leave you, please. This is my home."

The old woman's voice crackled like a dry leaf underfoot, all color and life gone from it. "So, my daughter, it is come. I had hoped they would forget you, leave you here to warm my last days, but it is not meant to be. You must go."

Grandmother turned and shuffled slowly up the steps and into the cottage.

Megan watched her go, feeling nothing, seeing, hearing nothing as the others helped her remove the laden *chiggi* from her back. Was this all? So much had happened to her in the last four months here. She'd changed so much. Disbelief numbed her.

With tears sliding down her round golden cheeks, Sanyŏ touched Megan's shoulder with a plump hand. "May-khan—" A sob stopped the rest of her words.

"Little Sister, thank you for all you have taught me."

Biting her fist to stop the sobs, the girl turned and fled after Grandmother.

Then Tai's Mother, still clutching the squirming child on one hip, clasped Megan's hand. "We will miss your help when we work, May-khan. You are a good diver, a true *haenyo*." The young mother turned and buried her wet face in the child's silky black hair.

Then Grandmother reappeared in the doorway and handed Megan a paper-wrapped package. The muffled click of metal on metal belied the packet's soft bulk. Her locket!

"May-khan, Little Fish, these are the garments you wore when you came to us out of the sea. I have cleaned them and kept them for you against this day." One gnarled hand brushed a tear from her lined cheek. "We both knew you would leave someday, as all daughters leave their mothers to begin their own lives. Only this I ask, my daughter: Come back to me, if you can."

How could she go? How could she leave these people, people she loved and respected, people who loved and respected her? "Please, no, *Ŏmŏni*, my mother. Do not let them take me. Do not make me go. I cannot."

"Fool!" Koh's voice cut through her. He gestured to the two strange men. "Take the stupid creature away!" They grabbed Megan's wrists. Memories of Devlin's tortures swarmed before her eyes. She twisted and turned, trying to free her hands to strike back at the attackers, but they held fast.

With all her might she wrenched her body around and brought the toe of her straw slipper up between the legs of one of the servants. The man howled but held fast to her and pulled her arm up behind her back.

She twisted to face the other attacker. Across the yard,

Grandmother's gnarled brown hand clenched the taller man's topknot, while with her free hand she slapped and beat him.

Then Koh's face appeared next to Grandmother's. He pulled the sobbing woman from the man's back and drew her into his arms, then looked straight into Megan's eyes. "Stop! You are a demon after all. You have bewitched an old woman who shames herself out of love for you. You will bring the King's wrath on all our family."

Megan's heart constricted at his words. She had repaid the kindness of her family by endangering them. She stood rigid, willing herself not to fight while the two servants bound her wrists with a leather thong.

The man she'd kicked grabbed the tether and pulled her so close she could smell the sweat and dust on his clothes and the garlic on his breath. He raised his hand to strike. She cringed, but the blow never fell.

The other man caught the menacing fist in midair. "Enough." They stared at one another, then the smaller man dropped his eyes. His upraised fist followed.

Megan turned for one last look at her family. The wives and children had disappeared, leaving only Grandmother, still sobbing quietly in Koh's arms. For the first time Megan saw how small and frail the old woman was. "May-khan, my daughter," she wailed, holding out her empty arms.

"*Ŏmŏni*, Mother." Tears choked her. Megan turned as the leather thong jerked taut, cutting into her wrists. She stumbled, then fell into step with the men. They pulled her away from the new life she'd worked so hard to earn. She did not look back.

A pox on the man! The butcher came puffing up, reeking of blood and offal, wiping his carmined hands on a ragged apron. He reached out a greasy paw and tugged on Megan's orange plait, snapping her head back for a moment. She tried to use her bound hands as a club, but the thickset peasant danced out of reach like a trained bear. His nasty, high-pitched laugh was as disgusting as his odor and appearance, and his actions seemed to entice the rest of the crowd to follow his example.

The tight ring of villagers made it impossible to move through the town's main street. Excited chatter drowned out Megan's pleas to leave her alone. Her two captors kept their eyes averted, ignoring her cries.

As they passed a new cluster of hovels, the fat butcher shambled off, braying the news of the strange creature to the rabble in the streets. Soon she knew he'd circle back, dragging more and more peasants to gawk and cackle.

The crowd edged still closer, the fetid odor of unwashed bodies filling the air.

The butcher chuffed back, pushing his bulk through the wall of bodies until he stood beside Megan again. Suddenly the great raw slab of his hand cupped one of her buttocks and squeezed. It was too much! If no one would help her, she'd fight for herself.

The roar of his laughter turned to one of pain as she twisted her head and sank her teeth into his shoulder. He jerked back and swung his other hand in one motion, his huge open palm crashing across the side of her face from the cheekbone to the white scar on her temple.

Her knees buckled and she sank to the sandy road, her wrists still tethered to her captors. Blood pounded in her head, or did she hear hoofbeats? The red cleared from her eyes. A mounted archer held a bow and arrow pointed straight at her tormentor. The butcher lumbered away and disappeared down an alley, moving with surprising speed.

"Yang, Pu, you useless bastards, get me down from here and fetch clean water." He unslung the bow and dismounted, then knelt beside her.

Where had she seen him before? Those slanted gray eyes and those high cheekbones looked familiar. She licked her dry lips. Metallic-tasting blood trickled from one corner of her mouth.

He lifted her head onto his lap against the white embroidered front of his blue silk coat. With clean fingernails he untied the cruel knots in the stretched leather thong. Raw stripes encircled her delicate wrists, cutting deep grooves into her white flesh.

Her jaw smarted and her cheek still stung from the butcher's blow. With gentle fingers her rescuer bathed her face and hands in the cold water brought by one of the servants. Then he lifted her onto the back of the wooden saddle.

As soon as he settled himself in front of her, she slumped against his back, her head on his shoulder, arms loosely encircling his waist.

She breathed in the clean man-sweat and horse. Who was he? Why had he helped her? The heat of his body soothed her. The horse stepped forward.

Megan's spine stiffened. She remembered! She knew where she'd seen him before. His was the face from her dream!

Cool white hands caressed his chest and stroked his belly, gliding closer and closer to his throbbing groin. Jongwhan awoke and loosened the tight *paji* from his throbbing groin.

From the far corner came a glimmer of white cloth marking the place where the foreign woman lay atop a pile of straw, wrapped in the horse's saddle pad. He could barely discern her soft, regular breathing beneath the snoring of the two footmen across the stable.

It had been an exhausting trek across the island in the failing light. Then, with the dusk came snow. The light from the lantern on his saddle showed little of the narrow track as the wind blew heavier and heavier flakes against their faces and bodies. The woman snuggled closer to him for warmth, and a sweet longing radiated through him. With his padded jacket and the glow of her body, he was chilled but not painfully cold, but the straw shoes of the footmen slipped on the wet rocks and their breath rose white in the dim light. The sound of their chattering teeth competed with the ring of the horse's hooves and their mumbled oaths.

At last an answering light twinkled through the snow ahead. "Master, it is a Buddhist temple. The monks there will grant us shelter for the night." Pu's panting voice echoed in the hushed night.

A thick layer of snow muffled the sound of their passage across the empty courtyard. A high stone wall and tall trees sheltered them from the howling of the wind, providing them with relative warmth.

Yang and Pu beat their fists against the high wooden gate. Lines of white snow etched every crack and chip of its red-painted surface. After a long wait, one side of the portal inched forward, creaking. A head appeared, black stubble thinly covering the shaved dome. Sleepy eyes peered out. "Yes?" The voice sounded rusty with little use.

"Open up! Can't you see that our master awaits entrance?" Yang growled through clenched teeth.

The man hesitated, then withdrew. The tall doors swung open wide enough for the horse, then closed with a hollow thud behind them as they hurried inside.

"Make ready your finest room for our master. He is a messenger of the King Himself," Pu ordered, but the monk stood with his lantern held high, watching Yang help first Jongwhan, then the foreign woman from the saddle. The gray-robed man edged closer, bobbing his head as he recognized the blue coat and winged hat of a gentleman. Then the lamp in his hand cast a pool of light across the woman's snow-flecked halo of copper hair. Her green eyes looked straight into the monk's dark ones. The man drew in a hissing breath, then turned and ran through a nearby archway.

Jongwhan had no choice but to follow. A stately abbot met them, his acolyte hovering behind. Without a word the saffron-robed man walked to the woman and looked deep into her face, then turned to Jongwhan. "We will have no demons here, Sir, King or no King. You and your men may enter, but this one may not."

Jongwhan's heart sank. "Now see here," he began, then stopped. Monks were *chunmin*, the lowest rung of society, as low as butchers and entertainers, but this man held the key to life or death for them. "We shall surely die if you turn us away. Would your Buddha have turned away a creature in need, no matter how strange it looked?"

"What do any of you know of the *Pulta*, the Buddha?" the older man scowled. "Very well, it may stay in the *magutkan* with your mount. You and your men are welcome. It grows chilly here, Sir. Let your men tie the beasts in the stable and join us inside by the fire."

"Thank you, Uncle, but if you will not admit my prisoner, we shall all sleep in the stable."

"As you wish." The abbot turned to the younger monk. "See that they receive food and drink in the stable and be quick about it!" He turned and bowed deeply to Jongwhan. "Goodnight, Honored Sir." He had vanished inside the temple, and they had hurried to the shelter of the straw-thatched mud hut where a few shaggy ponies and a flock of chickens slept.

Jongwhan burrowed deeper in the straw. Never had he spent such a miserable night. Not even an *ondol* under the floor to bring heat from the kitchen fire. It seemed almost as cold in here as outside. How could his servants sleep so soundly? He closed his eyes.

White arms reached up to him from the *yo*, pulling him down, down onto the glowing white body, to lie atop the soft breasts, resting between the firm round thighs, spread open to receive him.

He jolted awake. A hinge creaked and a puff of colder air blew across his cheek. Without turning, he spoke, pitching his voice so as not to wake the others.

"I know the last thing you want from me is my pity, but I am very sorry that I must be the one to bring you pain. Yet it is as the King commands. You and I, we have no choice. I must bring you to Him, because He orders it, and for reasons of my own." He paused, listening, but heard nothing.

"Where would you go? Even if you survive the night, you cannot return to Koh without bringing ruin upon his family." He struggled to keep the pleading note from his voice. "Only I can protect you in the name of the King. Now that the people know you are from another land and not a demon after all, they will obey the law, the law that only the King or his messenger can set aside." He took a breath. "In a square in our capital stands an ancient stone bearing the oldest law in our land. It exhorts all people of the *Chosun* to kill any foreigner who sets foot on our soil."

Again he listened. Snowflakes swept through the open door, chilling his face. "You are alone now. You need me, and I need you." If only she knew the truth behind his words.

Her strangled sob knifed through his heart. "I go only to relieve myself," she said at last.

He lay, rigid with anxiety. What if she didn't return? But he couldn't stay with her every moment. She had no choice but to return.

At last the door creaked open and closed again, and her straw shoes rasped across the earth floor. Faint sounds came to him from her makeshift bed. She settled into the straw and cried herself to sleep.

His arms and legs ached from clenching his muscles, keeping himself from going to her, soothing her to sleep. She'd made it clear she blamed him for his servants' cruel negligence. Damn the ignorant bastards! He tossed and turned in the straw, trying to find some small comfort. This promised to be a long night, and a still longer trip to Seoul on the morrow.

11

The Yellow Sea, near Chemulpo

The blackened inkstone slid across the table, then back again with each roll of the ship. Jongwhan's bamboo pen scratched across the smooth surface of the rice paper. A slim figure in baggy men's clothes took shape in the circle of lantern light. He frowned. The features were accurate, but somehow the expression eluded him. Sighing, he set the pen in a groove in the tabletop and put the sketch aside near a stack of other unsuccessful attempts.

He strode across the stuffy cabin and stared out the porthole. Stars twinkled in the clear predawn purple of the sky, but a trickle of icy wind reminded him that it was the time of *dai han*, the senior cold, when rivers froze solid and snow covered the ground.

The trip across the island had been uneventful. After the monks had served them a hot breakfast, Yang and Pu lifted the woman up behind him on the padded green leather saddle. The sturdy island pony had no trouble navigating the path through the slush. Sunlight and the woman's body warmed Jongwhan, and the jasmine smell of her skin blended with the crisp clean air. His hands ached to paint the beauty of the stunted pines and the crystal rills that cut the snowdrifts. Drops of melting ice ticked and tocked from the clay banks onto the shiny black stone trail in counterpoint to the ringing of the horse's hooves.

The trek had lasted a few short hours—too short. Too soon they were aboard the *totan pae*, sails billowing in the winter winds. And today, in a few hours, they would take harbor in Chemulpo. By tonight their fates would be sealed.

He held no hope of ever seeing the woman again after he presented her to the King. His Excellency might do anything with her—might send her to prison, have her tortured, or even killed.

Jongwhan's belly chilled. He should have left her safe on the island. But it was too late for regrets.

He leaned his forehead against the cold circle of glass. No, he must believe she'd please the King. She might become a member of the court, maybe even a concubine. Hot blood rushed in his temples. No! No other man would have her, not even his sovereign.

What was happening to him? The thought of her obsessed him. She was foreign, *oegugŭi*, not to be tolerated. He should shun her. Foreigners always brought trouble. He ground his teeth. Hadn't he read and reread the history of his people? For centuries outsiders had swept in wave after wave over Korea's fertile lands, using the peninsula as a bridge from one powerful nation to another, exacting tribute.

The people resisted, sometimes with arms, but more often with patience. A land of scholars, not warriors, a dove among tigers, they clung to their own ways, maintained their language, their customs, their art. He longed to take part in this war of preservation, to record for all time the scenes of everyday life—life as it had been for more than three thousand years. A familiar hunger gnawed at his belly. He must finish up this sacred duty to his father, restore the family honor, and return to his true work, his art, his life.

Blast the woman! Her beauty bewitched him. He'd told himself over and over to put aside his unnatural desire for her. Yet no matter how often he steeled himself to indifference, her presence dried his mouth, sped his pulse. It would be better for him if he never saw her again, but the prospect left him hollow.

He had to get control of himself. If only he could have slept instead of sketching all night, but the dreams had persisted, delighting and exhausting him. Outside the porthole, the first rays of dawn streaked the sky. A walk on deck might calm him.

Cold pressed around him at the cabin door. His feet crunched the fine frost covering the deck. The smell of brine and decaying wood stung his nostrils in the wintry air. The wind had died, leaving only the slap of the waves against the ship's wooden sides. Alone on deck, the pilot held the giant wheel. The rest of the crew must be sleeping below, out of the bitter cold.

Something rasped against the lea siding. A rope squeaked, then a pale hand slapped the wooden railing. Jongwhan stepped into a shadow just before the head appeared, haloed a deep crimson in the dim light.

The woman's lithe body jumped over the rail and landed with a soft thud. The breath caught in his throat, and his muscles tightened. She was even more beautiful than he remembered without scrapes and bruises marring her perfection in the silvery half-light.

Seawater streamed from round buttocks and smooth thighs. Drops of water fell from crimson nipples and froze as they touched the icy deck. A warmth spread through Jongwhan's loins. His hand stroked the smooth cold wood of the railing. With a faint rustling, the woman drew on her wrinkled men's clothing and glided across the deck and through the hatchway.

Why had she been in the water, in the dark? Did she hate him so much she wished to die? He shuddered. Was she a creature of the sea, a demon after all? Nonsense! He really must get hold of himself. She was *haenyo*, used to diving in winter seas. She must have chosen early dawn hoping not to be seen. She may have thought the ship was close enough to land for her to swim ashore.

In the growing light, a blue-green smudge of land appeared to starboard. She could have made it easily. She must have changed her mind, decided not to try to escape.

Whatever the reason, no harm had come to her. He rubbed his face. And now he had even more memories to torture him. His mind filled with images as he followed the woman across the deck and into the bowels of the ship.

Megan teetered down the gangplank. The soles of her gillie shoes slipped on the frosty surface of the wood. She clenched her teeth. Why hadn't Jongwhan let her wear her straw sandals?

She sighed. He'd come to her cabin at dawn, his face red, stammering a greeting. For a moment she wondered if he'd followed her on deck. She'd wanted one last swim—no telling when she'd have the chance again. She grimaced at the thought of him seeing her naked, but a hint of warmth stirred in her groin. Why else would he be awake so early? Nonsense. He probably couldn't sleep.

He'd asked her to wear the clothes from her country. Did he think the King would like her better in her native dress? She shuddered. He'd warned her of the consequences if she failed to please His Excellency.

Jongwhan had also convinced her of his concern for her safety. His compassion in the stable had confused her. If he hated hurting her as he said, why did he take her from the village? And why had he let those smelly servants bind her and the peasants maul her?

"For reasons of my own," he had said. He must have something to gain by keeping her alive until they reached the King. Probably money or power, like Devlin, like all men—only concerned about themselves. He didn't really care about her, only what she could buy him. One more reason to hate him. But did she really hate him? She loathed him! And yet . . . Nonsense!

It was only that she depended on him to protect her. She had thought she no longer needed a man on the island. And now she was back where she had been with Devlin, relying on a man she hated. Only this time she wouldn't be fooled by his seeming friendship.

Her feet slipped on the snow-covered clay bank. The odor of dead fish filled the chill air. Jongwhan took her elbow and without a word hurried her toward a cluster of ramshackle buildings. White-coated men stared at her. Why had he made her wear this? Even in her white clothes her red hair marked her a stranger, but with this dress . . . He pulled her into a dusty shop filled with stacks of clothing.

He spoke a few rapid words to the shopkeeper. His accent differed from the island dialect. She couldn't follow the conversation, but the man soon produced a green silk coat. Jongwhan handed the man a string of coins, then flung the coat over her hair and fastened it beneath her chin. The empty sleeves hung down the sides of her head. She'd seen merchant women wear coats like this in Sogwipo. Whatever their reason for covering themselves, it served to shield her copper hair from the crowds in the street. She sighed in relief.

Jongwhan tugged at her elbow again, then led her to a stable. This time she caught the gist of the conversation— they seemed to be dickering over the rental of a horse. She pulled the green silk coat closer and looked around her.

Shops lined the streets. From their eaves hung strings of dried fish and seaweed. People wrangled over piles of fresh seafood. Money changed hands on all sides. A fishing village, like Taejong, only dirtier, more squalid. This couldn't be the mighty capital.

Jongwhan concluded his dealings with the owner of the horse and hurried her away. Two hired grooms followed, leading the shaggy horse by its bridle. At the edge of the village Megan recognized a spirit tree. In front of it, people had piled rocks as they passed by on the roadway. Ribbons and streamers of paper hung from the branches, along with articles of clothing and shoes, all gifts to appease the spirit dwelling in the tree.

Nearby, large planks of wood stuck up out of the ground. The top of each had been carved into the likeness of a horrible face, then painted gaudy colors. Some kind of markings decorated the posts. She wondered if the people on the mainland believed the demon posts protected the village, as the islanders thought the stone grandfathers protected them.

A group of ragged peasants approached them, carrying a sort of wooden box half Megan's height. Red silk curtains hung in the window of a small door. The box sat atop four poles, which rested on the fellows' shoulders. They stooped and lowered the strange contraption to the ground. Jongwhan dickered with them for a moment, then gestured for Megan to enter.

She hesitated, then bent forward and opened the door. Inside, red silk cushions covered the wooden floor of a cozy chamber. Another curtained window opened in the opposite wall.

Megan clambered in and settled herself cross-legged on the cushions. She clung to the wooden sides as the box rocked once, then rose in the air and moved forward. Megan pulled aside the curtains and caught a glimpse of Jongwhan's grooms helping him into a tall saddle.

She dropped the soft material and leaned back. Her heartbeat slowed and she tried to relax. At least the little house protected her from the wind. She stretched out her legs. Might as well rest while she could—no telling what the rest of the day might bring.

The sudden stop jolted Megan awake. She leaned forward, careful not to overbalance the eight runners carrying the closed litter. The men stayed quiet, some wheezing from the steep climb, others chuckling at a whispered joke.

She put her face near the tiny window. A faint scent of lilac came from the scarlet silk curtains, probably from the last lady to ride in the covered chair. Below in a deep valley, lay a huge city, like a bowl filled with white flowers.

A shiny ribbon of blue cut through the center, and a wall marched up and down the surrounding hills. So this was Korea's ancient capital, Seoul.

The litter leaned sharply as the bearers started down the steep trail. A few more hours and she would be down there, inside the city. If only the time would pass quickly, no matter what the outcome. She could endure anything but waiting.

Megan had been riding since early morning. She sat back against the soft cushions, trying to find a comfortable position. No matter how her bladder ached, she'd resolved to wait for more privacy before humiliating herself again. Once they'd stopped so she could relieve herself. Her gillie shoes gave little purchase on the slick, snow-covered clay. She squatted behind a scrubby bush. The men didn't even pretend to look away. Her cheeks burned again at the memory.

She tried to go back to sleep, letting the darkness and the rhythm of the runners lull her. She sighed and opened her eyes again. She scratched her hard nipples where the wool gown itched and bound her. How could she ever have worn such things every day? At least it was warm. By why had Jongwhan insisted she wear it?

She wrung her hands and stretched as far as she was able in the tiny litter. A pulled thread in the tartan skirt caught her eye, and she took pains to work it back into the rough weave of the wool. Time wore on, leaving her restless mind numb with anxiety and boredom.

Finally the compartment leveled. Voices shouted, and horse's hooves clattered with hollow thuds onto what sounded like wood. The sweet-nasty smell of water plants and quiet slurping sounds announced their arrival at the river.

The covered chair lowered. Megan peered from behind the silk curtains at the afternoon sun glinting off the muddy surface of the water. Her eyes took a minute to adjust to the light. The bearers shivered and slapped their arms in the chill wind. They seemed to be on a boat or a ferry. Nearby, two men poled a raft loaded with oxen. Each bullock bore huge baskets of what looked like soil. As the breeze freshened, the stench of solid sewage turned Megan's stomach.

At the far shore, the chair rose up again, amid swearing and laughter by the bearers. Through the parted curtain came noises and smells she'd long forgotten. Cities—how she detested them! London had seemed so grand when Devlin first drove her through the streets, but later she remembered the beggars, the heads on pikes over London Bridge, the smell of the open sewers.

London was a city of tall buildings, rooms stacked on top because there was nowhere to expand out. Seoul's buildings were all low to the ground, with blank mud walls turned to the street. On planks across the ditches, little shops took the place of London's Cheapside market. The people looked and sounded different.

But ragged urchins played in the vile-smelling ditches, and people hurried on their way with no regard for other people in this great city as in the other. She held her woolen shawl over her nose and closed her eyes. If only she were back on the moors with sweet purple heather blowing in the sun. Instead, she faced a world she could never understand and a tyrant who might end her life on a whim. Tears left hot tracks on her cheeks. She let them fall.

The bearers picked up speed, each jogging step jolting her aching bones. Suddenly the noise faded. The litter swerved right, then left, then right again, until Megan lost all sense of direction. Neat houses with tiled roofs and empty courtyards flew past the small window.

Then the images slowed and the sedan chair lurched to the ground. The tiny door opened and Jongwhan pulled her out. He hurried her through a scarlet archway into a large room.

A hundred men in white sat on pillows around the room, each wearing a high-crowned black hat like Koh's. At the far end a thin man wearing a yellow coat and a black silk crown sat on a platform surrounded by others in a rainbow of colors.

In the center of the vast floor, two women faced each other. They wore round black hats and long frocks over their skirts, with the front tails tied behind their backs. In

time with the stately rhythm of the squeaky reeds and
gongs, the dancers thrust and parried with play swords that
rattled when shaken. The graceful women circled the floor,
alternately hiding the swords beneath their arms and
tapping the weapons against their hips. With surprising
agility, each did a backbend to rival the traveling acrobats of
Scotland.

The rhythm of the strange music increased. Two more
dancers entered. All four faced the audience, swords
clacking high above their heads. Then, very slowly, the
dancers knelt and brought the tips of the swords to rest in
front of them on the floor.

The music ended and applause erupted from the
audience. The dancers rose and floated to each side, then
settled like drifting leaves onto cushions on the floor. A
longing filled Megan. Never had she seen such grace and
beauty. For a moment she wished she could learn their
secrets, could move like a spirit, without weight or
substance. Who were these women?

Jongwhan tugged at her elbow and gestured her
toward the high platform. She stood for a moment, looking
up the score of steps to the slight man on the low red chair.
Behind him stood a brightly colored screen with green
mountains, a red sun, and a white moon. On the ceiling
high above, two painted birds circled in the rafters.

"Kneel," Jongwhan hissed.

She started. This, then, was the King of this strange
land. This little man held the power of life and death over
all those present, and most especially over her.

She bowed, touching her forehead to the ground. If
she failed to please him, he could order her tortured or
killed. But if he liked her, he might grant her anything,
even a trip to Nagasaki, and from there to her father in
Virginia.

A high laugh echoed through the hall. "Tell it to arise.
We are pleased!" She hurried to her feet and glanced up at
the small monarch. He laughed again and peered down at
her. "Does it understand speech?"

"Yes, Excellency!" Jongwhan's rich voice sounded
strained. Megan nodded, then looked down.

"So, Foreign Woman," The words came slowly and distinctly. "You understand me?"

She nodded again.

"Good. Here it is the custom for women to entertain men, to please them. Our *kisaeng* have just finished performing for us. Now it is your turn. Show us how a foreign woman entertains the King of the *Chosun*."

She knelt again and pressed her face to the floor, thinking furiously. How could she entertain him? She had no bagpipes, nor could she have played one. He wouldn't understand the Gaelic if she sang a ballad. Besides, their music sounded so strange, she was sure he wouldn't be pleased with her idea of melody.

It was important that she please him. She must think fast. A dance would be the thing, but without a partner—only men danced alone. Wait! The sword dance that Jemmie had taught her. No, that was a man's dance. But not here—hadn't four women just danced with swords in their hands? Besides, she could think of nothing else. She would worry about her boldness later.

She walked to two of the dancers and bowed. She pointed to the swords lying in front of them on the wooden floor. "Borrow, please?"

The nearest dancer, a dark beauty, scowled and pulled her swords closer, shaking her head. But the girl beside her smiled and nodded.

Crossing the ornamental swords on the floor, she lifted the hem of her wool gown and tucked a corner into the white Korean pantaloons. Lucky she had thought to wear her *paji* underneath her tartans.

With one hand on her waist and the other curved over her head, she touched her toe on either side of the bottom sword, then turned a quarter turn and repeated the step with the other sword. She turned again, touching with the other foot and switching the positions of her hands.

Faster and faster she touched and spun, changing hands and feet, until she could barely stand. Then she leaped to one side and bowed from the waist. For good measure, she got down on her knees and touched her forehead again.

"Ha! Ha!" crowed the thin man on the throne. He clapped his hands. "Yes! Yes! Southern Barbarian, we would like to give you a gift. What do you wish for?"

Jongwhan stepped forward and bowed. "No gift but your pleasure, Sire."

She must take the chance, ask for what she wanted so badly, even if it meant death. It was her only hope. "I want to go home, Sire, please!"

12

Jongwhan held his breath. She was beautiful. Red hair pooled around her bowed head. Scarlet skirts formed a larger pool around her bent body. Like melted copper, or a blown poppy. Would she die for her words?

Only the gold eyes seemed alive in the blank mask of King Injo's face. The slender monarch stared at the prostrate form. Then the corners of his mouth twitched. A rusty chuckle bubbled out between thin lips. The chuckle built to a hearty laugh. Others joined him until the audience hall echoed.

"Arise, Southern Barbarian. We shall consider your request. We know you to be ignorant and therefore forgive you for desiring to leave us. For now, you shall be trained as a *kisaeng* under the guardianship of Madame Lee Insung."

In one fluid movement, the leader of the *kisaeng* troupe stepped forward and bowed. Insung was still beautiful. She looked for a moment like a young woman flirting with her first lover. Soft brown eyes peered at the King through silken black lashes. The sovereign's smile softened and his thin cheeks glowed. He nodded to her. If only Jongwhan knew what lay between them. Maybe he could use it to help his father.

The King turned shiny gold eyes toward him. "And you, Yi Jongwhan, we are pleased with you. You shall assist Madame Lee and await our further pleasure."

Jongwhan bowed, then tapped Megan on the elbow. He motioned her to follow and stepped back to sit on his cushion. The remainder of the performance became a blur of color and sound. What unbelievable luck! They'd won the King's pleasure. He could stay at the court and find his father's accuser.

And best of all, he could be with this puzzling and irritating creature beside him. Without turning his head, he drank in the sight of her, breathed in the jasmine scent of her skin and the sheep smell of her clothing. No matter what others thought, the time had come to face the truth— even if she hated him, he wanted her!

Megan lay back exhausted against the red silk cushions. The sedan chair swayed with the steps of the runners like a schooner at sea. Whatever had possessed her to speak up to the King like that? Sweat trickled under her armpits and between her breasts. Jongwhan had told her the story of how this King's predecessor had destroyed his nephew, the crown prince. He locked the poor laddie in a room, then stoked the fire and heated the vents under the floor until the boy was roasted alive. She shivered. If they could do that to a prince, what might they have done with her? What might they still do if she couldn't learn to be a *kisaeng*?

No, she must succeed! Once more she must build a life for herself here. It was the only chance of finding her way home to the Colonies and Father. Well, at least she still lived, but she wouldn't stay that way long if she didn't curb her tongue.

She was alive! She hugged herself and laughed without sound. God, it was good to be alive! Even if it meant facing hardships ahead, she was alive!

The footsteps of the runners slowed and Megan braced herself. The chair tilted to one side and turned. Yellow light filtered through a slit in the curtains, revealing a courtyard filled with horses and servants. With grunts from the porters outside, the covered litter settled to the ground in front of a large building. A door opened. A beautiful young woman stood in the doorway, wearing a short jacket of spring-green silk over a long pink skirt. She smiled and held out her hand.

"Come. I am Soonhee. My mother sent me to help you find your way." The young woman's voice was as clear as her glowing complexion.

"What is this place?" Megan whispered, pulling the green cloak over her head. Would the servants react like the villagers? Would she have the strength to fight?

"Why, this is my home. And now it is also your home. You are to be *kisaeng*. We will teach you all you must know to be a fitting companion for the gentlemen who visit here."

"Companion! You mean 'whore'? I'll not sell my body!" To be rescued from the Shogun, then turned into a heathen's doxy, that would be more than she could bear.

Soonhee's laughter was like a tiny bell. "This is not a *changga*, a whorehouse. We do not sell our favors. We entertain gentlemen with conversation, with dance, with music, with poetry." The golden face stilled. "Sometimes a *kisaeng* falls in love and shares her body with a man, but often such a one ends her life with a broken heart."

Again the golden eyes twinkled and the smooth lips curved upward. "That is why it is better to be like me. I never fall in love." Her laugh deepened and she swept the courtyard with a glance. "But we must go in. It is cold and you are shivering."

Madame Insung waited, smiling in the open doorway, the warm glow of lamplight silhouetting her slender figure. Music and laughter echoed faintly from the room beyond. "Welcome, friend." Her voice purred a tone deeper than her daughter's, rich and warm like the peach silk gown she wore. "Come inside, please."

Soonhee stepped out of silken slippers and across the threshold. Woven white stockings covered her tiny feet, tied around slender ankles.

Megan hesitated, then bent on the snowy step to untie the ankle laces of her gillie shoes. With numb fingers she worked the knots from the wet leather strings.

A servant took Megan's green cloak and closed the heavy wooden door. Her damp wool skirts dragged against her ankles, but at least they partly covered her chafed bare feet. The warm floor baked the cold from her numb toes.

Megan sneezed, then stood with her hand to her nose, unsure where to wipe the moisture in her palm. Finally she squeezed her nose between her thumb and two fingers and pretended to smooth her skirts. The older woman smiled and cocked her head.

"What are we to call you?"

"My name is Megan." She curtsied.

"Welcome, Megan. You must rest while we find you some clothing. A *kisaeng* is known for her beautiful attire."

Insung gestured toward the interior. Men in coats of blue and green sat on pillows around the large room. Each had a cup and a bowl before him on a tiny low table. Like many-colored jungle birds, the *kisaeng* perched on pillows beside their customers. The graceful creatures poured and served, laughed, talked, and openly caressed their guests.

In all her months in Korea, Megan had never seen men and women show affection for one another before. Although it would have seemed normal in Scotland, here such openness shocked her.

Insung's low voice commanded Megan's attention once again. "You are taller than Soonhee. I will ask Pilsu to share with you until we can have your own things made." She nodded toward a stunning woman dressed in scarlet and purple. Pilsu's long fingers stroked her tablemate's cheek. "She is just your size."

Insung glided across the room to Pilsu's side. The young woman smiled and nodded at her mistress. Yet when the other woman turned to make her way back, Pilsu's eyes met Megan's for a moment with open hatred. What now? How had she made an enemy so soon?

"Soonhee will show you your room. Pilsu will join you as soon as she can. She says she is delighted to share with the King's new favorite *kisaeng*." She patted Megan's shoulder, then glided away again.

Soonhee linked her arm through Megan's "*Oshio*, come. It is not far." She led the way through a low arch into a long hallway. "Our rooms are on either side, like a *yogwhan*, an inn. This hall goes to the kitchen." She pointed to an archway ahead. "On the other side are more rooms. A *kisaeng* must have privacy."

She stopped before a paper-and-lath door. "Look closely at the design. Each door is different to prevent embarrassing mistakes." She pulled two tiny knobs in the middle and the double doors opened out like window shutters. "This is your room. I hope you will be comfortable."

An oil lamp lit the small cubicle. A pallet occupied one corner, a shiny dark chest another. Clean oiled paper covered the floor.

Soonhee pointed at the door opposite. "My room is there. Pilsu's is next to the kitchen." The girl squeezed her arm, then nodded and left.

Megan stood for a moment in the open doorway before she pushed the doors closed and sank onto the soft *yo*. Her own room. She stroked the smooth brightly colored squares of silk that made up the coverlet. She hadn't slept alone since those awful nights right after Jemmie's death. Since then she'd slept in the women's hold on board Devlin's ship and in Grandmother's room on the island. Loneliness filled her at the thought of her foster mother. She sighed. A faint scent of lavender and burning oil mixed with the wet wool smell of her gown.

She should undress. Pilsu might arrive any moment with clothes for her. She clenched her fists. Why did the woman hate her? What had she done? She took a deep breath. Maybe she imagined that look. Small wonder, after today.

It was too much. Events had moved much too quickly. Hours before, she'd risked death or imprisonment for a chance to go home. Now she sat in her own room on a soft bed draped with silk. She lay back and closed her eyes, enjoying the warmth of the room.

The events of the day spun through her mind: her early morning swim, the long ride in the sedan chair, her dance. She rolled onto her side and pulled her cold feet under her skirts. Now she would be trained as an entertainer. In London, many minstrels eked out a living as whores. But no London whore wore silks and furs.

She'd be an entertainer, the best in the kingdom, if

that would make these people send her back to the New World. She must do whatever she could to please them.

If only all the people were as warm as Soonhee and Madame Insung. They'd treated her kindly, with more warmth and friendliness than all the *haenyo*. Her chest tightened. Tears filled her eyes. She should be in Grandmother's room now, snug under her ragged white *ibul*.

It was Jongwhan's fault. How she hated him for taking her from Grandmother! And now the King had made the man her guardian.

An angry smiled curved her lips. He'd looked stricken when she blurted out her petition to the King. The way his clear gray eyes had widened and his smooth golden skin paled—it served him right.

What was he doing now? Sitting somewhere with some slant-eyed drab drinking rice wine, no doubt. Probably someone like Pilsu, stroking his face, leaning against one of his broad shoulders.

With a clenched fist she struck the coverlet. Her cheeks burned. The fool! If only—but it didn't matter how she felt about him. He was only interested in doing his duty. She should have been glad to get rid of him, but somehow it was comforting to know he was trapped by the King's order, too.

She shook herself and stretched, then got to her feet and untied her laced bodice. The stiff wool had left blotches where the gown chafed her bare breasts. How had she ever worn such stuff every day?

She tugged off one tight sleeve, then the other. If only she had her old white jacket. Well, at least she still wore her *paji*. When she loosened the laces at the point of her stomacher, the gown fell to her ankles. She stood for a moment in her baggy cotton pantaloons, bare from the waist up.

The white paper doors swung inward. Pilsu entered holding a bundle of bright cloth. Hatred flashed from her dark brown eyes, and her delicate lips curled in a sneer. "I bring you clothing as ordered."

Megan crossed her arms to cover her naked breasts. She must be polite, no matter what happened. Soonhee and Insung respected this woman. "I thank you. I will be most careful of them and return them as soon as I am able."

Pilsu laughed, a sharp cruel bark. "Foreign Pig! You think I would give you anything I value? They are castoffs I was going to give my maid. I wouldn't touch anything that came near your ugly white skin!" She flung the bundle and stormed away.

Spicy musk hung in Pilsu's wake. Megan stood clutching the soft cloth to her breasts. Why did the woman hate her?

Long shadows cut the frozen mud and crept up the anonymous walls and the roofs of the houses beyond. A skin of ice floated on the sluggish green waters of the open sewer at the street's edge. Some half-naked children stopped teasing a mangy dog, stared for a moment, then slunk away.

Megan clutched the padded silk *chogori* to her body in the icy wind. The former owner's musk still clung to it. Her fists clenched. Why did Pilsu hate her? She forced herself to breathe deep, the cold air burning her nostrils. No sense brooding about it. At least the jacket kept her warm.

She wiggled her toes in the padded white socks. No stockings for the last year or more. Strange, with their little ankle ties, but at least they warmed her feet and kept the *kudu* from chafing. The leather outdoor shoes clacked in the frozen silence of approaching twilight.

Jongwhan walked close beside her, staring straight ahead. The heat of his body reached out to her even though they did not touch. His smooth face held no expression in the harsh brightness and deep shadow of the late winter afternoon.

He'd come to take her for a holiday. Tomorrow they would celebrate the New Year. It was the custom of the *Chosun* to visit a *pansu*, a fortune-teller, to advise them on the coming year. She shivered.

A few months before Jemmie died, a Gypsy caravan had come to the Highlands. The fortune-teller had foretold great trouble. Her mouth twisted. Widowed, lost, half a world away from home—great trouble indeed! But Jemmie had laughed. They only wanted to scare you so you'd buy their charms. If only he'd listened.

She flinched when Jongwhan touched her elbow. A smile flashed across his handsome features, then he gestured to a nearby door. Ice etched the wooden plank over the sewer ditch. The smell of human waste brooded above the makeshift footbridge.

Megan held a hand over her nose and followed Jongwhan through the gate and up the steps. Frost circled the nailheads that pockmarked the thick wooden door.

Jongwhan coughed loudly and scuffed his leather shoes on the top step.

Why didn't he simply knock? She reached out a hand, then drew it back. She would ask Soonhee.

The heavy door swung inward on complaining hinges. A sweet-faced young girl hung her head. "Won't you enter, please?"

Megan lifted one leather *kudu,* then remembered and stepped out of the shoes and across the threshold. The floor warmed her stockinged feet. When the door shut, the inner darkness blinded her for a moment.

"We come to see the *pansu,* Little Sister." Jongwhan's gentle voice fell into the close darkness.

Megan could barely make out silhouettes. The girl's head still tipped downward. "This way, please, Sir."

The paper-and-lath door, closed tight against the winter cold, lay in shadow. Brght twists of paper, scrolls, and unrecognizable objects decorated the walls.

One lamp smoldered on the low table. Behind sat what remained of a once big man. Gray-streaked white hair ended in a topknot at the crown of his large head. A white mustache drooped past his chin on either side of a near toothless mouth. But the eyes! Empty sockets stared at her.

"Welcome. Please sit." A bony hand gestured to bright silk cushions across the stunted table. "Ahem, a fine gentleman and a lady."

Megan's heart thudded. How had he known who they were?

The corners of the ruined eyes crinkled, and the thin lips curved upward. "You wish to know what lies ahead for you." It was a statement, not a question.

"Yes, *Harabŏji,* Grandfather," Jongwhan said. He'd explained to Megan the polite title for an old man.

"And the lady?" The eyeless sockets turned toward Megan.

She opened her mouth but no sound came. Finally she croaked, "Yes, please."

Jongwhan gazed down at her, eyebrows lifted, head cocked to one side. At least he couldn't see her flushed cheeks in the dim light. She coughed, then nodded at him.

"Ahem." The old man reached for a white ceramic plate covered with fantastic creatures in bright red, green, and blue. "What year and month were you born, Young Sir?"

"On the fifth day of the fifth month of *pyong chin,* Grandfather."

The old man nodded. "What hour?"

"The second after sunrise."

The yellowed hands skimmed raised figures on the plate and stopped on the picture of a man with a head like a dragon. "Very good. Much wisdom and power." The ruined sockets turned to Megan. "And the lady?"

"Eighteen years ago, the sixth day of the eighth month, right after midnight." Her whisper echoed in the tiny room. She shivered again.

"The hour of the rat." The white topknot bobbed. "You will love others." The wrinkled fingers traced a serpent's forked tongue. "The day of the serpent. You will be a clever student." A long yellow nail traced the horns of a ram. "You will travel much." He smiled. "You have already wandered far." The fingertips slid to a man with a horse's head. "You will have the blessings of Heaven." He wrapped the plate carefully in scarlet silk and set it to one side.

"Now we shall see what lies ahead for you both in the next dozen moons." The *pansu* reached for a small box shaped like a turtle. Inisde lay three small gold coins. With folded hands he murmured something about people and symbols, then tossed the coins in the air. His fingertips glided over the coins, then he scooped them up and tossed them again, then again.

The creases in the old man's cheeks and brow drew

downward. He sucked on his teeth and hummed beneath his breath.

Megan squirmed on her cushion. Waiting made her nervous. In fact, this fortune-telling business made her nervous. In Scotland this old man would be burned as a witch. But they weren't in Scotland.

The old man sighed, shook his head—like the Gypsy fortune-teller at home. Why was he trying to scare them? She didn't want to believe, but maybe he could see the future. She shuddered.

His voice, when it came, sounded rusty and far off. "The one with blazing hair will bear much pain and sorrow before the New Year returns twice." The sightless sockets turned toward her. "Those you love and those you hate will die, and you will be helpless, as you have always been."

Now the wrinkled face turned to Jongwhan. "You will gain what you think you want, but lose what you value most." Not a breath stirred the room when he paused. "But there is hope. There is always hope if you are strong."

13

Jongwhan followed the warm glow of the oil lamp in Chang's hand. The *pansu* led the way down a dim hall, one hand grazing the thick inner wall. Except for the fortune-telling room, the home symbolized the Confucian ideals of simplicity and comfort. Even here the yellow-papered floor warmed his stockinged feet. The old man had invited him to a private room.

From behind, the odd accent of the foreigner's clear voice joined Youngsook's breathy murmurs. The women had retired to the *chubang*, the kitchen, for a cup of scorched-rice tea.

Real terror had shone from Megan's eyes at the old man's words. The charms he had bought only calmed her a little. True, Chang's words had been frightening. But if trouble lay ahead, what use to worry? One must bear one's fate.

Still, her passions fascinated him. Like Pilsu. He smiled. Much joy he had taken in that dark beauty's arms, but he'd been right to stop. She wanted much more than he could give. He sighed.

Chang turned. "What grieves you, Young Sir?"

Jongwhan's cheeks burned. "Nothing, Grandfather."

"Ahem." The old one turned and held the lamp a little higher. Cotton stockings whispered again on the paper floor.

He didn't want to insult the *pansu*, but what could he say? Still it was ironic—he didn't want the woman who wanted him, and the one he wanted despised him.

Or did she? For just a moment he'd thought she warmed to him tonight. No, she was afraid and vulnerable. He breathed deep. The sweet smell of rice cakes and the rich odor of New Year's soup filled the hallway.

New Year's Eve was a special time when he was growing up. Would his family celebrate tonight and tomorrow in exile? It had been two years since his honored parents sent him from the estate in Kyŏngju to regain the family's honor. Life had been so simple once. He started to sigh, then turned it into a cough.

Chang pushed aside a bamboo curtain. The room held simple furnishings—the usual marriage chests with brass fittings and age-mellowed lacquer. A bright *ibul* covered a pallet in one corner. A small table squatted in the middle of the deep-yellow floor.

"Welcome," he whispered, and gestured to a cushion. "Please sit."

Jongwhan picked up a small red top and set it aside with a smile. He'd enjoyed one very like the wooden toy as a child.

"My grandson sleeps in the next room. He is the reason I asked you here." When the old man smiled, years vanished from the withered face. "Like any boy of five, Kwangin longs to stay awake until the New Year arrives. His sister has told him his eyebrows will turn white if he

sleeps before midnight tonight." A soft chuckle slipped
between withered lips.

Chang knelt and rummaged about in a small trunk,
then held up a tiny silk bag. "I have white powder, but as
you can see, I cannot complete the joke without eyes, so I
would borrow yours. Please, Sir, would you do me this
great favor?"

Jongwhan bit back a chuckle. He remembered his
horror the first time he awakened on New Year's Day with
whitened eyebrows. He bowed. "Of course, Grandfather. I
would be honored, but wouldn't the boy's father wish to
help?"

"My son joined our ancestors before the child was
born. His mother died bringing him into the world. He and
Youngsook are all the family I have." Chang straightened
and cleared his throat. "But come, take a look for yourself."
He handed Jongwhan the bag and carried the lamp through
the doorway.

The small boy slept on his back, arms flung out, mouth
open. Damp black tendrils clung to his wide forehead and
smooth golden cheeks. A silken black braid curled over one
shoulder.

"Grandfather, he is a fine boy." A new longing crept
into Jongwhan's throat. Word had come from his father. His
brother's wife was with child. Why could he not have some
of his brother's luck?

The sleeping child kicked against the *ibul* and turned
his head. Better finish the task before he rolled over or
woke up. Jongwhan pushed the drawstring open and
dipped thumb and finger into the contents. He sprinkled a
generous amount of the white powder on the boy's smooth
brows. It clung to the dewy black hairs. A clean child-smell
mingled with the dusty odor of the powdered seashells.

"Done, Grandfather."

With a nod the old man led the way back to the other
room. He chuckled, then wiped the damp skin below the
empty eye sockets. "Thank you, Young Friend. You have
given me much joy tonight."

"It is nothing. It gave me pleasure, also." It was true.
He hadn't enjoyed a New Year's Eve so much since he was
Kwangin's age.

The old man leaned forward. "Would you care to see another surprise?"

"I would be honored."

Chang opened a large chest and drew forth a large paper package. He laid it on the table in front of Jongwhan. "Go ahead, open it," he whispered.

The finely crafted kite gleamed in the dim lamplight. A dragon swirled its green-scaled tail in loops and circles over the scarlet surface. "I made it myself. My granddaughter painted the dragon. It will be his first kite."

"It is beautiful, Grandfather. It reminds me of my first kite."

"I have already asked too much, Young Friend. I could not ask you to help an old blind man teach his grandson to fly such a humble kite."

Jongwhan smiled. The old scoundrel! How could he resist? "Grandfather, it will give me great pleasure."

The old man sucked on his teeth and nodded. "Thank you. I am most grateful."

Jongwhan cleared his throat. "I shall call tomorrow, then. And now I must see the young lady home." He rose.

Chang's hand caught his elbow. "Take care with her. She is a treasure." The sightless eyes stared up at him. After a moment he smiled. "And now I will take you to her."

With one yellowed hand, he took up the lamp once more. With the other he held aside the bamboo curtain. "This way." His white topknot bobbed as he shuffled ahead.

Jongwhan glanced through the open doorway at the sleeping child, then back to the dazzling kite before he followed.

A son. The words echoed in his mind. To have a child so beautiful, a child of silk and gold. He shook his head. Munja would never conceive. He'd accepted the truth, even if she hadn't. She spent all her time buying charms and visiting shrines, trying to appease the spirits of the ancestors who denied her a child.

He could divorce her, choose a bride of his own. But then she would return to her family in disgrace, to live on their sufferance for the rest of her life, or starve herself to death as many divorced women did. She'd never be allowed to marry again.

No, he could never divorce her. She'd tried to be a good wife to him. She couldn't help being barren. If he was to have a son, he must find another way.

The lamp disappeared for a moment, leaving him in darkness. Then the edges of a doorway glowed. The old man replaced the light on the low table in the fortune-telling room. "Please be comfortable. I will call Young-sook."

Idly he inspected the dried fishhead nailed to the doorpost. Charms, incantations, did they really appease the spirits? What must he do to get a son of his own like Kwangin?

A clear voice startled him. "I am ready, Jongwhan."

He mastered his impatience. She wasn't intentionally discourteous. He must teach her *kichim,* the polite cough to announce oneself.

Still, her voice made his blood rush. He turned and drank in her beauty. Here was a woman to give a man sons. Perhaps, someday—but no. She was a foreigner, and she despised him.

Megan smiled and held out her hand. His heart skipped a beat. Maybe they could be friends, at least. He fought hard against his hope for more, but a warm glow filled his head and a smile touched his lips. He took her arm and turned to leave.

Pilsu jumped hard on the seesaw. Soonhee flew into the air, then landed again feetfirst on the board. Youngsook laughed and clapped her hands. "Did you see any boys outside the wall, Soonhee?" The girl giggled.

Soonhee squeezed the younger girl's shoulders. "Dozens. But I think they've come to see you. Your turn."

Only Megan saw Pilsu's nostrils flare and her eyes narrow. The dark beauty turned, folding her arms across her chest, and wandered over to inspect a stunted pine.

A warm New Year's sun had uncovered grass and mud in the courtyard of the *kisaeng* house. Hillocks of white snow lingered in the shadows.

"Now stand straight and don't look down." Soonhee fussed, arranging Youngsook on the seesaw. "Look over the wall and smile. And don't be afraid."

"I know how." Chang's granddaughter frowned. "I did it last year, remember?" She smoothed her bright orange silk *chima* over her slim waist and hips. "I'm ready. Do hurry, please."

Soonhee gathered her turquoise skirts in both hands, exposing embroidered white pantaloons and embroidered silk shoes. She leaped high and came down hard on her end of the seesaw.

Youngsook's face paled as her slender body rose in the air, but she managed to smile. Her *kudu* clacked. She landed on her feet on the board and both girls hopped to the ground giggling.

Youngsook clasped her hands and jumped up and down. "Oooh!" she breathed. "So many! And the gentleman who brought you to see Grandfather just arrived, Megan."

Pilsu whirled around and rushed to the seesaw. "My turn!" she announced, taking her place on the end of the board nearest the wall.

"Megan, you jump her up this time," Soonhee coaxed.

She started to decline but changed her mind at Pilsu's grimace. She raised her emerald-green *chima*. Her *kudu* crashed onto the board, sending Pilsu into the air. Megan waited for the other girl to come down before she bounced off the board.

"Your turn, Red Hair." Pilsu pushed Megan into place on the board.

"Be careful, Pilsu! She's never jumped before." Soonhee pursed her lips and clasped her hands.

"Oh, are you afraid, Red Hair?"

"It's all right, Soonhee. I can do it." She'd never give such a cat the satisfaction of seeing her fear.

Leather soles clapped against the board. She went straight up, and the bottom fell out of her stomach. With one hand she pressed her mother's locket against her chest. A dozen or more men stood outside the wall, but not Jongwhan. Where had he gone? Then the crowd disappeared and the ground came up to meet her. A thrill of fear twirled in her belly.

Her feet hit the board square, ready to bounce up and off. Instead the board lay slack, and she fell hard on her backside in the mud.

A peal of nasal laughter explained what had happened. Pilsu had jumped off her end of the seesaw before Megan landed.

"It's not funny, Pilsu!" Soonhee hurried to Megan's side.

Pilsu sobered. "It was only a joke, Soonhee. No harm done, right, Red Hair?" Did the voice hold a challenge or a threat?

Pain squeezed tears from Megan's eyes. She nodded once at Pilsu.

Soonhee ignored both question and answer. "It was cruel and senseless. You ought to be ashamed." Pilsu glared, then turned and flounced away.

Soonhee and Youngsook helped her to stand. The whole back of the green silk *chima* must be covered with mud.

From behind her came Pilsu's high voice. "Oh, Jongwhan, your foreigner has had an accident. She can't seem to learn our games."

"Pilsu!" Soonhee started forward, but Megan clasped her arm.

"Excuse me, Sir, but as you see, I must change my clothing." She forced her lips into a smile. If dissembling was the game, two could play it.

"Go ahead, Red Hair." Pilsu feigned friendly concern. "I shall be happy to entertain my old friend in your absence." A bewildered smile settled on Jongwhan's handsome face when the woman linked an arm through his.

Soonhee took his other arm and glared at Pilsu. Her voice purred, but her eyes flashed. "Yes, go ahead and change. We will all entertain the gentleman for you." With her other arm around Youngsook's shoulders, she nodded at Megan. The foursome turned toward the door of the visitor's hall.

Megan stood still for a moment, then put a hand to her aching tailbone.

14

"Grandfather, do you not hear? It's the candy man!" Kwangin's sweet voice penetrated the noise of the crowd in the marketplace. A young man held up an enormous pair of shears, clacking the blades together to attract customers.

"Really? Is it barley and mint I smell? I thought maybe it was garbage," Chang teased.

"No, Grandfather." Solemn dark eyes stared up at the lined face. "It is not garbage at all. It is *yot*, Grandfather, and very good *yot*, I'm sure."

Jongwhan's laugh brought a bewildered frown to the small countenance. He pretended to cough instead. "Please, Uncle, the boy must have some of this man's sticky toffee. And the lady has never tasted our *yot*. Allow me to buy them some."

When the fortune-teller nodded, Kwangin ran as if he'd been shot from a bow. Jongwhan laughed and followed. The man took the offered coins and snipped off bite-size pieces of the sticky mass.

Kwangin popped the whole piece in his mouth at once. He smiled and twined sticky fingers through Jongwhan's.

Megan strode toward them with her back straight and her head high, leading the blind man. Copper hair wove a crown around her head, *kisaeng* fashion. Coral brushed her pale cheeks and smiling lips. Perfect white features framed jade-green eyes. How could he be only her friend?

Something tugged at his hand. He looked down into Kwangin's shining dark eyes.

"Look up there!" Above them, dozens of kites bobbed and danced. Tiny figures on a nearby hill held the reins of these sky monsters. The small boy's awe and excitement infected him—to fight the pull of the wind against the string, to soar in spirit with a creature of paper and wood at the other end!

"Please, Elder Cousin, may we fly my kite now?"

Megan's faint jasmine scent announced her arrival with Chang.

The old man cleared his throat. "Patience, Grandson. You mustn't pester. The gentleman will say when he is ready."

"I am sorry, Sir." The small face fell.

Jongwhan laughed at Kwangin's solemn reply. "The gentleman is ready now. And the lady?" He held out his arm, but she turned to Chang.

"Certainly. Old Father, will you guide me?"

"If only I could, Little Blossom." The ancient one straightened. "Thank you, Daughter. Let us go arm in arm, and none need know who leads and who follows."

Jongwhan winced inside. Perhaps she hadn't seen him hold out his arm to her. He'd assumed she would walk with him, but of course the old one needed her. She became more Korean each day, saving the blind man's honor by asking him to help her, instead of offering to help him.

Kwangin tugged on his hand again. "Yes. Let's go."

The old man stroked his chin. "I recall my first kite." He and Megan followed Jongwhan and the boy across the marketplace to the bottom of the hill. "Do you recall yours, Young Sir?"

"Yes." He could see it still, cobalt blue with a rearing stallion. "All men remember that first battle of wills against the winds and the older boys."

Father had run partway down the hill to get it aloft, but once it was in the air, he'd flown it himself. It had gone higher and higher, until it reached the end of the string, pulling his little hands up over his head.

Then an older boy had run by, laughing. His string had cut Jongwhan's kite free. The older boys dipped their strings in fish glue and rolled them in ground glass to cut each other's strings. He even did it when he grew older. But that first day when he saw his beautiful kite soar away until it disappeared into the sky, his lips had quivered and tears had rolled down his face.

His father had said, "Be happy, my son. Your kite does not fall and lie broken at your feet. It is free. It flies up to God."

The pressure on his hand increased with the steepness of the climb. Kwangin's breath came in little white puffs and his smooth forehead glistened with sweat.

"Come, Little Man. Let me by your sturdy mount." He swung the wide-eyed youngster onto his back. The clean boy-smell mixed with the minty scent of the candy. Strong legs wound about his waist and two sticky fists clung to his shoulders. The longing for a son closed his throat again. He turned to look down the hill at Megan.

She and Chang seemed deep in conversation, but when she saw him she smiled and waved.

His heart lifted. "Only a little way left."

She nodded yes and turned to help Chang around a boulder.

The voices of the other boys came on the wind like the cawing of giant birds. He set Chang's grandson down on the green slope. "Here is good enough," he said.

Kwangin removed the paper wrapping from the kite. The scarlet and green dragon glowed in the clear, cold sunlight. With chubby fingers he tied the loose end of the string to the wooden crossbars and unwound a length from the stick.

"Please, Sir, could you get him into the air? My legs are too short." He sighed.

Jongwhan nodded, keeping his face serious. "I would be most pleased to." He held the stick loose in one fist so it could turn freely, then tossed the diamond-shaped kite into the air and ran down the slope. A gust of wind caught it, toyed with it a moment, then pulled it up almost out of his grasp.

Kwangin danced about like the kite when Jongwhan ran back up the slope and handed the stick to him. The red and green paper diamond tore upward like a thing possessed, dipping and swaying on its thin string leash.

Kwangin's stubby fingers held tight to the stick, turning it to play out more and more string. "It goes up, Grandfather! Up and ever up! Now it is dancing. It plays with me, dipping down and then soaring up." Wonder lit the five-year-old's face. "Oh, Grandfather, it is the best kite here, the most beautiful. It flies higher than all the rest!"

The truth of his words brought uneasiness to Jong-whan. Most boys looked upon kite-flying as a competition. A boy of about ten ambled down the hill toward them, paying out string as he walked. His kite sported the symbol of yin and yang in orange and purple. Another joined him, his creature a green diamond with two cranes in flight. A third came running, towing a brown rabbit on a field of bright yellow. Perhaps they only wished to share an excellent vantage. Perhaps not.

Kwangin's radiant eyes never left the dragon kite, soaring among the clouds. But Jongwhan caught the glint of ground glass on string as the other kites flew closer. Surely they would spare such a young one.

But he knew they wouldn't. Boys have little enough mercy. And he dared not interfere to ask forbearance. If they gave it, which he doubted, it would crush Kwangin's honor, ruin the pleasure of his first kite. Honor was important, even to one so small.

Just then it happened. The rabbit kite caught a freshet of wind and crossed strings with Kwangin's. The small boy's mouth opened in horror, but no sound came forth. The strings sawed against one another in midair, then the rabbit kite's string bit through Kwangin's. The owner of the yellow kite shrieked victory and led the others back up the bluff.

The scarlet and green diamond bobbed free and danced in a circle. Jongwhan held his breath. Let it go up and up and carry good luck to Heaven for its owner.

The nose dipped suddenly and swayed side to side as if looking for something, then floated down like an autumn leaf. At least it might land in one piece. He could get glue and ground glass and send it up again for Kwangin.

Tears streamed down the child's plump cheeks. The spindle of string hung from his limp hand, but his dark eyes

never left the paper diamond. A downdraft caught it,
tipped it on end, and it plummeted to the bottom of the
hill.

Kwangin ran down the steep slope as fast as his short
legs would go. Jongwhan found him standing, looking down
at a wad of shredded red paper and splintered wood. The
dragon twisted in agony, its neck severed.

"You think she is beautiful, your foreigner?" Pilsu's
voice broke his daydream. His face grew hot. He must have
been staring.

He smiled, hoping his voice showed an indifference far
from the truth. "Very different, anyway. And what do you
think?"

Pilsu's lips curved up, but her eyes remained cold
black. "She is interesting, as you say, different, like an
animal. Your move."

He frowned. He didn't want to contradict her, but he
wanted to make sure she didn't carry that comparison to
Megan as his.

She'd wheedled him into a game of *yoot*. Evening
shadows filled the visitor's hall. Soon the New Year's
celebration would end, and he must play one game with
her. Megan had refused to play, saying she'd watch until she
understood their games more clearly. Pilsu had colored at
that remark. What lay between them? They'd only met a
few days before.

Now Pilsu's marker jumped his, "eating" his man and
sending him back to the beginning. Pilsu had over half of
her men "home," while he had none. He couldn't concentrate with Megan so near, close in conversation with
Soonhee.

Pilsu scooped up the four ivory sticks and tossed them
in the air with a twist of her wrist. She moved another man
abreast of the first one and "carried" them both the number
of squares notched on the sticks.

"Truly, Little Flower, I do think the foreigner beautiful
in her own way, don't you?" Did her eyes narrow a tiny bit?
Did her nostrils flare ever so slightly?

She cast her eyes down, her voice demure. "As
beautiful as I, Dear Friend?"

He smiled. How could he resist teasing her? "Perhaps, but as you say, in a very different way." He tossed the sticks and moved his man a few squares closer to home, "eating" one of Pilsu's men.

Pilsu's lashes still hid her eyes, but her smile had left. Her voice fell cold and hard on his ear. "She hates me, you know. I do not know why, but she does. That is why she smiles at you, only to mock me because she knows I love you."

He laughed and shook his head. "You imagine it." Megan was not capable of such deception. Or was she? He glanced at her. She smiled at him and color tinged her cheeks.

"Do I?" Tears softened her voice. "Did you not notice a change in her these last few days?"

He started.

"It is since she learned of our love. She knows I would have you back for my own. She told me she does not want you for herself, only to keep you from me." She sniffed and wiped her eye.

So, Megan did still hate him, and this was her revenge. How could so beautiful a shell contain such a demon?

15

Moon of Spring Harmony

Megan swept the writing brush down, across, up, and back, then pressed her lips together. "M-m-m, right!" She wet the brush again before she made the double staff, completing the first part. Beneath, she stroked across and down, then added another staff with a tiny branch. Last, she stroked down and across.

"There—Megan!" Just like a schoolboy, the first thing she wanted to write was her own name. She wrinkled her nose at the burnt-oil smell of the black pigment. Madame Insung had spent the day before showing her how to ink the brush and write the symbols of *hangŭl*.

She set the brush aside and admired her work in the soft morning light. The piece of rice paper didn't look anything like the sampler she'd stitched at age five. Then, too, her main interest had been in her name. Indeed, she'd never learned much more of writing than the alphabet.

She'd relied on her father, then Jemmie, to read and write all that was needed. It would have been uncommon for her to know as much as a man.

That scurvy Devlin had known it, too. All those papers he showed her, claiming they were debts Jemmie owed him. And the indenture to pay him back, the paper promising to take her to the New World. She'd only been able to read her own name.

Devlin had smiled and promised to handle everything. Her mouth twisted. He'd handled everything, all right! She clenched her fists. The bastard! But he'd paid for his lies. She shook her head to clear the memories.

Most *kisaeng* learned to read and write as children. Soonhee said other Korean women did not bother, but *kisaeng* must be able to read the old songs and poems, and even write their own. Gentlemen expected them to be well-versed in literature.

And she would learn. She picked up the brush and inked it again.

The door swept open. Megan frowned. Jongwhan had explained the courtesy of *kichim* to announce oneself. She'd heard no polite cough. Who would be so rude?

Pilsu stood glaring down at her, a sneer twisting her delicate mouth. "So, the baby plays with ink and brush."

Megan opened her mouth, but before she could respond, Pilsu barked, "Come!" She wanted to refuse, to question her, but the woman had already turned and swept out again.

What if Madame Insung or Soonhee had summoned her? Or what if Jongwhan had arrived? He hadn't visited for many weeks, since New Year's. If she didn't follow, she might insult someone—worse yet, she might miss a welcome visitor.

The tall *kisaeng* stood in the archway to the kitchen near an open door. Soonhee had said Pilsu's room was near the *chubang*. Why would she invite Megan to her own room?

She shrugged. It would do no harm. Besides, maybe the bedchamber would give some clue to its puzzling occupant.

She stepped across the threshold. Pilsu's spicy musk stung her nostrils. Underneath the strong scent lay the odor of unwashed clothes, and something worse.

The sleeping room blazed with color. Heaps of bright silk cushions covered a sleeping pallet and dotted the yellow paper floor. Bamboo mats, scrolls, and fans, all in gaudy hues, lined the walls.

Pilsu inspected her perfect long nails. "My maidservant is ill. But Madame has said you will do instead. You will empty the chamber pot and rinse it, then bring it back." She pointed to a silk-draped bowl in the corner.

Megan longed to rebel. Madame would never ask this of her. Or would she? She couldn't be absolutely sure, and it might be dangerous to refuse. "If Madame wishes it, of course I will obey." She looked down at her feet to keep Pilsu from reading her face.

"Insolent bitch! I order it!" Her brown eyes blazed hatred. The sneering mouth opened as if she would say more, but she stopped, her head cocked toward the hallway. "Now go!"

The bowl smelled as if it had been neglected as long as the rest of the room. She held her breath and walked steadily to keep the contents from sloshing. Once in the courtyard she hurried to the night-soil pit and dumped the odorous liquid. Her stomach turned over at the stench. She raced to draw fresh water from the well and rinsed the container, then scrubbed her hands.

She'd put up with worse in her life, but not often. At least it was done. She didn't envy Pilsu's chambermaid.

Megan stopped to enjoy the tingly morning air. It was quiet. Her thirst for knowledge had awakened her early

The snow had vanished and a late-winter sun glinted over a steep hill. The chickens scratched and fussed around her feet, and the pig rooted in his pen.

Even emptying chamber pots could be endured if you lived with such beauty every day. She stretched, then picked up the bowl and cloth.

She grimaced. Better get this back to its owner and hope the woman hadn't found any other tasks for her. She wanted to practice her writing before time to eat *choban*. What she wouldn't give for a bowl of porridge! Instead, she got rice and vegetables morning, noon, and night—better than going hungry, but not much.

Pilsu stood in the doorway with her back turned. Just as Megan reached the room, the tall *kisaeng* stood aside and smiled. Jongwhan stepped out of the shadows and frowned down at her.

"See what good friends we've become? Red Hair offered to help while my maid is ill."

Megan bent her burning face toward the offending pot. "Excuse me," she mumbled, and pushed past them through the door. She set the pot in the corner. Damn! She should have handed it to the lying strumpet.

She looked down at her wrinkled white cotton robe. Her hair hung in snarls and ink smudged her hands. She must get back to her room!

She hurried out, but Jongwhan's brusque tone stopped her. "Why are you not ready? I left word that I would call for you early. Have you no respect for the dead?"

Shock stopped her. She whirled, her mouth open to protest, but Pilsu interrupted. "Yes, Dear, remember I told you to expect a visitor." She rushed on before Megan could deny a word. "It was sweet of you to offer to help me, but now you must get ready. The gentleman should not be left waiting. But don't worry, I'll entertain him for you."

"My dear, you are too kind." His voice held genuine appreciation. So that was it! If he wanted Pilsu and she wanted him, why involve Megan?

Something twisted painfully in her chest. "Your pardon, Sir. Be assured, I will hurry!" Did Jongwhan's eyes widen at the ring in her voice? Fine, let him wonder. She flew down the hall to her own room.

She closed the doors and stood with clenched fists, trying not to cry. Even if she had no practice at this game Pilsu played, she could learn! But what did any of it have to do with respect for the dead?

"Now bow," Soonhee whispered. Damp earth penetrated Megan's *chima* and chilled her knees. The gold locket burned cold against her skin inside the silk *chogori*. She touched her forehead to the ground. When Soonhee raised her head, she followed suit.

Jongwhan stood and picked up a cup of *makkŏlli* from the low table. Savory steam rose from hot rice and vegetable dishes. He walked to the rock-walled side of a smooth green mound and bowed from the waist, then filled a cup with milky-white rice wine and set it near the grave.

"What happens now?" she whispered to Soonhee.

"We wait," she answered. Still on her knees, she rocked back so her silk-covered buttocks rested on her heels, her hands loosely folded across her lap.

Megan imitated the pose, but after a few moments her legs ached. She pulled her silk-slippered feet to one side and rested flat on the damp grass. It would leave an awkward stain, but she really didn't care. What did all this mystery mean, anyway?

Jongwhan gazed out across the hillside, hands clasped at his back. What was he thinking? His handsome profile betrayed no emotion. What did he see? Green domes and low gray stone walls of grave mounds filled the view. Here and there tall pine trees swayed in the early spring breeze.

Steam no longer rose from the viands on the table. Her stomach growled. She'd had no time for breakfast before they left the *kisaeng* house. "For what do we wait?" she hissed.

Soonhee smiled. "The spirits of Jongwhan's revered ancestors will take the nourishment they require from the food. When it is cold, we shall eat it. That is why this day is called *hansik*. It means 'cold food.'" Her eyes flickered to Jongwhan and back. "I'm hungry, too!" She smothered a giggle.

Jongwhan knelt once more at the grave and touched his forehead to the green grass. Megan did likewise without any prompting from Soonhee.

Her locket swung out of the loose jacket. Let it stay. She'd remember her dead in her own way. With one finger she stroked the raised emblem. Following Soonhee's lead, she rose stiffly to her feet and joined Jongwhan at the low table.

A pity these people never used chairs. Her silk skirt would be stained beyond repair. Ah, well, she had others now. No need to wear Pilsu's castoffs. No, she wouldn't let thoughts of that hellcat ruin the rest of this day. She took a deep breath and pushed the woman from her mind.

Jongwhan poured a cup of rice wine and held it out to her. She accepted it with a little bow, then smiled directly up at him. His mouth blossomed into a full smile and the corners of his liquid gray eyes crinkled.

"You look lovely today, Little Poppy."

She cast her eyes demurely at the table and nibbled at a sweet rice cake. She could play Pilsu's game, too. Damn the woman! She'd promised herself not to think about any unpleasantness and just enjoy the day. She looked up. "Thank you." She longed to say more, but all she could think of was, "This food is very tasty."

Had she erred? Perhaps it wasn't polite to comment on the meal. She looked across at Soonhee, but she was smiling and nodding.

"I am glad you grow accustomed to our ways, my friend. Your joy gives me pleasure."

Did he mean it? She realized she was cradling the heavy gold locket in her hand. She hadn't meant to draw attention to it.

"What is that you wear?" His voice held genuine interest.

Nothing to do now but explain. "It was a gift from my honored mother. She is *chugŭn*, dead, like your revered ancestors." She paused. "This is a symbol of my father's family." She traced the design with a fingertip.

Should she continue? She wanted them to understand, to realize she wasn't a barbarian after all, that she mourned for her mother, and most of all for kind, sweet Jemmie.

She slipped a fingernail into the catch and opened the face of the locket. "And this is the likeness of the man who was my *tongsin*. He is dead, also, since two springtimes past."

Soonhee's indrawn breath made her look up. The girl's mouth hung open, eyes wide, cheeks pale.

Jongwhan's silky black brows furrowed. His face darkened. "*Kwabu!* You are a widow?"

What was wrong? She closed the locket and slipped it into her *chogori*. Being a widow was common enough. People died, after all, men as well as women. She looked him in the eye. "Yes."

Dishes jumped as two strong fists crashed down on the low table. Jongwhan leaped to his feet and strode away, hands clenched at his sides.

She leaned across the table, a question on her lips, but before she could ask, Soonhee spoke. "Oh, Megan! Do you not see? You cannot take another man if you are a widow. It would be disrespectful to your dead husband!"

16

The heaviness in Jongwhan's chest made it difficult to breathe. Blessed ancestors protect him when the King learned the truth about the foreign woman. No wonder she hated him! Not only had he torn her from a happy life on Cheju Do, he'd insulted the memory of her husband. She'd never forgive him. Something twisted in his chest. It wouldn't help if she did. He could never have her now.

"Nephew!"

He turned. Scents of jasmine, lotus, and pine masked the odor of many bodies. Men in coats of blue, green, and red milled about in the audience chamber. Each coat bore royal insignia of cranes and other symbols of long life. The more insignia, the higher the office.

A fat man with five cranes embroidered on his coat puffed toward him. "Nephew!" The man looked right at Jongwhan. He turned, but no one stood behind him. The man must mean him.

"Your servant, Uncle." He bowed. Who was this man? They would both lose face if he admitted he didn't remember someone so obviously important.

"And how is my friend, your father?" The fat man chuckled. A wave of sour *makkŏlli* mingled with a rancid-oil smell. So the man knew the elder Yi. Should he dissemble? No, whatever got back to the King must ring true. Here, all mouths whispered in one ear.

"He is sad, yet hopeful, Uncle. He longs for His Excellency's favor as a babe for the breast, yet he knows not how he has offended." The fat man's mouth smiled, but his eyes remained cold and hard. Should he press the advantage? After his audience, he might not get another chance.

He took a deep breath. "You remember him, Uncle. Could you not help?" The small black eyes flashed, but there was no going back now. "You have the King's ear. Could you not ask what my honored father's error was, so that he might make recompense?"

The man's wheezing filled his ears. The din of the other courtiers sounded distant. Only the two of them mattered. The round face held no sign of emotion. Then the cheeks jiggled as the head swung left, then right. "I am sorry, Son. I know nothing and cannot risk His Excellency's wrath by asking." The corners of the thin mouth turned down, but still no feeling touched the eyes.

"I tried when first he was sent from the court, but His Excellency forbade me to ever mention your father's name in His presence."

Jongwhan sighed and unclenched his fists. No hope. He'd failed. A taste of metal filled his mouth. "My thanks to you, Uncle."

"Tell Yi Dong Chul that General Kim On Yun is still his loyal friend." The fat man bowed, then flashed a smile and hurried away, no doubt on important business for the King.

"Yi Jongwhan," the voice rang out. His heart pounded.

The King's chamberlain summoned him. Soon he'd be on his way home, in exile like his father. His family was ruined. He lifted one heavy foot, then the other. Perhaps his brother could succeed where he had failed.

A court official shooed him through the brightly painted archway and stopped beside him in front of the huge scarlet-painted throne. The man bowed, then approached the small monarch, the memorial scroll extended. The King waved an impatient hand.

Jongwhan's heart rose in his throat. His Excellency already knew he brought bad news. That explained his refusal of Jongwhan's carefully written memorial. Perhaps his punishment would be greater than mere banishment. This could mean prison or even death. He swallowed and stood erect. If he must go, he would go with honor.

The thin sovereign whispered something to the red-coated official and waved his hand again. Maybe the King wouldn't even speak to him. The chamberlain scurried out.

His knees shook. The guards would storm in any moment. How had the news come? He himself had only just learned the truth about Megan this morning.

The King beckoned. "Come closer, my son, so We can speak to you in comfort." His pulse raced. What did this mean? He hurried to obey.

The thin face wore a warm smile. "Please, sit. We wish to be informal with you."

"I—I thank you, Excellency, for your great kindness."

"You are most welcome. Your visit gives us much pleasure." He leaned forward on the red and gilt platform. The scent of lilacs enveloped him. "How fares your charge?"

So he didn't know. Or was his sovereign merely toying with him? He took a breath. "She is healthy and learns quickly, Sire. She is like a child who sees the world with new eyes."

"Good. We are pleased. Yet there is more. You are troubled. You need fear nothing here, my son." Sincerity rang in the reedy voice.

"Excellency, I do not know how to tell you. The lady is not a maiden as we supposed."

The King's thin laughter echoed through the hall. All heads turned, then the messengers scurried about again and the din of voices rose to its previous level.

"I shall not ask a likely young gentleman how he discovered this grave news. Surely she is not the only *kisaeng* to bear this distinction?"

"Sire, she has been married, and the man is now dead. She is *kwabu.*"

The thin mouth drooped. "Hmm, that is unfortunate. And yet—" The small eyes twinkled. "What if We choose not to accept a foreign marriage as valid? After all, the woman is now *kisaeng*, and what she was before she came to the Land of Morning Calm is of no consequence to us." The small man sobered. "She is too valuable to us to set her aside in a nunnery."

He looked out over the vast hall. "If We were younger, We would taste her exotic fruits ourselves." He winked. "As it is, We leave that to one who is younger and abler."

How had he guessed? Jongwhan's face flushed and he started to protest. Laughing again, the King clapped him on the shoulder. "Now, get you back to her and away from all this conspiracy. See that the foreign woman dances in the Secret Garden at *Tano.*"

Jongwhan bowed. The King's laughter followed him through the archway. "Well done," a low voice murmured in his ear. He looked up into a smiling face.

"Pongnim!" He stopped and grasped the square-faced prince by both arms.

"Fool! Keep walking!" The prince's gruff tone contrasted with the merry expression on the square face. He took Jongwhan's arm and slowed his pace to a stroll, nodding and smiling at courtiers they passed. At the doorway he turned sharply. "We go to my quarters. Act like you have been there many times before."

Not until they had reached the royal chambers and the servants had all been sent on errands did Pongnim explain.

"Brother, I have tried many times to get word to you since I heard you were in the capital, but no one knew where you were staying." The golden eyes brimmed with tears. Suddenly he embraced Jongwhan and pounded his back. "My friend, I have missed you!"

"And I you. I never dreamed you sought me, or I would have come. I waited for your summons, but I thought my family's dishonor—" He shook his head. He couldn't tell Pongnim he'd mistrusted the depth of their friendship. "But why all this playacting?"

Pongnim's mouth turned down. For all the breadth of his face, he sometimes looked very like his thin-faced father. "We are surrounded by fools." He shrugged. "After the mess with the Manchus, trust is in short supply. Neither of us needs to incur more gossip."

Jongwhan nodded. He'd heard stories of the insults heaped on the Tartars that spring. The Koreans had played tricks on the envoys and threatened to imprison or even kill them.

Pongnim looked around, then lowered his voice to a level only slightly above a whisper. "My dearest friend, there is one in this city who seeks your destruction."

Jongwhan's heart pounded.

Pongnim's lips pressed together. "I have intercepted three messages meant for my father, each signed by a different lord and in a different hand. Yet when I questioned those named on the memorials, they protested they knew nothing of the messages." The prince turned and paced the shining floor.

"Each letter accused you of treachery against the King. None could be proved, yet they could not be completely disproved, either."

Pongnim faced him again, a frown creasing the broad forehead. Each quiet word rang in the still chamber. "You have made a very powerful enemy."

"Imagine yourself floating from a string attached here." Madame Insung touched a spot just below the nape of Megan's neck. "Now move across the floor. Good!"

Megan concentrated on flowing from one position to the next and keeping all the lines of her body in smooth curves.

"Again. Remember, all movement begins in your heart." The *kisaeng* tapped Megan's breastbone.

She took a deep breath. Strange, to spend so much time learning to walk. She'd thought that learning these dances would be as easy as doing the sword dance with Jemmie. She pointed her toes up and rocked back a little on her heels. Lifting her torso, she flowed across the oiled-paper floor.

"Better, much better, Megan." Insung's always quiet voice echoed in the empty visitors' hall.

It was early evening, a time when the other *kisaeng* prepared themselves for the evening's guests. Madame's voice held sympathy. "Rest now. You are tired." She sighed, then continued. "It is easier for a young girl to learn than for a woman grown. I know, it was so with me also."

The older woman cocked her head to one side and looked Megan up and down. "But no matter. It is your *mŏt* and *hung* that entertains the King, and other gentlemen also."

She must have looked puzzled, because Madame explained. "*Mŏt* is inner beauty. Without it, a dance is empty movement. *Hung* is a sense of joy expressed in dancing." Smiling, she stroked Megan's cheek.

"These qualities you have. Your movements grow more graceful each day. Tomorrow you will begin to train with the others for the festival of *Tano*."

"Thank you, Madame!" Megan squeezed the woman's fingers.

The matron's handsome lips pressed together, but her brown eyes smiled still. "You must work hard! You have only two moons to learn a lifetime of dance. Now, go rest before *manchan*. You must eat and rest well!" She smiled and shooed Megan down the hall with both hands.

Her feet barely touched the warm floor as she sped down the hall to her own room. She flung the doors wide and stopped. A small woman lay face-down across her sleeping pallet.

The dark head raised. Youngsook turned her tear-stained face toward Megan. She sat up. "Oh, Megan, I am sorry. I thought this was Soonhee's room." She bit her thin lips and twisted her delicate hands in her lap. "I must see her."

Megan's heart pounded. Chang! Had something happened to the blind fortune-teller, or to Kwangin? "Your grandfather and your little brother, are they all right?"

Youngsook nodded. "They are well, thank you." She stood. "Could you please tell me where to find Soonhee?"

"Stay here. I will get her." She whirled and sped across the hall. She coughed politely, then opened the paper-and-lath doors. "Please come. Youngsook asks for you."

Soonhee followed without asking any questions and knelt to take the younger woman's hand. "What is it, Little Cousin?"

Megan stood with her back to the closed doors. The soft brown eyes looked up at her. She nodded to the frightened girl. "You can trust us both."

The girl's voice sounded devoid of hope. "It is the matchmaker. She visits my grandfather for the third time. He casts for the most auspicious day. It will be soon." Her voice caught in a sob.

Soonhee's lips tightened. She stroked the girl's smooth black hair. "Perhaps it will not be so bad. You will have many sons. And we will visit you, won't we, Megan?"

"Certainly." What did it all mean?

"Little one, you wait for us. We will bring you a cup of tea." She motioned Megan out and closed the doors behind them.

"Poor girl." She sighed and leaned against the wall.

Megan shook her head. "I don't understand. What is it? What's wrong?"

Soonhee's eyes widened. "Don't you see? Her childhood is over. Soon she must be married."

17

Moon of Flower Rain

The youth strode to the center of the low platform and hesitated. The old gentleman in charge took the boy's shoulders and turned him until he faced due west with his back to the rising sun. Chang had earlier chosen this as the luckiest direction. The young man knelt on the scarlet cushion.

Jongwhan stood well back from the platform. He hardly knew the family and didn't wish to intrude on a private ritual. He only agreed to attend at Chang's request. Someone must represent the bride's family. It was a young man's place to witness the manhood ceremony of the bridegroom, not fitting for an old blind man or a young boy.

The scene stirred memories of his own *tabal* ceremony. He'd been twelve summers old, about the age of the lad before him, he guessed. Im Young June looked like a sturdy young man, tall and strong, with clear skin and good teeth. His young face held no sign of cruelty. Jongwhan nodded. He'd grown fond of Youngsook and wanted her to be happy.

The old man spoke the ceremonial words and undid young Im's long black braid. The sharp razor glinted in the slanting rays of the spring sun.

Jongwhan had faced the end of his own childhood with terror and pride. To kneel down a child and rise up a man in the eyes of the world! It was a ceremony he would never forget. He hunched his shoulders inside the padded blue coat. He hadn't known then what burdens manhood would bring.

He sighed. Would he ever succeed in restoring the family honor? Only the spring breeze competed with the scraping of the razor against Im's scalp. Gnarled fingers shaved a smooth circle on the crown of the boy's head.

The sound raised the hair on the back of Jongwhan's neck. He fought a longing to rush away, out of this courtyard, back to his room at the palace, to his paints and brushes. He'd worked and worked during the last two moons, but made little progress.

He needed—what did he really need? He must return to Cheju to study with Koh. And he must absolve his honored father before he could leave the capital. But even then, would he be able to concentrate? The image of white skin and copper hair lay in wait during every waking moment, ready to spring into his consciousness at any opportunity.

Damn the woman! And damn his own foolishness, pining for one who didn't even see him as a man.

With the usual words the venerable elder pulled all the boy's hair together over the shaved spot and cut off all but a handspan of the length. What remained, he folded to the front and bound with black cord.

Next came the *mangkun*. The tight strings of the black cap cut into the boy's forehead. He would never appear without it again, even in his own home. Jongwhan winced and touched his own brow in sympathy. The headaches had lasted much longer than his elation at being a man.

The next day he'd been married to Munja. His mouth twisted. Even that first night she'd been a disappointment. If only his bride had been more like Megan. No, no other woman he'd ever known was like the foreign woman. It didn't matter that she didn't want him. A sudden longing to see her, to be with her, rose up in him. He clenched his fists and forced himself to focus again on the ritual.

Im rose from the cushion and made his way around the circle, greeting and bowing to his male relatives. Each solemnly acknowledged the new Mr. Im. The boy had become a man, and tomorrow he would take a wife.

"They come! They come!" Kwangin burst through the gate and into the courtyard. Megan laughed in spite of herself at his earnestness. Excitement colored his plump cheeks and caused him almost to dance.

His sister frowned down at the boy. "Calm yourself, Little Man. Who comes?"

"The groomsmen come with the *ham*," he panted.

Youngsook blanched. "We must prepare the tables for the guests." The girl looked at Soonhee, her thin lips trembling.

"We would be most happy to help our friend, wouldn't we, Megan?" Laughing golden eyes turned to Megan.

"I am your servant. Instruct me." She hoped the formal answer would bring some explanation.

"It is the wedding chest, from the groom's family to the family of the bride. Food and drink must be offered to those who carry the gift." Soonhee tugged her along in Youngsook's wake.

Tiny tables, each knee-high, littered the floor of the *chubang*. Cold side dishes in small bowls formed patterns on the lacquered tabletops. Megan wondered again why Koreans couldn't eat together at one table. Instead, each man sat cross-legged on a cushion, with his own tiny table before him.

Youngsook knelt by the round brass stove. "How many, Little Brother?"

"Six." He held up one hand and an extra finger. "I counted!"

The girl returned her brother's proud smile. "Good boy! Now go to Grandfather. You must help him bargain for the chest."

Eyes wide, the child whirled and ran through the archway, leaving the bamboo curtain swinging crazily. Megan hid a smile behind her hand. The little scamp!

The sister's smile faded and she pointed quickly at each table. "Grandfather, Kwangin, Jongwhan. Nine. Just enough." She scooped cooked rice from the iron pot into graceful greenish-blue bowls.

Megan helped Soonhee put the filled dishes on the tables, making sure to follow the *kisaeng's* example exactly. Tiny pitchers of rice wine completed each setting.

From the front of the house came the sudden sound of chanting. "Buy this chest. Buy this chest."

The bride-to-be gasped and raised clenched hands to her breasts. "They are here," she whispered. Megan frowned. What did Youngsook fear? The slender figure crept to the archway and peered through the bamboo curtain into the men's room.

"Why must they buy it if it is a gift?" Megan whispered to Soonhee. The *kisaeng* shrugged and motioned her closer to the doorway. "It is custom."

Jongwhan, Chang, and little Kwangin stood silhouetted against the afternoon sunlight coming through the open sash. Six men crowded into the opening and dropped the brass-bound chest. The thud echoed in the flues beneath the *ondol* floor.

The leader swayed. Megan listened hard to his slurred words. "How much will you give for this chest?" Her nostrils twitched. The breeze carried the odor of fermented rice to the inner room.

Chang stepped forward. "How much is asked?"

"No, that is not enough! You must offer more!" the man crowed. His companions hooted at this brave response. The drunken man's features twisted into a confused scowl. He turned and muttered to a man in red, then faced the trio again. "Make an offer."

A smile lit Youngsook's face at Chang's reply. "He values you highly," Soonhee whispered.

Megan shook her head. "But—" she began, but Soonhee held a finger to her lips.

After several offers and counteroffers, the men agreed to Chang's price. "Now you must come in and partake of a humble meal, my friends." With much laughter and loud talk, the men lurched and fell to the bright cushions covering the floor.

"Granddaughter!" Chang roared.

Panic lit Youngsook's gentle face. She lifted a laden table and pushed the curtain aside with her elbow. "Do not look at them or say a word," Soonhee hissed. Megan lifted a shiny table and followed.

The young hostess bowed to her grandfather, then set the food before the spokesman and hurried out.

They returned to the kitchen twice. On her third trip,

Megan placed a table before Jongwhan. His hand brushed hers as if by accident. A smile played around his mouth when she looked into his handsome face. She hurried after her friends.

Once back in the *chubang*, her whispered questions burst forth. "Do we join the men now?" Soonhee smiled. Youngsook giggled.

"Only *kisaeng* eat with men. Youngsook must eat here, in the women's room."

"Please, join me." The girl set a large bowl of rice in the center of a short table. She motioned her guests to sit, then handed each a metal spoon. She arranged the cold side dishes where all could reach them easily before she sat.

"Thank you for your help." She smiled. "I have long dreaded this hour. It would have been most awkward without you."

From the men's quarters came the sounds of laughter and drunken singing. "Youngsook, you know we will always help you!" Soonhee's voice rang with sincerity.

"I am so glad you said that, my dearest friend. I have something to ask of you both." The slender young woman drew a deep breath and opened her mouth, but a cry from the outer room stopped her.

"Granddaughter!" Chang's rusty shout echoed against the clay walls.

Eyes wide, the hostess leaped to her feet, grabbed a huge clay jug, and swept through the archway.

Soonhee chuckled, then answered the unspoken question. "More wine." Sounds of laughter from without filled the silence.

Megan busied herself with the *pulgogi*, savoring the sweet-sour flavor of the chunks of braised beef. Youngsook could cook—she'd make a good wife. She frowned. Or did that matter here? She shook her head. So many customs she still didn't understand.

Youngsook bustled back in, cheeks flushed but smiling. "Forgive me. I am not used to guests." She cocked her head. "I wonder if my mother-in-law will have many." Her face fell.

Megan knew the girl would go to live with her husband's family and become the virtual slave of her mother-in-law. That much she'd pieced together.

Youngsook sat again and picked up her spoon, but only toyed with it, then put it down. She took a deep breath. "My friends." She smiled. "Because I have no mother or grandmother, Grandfather has hired an old woman to attend me and guide me tomorrow." The sweet young voice quavered. "But I hate to trust myself so completely to a stranger." She cleared her throat and looked down at the table. "As your last gift to me, would you act as my attendants?"

Megan lifted a hand to her mouth and covered a yawn, glad the day was almost over. Youngsook had hurried out several times to refill the wine pots. Each time the spokesman had taunted the young bride until the girl wept.

Megan had rejoiced when the tormentor fell across his table snoring. The others carried him out the door and the ordeal ended, but not before the bride's confidence had suffered some heavy blows.

What right had he anyway! The man might have been Pilsu's brother. And now Megan had to sit and watch that vixen monopolize Jongwhan.

"You are tired, my friend?" Soonhee sat nearby on a cushion.

Megan returned the younger woman's warm smile. "I have learned much today." She nodded toward Jongwhan and Pilsu. The *kisaeng's* long fingers stroked Jongwhan's face. "But I still do not understand all of your Korean ways."

Soonhee sobered. "You do not mean writing and dancing, do you?"

She shook her head in answer. Why did it bother her so to see them together? They were old friends, after all.

Soonhee spoke slowly. "You must understand Pilsu. She was not born *kisaeng* as I was. Her parents were poor farmers. They sold her to my mother when she was very small." The girl paused and cocked her head. "My mother has treated her well, but still she seeks love and attention constantly. It is as if she can never get enough."

Could she ask Soonhee? But she must know. She took a breath and fingered the beaded ornament hanging from her jacket. "And what is it she wants from Jongwhan? Marriage?" She held her breath.

Soonhee's quick peal of laughter drew all eyes to them for a moment. She covered her mouth to smother the giggles, then touched Megan's shoulder. "I am sorry for laughing at your ignorance. But it is funny—a *yangban* offering marriage to a *kisaeng*." Again she cocked her head. "Do not be angry with me, Megan. I will explain."

The small beauty drew closer. "*Kisaeng* are *chunmin*. We are at the bottom, you see, with acrobats and sorcerers. Our class is the same as slaves or butchers." She looked down and drew a deep breath. "For a *kisaeng* to marry, she must choose from one of her own class. For this reason we seldom marry." Megan could not read the emotion in her young friend's eyes. "*Yangban* are the top. A *yangban* man may only marry a *yangban* woman. You understand?"

Megan nodded. Despite the silks and furs, the future of a Korean entertainer looked cold and lonely. Still, another question nagged at her. "But what of love?" Her cheeks grew warm.

Soonhee blinked. Her fine black brows furrowed. "What has love to do with marriage? Parents and match-makers arrange marriages. The bride and groom never meet before the wedding. Men seldom love their wives." She wrinkled her nose. "I'm glad I shall never be a wife. A mother-in-law is a special type of demon."

Megan's mind whirled in confusion. Her need to understand overcame her caution. "But do you never want children?"

Soonhee's eyes widened. "One needn't marry to have children. A *kisaeng* can always become the *yobo* of a married man. He will buy her a house and spend most of his time with her. It is better than marriage."

"But what of an unmarried man? Might he not choose to marry a *kisaeng*?" she persisted.

Soonhee shook her head. "A widower must remarry from his own class."

"And what of a man who has never been married?" Her heart pounded. She must know.

"But there is no such thing. In Korea, a man is considered a boy until he weds, no matter how old he becomes. Look around the room. Every man here wears his hair in a topknot. It is the sign that a man is married."

Jongwhan leaned across the table and said something to Pilsu. His smooth black hair ended in a topknot beneath his sheer black hat. The room grew suddenly cold.

Soonhee's voice came from a great distance. "That is the other reason Jongwhan could not make Pilsu his wife. He is already married."

18

"I'm making a mess of this. You try."

Megan took the pot Soonhee offered. She wrinkled her nose at the fishy odor of the glue. Boiled cod livers. Poor Youngsook!

Soonhee had already undone the girl's long silky braid and pulled the shining black hair back into a knot. Now the young bride knelt in her white cotton underclothes.

Megan smiled down at her. "No wonder they won't stick. You've got to stop crying."

With the hem of her sleeve, Megan wiped tears from the dark-fringed eyes. "It's your own fault for asking us to help you."

She softened her voice to take the sting from her words. "We two know as little about this as you do, maybe less." She patted the girl's clenched hands. "But we'll get through it somehow."

A tiny smile touched the bride's lips.

Megan dipped the brush into the smelly glue and wiped the excess on the lip of the pot. "I think if you look up at the ceiling . . ." With delicate strokes she covered the lower lashes of one brown eye with a thin film. "There. Now close it." The upper lashes stuck fast.

"Can you look up with the other eye without opening this one?" The girl nodded. She repeated the process. Finally the bride's eyelids were sealed shut.

Megan shuddered. A barbaric practice! *I—will— never—understand—these—people!* Curiosity surged through her. How had Jongwhan's bride looked on their wedding day? Her throat tightened. She pushed the faceless image from her mind. Better keep busy, think of other things.

"I'm not good at this. You're much better," Soonhee said, and handed her a larger brush and another pot.

Megan shrugged and put the pot to her nose. The chalky odor of powdered seashells tickled her nostrils. Thank goodness! She had been given something to take her mind off herself—the task of finishing the makeup. "Where do I put this?"

"All over her face." The slender dancer tucked her slim hands under her bottom and rocked back on the cushion.

Megan smoothed the white powder evenly over the golden features. The tiny nose wrinkled and Youngsook sneezed, then squeezed her nostrils. "Are you all right?" The girl bobbed her head, but remained silent.

Megan glanced at Soonhee. "Did you glue her lips together, too?"

The *kisaeng* giggled. "No, she must not talk or smile today." Her face sobered. "If she does, she will bring dishonor on herself, and her grandfather as well. You understand?"

Megan shook her head. "Just for talking? Why?"

Soonhee shrugged her slim shoulders. "Silence is thought to be a virtue in a bride." The *kisaeng* handed her another small pot.

The faint odor of fish mixed with the tang of hibiscus flowers. "Where do I put the red?" She moistened a fresh brush.

"Circles here." Soonhee touched an index finger to each cheekbone.

When Megan finished, she set the pot and brush on the low table.

"Youngsook, you make a beautiful bride." Soonhee patted the bride's shoulder.

The girl nodded, shook her head, then shrugged. Megan touched her hand. "It's all right. We understand. Don't try to answer."

Soonhee pulled a length of blue silk from an open chest. "Now the *chima*."

Megan cupped one hand under the silent girl's elbow and helped her to her feet.

Together they slipped her hands through the shoulder straps of the gown, then secured it in back with cloth ties. Next they slipped the rainbow sleeves of her red *chogori* over her arms and knotted the sash over her left breast. They eased the bride onto a cushion.

"And now we wait. It is always the hardest part, yes?" Soonhee settled herself again and patted the pillow beside her. "It won't be long. It is almost noon."

Youngsook knelt with her head down, only the rise and fall of her chest and the white of her clenched hands showing any life. Poor little girl, only fifteen, no more than a child—the same age as when she'd married Jemmie.

She sighed. At least they'd known and loved each other. This girl had never seen the man she would marry today. And what of Jongwhan—did he love his wife?

"Megan." Soonhee nodded at the sightless girl. "You were married. Tell us of your wedding day."

Had the woman read her thoughts, or did she want to distract the nervous bride?

She cleared her throat. "I was just your age, Youngsook. My bridegroom visited my brothers often. We loved each other very much." She paused.

"Jemmie asked for my hand, and Father gave us his blessings." Tears welled up.

"Father and my brother, Robbie, raided an English village to get my dowry." She smiled.

"They read the banns in church three Sundays in a row. On the fourth, we were married." She cleared her throat again.

"It was a beautiful sunny day, with birds singing and the heather in bloom." She could almost smell the Highlands summer day for a moment.

"I rode to the church behind Robbie on his black stallion. I wore a new tartan gown and black gillie shoes." The same outfit she'd worn to dance for the King. One palm smoothed the silk of her *chima*.

She took a deep breath. "We stood before the curate and he preached about love—God's love and our love for each other. We vowed to be faithful until death." Her mouth went dry. "Six months later he died." Her voice sounded flat in the small room.

The silence lengthened. At last Soonhee rose and snuffed the silk-shaded lantern. The paper doors glowed with noonday light, but inside, darkness filled the corners of the bedchamber.

Soonhee's voice flowed into the dim silence. "I envy you to have loved so deeply." She paused. "Do you miss him very much?"

Megan nodded. "Yes. Very much."

A stockinged foot scuffed the paper floor of the hallway, then a polite cough sounded. Chang's voice came through the bamboo curtain. "The bridegroom comes." His footsteps shuffled away down the hall.

Jongwhan's eyes sought Megan's, but she looked away. She'd hardly spoken to him when he escorted her to Chang's home at dawn. His desire for her soared like a New Year's kite, only to be pulled back to earth again and again.

The bride appeared in the doorway, only the tiny red box of her hat and her gleaming black hair visible above the white-draped arms she held in front of her face.

Megan stood at her side, shoulders erect and head high, with one hand cupping Youngsook's elbow. The simple purple of her jacket heightened the red of her hair. Her beauty closed his throat. Then her eyes flickered toward him, green and hard as jade.

Had Pilsu been right? Was Megan only playing him for a fool out of spite or jealousy? Black doubt spread its wings in his chest. Or worse yet, did she grieve for her dead husband? One could not fault a woman for such a virtue, yet what hope had he against a ghost?

He turned his attention to the ceremony. Im knelt and touched his forehead twice to the cloth-covered doorstep, then rose and stepped back. Megan and Soonhee helped the bride across the threshold and into silk slippers.

The groom paced to one side of the courtyard. Two women servants hurried to flank him. Megan and Soonhee guided the helpless bride to a spot opposite Im across a tall table filled with ceremonial foods.

If only he faced Megan across such a table. Jongwhan clenched his fists.

An elderly official intoned the ritual words. Soonhee crossed the courtyard to dry the groom's hands after he washed them in a bronze bowl. One of Im's attendants dried Youngsook's hands.

Then the bowing began. First the bride touched her forehead to the mat twice. The groom bowed once in return. Then the bride bowed twice again, and again the groom answered with one bow.

Youngsook sat on the rush mat and lowered her arms. Such a beautiful bride. Though he attempted a proper indifference, pleasure flushed the groom's young cheeks. Jongwhan smiled. Good! Youngsook deserved to be appreciated. Munja's plain features crowded his thoughts.

She'd been seventeen, thin and sickly. He'd just celebrated his twelfth winter. What a wedding night they'd shared.

He followed his father's instructions and removed Munja's hat and hairpin, helping her off with her jacket and shoes. Once undressed, she dived beneath the *ibul* and turned her back. Miserable, he blew out the lantern, undressed, and followed her to bed.

She didn't resist when he turned her body toward him. She lay without moving, her face turned away while he did his clumsy best to make love to her as his father had ordered.

In eight years of marriage, no matter how he tried, she had never responded to him in bed. He sighed. May Im and Youngsook share a more rewarding marriage!

The groom's attendant poured wine into a gourd dipper and held it for Im to drink. Then she handed the cup to Soonhee, who held it to Youngsook's lips.

The sonorous voice of the elder intoned the final words of the ceremony. The married couple rose and turned toward the assembled guests and bowed.

With the ceremony thus ended, Chang urged the men into the main room of the house for a light meal. Jongwhan hesitated. Megan and Soonhee led Im's wife into the *anbang*.

Megan's arms and back ached with the strain of supporting and guiding the helpless bride for hours. She settled Youngsook atop the bed in her own room, then collapsed onto a cushion next to the bride.

"I'll be right back." Soonhee disappeared in the direction of the kitchen.

They'd waited while the groom ate a light meal, then clambered into a scarlet sedan chair for the ceremonial visit to the groom's parents.

Im led the way on horseback through the streets of Seoul to his home. After almost an hour, the sweating runners set the sedan chair down in the courtyard of the Im house.

Megan and Soonhee guided the new bride through the difficult task of serving rice wine to her new in-laws. With her eyes still glued shut and hampered by heavy clothing, Youngsook's hands must be guided in every gesture. Still, the girl had performed flawlessly, her serenity intact to the very end.

Megan scrutinized the bride's face. A little strain showed around her eyes and mouth. What must she be going through, unable to see, talk, or even smile, almost unable to move by herself? Why did these people believe this cruel custom guaranteed a good wife?

The return trip in the sedan chair had taken even longer. Traffic streamed around them in the warm spring air. The sounds and smells of a large city had filled the palanquin. Not even a breath of air filtered through the drawn red curtains. Sweat stuck the back of her purple *chogori* to her skin. Poor Youngsook, in all those layers of silk.

Well, at least the trip had ended at last. The bride and the groom would stay at Chang's home for three days, and then Youngsook would begin her new life with Im at his parents' home. How would she fare with the hard-eyed mother-in-law? Even sweet, pliable Youngsook might have a time pleasing that one.

Soonhee bustled through the door carrying a rag and a piece of green fruit. She handed both to Megan and collapsed at her side. "Green tangerine. You squeeze the juice on to unglue her eyelashes."

Megan twisted her mouth. Elected again. She knelt before Youngsook.

"Try not to ruin the rest of the makeup." Soonhee smiled.

Cupping the cloth under the girl's eye with one hand, she squeezed a thin stream of juice over the gummy lashes, then wiped the residue. Tiny balls of glue stuck to the rag. She repeated with the other eye. "Now, Im's Wife, try to open your eyes."

Dark fringes parted for a moment. Soft brown eyes glanced at her, then at Soonhee. Tears collected in the corners.

Megan wiped them away.

The bride bit her lip, then closed her dark eyes once more.

Megan looked a question at Soonhee.

"Come, we will wait in the *chubang*. It is best for her to stay alone and rest," Soonhee explained.

Megan stepped over the raised threshold and into her silk shoes, then followed her friend down the hallway. They entered the room between Youngsook's bedroom and the kitchen. Through the doorway they could see and hear the old woman Chang had hired, banging pots and muttering.

"What is she so upset about?" Megan asked.

"Oh, that's Auntie Soh. She thought she would attend the bride." Soonhee craned her neck to peer into the dark cooking room and shook her head. "Instead, she got stuck cooking and cleaning up. She's not a bad sort. She'll cheer up when the men finish eating."

Megan stretched and yawned. "Why, what happens then?"

"You'll see." The slim *kisaeng* smiled. "But now we should eat." A loud crash sounded from the kitchen. Soonhee giggled. "You stay here. I'll handle the old dragon."

Megan closed her eyes and leaned back against the *chaddae,* grateful for the chair's back support. If only they'd make one with proper legs so a body could stretch out.

The warmth of the *ondol* floor and the smells of cooking food lulled her. She yawned again and her stomach growled. If she weren't so hungry, she'd fall asleep.

Strains of music filtered from the front of the house. The tempo seemed to echo her pulse. To think she hadn't liked the sounds of flute and gong and drum when she had arrived. Now when she danced, the music seemed like part of her soul.

"Wake up, Sleepyhead!" Soonhee set a short table at her knee and uncovered the steaming dishes.

Soup, rice, and *bulgogi,* and of course, *kimchi.* She slipped the chopsticks into her hand and used them to ferry slivers of braised beef from the shared dish to her mouth, savoring every bite.

They chewed in silence for a moment, then Megan stopped with a sliver of *bulgogi* hanging from her chopsticks. "Shouldn't we feed Youngsook? She must feel faint, not eating since this morning." She set the chopsticks down and pulled her feet under her.

"No! She is fine. It is all part of being a bride." Soonhee pushed her back onto the cushion. "Now hurry and eat. The men are almost finished!" The *kisaeng* smiled again.

More mysteries. Megan shook her head and set to again. With her belly full, she struggled to stay awake.

Kwangin strode into the kitchen from the hall with two small tables and disappeared again without a word. A moment later he returned with two more. He grinned. "We're finished!" He scurried out.

Auntie Soh bustled in, all her complaints forgotten, wiping wet hands on a towel. The older woman perched in the open doorway to the outside, Soonhee at her side. Megan tiptoed over to join them.

Im crossed the twilit courtyard to Youngsook's door, slipped off his shoes, and entered. Megan sighed. He was so young. What kind of honeymoon could they have?

With a finger to her lips, Auntie Soh blew out the lamp and fetched a cushion up against the paper wall dividing the *anbang* from Youngsook's bedroom. Soonhee motioned for Megan to do likewise. When they all sat facing the thin wall, Auntie Soh scratched a small hole in the paper and put her eye to it.

Shock paralyzed Megan for a moment, then she grasped Soonhee's elbow. "Stop her!"

Soonhee tilted her head and furrowed her brows, then held a finger to her lips. "It is custom." The rice paper stretched for a moment before the girl's forefinger slipped through. "We have to see that the groom performs his duty." She put her eye to the hole and smiled.

Megan shook the *kisaeng's* elbow. "How can you?"

"Youngsook expects it. Otherwise she would have to sit up fully clothed all night because a bride is too shy to undress herself." Her golden eyes sparkled in the light streaming in from the peepholes. "Besides, aren't you a little curious?" Without waiting for an answer, the young *kisaeng* turned her attention once again to the scene in the next room.

A warm glow began low in Megan's belly. She should get up and leave. She couldn't look, mustn't.

With an eye to the hole, Soonhee giggled, then drew in her breath.

Unable to resist any longer, Megan poked a hole in the wall and leaned forward to peer into the bridal chamber.

Im placed the wine cup against Youngsook's lips while she drank. Then he fed her rice cakes with his silver chopsticks. His boyish face held a look of concentration, like a scholar recalling his lessons.

The young groom reached up and took the boxlike red silk hat from Youngsook's head and pulled the giant pin from the knot at the nape of her neck. Shining black hair cascaded over her red silk jacket and blue skirts.

Still not speaking, he lifted the hem of her *chima* and slipped the embroidered white stockings from her feet. Youngsook kept her eyes cast down and her face expressionless.

The young man's hands trembled when he tugged the knot from the front of his wife's jacket. He slipped the full sleeves over her hands, then sat back and looked for a moment.

A blush rose beneath the rouge spots still decorating the bride's cheeks. Her bared breasts rose and fell.

Megan's heart pounded in her ears. Sweat covered the palms she held clenched in her lap.

Im lifted the red and blue silk shade on the lantern and blew out the flame.

Megan sat in the sudden darkness striving for control. The warmth in her body centered between her legs. Pictures of Jongwhan flitted through her mind, his handsome smile, his broad shoulders, his easy stride. No! She could never have him. He was married. Even this heathen ceremony meant that he had pledged himself to a woman until death.

Her breath caught. Until death. The words rang in her ears. Maybe his wife would die. It happened. She grasped at this thin hope, then recoiled in horror.

How had this place changed her? What had happened to the girl she once was? A few minutes ago she became a Peeping Tom. Now she wished for the death of a woman she had never met because she lusted after a married man.

No! She pushed the images from her mind, but the warm ache remained.

19

Moon of Plum Blossom Rain

"Ninety-eight, ninety-nine, one hundred." Kwangin's clear voice filled the small porch.

Jongwhan bowed his head toward the child. "Congratulations, Young Scholar. You have studied well."

A rare smile lit the boy's face. "I can go on," he said. He ran to Chang and looked into the ruined face. "Shall I, Grandfather?"

The blind fortune-teller sucked on his long-stemmed pipe and smoothed the boy's shiny black hair with a gnarled hand. "No, Grandson, that is enough. You will tire our guest." He patted the child's shoulder. "Go now and tell Auntie Soh I said to give you a sweet rice cake."

Kwangin whirled and took two running steps, then stopped. He bowed to Chang and then to Jongwhan and walked into the house. As soon as the door closed behind him, the sound of running feet echoed from the hallway.

Chang cleared his throat. "You must forgive an old fool for being proud of his only grandson."

"Uncle, you have reason to be proud. I should be if he were mine." He swallowed a sigh, then lifted a small table and set it before him.

"Are the drawing materials sufficient, Nephew?"

Jongwhan nodded and smiled, then realized the blind man still waited for an answer. "Yes, Uncle, most acceptable. My thanks again."

He removed the lid from the inkstone. A carved dragon encircled the black surface. He toyed with a brush, the image of the boy still in his mind. *A child of silk and gold.* The longing for a son filled Jongwhan's chest, but he pushed it away. Why dwell on the impossible?

He sprinkled black powder on the dry stone. His nostrils twitched at the smoky odor.

At five, he'd been like Kwangin, serious, eager to learn the four cardinal directions and to count to one hundred. Had his father burst with pride at his young accomplishments?

He lifted the square stick and spread the ink dust across the smooth stone surface.

For the first time a note of hope sounded in the letters from home, along with a note of caution. He walked a dangerous path through the intrigues of King Injo's court.

He held the ceramic water-dropper over the stone. A crystal pearl hung from the tiny mouth of the dragon-shaped vessel, then splashed onto the dusty black inkstone.

Thank the gods for Prince Pongnim. Once again the prince had squelched a rumor intended to destroy Jongwhan.

Except for Pongnim, he'd stopped visiting friends at court. Now, when he saw old acquaintances, he wondered if they had betrayed his father, or if they knew who did. He declined their invitations to go with them drinking, gossiping, hunting with bow and arrow. Their pursuits suddenly seemed shallow and petty.

With a large, soft brush he stirred the water into the powder. He drained the excess against the stone's raised edge.

More than ever, he lost himself in his art. And when he could no longer stand to be alone, the honest companionship of the blind man and the beauty of the foreign woman drew him to the house of the *kisaeng* and the house of the fortune-teller, side by side in the shadow of the city wall.

A polite cough drew him back to the present.

"My courtyard must be beautiful." The lines deepened in Chang's face.

"Yes, Uncle." From the shelter of the porch, the entire enclosure of the *pansu*'s house lay before him. A soft breeze carried clean scents of new life.

The red-tiled roof of the *kisaeng* house rose beyond the thatch-topped wall. And what of Megan? Was she there? He twisted his mouth. His desire for her was as impossible as his desire for a son.

He shifted his backside into a more comfortable position on the cushion and drew a sheet of rice paper into the center of the low table. He dipped a small brush into the thin black ink and sketched in the outlines of the wall and the roofed gate.

The old man cleared his throat. "At this time of year more than any other, I miss my eyes."

Jongwhan stopped, the brush in his hand poised above the drawing. He shivered in the warmth of the spring afternoon. What must it be like not to see? He searched for a response. "I am sorry." His words came in a whisper.

"Do not feel sad for me, Young Friend. I lost my sight many years ago. I have grown used to it." He paused and spread his hands wide. "But come. Your brush is drying. Don't let an old man's ramblings keep you from capturing the glory of this day."

Jongwhan lowered the brush. "Uncle, I do not know what to say."

A rusty chuckle came from the old man's wrinkled lips. "Then say nothing. You paint, and I will talk. Would you like to hear how I lost my sight?"

"Yes, if you please, Sir." Warmth flowed back into his body. If Chang could laugh about something so grave, how could he feel sorry for himself over his small problems? He dipped the brush again.

"Good." The old man rested two gnarled hands on his knees. "But first, tell me—are the buds swelling on the cherry tree?"

"Why, yes." The tree stood in a corner near the wall, its branches bristling with new growth. Pink edges trimmed the hard green knobs hiding among the new leaves. "But how did you know?"

"Tomorrow the buds will burst. The day after, it will be *Tano*." The fortune-teller smiled again. "It was just so when I lost my eyes. The blossoms are the last thing I saw."

With a new sense of confidence, Jongwhan's fingers traced the lines of the tree onto the paper.

The old *pansu* cocked his head. "It was *Tano* day, more

than forty years ago. I had seen just fifteen summers. The string of red peppers still hung across the gate, announcing the birth of my son and barring visitors from our home." He tapped the ash from his pipe.

"The Imjin War was almost at an end, though we didn't realize it then. The yellow dwarves had retreated time and again before Admiral Yi Sun Shin and his armored turtle boats, but a fresh wave broke through and swarmed into the capital."

Pride and anger burned in Jongwhan. How dare the bastards violate Seoul? Thank the gods for the peace the kingdom now enjoyed. With a few swift strokes the leafy branches took shape from his brush.

Chang filled the bowl of his long-stemmed pipe with fresh tobacco and lit it. A stream of sweet-smelling smoke curled about his head. "I hid my wife and son in the outhouse." He chuckled. "It was horrible—they smelled bad for days."

Jongwhan smiled, then shook his head. After the way King Injo had ill-used the Manchus, many people believed the barbarians would invade. His heart pounded. If war came, Megan would be in danger. Her odd coloring, her exotic beauty, would draw attention to her. Would he be able to protect her?

The wrinkled face sobered. "The soldiers broke through the gate." He pointed toward the roofed portal, pipe stem extended. "They knew the peppers signified a son. They wanted slaves to take back to the Japans."

Jongwhan's jaw clenched. To have a son, such a one as Kwangin, and to lose him. It went beyond imagining. He twirled the sable brush to a fine point and dotted the branches with tiny buds.

Chang held the bowl of the pipe between thumb and finger, tapping it against his knee. "When I wouldn't tell them where I had hidden my family, they built a fire and burned all the trees, save that one."

The old man nodded toward the bud-laden tree. "The leader held his sword in the flames until it glowed red. He put it first to one eye, then to the other."

Jongwhan shuddered. Would he react so bravely if he ever faced a barbarian enemy?

The fortune-teller paused, stroking his long white beard. "The last thing I saw was that tree, heavy with pink blossoms." He sucked at his pipe for a moment.

"I lay there in agony, screaming at first, then moaning, smelling the perfume of the blossoms mixed with smoke and the stench of my own burned flesh, until long after the heat of the day had passed." The wizened head swung back and forth. "My wife was an obedient woman. I told her to stay hidden until dark, and that is what she did." He grimaced. "She thought I was dead when she saw me. When she shrieked at the sight of me, I almost wished that they had killed me."

The brush shook in his hand. The bastards! What kind of man would do this to another? He knew the stories of the war, of women captured, raped, artisans dragged off for the rest of their lives, and worse—the monument Hideyoshi erected for the noses and ears his men cut from living Koreans.

Chang shrugged. "But I lived and became a teller of fortunes, a giver of advice."

Jongwhan's belly crawled. How could the man speak so calmly about such horror? He laid the brush aside and sat back.

He looked from the tree to the paper, reality to art. The lines were crude, but at last his work began to show life. He'd captured something of the moment in the black strokes on the thick white paper. If only he could return to the island, to Koh.

The old man coughed. "Your painting is finished. So is my story." The knotted fingers whitened on the pipe.

A warmth grew in him. Peace flowed to him from this old, fragile man, so brave in his refusal to give in.

Chang smiled. "I have no regrets. I would give my eyes again to bring my son back. Without the grandchildren he left me, I would have nothing." The wrinkled face sobered. "Remember, my friend, no agony can compare to the loss of one you truly love."

Megan arched her spine to relieve knots of tired muscles, then slumped against the padded *chaddae*. The chair back supported her weary frame and the *ondol* floor warmed her outstretched feet in the dim corner of the visitors' hall.

She'd have to sit more decorously soon enough. In a short while the great bell in the center of Seoul would sound and curfew would begin. Many men would choose to spend the hours from eight to midnight in the company of the skilled entertainers of the *kisaeng* house.

It hardly seemed fair. After long hours of strenuous dancing, she must smile and sparkle, while *yangban* wives roamed the streets, temporarily empty of men, to shop, visit friends, and gossip. Or if they chose, they could go to bed early.

The prospect of lying on a soft *yo*, covered by a thick *ibul* called to her like the thought of food to a starving man. She blinked and covered a yawn.

Who would have guessed the simple movements of the *pogurak* dance would prove so exhausting? The lifted torso and floating walk took a surprising amount of strength even in the frivolous ball-throwing dance.

Behind closed eyes she saw again the fifteen other dancers swaying with the music, their bright skirts and jackets crossing and recrossing the floor. The rapid rhythm of the flutes and hourglass drums pulsed again in her veins.

Sound exploded everywhere, shredding the gentle memories of the day. The gong! Megan stiffened her spine and drew her calves close beside her thighs into a more seemly posture.

Paper-and-lath doors opened, spilling gentlemen into the lamplit room. Darts of late spring wind carried the splashing sounds of heavy raindrops hitting the clay of the courtyard. The scent of wet hair and wet cloth mixed with the sweet perfume of blossoms.

Girls rose and glided to the doors to escort patrons to waiting tables. Pilsu greeted a short, fat man in a jacket of bright blue. He pinched the *kisaeng's* smooth cheek and chuckled. Something cold and dark lurked behind that jovial-seeming smile. What did Pilsu see in the repulsive little toad?

Someday soon she'd have to imitate the woman's

decorum, turn all her energies to the comfort and delight of the men who requested her services. She closed her eyes against the thought.

Voices hushed in response to the first sounds of the *kayagum*. The bowed dulcimer sang sometimes sweet and sometimes sour, a little like the bag and horns of the Scottish pipes. The instruments had little in common except the passion they expressed.

Funny how she could almost imagine herself at home in Scotland when she heard certain sounds, but the smells always ruined the fantasy. Subtle odors permeated everything. Even the outdoors smelled faintly of ginseng, kimchee, and lotus.

A sudden sharp tang of musk raised gooseflesh on her arms. She opened her eyes.

Pilsu sneered down at her. "Megan, you must consider yourself very lucky tonight."

The syrupy tone grated on her ear. Pilsu never used her name, preferring a list of insulting nicknames. She smiled in spite of her suspicions. "I do. But what besides the honor of your presence makes you say so?"

The dark almond eyes narrowed, then widened. "Why, the gentleman at my table wishes to meet you." She nodded to the fat man in the blue coat.

How could she squirm out of this without insulting the customer? No doubt Pilsu would love to complain of her to Madame Insung. "I regret that I am so unworthy of the gentleman's attentions. Please tell him I am sorry."

The tall *kisaeng's* mouth sprang open, but Megan rushed on. "Perhaps when I gain more skill in entertaining visitors, he will ask for me again."

Pilsu's brown eyes snapped and her whisper shook with rage. "Fool, he doesn't expect you to be a *kisaeng*, a foreign pig like you! Don't flatter yourself."

Forcing herself not to smile at the woman's displeasure, Megan shrugged. "What could he possibly want with me then?"

Pilsu twisted her lips into a vicious imitation of a smile. "He wishes a baser type of entertainment from you, and since he has such exotic tastes, I'm sure even a barbarian like you could satisfy him."

Megan's stomach churned. How dare she! The thought of bedding that loathsome creature filled her with sick disgust. "I am *kisaeng*, not *changga*. There is a whorehouse down the street. Send him there." She fought a desire to spit in the smooth golden-skinned face.

"You are even stupider than I thought. He is General Kim On Yun, a personal confidant of the King. His friendship could help you; his ill will could prove fatal." The ugly smile grew wider.

A chill crept up Megan's spine, but she kept her voice even. "Still, I must decline his generous offer." She bit her lip to keep from saying more.

"Idiot, if you will not think of yourself, think of Madame and the blow to her honor if you refuse him and he tells his friends." The slender dancer leaned toward her. "And what of your dear friend Jongwhan? Such a denial could destroy him politically."

Megan wavered. "Madame told me only a *kisaeng's* heart dictated who her lovers should be." She swallowed. "And Jongwhan would never ask such a thing of me."

Pilsu's metallic laugh cut into Megan's soul. "And just who do you think bragged about the delights of your white flesh? Who put the idea in General Kim's head?"

Megan opened her mouth to deny Pilsu's words, but no sound came out. All she could do was shake her head. He couldn't, wouldn't. Or would he?

"Whoever it was, you perpetuated it." Madame In-sung's rich, soft voice came from behind Pilsu.

The willowy dancer whirled to face the owner of the *kisaeng* house. "But—"

The steel purr of Madame's words cut through Pilsu's excuse. "If you promised the general he could bed a *kisaeng*, then you must keep the promise—yourself!" The last word was an order.

The young woman turned her beautiful face, now distorted into a mask of rage, and glared at Megan. Then she gathered her *chima* in clenched fists and stalked away.

Megan let out a shuddering sigh.

Insung smiled down at her. "Never mind. She is a difficult person and was so even as a child. Poor unhappy thing."

Madame started to turn away, then glanced down at Megan again. "You did well to stand up to her." She paused. "Pilsu is not an easy friend, but she can be a dangerous enemy. Be careful."

The older woman glided away, her peach silk jacket and skirt glowing in the lantern light.

Megan bit back the tears. What choice did she have? She hadn't tried to become enemies with Pilsu. That all seemed to be decided when she arrived.

The woman hated her, of that she was certain. But how much of her story had been truth, and how much lies? What about Jongwhan? Who else could have put the idea into the general's head?

20

Shrieks of laughter drifted on the soft breeze like clouds of pink cherry blossoms. Jongwhan shouldered through the crowd of brightly dressed men and women. Vivid colors replaced the everyday white clothing on holidays such as *Tano*. Something tugged at the sleeve of his *chogori*.

Pongnim's smiling square face peered around the brim of another man's *kat*. "A little more slowly, if you please, Cousin." He sidestepped another man and panted up beside Jongwhan. "I'm not used to so many people moving about so freely."

An image of the orderly and sober gatherings at court flashed through Jongwhan's mind. "Sorry, I didn't think."

Pongnim chuckled. "They do seem to be having a good time." He stood on tiptoe and peered around. "But where is this foreign *kisaeng*, and how will you find her in all this confusion?"

"Once you see her, you won't need to ask." His pulse raced. "Her hair is like beaten copper. It calls like a beacon."

Pongnim laughed and pounded his shoulder. "You are smitten with her, all right. She must be a beauty, indeed, to melt your cold heart."

"She is, I tell you. But come, I think we'll find her at the swinging contest." He edged between two men and around a group of women.

The crowds grew thicker near the cherry orchard. The sweet smell of blossoms soothed and cheered Jongwhan. Ahead, the ropes of the swings rose high into the trees.

Suddenly he broke through the front ranks of the revelers. They stood just out of danger of being hit by the moving swings.

Jongwhan's heart raced. Megan stood to one side, the bright russet of her hair glowing against the sea green of her silk jacket. The pink of her skirt echoed the cloud of petals behind her. Her jade-green eyes focused on the women swinging.

He touched Pongnim's elbow and nodded toward her. "There."

The prince's eyes widened and he nodded. "She is lovely." He gazed in silence, then shook his head and faced Jongwhan. "Remarkable. But what of the girl in the swing? Do you know her?"

For the first time, Jongwhan looked at the contestants. Soonhee stood on a wooden board suspended from a cherry branch by two stout ropes, flying back and forth, impossibly high off the ground. In the other swing Pilsu pulled the ropes and pushed her tall, slender body to and fro, a handbreadth lower. At the height of each arc, the rivals reached for a row of brass bells. Whoever jingled the bells first would win.

"I know them both. Which do you fancy?"

Pongnim pulled his gaze from the swingers. "The tiny one in yellow and blue." He turned back to the competition, lips parted and gold eyes shining.

Soonhee had won another suitor. Jongwhan smiled. Hopeful swains pursued the young *kisaeng* continuously.

She remained friendly to all but laughed at their attempts to win her heart.

The two beauties blurred the air. Pilsu's long fingers just missed the string of bells. A buzz of whispers spread through the crowd. Soonhee strained against the ropes and stretched her small fingers as far as she could reach. Her fingertips batted the tiny bells and a high sweet jingling sounded through the clearing.

The crowd cheered and clapped. Some jumped up and down.

Pilsu arched her back in one mighty last push. Her fingers closed on the string of bells and she jerked hard. The cord came off in her hands.

Jongwhan writhed inside, embarrassed for her. How like Pilsu!

A shocked murmur ran through the onlookers. Some turned and walked away, shaking their heads. The swinging contests had ended for the year.

Megan ran forward and caught Soonhee's swing to slow her flight. Pilsu waited until she could safely leap clear, then strode away, the bells still gripped in her hand.

"Come, Cousin. You must introduce me to these two goddesses." Pongnim clasped his elbow.

He shook his head. His friend had a pregnant wife and a small daughter. But he'd never seen the man so enraptured. He hoped Soonhee would be gentle, for Pongnim's sake.

"Congratulations, Little Friend. You did well!" He bowed his head to the tiny *kisaeng.* "Allow me to introduce His Excellency Prince Pongnim."

Soonhee's eyes widened. She smiled up at Jongwhan and turned to the prince. Her color heightened and her gold eyes glittered, then she lowered her gaze and bowed. "Your Excellency, I am honored."

Jongwhan frowned. Soonhee seldom played at coyness.

The diminutive dancer raised her eyes once more. Her whole face glowed with a radiance he'd never seen before. Her enchantment matched Pongnim's!

Megan cleared her throat. He turned and caught her cold stare. "And Your Excellency, this is Megan, the foreign beauty I spoke of."

Pongnim drew his eyes from Soonhee's. "I am most pleased to see you at last."

Megan bowed. "Your Excellency." Her brevity bordered on insult, but Pongnim had already turned again to Soonhee. She took his arm and they strolled away.

Jongwhan frowned his displeasure, but Megan looked away.

"Hadn't you better greet your old friend, General Kim?" Her voice held cold anger. "Pilsu told me how close you two are."

Across the clearing the tall, dark *kisaeng* stamped her foot on the damp brown earth. Kim On Yun patted her shoulder and looked up into her beautiful, tearstained face. When had those two met? He shrugged.

"Perhaps later, but—" He turned back to Megan, but she was strolling after Soonhee and Pongnim.

Would he never understand this alien creature? Why, of all the women in the world, did this one have to steal his heart?

The musicians finished tuning their instruments and struck the opening notes of the first song. Megan stood with the other dancers in the shadows just outside the lantern-lit platform.

Her skin burned hot one moment and cool the next. Sweat stuck the new dance costume to her body. She feared it would stain the blue silk skirt and white jacket. Her legs shook. *Kalbi* rose into her throat, leaving a sour taste. Drat Jongwhan for insisting she eat the broiled beef ribs for lunch. What if they came up while she was dancing? She gave a shuddering sigh.

Soonhee squeezed her hand. At least they stood last in line and would enter after the others. She took a deep breath. She'd be fine once the dance started.

In the dim light, the *yangban* stood and sat in small groups among the cherry trees in the *piwŏn* garden. The King sat on his wooden throne platform. What must it be like to be king, to know this beautiful park belonged to you, and none could enter without your invitation?

The song ended and the audience applauded. "This is it." Megan's heart raced at Soonhee's whisper.

The first strains of the accompaniment for the *pogurak* dance sounded. Her body froze for a moment, then she forced herself to concentrate on the rhythm of the music.

The dancers streamed ahead of her onto the platform. Madame Insung led the troupe, carrying a large basket of fresh-cut peonies, and took her place to one side of the tiny gate at the back of the platform.

Pilsu followed, a large bowl of black paint in one hand and a soft brush in the other. She stood opposite Madame.

The line of dancers dipped and swayed, gliding in intricate patterns across the wooden floor. Soonhee stepped toward the stage.

Megan took a deep breath and followed. Toes up, spine arched, body floating, gliding.

From the basket, Madame pulled a small red silk ball and tossed it to the first dancer. The girl caught it and moved smoothly toward the gate. She tossed the toy through the hole in the top of the gate.

The crowd applauded and Madame presented the *kisaeng* with a peony. Without a break in the flowing movement of the dance, the dancer took her place in line behind Megan.

The next girl won a flower and the next, but the fourth dancer missed the hole. The onlookers laughed and whispered. The *kisaeng* stood swaying, her head bowed. Pilsu glided toward her and dipped the brush into the paint. She marked a small cross on the girl's cheek before she glided back to the gate.

Megan's hands twitched in sympathy, but she forced herself to maintain her rhythm. Pilsu enjoyed the role too much.

The game continued, each dancer taking her turn with the ball. About half the throws succeeded in their aim, while the others went astray. Megan's arms ached from the graceful gestures of the dance, and from her fear of failing when her turn came.

Suddenly Soonhee's turn came. She caught the ball and tossed it gently toward the target. It bounced off the red lacquer of the gate.

Megan reminded herself to keep dancing while Pilsu marked the girl's cheek.

At last her turn arrived. With trembling fingers she clutched at the soft silk toy. Madame smiled and nodded at her. She glided to the gate and held her breath, then tossed the ball into a high arc. Her heart sank. Too high. The ball bounced against the intricately painted rafters of the roofed gate and fell to the floor. The audience laughed.

She swayed in place, hanging her head, but her eyes followed Pilsu's gliding step. A broad smile of hatred and triumph distorted the dark beauty's features. She stopped in front of Megan and drew the dripping brush from the bowl. Paint spattered the front of the white jacket and blue skirt as Pilsu dragged the brush from temple to chin, across Megan's eye and mouth, then repeated the mark on the other side.

Dimly, Megan heard the crowd cheering and hooting encouragement. The black-drenched brush came again and again, until the sticky liquid covered every bit of her face.

"Now, foreign pig, see how Jongwhan likes you," the tall *kisaeng* hissed.

Megan moved to take her place behind Soonhee, sick with shame and hatred. She longed for the dance to end so she could hide from Jongwhan, from everyone. She glanced at Madame. Insung's dark eyes glittered and her lips pressed together.

The dancers circled the platform again, then flowed down the steps and disappeared into the night. The last to enter, the last to exit. Hoots and cheers followed Megan out of the light. She turned to run, but Soonhee caught her elbow.

"Come, there is a stream where we can wash."

Sobbing, Megan followed her past a knot of dark figures.

Madame's voice carried through the night air. ". . . cruel and senseless—"

"But it was a joke, and the King loved it. Did you not see—" Pilsu protested.

"Return to the house at once, and tomorrow . . ." Madame's voice faded in the distance.

"Here, dip this cloth into the water. Mother always brings towels for us to clean ourselves after the *pogurak*." She patted Megan's hand. "You were brave, you know, to stand there while she did that. I'd have run away or slapped her."

The thought of her tiny friend reaching up and slapping Pilsu struck her as funny and she laughed, then choked. Soonhee's arm circled her shoulder. The sobs came in earnest. She held her head in her hands, tears mixing with the sticky paint in her palms. "Oh, Soonhee, what am I going to do? She made a fool of me in front of everyone!"

A twig snapped in the dark silence. "She made a fool of herself, and I intend to tell her so," Jongwhan said.

21

Moon of Barley Harvest

The sweet-rotten smell of the river rose from the reddish mud at Megan's feet. She wiggled bare toes in the slick, warm clay and giggled.

With turned-down mouth and furrowed brows, Soonhee roughened her voice in pretended sternness. "Now quit playing and get to work, or your hair will never get clean." Her frown dissolved into a giggle.

Megan bent again to the wild iris, using a stick to push the soft mud away from the root. It gave a small plop when tugged from the riverbank. After twisting the stem and flower off the *changpu* plant, she tossed the white tuber into the basket.

She stood, kneaded the small of her back, and inhaled the perfume of the delicate blue iris in her hand. The morning sun, burning like a gold coin in the deep blue sky, stuck the rough white cotton of her jacket to her back.

After lunch they would wade into the green water and wash their hair with the slippery yellow liquid boiled from the roots. She smiled at the memory of the last *pok* day.

What a sight they'd been, twenty naked girls splashing and playing in the slow-moving water! Almost like Koh's wives. She winced at the comparison and moved into the shade of a stand of bamboo.

Her hands left green-brown stains when she wiped them on the coarse-woven skirt. Troupes of blue flowers danced in the breeze. She bent to loosen a large clump of bulbs.

A slender dark foot appeared beside the plant and Pilsu's voice split the morning calm. "So, finally a costume and an occupation that fit you, foreign peasant." The tall dancer stood resplendent in a *chima* and *chogori* of pale pink silk.

She gave a harsh laugh. "A shame to waste such earnest labor. Even *changpu* root cannot make your hair a normal color." The slender dancer laughed again and walked away, leaving the heavy musk of her favorite scent in her wake.

The bamboo stalks clicked together. Soonhee's basket thudded onto the wet bank. "Pay no attention to her, Cousin."

"I don't!" Even to herself, Megan's words lacked conviction. The last hair-washing party had been such fun without Pilsu. Too bad she'd decided to join them today. She dug harder at the tough iris bulbs.

Soonhee's gentle voice came again. "She is only jealous of the attention you get. Your hair makes you special, sets you apart, Megan."

She sighed. Yes, her hair and skin shouted "foreigner" at everyone she met.

Soonhee tossed a bulb into her basket. "Of course, if you ever wanted to look like a Korean, my mother could dye your hair and skin for you, you know."

Megan straightened. To look like everyone else. It had been so long, she'd forgotten what that must be like. To walk down a street with no one staring, and Pilsu—no, Pilsu would never let her forget she was different, no matter how she changed her looks.

But what about Jongwhan? Was it her hair and skin that kept him so distant? He acted as if he cared for her, and sometimes she thought desire shone from his eyes, but he never so much as touched her hand. Would he want her if she looked like a Korean woman—like Pilsu or his wife?

She set her mouth and gave the clump of irises an angry heave. Suddenly the huge bunch of bulbs gave way. She stumbled back, then savagely pulled the plants apart.

"Do you want me to ask Mother for you?" Soonhee cocked her head.

Megan tossed the crushed blue flowers into the stream. "No, thank you, Cousin." If he ever wanted her, he would have to take her as she was. The bulbs smacked against the others in the basket.

"Are you sure the farmer doesn't mind?" Megan dropped another handful of green onions into her basket.

"Don't worry. Mother asked him." Soonhee puffed out her cheeks and thickened her voice in imitation of the man. "He was honored." A giggle spoiled the illusion. "Come, the lettuce is this way."

Megan lifted her soiled skirt and followed her friend up the hill. The path led between rows of green plants stretching to the horizon. "But where is everyone?"

Heads of lettuce muffled Soonhee's voice where she knelt in the rich soil. "No one works on *pok* days. It is said those who do will go mad or die from the heat. Now would you hurry? I'm starved."

Megan's stomach growled in response and this time she giggled, too. A clean, warm smell rose from the chunks of earth hardening in the noonday sun. She knelt and stripped the outer leaves from a dozen ruffled green heads before Soonhee led the way back toward the shady riverbank.

A sour onion smell rose from a pot of thick yellow *changpu* liquid cooling in the shade. Rice bubbled on the fire and stacks of wet lettuce leaves and vegetables filled the picnic cloth. Megan hurried to rinse the contents of her basket in the cool water, memories of the delicious *sam* stirring her hunger again.

The chattering and laughter of the *kisaeng* almost covered the soft rushing of the stream and the calling of the songbirds.

The green water cooled Megan's hot hands. Even the woven bamboo bracelets only helped a little by keeping her sleeves away from the skin. She longed to slip her nude body into the caressing current.

"Megan, hurry!" Soonhee called from the fire. "They're starting! It will be gone soon."

She finished rinsing the last handful of garlic, tossed it in the basket on top of the other greens, and ran back to the clearing. Breathless, she added her offerings to the plenty spread out before her and took her place in the shade-dappled grove.

Twenty girls sat around the large picnic cloth. Most wore old clothes of plain rough cotton—digging *changpu* roots ruined silk gowns.

An air of camaraderie surrounded the making and eating of *sam*. A small bowl of hot rice and a pair of wooden chopsticks lay before each girl. Groups of three and four *kisaeng* shared dishes of sliced garlic, *kimchee*, and brown bean paste, as well as the piles of washed greens.

Soonhee tore a square of lettuce and laid it across her left palm. With chopsticks she scooped a lump of sticky rice into the center, then added garlic, onion, greens, and bean paste. She gathered the edges of the torn leaf to form a bite-size ball and popped it whole into her mouth.

Megan's fingers lacked her friend's smooth swift action, but she managed to get the food into her mouth without spilling any. The onion and garlic stung her tongue and made her nose and eyes water, but after four her hunger abated some.

Soonhee leaned toward her. "Don't fill up too much. I have a surprise for you."

Just then, two women servants appeared at the edge of the clearing with huge baskets balanced on their heads. Soonhee jumped up and ran to them and danced around them as they plodded toward the group in the grass.

The first woman lifted the heavy basket to the ground beside Megan.

"Look! Melons for everyone!" Soonhee's eyes sparkled. She dropped down at her place again and pulled a large, bright yellow ball from the basket. She sliced through the orange meat and scooped the seeds onto the ground, then handed dripping wedges to those around her.

The cool sweet juice dripped down Megan's chin and soothed her parched mouth and throat. She chewed the crisp-soft fruit and swallowed. "This is wonderful! But where did it come from?"

Soonhee's eyes danced and she leaned close to Megan's ear. "Prince Pongnim sent it." She giggled. "He said he wished he could bring it himself." She sobered and clasped Megan's arm. "He and Jongwhan have visited many times this last moon. Do you think he is beginning to care for me?"

The cool yellow *changpu* juice dripped down her forearm. Megan knelt in thigh-deep water, bare breasts breaking the surface with every movement of her arms. Head tilted back, she scrubbed the foaming stuff through her wet, tangled hair.

She leaned back until the water eddied across her brow, fingers working the residue from her copper tresses. The *kisaeng* believed hair washed on a *pok* day would become soft and obedient like the stream. Anyway, the smelly stuff soothed her itching, sunburned scalp.

She rose, water sheeting off her upper body, wet chestnut strands clinging to white breasts and belly.

Across the stream, Soonhee leaped and splashed with three other girls, throwing sparkling arcs of water on one another from empty rice bowls.

Megan smiled at the shrieks and giggles that filled the air. She knew from the last time the others couldn't swim, so she wandered upstream alone toward the deep pool she'd found. Clear green water streamed around her ankles and calves. Her feet found sure footing on the smooth round rocks of the riverbed.

The happy sounds of the *kisaeng* faded when she rounded a bend. Ahead, crystal water bubbled over a tiny waterfall and spread into a round green pool.

The smell of damp earth and pine needles wafted to her on a gentle breeze. Tall conifers and poplars threw cool shade from one rocky bank to the other. A lone willow trailed wistful blue-green branches into the clear water.

Songbirds called from tree to tree. A tiny yellow lark swooped across the pool, flickering in the deep shadows, and landed on a low branch. A deep sense of peace and rightness filled her.

Water splashed behind a boulder at the stream's edge. Megan stepped onto the bank and around the huge rock.

Pilsu knelt at the water's edge, struggling to rinse the slippery *changpu* juice from her long, blue-black hair. She still wore her silk skirt, now smeared with mud and moss.

Her long, slender hands caught at the water and splashed small amounts on her head—not enough to clear the thick foam from her hair. "Oooh!" she raged, and slammed her fists into the water.

Megan smiled at the cry of pain until the slender dancer sobbed and sucked at her bruised hand. She ought to leave Pilsu there to struggle on alone, after the vicious tricks the woman had played on her.

But then she'd have to give up her swim. If she offered to help, maybe the dancer would finish her wash and leave, or maybe she'd leave before she finished. Either way, Megan would get the solitude she wanted.

She waded into the pool. "Here, let me help." She cupped her hands and splashed clear water over the woman's head.

Pilsu sputtered. "You! How dare you sneak up on me like that!" The woman's long arm shot out and shoved Megan backward into the deepest part of the pool.

Pain lanced through her temple. She'd hit her head on a rock, the same spot where the mast had clipped her. Echoes of the old dark terror welled up in her mind. Her chest ached, blackness closed in. She forced the panic down.

A new hot rage replaced it. Pilsu didn't know she could

swim—the woman had tried to kill her because she offered
to help.

She marshaled her breath and dove deep, then shot
across the pool. Pilsu's feet and calves shimmered below the
surface. Megan swept them with her outstretched arm and
paddled backward to avoid the falling body.

The slender *kisaeng* sputtered and bobbed in the deep
water, the air trapped inside her gown bubbling around
her. "Help me," she gasped, her eyes darting wildly around
the pool. Her long arms flailed. "Help me." Then her head
disappeared beneath the surface.

Megan knew she couldn't let the woman drown, as
tempting as it seemed. She swam over and pulled Pilsu to
shore.

The tall dancer stumbled up the bank, dripping black
hair and transparent silk gown clinging to her slender body.

At least most of the *changpu* came out during her little
swim. Megan fought an impulse to laugh.

Pilsu turned and glared.

Megan shivered in the heat, her own rage cooled by
the sight of such hatred.

The veins stood out in the dancer's neck and her voice
shook. "Until now, I have only toyed with you."

Regret twined cold fingers around Megan's belly. Now
she'd done it. Now there would be no peace. The soothing
shade of the pool took on a sinister darkness. She shivered
again.

Pilsu's words sliced the air like a whip. "But now,
because of this insult, I will destroy you, and with you, your
precious lover, Jongwhan."

22

Moon of Monsoon Heat

Megan winced at the sour note. "I'm sorry, Madame. My hands each have five thumbs."

Insung leaned across and tightened a wooden key, then plucked a string. Her lavender scent surrounded Megan for a moment. The note rang true. She smiled. "Try again."

Megan squirmed a little on the cushion, adjusting the *kayagum* to a more comfortable position.

The big wooden box looked a little like a big dulcimer with a bridge, but the resemblance ended there. She'd played the little stringed box her father made her by striking sweet, clear notes with a tiny hammer.

She drew a bow across the strings of the *kayagum*, producing a whining chord, then ground her teeth. Would she never get it right?

Madame leaned nearer and showed her again. She forced herself to concentrate. This time, when Megan bowed the strings, the handsome *kisaeng* smiled and nodded.

"That is enough for today. You are tired." Madame's rich, gentle voice echoed in the empty hall.

Megan enjoyed the afternoon lessons alone with Insung while the others busied themselves elsewhere. The tile roof kept out most of the heat of the summer sun. A cooling breeze wafted through the open doors. Birds sang in the courtyard trees.

"Thank you. I am sorry to be such a stupid student."

She set the *kayagum* gently on the yellow paper floor and looked around the hall at the decorative screens. Madame had explained the significance of some, but many she knew merely added color and grace to the room.

"It is more difficult for a woman grown to learn the eight womanly arts. It was for me." Madame covered the instrument with a square of bright red silk.

"For you?"

Insung's eyebrows shot up.

Megan blushed. "Excuse me, I have no right to ask, but I thought you had always been *kisaeng*."

Madame smiled and shrugged. The gray streaks at her temples belied the youthfulness of her face. "Do not worry, Little Friend. I do not mind your curiosity. Would you like to hear how I came to be a court entertainer?"

Megan nodded.

"I was born *yangban*, to an aristocratic family. I lived in isolation with my mother and my sisters, learning only to sew a little and to manage the servants." The *kisaeng* rested her graceful hands in the folds of her lavender silk skirt.

"When I reached the age of seventeen, my parents chose a husband for me."

Megan cleared her throat. "Excuse me, but was that Soonhee's father?"

Madame started. "No. No, that was many years before my daughter's birth."

Megan bit her lip. No more questions. If she offended Insung . . .

The older *kisaeng* smiled. "My husband was not capable of fathering a child. On my wedding night when my eyelids were unglued, I discovered my parents had married me to a boy of seven."

It was Megan's turn to feel startled. Marry a woman to a child? Why? The question must have shown on her face.

"Perhaps they wished to secure the match, to form an alliance with his family. I do not know." Insung paused and looked down at her hands.

Megan sighed. Wedded to an infant. How dreadful!

"My mother-in-law made my life miserable, and I took it out on the boy." Insung frowned. "But later I realized it was not his fault, and I came to care for him. At last he grew to manhood, and we had a son." The dark eyes clouded.

Megan twisted the *norigae* hanging from her jacket. Soonhee had never mentioned a brother.

"It was winter. My husband caught a fever and died. Then my son—" The elegant woman slumped, wiped at her eyes with the edges of her soft pink sleeves, and cleared her throat. "My son died also."

Megan held her breath. So much pain. It happened, in fact, more often than not. She shook her head. To lose a child. How could a woman survive that?

"My in-laws blamed me. They tried to force me to drink poison." The elegant nostrils flared. Anger glittered in the dark eyes. "But I knew I was not to blame, so I ran away."

She looked down again and sighed, then raised her head and smiled into Megan's eyes. "I became a *kisaeng*. It was difficult, but I succeeded. As you will."

"You pleased the King." Megan's heart pounded at her own boldness, but she had to know. How could she get the King to send her home?

Madame's face blanched and her eyes narrowed for a moment, then she nodded. "He was not the King then, only a nephew." The narrow hands twisted together.

"When he ascended to the throne, he remembered our friendship." Insung's voice quavered.

Megan's heart thudded in her chest. Madame always stayed calm, even with Pilsu. What had upset her so?

"He gave me this house and granted me the right to live outside the palace walls. Before that, the *kisaeng* were nothing more than palace slaves." Madame rose from her cushion and turned away.

Megan pushed herself up onto her knees. "So Soonhee—"

Madame whirled on her. "What of Soonhee?"

The hardness of the voice chilled Megan. She gulped. "She was born a *kisaeng*, only free."

Insung bit her lip, then smiled. "Yes." She cleared her throat. "Yes. Free to read and write, to learn, and to think for herself."

She touched Megan's cheek with a cool hand. "You must excuse me. Our little talk has tired me." She turned, silk skirts whispering, and glided out the paper-and-lath doors.

Megan sat back on the thin cushion, a knot forming in the pit of her stomach. She'd never seen Madame Insung behave rudely to anyone. What lay behind the *kisaeng*'s friendship with the King? And why did she react so strangely to questions about Soonhee?

"But would you die for love?" Pongnim's square face glowed in the lamplight. A cool breeze carried the last dusty scents of the day's heat through the open doors.

Jongwhan shrugged. "I'm not sure I've ever truly loved." He sought Megan's green eyes, but she looked away. The curve of her neck called to his lips, the intricate coils of her hair cried out to be undone. "Perhaps, if I loved the right woman—"

"But our history is filled with stories of those who gave their lives out of love." The prince rested his left hand on his right foot in the *yangban* manner. How did he manage to look so cool in the terrible heat? Pongnim's cheeks colored. "What do you say, Soonhee?"

Jongwhan struggled to keep from smiling. Any fool could see how the prince felt about the young *kisaeng*. Would he ever gain the courage to confess his love?

And Soonhee returned the feeling if her blushes meant anything. Gold eyes looked up from beneath lowered black lashes. She smiled. "Yes, the *kisaeng* tell many such tales." She cleared her throat and looked away from Pongnim.

"When I was young, two of the King's counselors vied for the love of a young *kisaeng*, a friend of my mother's." She cocked her head. "In fact, one was named Kim, and the other bore your surname, Yi."

Jongwhan furrowed his brow. Could it have been his father?

Soonhee smiled. "A common enough name, to be sure. No matter. Soon, the one named Yi won her heart. He built her a small house and visited her often." She sighed. "But his passion faded. When he left her, she drank poison."

The young *kisaeng* looked down. Tears glistened on the black lashes. "I remember her well. She was always kind to me."

Megan touched the girl's shoulder.

Pongnim cleared his throat, regret etched into his face. "And you, Megan, in your country, do people die of love?"

She nodded. "One story tells of a girl named Barbara Allen, who scorned a young man's love. When he died pining for her, she repented and died soon after."

She cocked her head and smiled. "Some say a brier grew from his grave and a rose from hers, and they twined together in a lover's knot."

Jongwhan's heart beat fast. "But some pine for love and continue to live." He looked at Megan. Had she understood?

Pongnim rubbed his hands. "True! Does not our song 'Arirang' tell of a faithful woman awaiting the return of her lover after many years?"

Soonhee smiled. "And don't forget that tonight is *Chilsŏk*. But Megan doesn't know the story." She pointed out the door to the darkening sky.

"Once, long ago, a princess fell in love with a poor shepherd. Her father forbade her to see him, but she pined for him day and night." Soonhee clasped her hands to her chest in mock grief.

"The gods grew angry at such defiance of the proper order and cast both of them into the sky as constellations." She sighed. "Now, only once a year, on *Chilsŏk*, the Milky Way forms a bridge for the lovers to cross."

She giggled. "And tonight, young girls will go to sleep, hoping to dream of their own true loves."

Megan smiled and raised her eyebrows, first at Soonhee, then at Pongnim. Then her expression sobered. "In my country, we have a song about lovers parting."

"Please, sing it for us, Megan!" Soonhee pleaded.

"Yes, please," Pongnim chimed in.

Megan looked up at Jongwhan again, a question in her eyes.

He nodded, and she began to sing.

By yon bonnie banks and by yon bonnie braes,
Where the sun shines bright in the gloaming

Me and my true love forever shall we part
On the bonnie, bonnie banks of Loch Lomond.

The words made no sense to Jongwhan. He'd forgotten she spoke something other than Korean. He frowned at the reminder. A vision of her in her strange red gown swam before his eyes. He pushed it away and drank in her present loveliness. The soft purple of her thin silk jacket brought out the whiteness of her skin and the copper of her hair.

In spite of the strangeness of her words, her voice stirred something wild in his loins. All that passion—if only she felt like that about him! For one wild moment he saw her stretched out nude before him, scraped and battered, but beautiful.

As the last notes faded, her jade-green eyes looked into Jongwhan's for a moment. Was that a flicker of interest? She turned away. He must have imagined it.

Pongnim's voice broke into his thoughts again. "But if you won't die for love, will you die for honor? What do you say, Cousin?"

Jongwhan reflected for a moment. "It is easy to say 'I will do such and such,' but who knows until he faces death what he will do?"

Pongnim laughed and pounded his back. "Good answer, O Wise Philosopher!"

Soonhee smiled. "Honor means something different to a *kisaeng* than to a *yangban*." She smoothed her jade-green skirt with plump golden hands. "During the Imjin War, didn't a captive dancing girl lure a Japanese general to a cliff and leap to her death to kill him?"

She looked up at Pongnim and shuddered. "But truly, I hope I never have to choose between life and honor."

Pongnim touched her hand. "I share that hope." She colored. He drew his hand away and turned to Megan. "And what of you, Little Friend?"

Megan rose and walked to the open door. The silver light of the new moon edged her silhouette against the starry night sky. "I, too, was raised to value honor even above life. But when the time came to die, I could not."

A gentle night wind blew the jasmine scent of her skin to Jongwhan. Her voice came to him from a great distance. "I fought and fought to live, and I have no regrets."

She turned, her jade-green eyes looking straight into Jongwhan's heart. "No matter what shame I must endure, I will fight to survive."

23

Moon of Waning Heat

Jongwhan nocked the arrow, then pulled the string taut across his chest and sighted the shaft to a point slightly above the target. Smells of resin and dry pine needles filled his nostrils.

His fingers loosed the wooden shaft gradually, letting the missile find its own moment of release. The string sang and the metal head bit deep into the target.

"Bravo!" The cheering of the King's advisers filled the morning air. A late summer sun cast long shadows across the small glen. He lowered the bow until one end rested on the damp brown earth at his feet.

King Injo strode toward him, respendent in a yellow silk *chogori*. He clapped Jongwhan on the shoulder. "Well done, Nephew! We are impressed with your marksmanship."

"Thank you, Excellency." Jongwhan bowed.

The King turned to the target, then back to Jongwhan. "Why is it I never see you at the royal hunt?" His gold eyes peered into Jongwhan's.

He bowed again, his cheeks growing hot. "I would be greatly honored and personally pleased to ride out on the hunt in your company."

The King nodded, but the gold eyes continued to bore

into him. He couldn't lie to the man. "But I fear my performance would disappoint you."

The ruler cocked his head.

He hurried on. "I find it difficult to kill a living creature. Forgive me."

He dropped his eyes. He held his breath. The bow dug deep into the ground. Would the King be angry?

"Honesty and compassion are rare enough qualities in my court, Nephew. See that you attend me more often." King Injo looked across the clearing, then moved toward the other target.

Relief filled Jongwhan. He sighed.

"Well said, Cousin." Pongnim's square face appeared at his shoulder. "Now he respects you."

Jongwhan rubbed sweat from his palms. "Thanks." He had to laugh at Pongnim's mock-serious expression. "It's good to see you. And how is Soonhee?"

The prince laughed in return. "Radiant. I think she is falling in love with me." Color crept onto the high cheekbones.

"I told you that weeks ago." Jongwhan kept his eyes on the bow as he bent and unstrung it. "And how is Megan?"

"Refreshing. She asked for you." Pongnim's eyes twinkled.

"She did?" Jongwhan's pulse raced.

"Yes, she asked how her guardian could report to the King when he never visits her." Pongnim chuckled.

Jongwhan lifted the unstrung bow by its grip. "But I've been attending to court duties. That's unfair." He strode toward the target, knuckles white and jaw clenched.

The prince's teasing voice followed him. "That's what I told her."

He leaned the bow against the target, then grasped the arrow and rocked it back and forth to loosen the metal tip. A bowstring sang somewhere behind him. The air whistled beside his ear and another arrow thudded into the target a handspan from his own. He spun on his heel, his heart pounding.

Behind Pongnim stood General Kim On Yun, unstringing his bow, a broad smile splitting his round face.

"Forgive me, Young Friend, if I startled you. I merely wanted to try my marksmanship against yours." The fat man turned, blue coattails trailing in the morning breeze, and waddled away.

Pongnim ran to Jongwhan. "Aren't you going to follow him? He might have killed you!"

"No." Jongwhan cleared his throat. "No, he apologized." He thrust the arrow into his quiver. "Besides, he is a friend of my father's." He nodded toward the King, his voice suddenly bitter. "My father needs all the friends he can get."

The courtyard hung heavy with the smell of sweating bodies. The guests rose one by one and knelt before Grandfather Chang, then touched their heads to the woven matting.

Megan squirmed on the cushion and sighed. She looked sideways at Jongwhan. He frowned a warning at her, then turned back to the ceremonies.

Some birthday celebration! No singing or dancing, and the only one drinking was old Mr. Chang.

She dropped the round bamboo fan by her knees. It only stirred the moist, hot air, not really cooling her sticky skin. The sun beat down upon her head through the cotton awning.

Like a patchwork quilt, the crowd sparkled in the bright colors of their best clothing. Only for a very special occasion, she knew, would common Koreans exchange the everyday white *hanbok* for such splendor. The last time she'd seen so much finery was at Youngsook's wedding.

It had been four months since that day, and now, on the bride's first visit, they sat across a hot courtyard from each other, separated by fifty strangers. The young matron looked different somehow, sitting beside her child husband. She held her head erect for the first time in Megan's memory. What had changed her?

For once she wouldn't have minded being relegated to the kitchen with Youngsook and Soonhee, but this time the women were included in the festivities. If only the three of them could sneak off alone together for a gossip session.

She sighed again and picked up the fan. Maybe it helped a little, and besides, it gave her something to do.

She knew it was almost a miracle to reach one's *hwangap*. Imagine, to live for sixty years! Sixty seemed to be a magic number here, something about the twelve animal names and ten heavenly names for the years. This year had the exact same name as the year Chang was born.

Still, they could have made the celebration more fun for the guests. Another couple completed their bows and rose.

Chang downed another cup of *makkŏlli*. At least he seemed to be having a good time. She could go for a cold cup herself. She'd acquired a taste for the sweet, milky rice wine and the way it quenched a summer thirst.

Jongwhan rose to his feet and motioned for her to follow. She stood and reached her left hand behind her to grasp the edge where the blue *chima* overlapped.

She teetered a bit on the narrow leather soles of her red silk shoes, then minced after him in short steps. Not only was this gait considered ladylike, but the constrictions of her finest clothing made it the only one possible.

Jongwhan knelt on one embroidered square cushion and gestured her to the other. Before them lay a low table covered with delicacies. Megan's stomach rumbled at the delicious smells. White, green, and golden brown sweet rice cakes rose in neat pyramids, as did several varieties of fresh and dried fruits.

She bowed her head and looked up through her lashes at Chang's eyeless face. Sweat dripped in little runnels from his lined cheeks and his smile looked painted on.

"My most exotic flower!" Sour *makkŏlli* fumes accompanied his slurred words.

From the corner of her eye, she watched Jongwhan and did exactly as he did, but a few seconds later. He rubbed his palms together and asked for the old man's blessing for them both, then placed his hands palm down on the bamboo matting and rested his forehead atop them for a moment.

When she raised her head, sweat from her brow glistened on the backs of her hands.

Jongwhan stood, adjusted his metal belt, and waited while she got to her feet and grasped her skirts. When she turned to follow, an odd snorting sound rose behind her. Megan peered over her shoulder.

Grandfather Chang sat cross-legged, eyes closed, chin on his chest and a smile on his face, snoring. Her eyes swept the crowded courtyard. These Koreans cared so much about appearances. What would they do?

Youngsook stood in the center of the courtyard and smiled. She placed a finger against her lips in a signal for silence and gestured for the servants to bring tables of food to the guests. Those assembled smiled and nodded toward the sleeping elder and engaged in whispered conversation.

Megan threaded her way back to her place beside Jongwhan. So, it was true what Soonhee had told her. Adults who reached their *hwangap* enjoyed total indulgence. From now on, whatever Grandfather Chang chose to do in public would be accepted without question.

She sought Soonhee's sweet face in the crowd. Pong-nim bent and whispered something to the *kisaeng* and she smothered a giggle. For some reason, something in their faces looked a little alike today.

Funny, she'd never noticed the resemblance before. They had the same high cheekbones, the same squarish jaw, and the same rare golden eyes. She'd seen someone else with eyes just that color, but whom?

Her mouth twisted. Maybe they looked alike because they loved one another. She glanced up at Jongwhan, sitting like a statue beside her.

A look of composure lay across his handsome face. She breathed in the clean, man-sweat smell of him. If only she could grab his broad shoulders and shake him. She wanted to scream, "Look at me! I love you!"

But she couldn't. He'd made it obvious by his absence how little she mattered to him. Well, next time he could just stay gone forever!

She'd only been fooling herself anyway, thinking he cared for her. The man had a wife. He belonged to another woman. She should just give up hoping for his love. This time she would.

She twirled the handle of the fan between her fingers. A cold, tight knot of misery began to form in the pit of her stomach. If only she could.

A cooling breeze ruffled the trailing branches of the willow tree shading the *anbang* from the late afternoon sun. Megan stood in the open door of the women's room and loosened her jacket to let the sweat dry beneath her arms. She lifted the heavy gold locket from her chest and blew a stream of air between her breasts.

At last the guests had all taken their leave. Grandfather Chang lay in his room, snoring still. Kwangin curled beside him, exhausted as only a small boy could be after a day of such excitement. Jongwhan, Pongnim, and Im sat drinking *makkŏlli* and playing *yoot* in the courtyard.

"Finally we can talk." Youngsook bustled into the room carrying a tray with three small cups. Soonhee followed with a plate of leftover rice cakes.

Megan smiled at her two friends and seated herself on a soft floor cushion. The icy, sweet fruit tea refreshed her. She swallowed a tiny rice cake and licked the honey from her fingers, then looked across at the others and laughed. "All day long I've been dying to talk, and now we're all so busy eating we haven't said a word. Youngsook, tell us everything!"

"Yes!" Soonhee set down her empty cup. "Is your mother-in-law a dragon?"

Youngsook blushed. "A little. She works me very hard, but she is not as cruel as some."

Soonhee shook her head. "You would find something good in a demon! But tell us about the house. Is it like this one?"

"Oh, no! It is much larger, with a tile roof. We have a separate wing to ourselves." The color came and went from her cheeks. "I have three tall chests for my clothing." She bit her lip. "My revered mother-in-law forced me to give away everything I had and make more. She said my things were not worthy of the house of Im."

"Poor Youngsook!" Soonhee patted her hand. "Well, at least you have new clothes."

Youngsook nodded.

If Im's mother was kinder than some, what must other in-laws be like? Megan kept the thought to herself. No use making Youngsook feel worse.

She wriggled inside her hot clothes, suddenly glad *kisaeng* couldn't marry. At least she'd never go through that. She grimaced. Or any of the other joys of womanhood, it seemed.

"But what about the rest of the family?" Soonhee asked.

"Are there any other girls your age?" Megan reached for another cake.

Youngsook giggled. "Im's sister is almost my age, but she is so homely they are afraid to arrange her marriage for fear a bridegroom would send her back." She folded delicate hands in her lap. "But she has a good heart." She giggled again. "She is so funny! She says she will become a Buddhist nun before she makes a husband miserable."

Soonhee joined the laughter. "Poor girl!"

Megan frowned. "What's wrong with being a nun?" In Scotland, rumors accused nuns and priests of greed and lechery, but she'd never given the stories any credence.

Gales of laughter answered her. "Buddhist nuns are worse than whores. They beg for a living, and they'll couple with any man for free!" Soonhee giggled.

She shook her head. Was everything backwards in this country?

Youngsook sobered. "But I worry about my sister-in-law. She suffers from *singbyŏng*. The family will make her drink poison if they find out."

Megan's mouth fell open. What kind of people would poison someone for being ill? "But why?"

Youngsook's eyes widened. "It would be a grave disgrace for the family if she became a *mudang*."

Now she was truly confused. "What's that?"

Youngsook frowned at Soonhee. "But, Megan, you must know the *mudang*. One calls on them to satisfy the household spirits."

Soonhee shook her head. "Mother refuses to have them in the house since they stole two of her best dancers during a *kut*."

Megan slapped the floor. "Slow down, would you? One new word at a time. What is sing—, sing—, whatever you called it?"

Soonhee smiled. "*Singbyŏng*. Spirit sickness. The spirits of the ancestors possess a woman and call her to serve them."

Megan nodded. Witchcraft. She'd seen a witch-burning in London. The stench of roasting human flesh came back to her for a moment. "And they are allowed to live?"

Youngsook frowned. "Of course. They become *mu-dang*. They are respected in their own way."

Soonhee nodded. "A *mudang* performs ceremonies to appease the spirits. The women of the household pay her for the *kut*."

She nodded again and shuddered. Witches allowed to consort with spirits! "But will your sister-in-law really take poison?"

Tears dewed Youngsook's eyelashes. "I hope not, but sometimes it happens."

Now she'd done it. She'd made Youngsook cry. "Let's talk about something else." She strove to make her voice merry. "This is supposed to be a celebration!"

"Tell us about Im!" Soonhee prompted.

"Yes, tell us about your handsome husband."

The young wife looked down at her folded hands, then tossed her head and looked from Soonhee to Megan and smiled. "He is very kind and gentle." She blushed and looked down again.

So, despite everything, love still bloomed in this strange Oriental garden! Megan sighed.

"But what about"—Soonhee giggled—"in bed!"

Youngsook covered her reddened cheeks. "He—" She took a breath. "He pleases me very much." The bride covered her eyes, but a giggle emerged from behind the tiny hands.

"Really?" Soonhee breathed. She looked out the open door, her eyes glittering.

"But you know how it is between a husband and wife, don't you, Megan?" Youngsook sat up straight, hands loose in her lap. The giggling, blushing girl had disappeared. Instead a very self-possessed matron sat in her place. Their little friend had changed indeed!

"And you, Soonhee." Youngsook smoothed her skirts. "Do you know how it is between a man and a woman yet?"

The young *kisaeng* didn't turn her head. "No, but I think I will very soon." She turned, a radiant smile lighting her lovely gold eyes. "I think the prince will ask me to become his next wife."

"Soonhee, that's wonderful!" Megan squeezed her friend's hand.

"You have a wonderful surprise awaiting you!" Youngsook's matronly air dissolved once more into laughter.

So, both her friends would be married, and she would be the old maid. She clenched her fists. Well, what do you expect! You're a freak, a red-haired, green-eyed, white-skinned demon! No one would want her for wife or lover.

Youngsook looked up at her, brown eyes shining. "And what of you and your Jongwhan?"

Her cheeks grew hot, but she tried to keep her voice even. "He doesn't care for me. He belongs to another."

Youngsook gasped. "Not Pilsu!"

Megan smiled. "No, she's left us both alone since early summer. She spends all her time with that fat General Kim."

"Then who?" Soonhee demanded.

"His wife." She couldn't keep the bitterness from her voice.

Soonhee shook her head. "She still doesn't understand." She turned to Youngsook. "You try to explain it."

The bride chewed her lip. "Megan, I am very lucky to have a kind husband who cares for me." She leaned forward slightly. "For most women, this is not so." She paused.

"A man loves his mistress, not his wife." She sat back and pulled her skirt tight over her abdomen. Her shining brown eyes smiled into Megan's. "A man and a wife couple together for only one reason—to have a child to live after them and bring honor to their ancestors."

Soonhee clasped the younger girl's elbow. "You mean—you're with child?"

Youngsook nodded.

Soonhee leaped gracefully to her feet and danced a few joyful steps. "Megan, isn't it wonderful?"

She laughed and nodded. She couldn't let her friends see how she envied them. No matter what they said, Jongwhan could never be hers. She couldn't allow herself to think that he might want her. Her heart raced. Or could she?

24

Moon of Autumn Cool

Jongwhan willed the young boy's hands to steadiness. Savory steam rose from the bowl of dumpling soup, curling in wisps around Kwangin's shining face. The boy's brown eyes never left the brimming vessel from the moment Auntie Soh handed it to him until his slow careful steps brought him to the altar.

After placing the dish on a tray already crowded with plates of peeled apples, pears, and sliced chestnuts, the boy knelt and bowed, touching his forehead to the yellow *ondol* floor. Then the child stood and glanced at Jongwhan.

He fought to restrain a proud smile and nodded.

At this signal, Kwangin paced to the door again and fetched a covered bowl of rice. One stockinged foot slipped on the shiny surface of the oiled paper floor. The lid rocked atop the metal dish.

Jongwhan held his breath until the stubby thumbs clamped the top down. Round dark eyes, dewy with tears, looked up at him. A soft lower lip quivered.

Jongwhan nodded again. Kwangin placed the rice bowl on the *chesa* tray. His tiny hands lifted a flagon and poured brimming cups of rice wine, then tapped a pair of chopsticks against an empty bowl. He laid the silver sticks to one side and tilted the rice bowl lid ajar. With a flat silver spoon the boy scooped a few white grains into the soup.

Jongwhan's heart filled his chest. His pride couldn't be greater if he'd sired the boy himself. His mouth twisted. If only he had.

Kwangin's perfect bow brought his forehead again to the mulberry paper covering the floor.

When the dark silky head turned toward him this time, Jongwhan couldn't keep the corners of his mouth from turning up a little. He nodded again and turned his back on the ancestral meal, taking his cue this time from the boy. Let the ghosts feed in private.

Morning sun streamed through the open doors in front of him. A frigid gust blew a hint of frost and decayed leaves into the room, but heat seeped through his stockinged feet from the ducts under the floor.

Chusŏk had always been his favorite holiday, the best of all the other celebrations rolled into one. After the offerings to the ancestors, the day held nothing but gaiety—wrestling, archery contests, plenty of food and drink, and in the evening, music and beautiful *kisaeng* dancing in the light of a full moon.

And this year, Megan. Today she would walk beside him, and tonight she would glide across the stage, twirling and swaying for the King and his court. If only she danced for him alone. He had almost given up hope of breaking through the walls keeping them apart.

But she'd warmed to him the last few weeks, jade eyes twinkling, soft coral lips smiling. Muscles tightened in his groin. He took a deep breath and forced himself to relax. Not yet. No matter how much he wanted to take her into his arms, he could not risk crushing the flower of trust beginning to blossom between them.

He started at the old man's cough, then signaled the boy to bring the *chungmun* papers to the courtyard. Behind him, Auntie Soh's heavy steps crossed the floor to clear away the ancestral feast.

He took the thin rice papers while Kwangin ran to the back of the house. Each contained the name of Chang's ancestors to the fourth generation, each with the honorary title "student."

Chang had insisted Jongwhan guide his grandson through the *chesa* ritual. "I may not be here to teach him when the New Year arrives." Deep lines sagged in the usually cheerful face. "This child is my only male issue, the only one who can nourish my soul and the souls of those before me once I am gone."

How could he refuse, even though it meant holding his own *chesa* as the sun rose, then hurrying to the fortune-teller's home?

Kwangin came panting back, carrying a glowing twig from the kitchen fire.

Jongwhan took the brand and touched it to a corner of the ancestral papers where they lay on a flat dish. He rubbed his palms together and bowed from the waist, offering a prayer for peace to Chang's forefathers in the hereafter. The sweet smoke rose and hovered above his head, then undulated like a tiny dragon and spiraled up into the clear sky.

He carried the dish to the corner of the courtyard. He scattered the ceremonial ashes among the waist-high black storage jars standing sentinel there.

Kwangin slipped a chubby hand into his. He looked down at the top of the boy's head, the silky black hair. Chang's words echoed in his ears—"only male issue." Would he stand childless at his own *hwangap*, or would he be forced to adopt a nephew on his deathbed?

He squeezed the tiny hand. No, he must have his own son. If his wife couldn't give him one, he would take another woman as his own. An image of white limbs filled his mind, a cloud of copper hair, round jade-green eyes. His pulse raced. Not today, but soon—very soon!

Strings of bright orange dried persimmons hung from the awning of the small shop, filling the afternoon air with their peachlike fragrance. Megan rolled a tangy sweet bite on her tongue, sucking to soften the chewy morsel.

When she smiled her thanks into Jongwhan's gray eyes, two red spots appeared high on his cheekbones.

She turned her attention to the wrestlers sweating and

straining in front of them on the grass. Both wore red
cotton breechcloths and black headbands, and little else.

The stouter of the two grabbed the other man by the
cloth on either hip. They rocked back and forth, sweat
glistening on the ropes of sinew in their bare backs. Groans
and panting bellows from the wrestlers punctuated the
excited cries of the crowd.

The sight of their straining muscles started an ache
churning low in Megan's belly. Heat rose in her cheeks. She
wanted to look away, but she couldn't look at Jongwhan
again. Instead she turned to Soonhee.

The competition held the young *kisaeng's* full attention. Her red lips parted and her eyes sparkled. She
clapped her tiny hands and laughed aloud.

Pongnim stood beside her. His golden eyes smiled into
Megan's for a moment. When he turned back to Soonhee,
the prince's square face showed such tenderness it brought
tears to her eyes.

A cry from the crowd brought her attention once more
to the wrestlers. The slender man lay gasping on his back
on the yellowed grass. The victor raised two clenched fists
and turned to acknowledge the crowd's cheers, then bent
and helped the loser to his feet.

A blue-coated official led a young bullock onto the field
and presented the lead rope to the winner. With the prizes
awarded, the wrestling tournament ended. The crowd
milled about and began to disperse.

Soonhee tugged at Megan's sleeve, gold eyes shining.
"Come, the mask dance is starting!"

She allowed herself to be led toward a grassy square.
Dark-haired men and women sat or strolled around the
playing area. Tolerant smiles followed the children racing
among their parents through the dry grass, laughing and
playing, pursuing goals only they knew. Toddlers clung to
their mothers' skirts or nestled in their fathers' arms.

Only the poorest wore the everyday white *hanbok*
today. Rich and poor alike sported their finest bright
plumage on feast days. Middle-class women accompanied
their husbands, but Megan knew the richly dressed
yangban left their wives at home. Instead they escorted
gaily dressed *kisaeng* like her and Soonhee.

She pushed down a twinge of guilt at the image of Jongwhan's wife, secluded in a back courtyard, peeping through a bamboo screen at jugglers hired to entertain the women of the house. Somewhere Youngsook sat with her spiteful mother-in-law.

Her mouth twisted. They wouldn't want her pity. Youngsook had explained that a man's seclusion of his wife showed how much he valued her. Only a man too poor to hire servants allowed his wife outside the women's quarters in broad daylight. Still, she wouldn't trade places with them and miss the sights and sounds of *chusŏk*.

The band struck tentative notes, heralding the beginning of the dance. Jongwhan and Pongnim ushered them to cushions in the grass.

Soonhee nestled against the prince, her hip pressed against his bent knee. She gazed up at him, head thrown back and hands resting palms up in her lap.

Megan chewed her lip and glanced at Jongwhan. The blue silk of his trousers pulled taut across his muscular thighs. She forced herself to look away and let her eyes rove across the meadow.

Inside a nearby tent, two men wrestled with the head of the most fantastic creature she'd ever seen. Huge eyes bobbled and bounced as the men struggled. Round red jaws opened and closed beneath a wide black nose. Strips of tan paper covered the head, with darker strips forming a mane.

One of the men succeeded in thrusting his head up inside the giant mask. The other quickly cloaked them both in a huge hide covered with yet more tan paper.

Another man in a devil mask strode across the meadow and introduced the lion dance. He led the creature forth amid shrieks of laughter from the audience. It pranced along, swishing a paper tail and thrusting out a long red tongue.

The devil ordered the beast to dance to the band's lively music. The lion gamboled about the stage for a moment, then stopped, shook its head, and refused to move.

The devil leaned across and rapped the creature on the head with a long stick. Megan screamed her approval along with the crowd, then cheered the lion on as it chased its master around the grass, trying to bite his backside. The devil avoided the snapping teeth and smacked the stick down again and again.

Finally, when her sides began to ache with laughter, the lion settled down and danced his way around the playing area. Then, all of a sudden, the beast circled in on itself and the jaws snapped on its own backside. Megan joined in the fresh gales of laughter at the fantastic lion chasing an itching tail around and around in circles.

At last the devil succeeded in shooing the lion off, but not before it hung over the crowd, rolling its eyes and snapping its teeth at those sitting nearby.

Once back in the tent, the dancers shrugged off the heavy costume and served each other brimming cups of *makkŏlli*. Another devil joined the first and the two began a mock battle, but she missed the reason for the conflict and lost interest.

She glanced again at Jongwhan, at his broad shoulders and strong legs. He turned and smiled down at her. She lowered her eyes. If only she could be sure of his interest.

Perhaps he didn't want her as Jemmie had, as a wife. She was a foreigner, and *chunmin*. That's how things were—she'd have to accept it. Besides, she wanted to go home, to Virginia and the New World. Did she really want to give that up to marry Jongwhan?

She pushed the thought away. It would never happen—she needn't make that choice. Maybe he only wanted her body, to be able to boast of his exotic lover. She looked up again at his handsome profile. No, she couldn't believe him capable of such vulgarity.

Anyway, what if he did only want her body? What if he left her after only one night? Her spine stiffened and she tossed back her head. Well, what if he did? If he truly wanted her, she'd have to take that chance. A warmth swirled slowly through her loins.

25

A sliver of orange moon peeked over the black edge of Namsan mountain. Megan shivered in her thin white gown. At first she'd welcomed the cool darkness after the damp heat of the day. But now the shadows chilled her spirits as well.

At least in Scotland, folks knew enough to stay indoors when the moon hung full in the sky. Especially a harvest moon. She inhaled the pungent, raw odor of dead leaves and sneezed. Didn't these fools realize poisonous humors filled the night air?

She'd breathe easier when the dance began. As if in answer, a servant lifted a red and blue silk shade and lit the first of the lanterns surrounding the stage. A circle of light glowed yellow on the wooden platform and reflected off the huge drum occupying the center of the dais.

She checked the knot of her white *chogori* and wiped sweat from her palms. Where was Soonhee? The girl had gone off alone with Pongnim, swearing Megan to silence and promising to arrive at the palace in plenty of time for the dance.

Madame Insung frowned and scanned the crowd in the King's Secret Garden. Megan knew only members of the royal family had access to the *Piwŏn*. The King did them a great honor by asking them to dance here.

Megan bit her lip. Just as well Soonhee hadn't mentioned a destination, or she'd have to tell. She only hoped Jongwhan could find them.

She twisted the *norigae* ornament hanging from her sash. How could the girl put her in the position of lying to Madame? How could she put them all in this position? Soonhee led the dance—without her, the rest couldn't go on. She shivered at the thought of the King's displeasure.

She shook her head. Even Pongnim would feel the royal wrath if the King discovered he had a part in delaying the *Chusŏk* celebration.

She checked the crowd again. Still no Soonhee. A hand grabbed her shoulder and yanked her around. Pilsu sneered, "Your little bitch friend had better show up, or I'll scratch her eyes out myself!" She let go with a shove and flounced away, her bright red skirt and jacket glowing in the warm yellow light.

Megan clenched her fists until the nails dug into her palms. Leave it to Pilsu to blame Megan for Soonhee's absence. She drew a ragged breath and surveyed the clearing.

The servant lit the last of the lanterns and trudged away. Swirls of red, blue, and yellow glowed from the top of the giant drum. Musicians sauntered in, finding their places and tuning their instruments.

She took a deep breath and rehearsed the dance in her mind. The four *wŏnmu* would enter first, each in one of the colors of the cardinal directions, blue for north, red for east, black for west, and white for south. They would walk to the front, pick up the drumsticks, and circle the drum.

As one of four white-clad *hyŏpmu*, she would enter and station herself between Soonhee and Pilsu. While the inner circle danced and drummed, she and the other dancers would sing.

She muttered the words under her breath. Nonsense sounds made up all but two lines. "The moon is rising high, ever so gently . . . By favor of our illustrious Admiral Chungmu."

"I'm sorry to be so late." Soonhee's whisper startled her. The young *kisaeng* wore her deep blue skirt and jacket with the rainbow-striped sleeves, like Joseph's coat of many colors.

"Well, at least you're ready to dance. It's almost time." The gruffness drained from her voice at the sight of the young *kisaeng's* face shining in the moonlight. "What happened?"

The girl caught her elbow and squeezed. Excitement danced in her eyes. "I should tell my mother first, but I can't wait." Soonhee's voice quivered between laughter and tears.

"Well?" Megan took the girl's cold hands in her own. She knew the answer, but she had to hear the words.

"Pongnim has asked me to be his wife, to live in the palace and bear his children." The golden eyes begged for her understanding, her approval, for her to share the joy.

A bitter taste filled Megan's mouth. Happiness for her friend could not soothe the knot of jealousy forming in her belly. As a member of the royal family, the prince could marry again, but a courtier such as Jongwhan could not.

She forced a smile to her lips. "That's wonderful!"

The first notes of the *toduri* sounded. Soonhee's eyes sparkled. "I'll tell Mother as soon as we reach home. Until then, it's our secret!" The girl glided off to take her place in line for the beginning of the dance.

"Eat all of your *chatchuk*, My Friend!" The prince's red face hovered nearby, his sour *makkŏlli* breath wrinkling Jongwhan's nose. "You'll need it!" Pongnim laughed and slapped his own knee.

Jongwhan nodded and slipped another spoonful into his mouth. The smooth pine-nut porridge coated the stomach and allowed a man to drink as much rice wine as he wished without getting sick.

He swallowed the slick, tasteless stuff, but without any intention of getting drunk. He'd never seen his friend like this—loud, careless, but so happy. Someone had to look after the man and make sure no harm came to him.

A white-coated servant took the empty wooden bowls away and replaced them with dishes of *sanjŏk*. He slid the chunks of crisp broiled vegetables, fish, and meat from the long skewer. His stomach growled at the rich aroma. He'd missed dinner trying to find the two lovers before the dance, and the *Chusŏk* entertainment had lasted until almost midnight.

But oh, what entertainment! The dancers twirling, their rich colors delighting the eye. The sweet, high strains of the flute, the deep, fast rhythm of the huge drum. His pulse kept time again for a moment with the remembered beat.

And best of all—Megan. Megan, all in white, whirling and chanting, her red hair glowing in the lantern light.

Pongnim leaned across the low table and refilled Jongwhan's tiny wine cup, then waggled the flagon in his face. He sighed and filled the prince's cup for him, then set the bottle behind him on the floor.

The man downed the milky white liquor, then looked around. He pointed to the bottle. "Shame, shame, Cousin!" The words slurred together. "You mustn't deny a friend when he's thirsty!" Eyelids hung heavy over the golden eyes, but the smile never wavered.

"But don't you want to eat?" The skewer lay untouched on the prince's plate.

He breathed a sigh of relief when Pongnim looked down at his plate.

"Yes, yes! Eat! I shall eat, and you shall eat! Everyone shall eat!" The black-coated shoulders swayed back and forth.

The prince tried several times to pull the food from the bamboo skewer with his chopsticks. Finally he dropped the silver utensils, pulled a chunk off with his fingers, and popped it into his mouth.

Pongnim chewed and swallowed. "M-m-m, delicious!" He popped three more pieces into his mouth at once, chewed for a moment, then opened his mouth to speak, spraying bits of food. "Where's the wine?" He tugged at a servant's trousers. "See here! We must have more wine!"

The man bowed low and trotted off.

Jongwhan captured his friend's hand. The square red face beamed goodwill at him.

"Pongnim, this is not like you." He strove to keep his tone gentle. "Cousin, why are you doing this?"

The prince wove toward him and away, his expression never changing. "I'm happy!" He stared at his hand, then pulled it from Jongwhan's grasp and slapped him on the shoulder. "Celebrate! We must celebrate!"

Jongwhan placed a hand on each shoulder, steadying the prince. "But why? It's only *Chusŏk*."

The square face swung from side to side. "No, 'smore—much, much more." Suddenly the smile faded. "'Sa secret! But I can tell you."

He leaned close, blowing sour breath into Jongwhan's face. "I'm going to take a wife. Not my parents' choice, but a wife of my heart."

Pongnim looked from side to side. "I haven't told my father yet. She wants her mother's blessing first." He paused. "Soonhee. My beautiful *kisaeng*." He rocked back and lifted his empty cup. "Wine! We must have more wine!"

Jongwhan's pulse raced. Perhaps, somehow, Soonhee's marriage would smooth the way for him with Megan. When she saw how happy the other couple was, she might decide she could love him.

He clenched his fists. He wasn't a prince—he couldn't offer her marriage, but short of that, he'd give her the world!

Megan tossed on the thick *yo*, unable to find any comfort in the soft, warm bedding. The hours had eased her cold, aching jealousy, but each time she tried to sleep, visions whirled through her head.

Soonhee, laughing, smiling up at Pongnim, his serious square face lit with love. And Jongwhan, his shoulders square and proud, standing before the King, then squatting beside Kwangin, touching the boy's round cheek. And last, Jongwhan's gray eyes smiling down into hers.

She scissored her legs, then kicked the thick *ibul* aside. Warm air rose from the *ondol* floor, pressing against her bare skin, suffocating her.

It wasn't fair! She'd loved Jongwhan long before Soonhee even met Pongnim. And now they would be married, live in the palace, have children, perhaps even grow old together in their love.

She flipped onto her belly and pressed her face into the tight roll of the sawdust-filled pillow. The bed smelled of hot water and soap, with a faint jasmine smell of her own sweat. She pounded the hard *pyogae* with both fists.

Bile rose in her throat and burned her tongue. How

could she begrudge these two their good fortune? They had a right to as much happiness as they could gather from life.

She could hardly blame them for the mess she'd made of her life. If only she could forget Jongwhan. She turned on her side. She should have died in the storm or never set foot on that ill-fated ship in London, never trusted Devlin.

A chill seeped under the paper door. She shivered and pulled the quilt over her again. If only she could have stayed on the island with Grandmother, diving and working in the fields. Life was simple there.

But no, she'd have grown dissatisfied someday, without a husband or children. And from the moment she saw Jongwhan on horseback, his bow drawn to drive away her tormentors, she'd known he was the only man she'd ever want.

She sighed and sat up, drawing a heavy cotton gown over her bare shoulders. With one hand she searched for the firepot and uncovered the live ember. Poking a rice straw into the orange glow, she blew until the tinder caught and flared.

She held the brand to the wick sticking out of the tiny white oil bottle, then set the tiny lamp in its black wood stand. Her fingers found the silk cover of the book Jongwhan had given her "to better understand the thoughts of our people."

She sighed again and opened the slim volume. With moving lips, she spelled out the title *Songs of the Common Man*. She flipped through the small pages, impressed by the clear and regular characters and the smooth, sheer rice paper.

Her eyes stopped at a short stanza with a two-word title. She squinted and drew the book closer. "Flower Song." She wet her lips and whispered the words to herself.

> *The bloody linden slashed by a sword*
> *The stuck-in-the-throat thorn bush*
> *The trembling poplar*
> *The dried-out bamboo*
> *The sat-on and crushed boxthorn*
> *The kissing, smack, smack, indigo plant.*

Cheerful stuff! It fit her mood. She flipped the pages again. A stockinged foot brushed the wooden tile of the hall floor outside her door.

"Megan?" Soonhee's voice sounded hollow through the paper partition.

She clenched her teeth. Could she bear to hear and see her friend's joy? Too late to feign sleep. "Come in."

Soonhee stepped into the room and closed the door. She leaned her head against the wall and covered her face with her hands. A dry sob shook her tiny frame.

Megan clambered to her feet and pulled the sobbing girl into the lamplight. "Soonhee, what is it?" She tugged the hands from the girl's face. Tears spilled from the golden eyes, streaking fresh courses down the already-stained face.

Confusion touched her, and a tinge of fear. "What's wrong? What has happened?"

The girl closed her eyes and hung her head.

"Is it Pongnim? Has he been hurt?"

A fresh sob racked the small body, but she shook her head no.

Megan clasped the heaving shoulders and gave them a little shake. "Then what!"

The tiny *kisaeng* bit her lip until a tiny drop of blood appeared. With a last shuddering sigh, she spoke. "You must swear never to tell anyone, not Pongnim, not Jongwhan, not anyone!" She took another deep breath. "And you must never tell my mother I told you."

Megan nodded and loosed the girl's shoulders. "I swear."

Soonhee smudged tears across her cheeks with her hands. "I went to my mother after we returned, to tell her what"—she sobbed again, then continued—"Pongnim had asked me."

She twisted her hands in her lap. "I thought"—she cleared her throat—"I thought she would be happy, but when I told her, she looked very old and sad."

Megan nodded.

"She began to cry, and she forbade me to marry him."

Megan's breath caught in her throat. No! Was there no

mercy in the world? They loved each other! They must
marry!

Soonhee looked down at the floor. "At first she would
not tell me why. I—I defied her!" She sobbed again. "I told
her I would marry him, with or without her blessing."

Megan lay her hand across the tiny *kisaeng*'s. It must
have cost her dearly to go against her mother's wishes.

Soonhee drew her hand out of Megan's grasp. "Then
she told me why." Her voice sounded dry and hollow in the
tiny bedchamber. Her golden eyes looked straight in
Megan's. "I can never marry Pongnim, because he is my
brother."

26

Soonhee covered her face again and wept.

Megan sat, dazed, not sure what to say or do. Finally
Soonhee's sobs slowed and the girl wiped her face.

"But how?" Megan bit her lip.

Soonhee nodded. "I asked the same question." She
crossed her arms and hugged herself. "It seems my mother
met the King, my—my father, when he was but a nephew,
not even in line for the throne." She rocked back and forth
for a moment.

"He had a wife, and two sons." She looked into
Megan's eyes and shrugged. "You know how these things
are. He was a prince, she was a *kisaeng*."

Megan nodded. Suddenly she knew how it must have
been—two young lovers. She shivered and drew the quilt
around her. Like her love for Jongwhan.

Soonhee placed her hands on the floor at her sides and
looked down. "When she found she carried me, she went to
Pusan. She has friends there, other *kisaeng*."

Megan bit back tears. Insung had endured so much,

the death of her husband and son, then to choose to bear a child alone.

Soonhee's voice quavered. "She never told my father about me. If I'd been a boy, she'd have given me to his first wife to raise." She stopped, the color draining once more from her cheeks. "Pongnim and I would have been raised as brothers."

Horror clutched at Megan's bowels. To love as they loved, never knowing they shared the same father!

Soonhee grimaced. "But since I was a girl, my mother kept my birth a secret. She didn't want her daughter raised in ignorance in the back courtyards of the palace."

Insung's words came back to Megan. "Free to read and write, to learn, and to think for herself." It all made sense.

Soonhee buried her face in her hands once more.

"But what will you do?"

The *kisaeng* raised her haggard face. "Only what I must. I leave tonight for Pusan." She grabbed Megan's hands. "Pongnim must never know why—never!"

Megan nodded. Better to have him think she didn't really love him than to know the awful truth. Her heart sank at the thought of losing her friend. "But will you never come back?"

A ghost of a smile crossed Soonhee's face. "Dear Megan. Yes, I think so, someday when temptation has passed, for both of us." She dropped her eyes, then looked up again. "I have one more thing to ask of you, My Friend. I will understand if you say no."

Megan reached out a finger and traced a tearstain down the younger girl's cheek. "Anything. You know that."

Again a faint smile flitted across the *kisaeng*'s lips. "Only this—if Pongnim ever needs help, if he's ever in any kind of trouble—do everything you can for him, as if you were me."

Megan nodded. "I promise. Whatever I can do, I will."

Soonhee rose and rubbed her face. "Thank you. You are a true friend." She turned away, then raised her head high. "I must prepare to leave in a few hours. I will see no one else."

Megan ran to her and swung her around into a hard embrace. The girl's composure broke again and sobs shook her. Megan patted and rubbed the thin back through the blue silk jacket, the same she'd worn at the dance.

At last the sobbing ebbed and the girl's whisper filled the silent room. "Oh, Megan, I am so frightened."

She cupped the girl's face in her hands. "Soonhee, this is the worst thing that could possibly happen to you. You never have to be afraid again."

The tiny *kisaeng* shook her head. "But you don't understand. There's something else you don't know."

Megan shook her head, confused. What could be worse than what had already happened?

"Pongnim and I could not wait for marriage. We became lovers." She took a deep breath. "I may be carrying his child."

Jongwhan laughed at the expression on Pongnim's face when they passed a *bulgogi-jip*. The odor of the rich sweet sauce and broiling beef ribs filled the street. The prince rolled his eyes and groaned.

"Why didn't you stop me?" He shaded his eyes from the glare of the early morning light. "Some friend you are, letting me drink myself stupid the night before the most important day of my life."

Jongwhan chuckled. It served his friend right. "With due respect, Your Excellency, I think the 'stupid' may have come *before* the 'drink.'"

The prince pressed his palms against his temples. "I think my *kat* is too small." He fiddled with the strings of the shiny horsehair hat.

"Or your head made too large by the lady's love?"

Pongnim fixed him with a sour look. "That's right, laugh at me in my weakened condition. You don't have to ask a woman for her only daughter's hand in marriage, then approach my father the day after a feast." He gave a thin chuckle. "His head is twice as bad as mine, I'll wager."

Envy clenched Jongwhan's fists for a moment, but he kept his voice even. "No. You are luckier than I in that. Soonhee will make a fine wife and give you many sons." He paused to savor the next good-natured jibe. "But I would not have your head in any case, because I would not drink so much *makkŏlli* on such an important night."

Pongnim grimaced. "I wonder!"

They let themselves in the gate and scratched at the nail-studded wooden door. It swung in on heavy hinges, but instead of the serving girl, Megan stood in the doorway.

Jongwhan drank in her beauty, the copper sheen of her hair, the flawless white of her skin, the deep jade of her eyes.

Color came and went from the woman's cheeks until Pongnim elbowed him and he realized he'd been staring. He bowed to hide his confusion.

Megan bowed in return. "Gentlemen, you are our first visitors of the day." She held the door open for them. "Won't you join me for some refreshments in the visitors' hall?"

Pongnim hummed a tuneless song as they followed the exotic creature to the large, empty hall. They seated themselves on square blue pillows and leaned back against the padded *chaddae*.

The foreign *kisaeng* smiled down at them. "Now, what can I get you to drink? *Makkŏlli?*"

Jongwhan cleared his throat to hide a chuckle.

Pongnim paled and shook his head. "Could we have *yoolmu cha* instead?"

Her chestnut eyebrows rose, but she smiled and nodded. "Of course. I'll get it." She turned and glided away, her stockinged feet barely whispering across the yellow mulberry paper of the *ondol* floor.

When her back disappeared through the doorway, Jongwhan could restrain his laughter no longer. "*Yoolmu?* Couldn't you think of anything more manly than buckwheat tea?" He clapped Pongnim on the shoulder.

The prince belched and breathed stale alcohol fumes. "My mother used to give it to me for upset stomach. After that remark about *makkŏlli*, it was all I could think of." He pressed his hands against his forehead and moaned. "I will never drink rice wine again."

"Until the next time!" Jongwhan laughed, then sobered when he saw Megan returning with the tea.

She knelt and poured sweet brown liquid into three cups. Jongwhan memorized the line of her neck and her arm as she bent over the tiny table. His heart thudded at the memory of the soft white skin beneath the yellow jacket.

They sipped tea in silence until Pongnim cleared his throat. "May I speak with Madame Insung?"

Megan looked down at her hands. "I'm sure Madame would welcome a chance to speak with Your Excellency, but she is ill and cannot be disturbed."

A chill ran up Jongwhan's spine. That was not what she was supposed to say.

Pongnim blanched, but he kept his voice quiet. "I'm afraid I must insist."

Megan turned the handleless cup around in her hands. "Forgive me. Even if you insist, I am afraid I may not disturb her." She looked up, tears dewing her long chestnut lashes.

"Then I must ask to see Soonhee." His voice rang in the empty hall.

"Forgive me again, but you cannot."

Color rose in Pongnim's cheeks. He stood and looked down at her. His soft voice held a threat of danger. "And why not?"

Fear paralyzed Jongwhan's chest. Why was she doing this? What had gone wrong? Didn't she know she was refusing a prince?

Megan still looked down at the cup clenched tight in her hand. Her sweet, clear words fell into the silent room. "She is not here." She looked up, tears coursing down her white cheeks. "I'm sorry."

Pongnim half fell to the cushion, then hunched forward. The silence lengthened in the still room. When he finally spoke, his voice sounded rusty and far away. "Where?"

Megan sobbed. "I cannot tell you."

The prince nodded, his face haggard. "Why?"

"I cannot tell you that, either." Her white hand

covered his. "I know you love her. I love her, too." She pulled back her hand and squared her shoulders. "But I—I swore on oath."

Pongnim's fist crashed down on the tabletop. "Your oath be damned! I want to know where she is and why she left!"

Megan bit her lip, then rose to her feet. "I cannot betray Soonhee's wishes, no matter what you say or do. Only believe this—what I do comes from my friendship for you as much as for her."

Pongnim leaped to his feet. Veins stood out in his neck, and each word he uttered raised the hair on Jongwhan's neck. "I spit on your friendship!" He whirled and stomped out the door.

Jongwhan got to his feet and looked down at the beautiful tearstained face. He crooked a forefinger under her chin and raised her eyes to his. "Tell me." It was an order, a question, a plea.

She shook her head. "I can't." Her voice broke and she dropped her head into her hands and sobbed.

A hot wave of anger washed through him. He clenched his jaw. "Someday you'll be sorry you didn't trust me."

She took her hands from her face and tossed her head high. Jade green flashed cold and hard from her eyes. "I have no choice. I can never regret doing what's right." She turned and glided out of the room.

His shoulders slumped. He longed to call her back but stopped himself. What if she didn't come? Better to wait until another day and try to begin anew, to bury their words as if they had never been uttered.

He turned slowly around, remembering the bright hopes he'd cherished when he entered this room moments before. Swallowing the bitter taste of ashes, he straightened his jacket.

Jongwhan took a deep breath. Besides, he had to go after Pongnim. No telling what he might do in this mood.

Megan's chest ached, but still the sobs wouldn't stop. She pounded the hard pillow. She'd lost them all now. All the friends she had in the world.

Soonhee was gone, to return no-one-knew-when. Pongnim hated her, blamed her, and she couldn't destroy him by explaining. And Jongwhan—her chest tightened. Now she'd lost him for good, told him she couldn't trust him, that her promise to Soonhee and her own honor were more important than her love for him.

Why did she have to be the one to tell them? But she knew the answer. She'd promised Soonhee she would help Pongnim. She couldn't let a servant give him such a message.

A hand smoothed the hair on the back of her head. She sat up and scrubbed her cheeks with her palms. "Madame, I—I miss Soonhee!"

Dark circles smudged beneath the older *kisaeng's* eyes. Megan had never noticed the lines around Insung's mouth before, the sadness etched deep into her face. Of all the hardships the woman had endured in her life, breaking her daughter's heart and sending her away must be the worst.

"I miss her, too." A thin smile touched the pinched mouth. "Don't worry. I know she told you everything." She sighed.

Megan started to protest, but a quick shake of Insung's head silenced her.

"Don't worry, truly. I heard what you said to Pongnim and to Jongwhan. I know what it cost you. Our secret is safe with you."

Madame pulled her into her arms, cradled her as if she were a child. "It may still turn out all right for you. Life is never easy, but the choice is to continue or to give up."

Megan rested against the soft shoulder. A warm peace dissolved the sharp icy edges of her misery.

Insung's soft, smooth fingers wiped tears from her cheeks. "You are not the kind to ever give up."

27

Moon of Falling Leaves

Jongwhan's leather shoes crunched on the broken white seashells of the garden path. Papery leaves skittered away from him on a knife-edged gust of wind. The chill air, redolent of pine and dead leaves, burned his nostrils.

The bleakness of the gray sky suited his mood. The words of his father's most recent letter echoed in his mind. His wife spent months at a mountain shrine, praying to phallic stones for a child, and his mother found a book of Buddhist prayers in Munja's sleeping room. His own wife, turning to Buddhism!

He sighed and kicked at a frost-rimed pile of brown leaves. On top of that, Pongnim refused to see him, or anyone, since Soonhee left. Damn the little tease, anyway! She'd almost killed the man with her trick of disappearing with no explanation.

No, that was unfair. She must have had a reason, and a good one, to give up a chance to be the favored wife of a prince, maybe one day a king. Besides, she loved him— he'd seen that with his own eyes. Then why?

He didn't dare ask Megan again. She still refused to meet his gaze and answered his attempts at conversation with one-word replies. Another gust of wind cut through his thick padded jacket.

He pressed his arms against his sides and quickened his pace when he saw Pongnim sitting beside the path ahead. "Cousin, walk with me. It's too cold to just sit."

The prince lifted his haggard face. Hollowed cheeks made the square jaw and high cheekbones stand out even more. A haunting sadness hovered behind the gold eyes.

The corners of his pale mouth turned up. "All right." He stood and dusted the back of his *paji*.

They walked without speaking for several moments. Finally Jongwhan broke the silence. "Cousin, I am glad to see you. I was hoping to find you here in the garden today."

Pongnim nodded but made no reply.

Jongwhan cleared his throat. "May I speak openly?"

Pongnim smiled, the first true smile he'd seen on that square face since *Chusŏk*. "Of course, Brother. No ceremony can stand between us. Speak of anything you like." The prince clapped a hand on his shoulder.

Jongwhan took a deep breath. "The King has asked again what ails you. He fears for your life." Pongnim held up a hand to stop him, but he rushed on. "He says you do not eat or sleep, that you avoid your wife and your children. He says you live on rice wine and books of poetry."

He stopped walking and turned to face the shorter man. "You must stop grieving for her. She left you. She's never coming back."

A hard light came into Pongnim's eyes. "No! She is not gone. She lives in here." He pounded his chest. "I will always love her, and no other." Tears sprang to his eyes and he turned away, choking back a sob.

Jongwhan touched one heaving shoulder. "Brother, I know what you must feel!"

The prince whirled on him, grabbed his arm. "Do you? Do you really?" Anger twisted the handsome features. "What do you know of my pain? You think because your wife does not give you a child, you know pain? Because some white-fleshed foreigner holds you at arm's length, you know what I feel!"

Jongwhan turned away, unable to watch the man's suffering any longer. Pongnim's gasping breath filled the silence. A squirrel chattered on a limb above their heads.

A hand squeezed tight around Jongwhan's arm. "I am sorry." The voice sounded old and dusty, as if it came from a tomb. "You are not to blame. You alone care enough to risk my tirades." The hand suddenly let go. "Thank you."

Jongwhan turned and took Pongnim by the shoulders. The man swayed under his grip. "You must stop trying to kill yourself. You must live! For your father, for your ancestors. For your own small daughters."

He gave the shoulders a gentle shake. "For your people. You are not just a man—you are a prince! If the unthinkable should happen, if Sohyon couldn't rule, you would be crown prince in his place, and someday king."

A fire kindled in the gold eyes. He nodded. "Yes, Cousin, you are right. I have been selfish and irresponsible. No matter how I love or how I suffer, I must do my duty."

Jongwhan dropped his hands. "Please, my dear friend, come with me to your quarters. You will eat, and then you will sleep. When you awaken, we will visit your children."

The haunted eyes looked long into his. "She will never come back to me, will she?"

He bit his lip and shook his head. "No. Will you come with me?"

The courtyard reeked of raw cabbage, garlic, and red pepper. Megan sneezed, then picked up the tiny mortar and rolled the stone cylinder around and around the bowl, crushing the hot peppers to a fine red dust.

Youngsook's sweet voice chided her. "Dear Friend, you do not need to help with the *kimchee*. Auntie Soh and I can manage."

The old woman grunted and mumbled under her breath, but the young girl just laughed.

"Nonsense. I want to help." Megan realized the truth of her words. She'd been happy to see Youngsook. Since Soonhee's departure, she'd known a gnawing loneliness.

Besides, making *kimchee* reminded her of the island and her long afternoons with Sonyŏ, cutting cabbage and placing vegetables in salt.

A chill wind stung her cheeks. It had been cold then, too. She'd been in the *Chosun* kingdom for more than a year. Would she ever get home?

She emptied the fine red powder into a larger bowl and refilled the pestle, wrinkling her nose at the odor. How could anything that smelled so bad taste so good?

When Auntie Soh puffed to her feet and lumbered off to the kitchen, Youngsook leaned closer. "So, tell me what happened. Why did Soonhee leave when he wanted to marry her?"

Megan shook her head and shrugged her shoulders. She hated to lie to Youngsook, but it would hurt more to admit she knew and then refuse to tell. Better to change the subject. She forced herself to smile. "But what about you? How is Im, and your mother-in-law?"

Youngsook beamed. "My husband does extremely well. He studies all the time. He will take his government exams next year, and I know he will pass and receive a high post." She blushed. "Forgive me for boasting, but we are friends, so I can tell you the truth."

They worked in silence for a moment, Youngsook chopping garlic and Megan grinding peppers.

"But what of the child?" Megan prompted.

Again the sweet-faced young matron beamed. "I am sure I carry a boy. He gives me many lusty kicks." She smoothed her hands over her round belly and frowned. "My mother-in-law says he is too large and will give me much pain when he is born."

The brown eyes flashed defiance. "But I don't care! He will be strong and healthy, and then she will have to treat me better!"

Megan nodded and bit her lip. "Is she very cruel?"

"No, not so bad." Youngsook smiled. "Sometimes she makes me cry, and then Im scolds her for breaking the peace of the household."

The girl shrugged her thin shoulders. "But then she is twice as cruel when he is not around, so I've learned to keep my feelings to myself." She gave the garlic a vicious cut. "Anyway, I am as strong as she. I will show her someday."

Megan sneezed again, then laughed and poured out another bowl of red dust.

Youngsook giggled and tipped the chopped garlic atop some strips of cabbage, then fixed Megan with an appraising look. "And what of you and Jongwhan? Has he told you he loves you?"

Megan twisted her mouth and shook her head. "We— we had a disagreement."

The girl leaned forward, dark eyes sparkling. "About what?"

Megan's cheeks grew hot and she lowered her eyes. When she'd made the promise to Soonhee, she had no idea what it would cost. She sighed. "You know how it is between a man and a woman." She hoped that answer would satisfy Youngsook.

A small hand reached over and patted hers, scenting the air with the pungent aroma of garlic. "Of course, I understand. Let's talk of other things."

Megan took a deep breath. If only it *were* a lover's quarrel. She chewed her lip. They weren't lovers yet, might never be. She had refused to trust him, and she could think of no way to heal the breach short of telling him Soonhee's secret. She shook her head. That she could not do.

"Really? You think not?" Youngsook's question startled her.

"What? I'm sorry. I wasn't listening."

The girl giggled and waggled her forefinger. "Thinking of Jongwhan?"

Megan nodded.

The smile left the young mother's face and her voice held a new earnestness. "I asked if you thought the Manchus would invade. My mother-in-law says we must prepare, that the Mandarins can no longer protect us."

Megan's skin grew cold. A war! She shivered. Bloodthirsty barbarians riding through the streets of Seoul. "Yes. Yes, I heard some rumors."

Youngsook cocked her head. "Really? What does Jongwhan say? He is at the court. He must know something!"

"He says very little, only that the Manchu envoys were insulted, and he's sure the King will make amends."

Youngsook laid aside her knife. "Did he really trick them and have them driven from the South Gate?"

Megan nodded. "And now the Manchu emperor has threatened to invade if the King doesn't send an envoy." She shivered again. Surely the King was no fool. He would send the envoy rather than bring his kingdom into a war they could never win.

Youngsook lifted an oval head of cabbage and cut it in half with one blow. "My mother-in-law says it will do no good. War will come. Omens never lie."

A chill ran up Megan's spine. "What omens?"

The girl continued cutting the cabbage into strips. "Large stones have been seen to move of their own accord. Ducks fought on the water and killed each other."

Megan's belly chilled. The Gypsy had spoken of omens years ago in the Highlands, and Youngsook's grandfather had predicted sorrow and loss for her in the years ahead.

The young mother stood and leaned her big belly against the lip of a huge earthenware jar, then bent and dumped the cut cabbage inside and sprinkled it with salt and spices. "They say the frogs had a war outside the South Gate, and one of the palace ponds turned red like blood."

Youngsook eased herself down onto the open porch again and began to cut another cabbage. "Everyone knows the river rose so high last summer it lapped the foundations of the East Gate, and the ground rose and fell all around the city."

Megan swallowed. "I had not heard." She filled the bowl with peppers and began to grind them.

The young matron stopped chopping and rubbed the small of her back. "That is why I must leave tomorrow. My mother-in-law has sent for me. She is moving the household to Cholla Province, to the family's country home."

The girl put her arm around Megan's shoulder and squeezed. "I only came to say good-bye. I don't know when I'll see you again, or my grandfather and my brother."

Megan's chest tightened. Must she lose everyone she loved?

Tears thickened her friend's sweet voice. "Grandfather refuses to go with me. He says he lived through the Imjin War and he'll likely live through another."

Youngsook rubbed a tiny hand across wet eyes. "I begged him to let me take Kwangin, but he says he'll not have his grandson raised in another man's home like an orphan."

Megan clenched her fists. Men and their pride! They were fools, all of them!

A tiny hand touched her cheek. "Take care of them for me, please?"

Megan nodded, but her heart sank. She couldn't even take care of herself. If war came, how could she take care of a prince, an old man, and a young boy?

28

January, 1637, Moon of Drifting Snow

A smooth blanket of pale gray cloud hovered low above them, scattering large flakes of snow and muffling the shrieks of laughter from the children already out upon the ice.

Kwangin ran to the side of the frozen river to watch, then back to where Megan stood. She shivered and rubbed her cheeks, then blew on her fingers and stamped her feet.

A few paces away, Jongwhan hunched over a slab of wood, struggling to attach wooden runners to the bottom. Her heart swelled at the gentleness in his voice when at last he rose and called to the boy, then plodded through the snowdrift to the water's edge.

"Nephew, wait while I test the ice." He jumped hard, but the smooth, clear surface didn't crack. "It must be a handspan thick or more. Come, climb aboard!"

Kwangin clambered out to the makeshift sled, weaving and bobbing as his feet slid on the glassy surface. The boy wiggled his bottom and scooted to the front of the small platform. "Megan, too!"

Jongwhan laughed. "All right, Megan too." He bowed low. "Madame, allow me."

Her fingers tingled at the warmth of his touch. He guided her to the sled and helped her arrange her skirts. She slipped her arms around Kwangin's wiry body and breathed in the little-boy scent of snow and sweat and excitement. He nestled into her arms, his dark eyes shining and his round cheeks red with the cold.

Poor child! His sister was the closest to a mother he'd ever known and now she was far away to the south, with a child of her own to raise.

Jongwhan stepped through the loop of rope at the front of the sledge. He turned in his traces, his voice full of mock seriousness. "Prepare for the ride of your life!"

With a lurch, the little sled floated over the ice. Jongwhan ran with sliding steps, farther and farther away from shore.

The snow stopped abruptly and Megan's breath caught in her throat at the beauty of the day. The Han spread all around them, acres and acres of smooth white ice.

It seemed a mile wide, and on the other shore, white-topped houses climbed the hillside. Only the wisps of smoke rising from the chimneys gave any sign they were not alone in the world.

Muffled cries rose from the nearby shore. Jongwhan pulled the sledge in a slow arc. Coming around a bend, he ran headlong into another sled. His feet went one way and his body another. He landed with a thud on the seat of his blue britches.

Kwangin squealed with delight, a laugh so infectious the occupants of the other sled couldn't help but join in. Megan bit her lip, but when Jongwhan glowered, her resistance dissolved into giggles.

His gray eyes sparkled as he pulled himself to his knees and crawled toward them. "You'll be sorry for laughing at me!" His smile contradicted the gruff words.

Like lightning his arm shot out and flipped the sled, spilling his two passengers onto the snow-covered ice. Megan rolled to her side to see how Kwangin fared.

The boy jumped to his feet and still laughing, slipped and slid to where Jongwhan knelt, then leaped onto the broad back, pummeling the shoulders with his tiny fists.

Satisfied her charge had survived the fall unhurt, she lay back, still giggling, trying to catch her breath.

Jongwhan's handsome face appeared, looking down at

her. For an instant it seemed he'd looked down at her like that before, but then he smiled and took her hand to pull her up.

Lights danced in his gray eyes. "I hope you're not hurt. I don't know what came over me." A smile curved his lips and dimpled his rosy cheeks. "But you really shouldn't have laughed."

Kwangin came toward them, towing the sled, but lost his footing. He landed on his backside and slid to a stop at their feet.

The small round face pouted at the sound of their mirth. "You really shouldn't laugh, you know!" Before they could stop him, he'd swept them both off their feet. Merriment lit the dark eyes. "Now let's have another ride!"

Jongwhan settled them both on the sledge and pulled toward the near shore. Megan rested her chin atop the small boy's head, clinging to the warmth of his small body.

A yearning built in her loins and spread like a fever through her body. To have a child like this. She nuzzled the small cold ear, but he wriggled away from the caress.

She sighed and memorized the gliding grace of Jongwhan's steps. Long slender fingers held the rope in place, and in spite of the heavy padding of his *paji,* the muscles of his calves and thighs bunched and narrowed with each stride.

She cuddled Kwangin closer, and this time he didn't resist. So this was happiness. She'd never expected to find such complete contentment again. If only they could stay on this tiny sled forever.

They bumped to a stop at the shore. Kwangin tugged at Jongwhan's sleeve. "More, please?"

Jongwhan knelt beside him. "It's time we went back to your grandfather's house, so Auntie Soh can change you into some dry clothes and give you some hot fruit tea."

The boy drew his small body erect. "I'm old enough to dress myself, you know. On New Year's I shall be six."

Jongwhan nodded without a trace of a smile. "Of course. But are you too old to ride on my back?"

Kwangin cocked his head and paused. "No, I don't think so."

Jongwhan held out his hand. "Then climb on!" With his small passenger in place, he stood and plodded up the snow-covered bank.

Megan caught the rope and dragged the sled up the slope. It clattered behind them through the streets.

Kwangin's clear voice startled her from a contented reverie. "And how old shall you be at the New Year, Uncle?"

"Twenty years, Nephew." His hands clasped the boy's sturdy small thighs.

"And you Megan?" Kwangin lay a rosy cheek against Jongwhan's shoulder.

"But my birthday falls in the summer." She shook her head. Were they both born on New Year's Day? How odd!

"Doesn't matter." The small head nodded. "You shall still be a year older at New Year's."

Jongwhan smiled down at her. "Here we remember the day of our birth only on the first and the sixtieth years. But we all add a year to our age when each new year is born."

"How old?" The boy smiled.

She returned his smile. "Then I shall be eighteen."

The boy nodded and his dark eyes closed. Soon the soft lips parted. Megan held a finger to her lips and whispered a warning. "He is asleep."

Jongwhan nodded, then smiled. "I had no idea you would be so good with children."

She slipped a finger into the sleeping child's fist. "Nor I you." Her heart raced, but she forced her voice to a calm she didn't feel. "Are you this good with your own sons?"

He stopped and turned to her, his eyebrows raised. "But I have no sons."

She stared up at him, unable to keep from asking what burned in her heart. "Why?" Please let him say he didn't love his wife.

He returned her steady gaze, his soft answer falling slowly into the silent street. "It is a great sadness. My wife is barren. It is not her fault, but we share no joy in our coupling." He dropped his eyes and color rose in his cheeks.

Megan's heart swelled in her chest until she thought she couldn't breathe. A fierce joy shot through her veins. He could be hers—she would make him hers!

Jongwhan inhaled the frosty afternoon air, the warm, faint scent of jasmine rising from Megan's hair and skin. Her shoulder brushed his with each step. Snow cloaked the trees and buildings of the Secret Palace Garden. Only the scratching of their leather shoes on the seashell path disturbed the silence.

He longed to talk to her, to tell her his feelings, but fear kept him mute, ambling beside her through a winter fantasy of snow. He could not bear to risk their new closeness, even for a chance to live his dreams.

The warmth they shared seemed to him as fragile as a delicate celadon vase. To push for more might cause his joy to shatter and crumble into blue-green shards.

At last he spoke. "It was—" He stopped, embarrassed at the sound of her words, spoken in the same moment as his own.

"Pongnim—" She looked at him and giggled. Her green eyes sparkled. "Go ahead."

He cleared his throat. "It was good of Pongnim to invite us to the garden today. Few ever see this beauty." He looked away, cursing his stilted words.

"Yes." Her voice hung soft in the air, almost a tangible presence. "He looked well, but tired, as though he's been ill."

"So he has, with grief. He almost died." He bit his tongue, regretting his sharp tone. Fool! Now she'd think he blamed her. "But he is better now." He tried to soften what he could not unsay.

Her green eyes clouded for a moment, then she smiled up at him. "I am glad he is better."

Now that the conversation had turned to this, he must ask. He owed Pongnim that much. "Any word from her?"

She lowered her eyes and shook her head.

Misery weighted his shoulders. He'd broken the spell. The snow seemed ugly now, pockmarked with rain and dust. His feet kept walking forward, but his heart sank.

Suddenly she was no longer beside him. He turned back, alarm causing his pulse to race. She stood smiling in the path. "May we sit?" She pointed to a pavilion jutting out over a square, ice-filled pond, half of its floor on land, the other half supported by stone pillars reaching down into the surface of the gray ice.

He nodded and cupped a hand beneath her elbow to help her up the wooden steps. His heart leaped at the warmth of her arm beneath his fingers. He didn't know why, but she'd forgiven him.

He shook dry snow and dust from a square cushion and set it near the edge of the platform, overlooking the frozen pool.

She sank to the floor, her red skirts opening around her like the petals of an exotic flower, her beauty filling his senses. His loins tightened. He took a ragged breath. Not yet.

She found a pinecone on the wooden decking and tossed it over the edge. It skittered to a stop far out on the ice. She reached for a dry leaf and sailed it into the bright crisp air. It floated and spiraled like a New Year's kite, like his heart. This time, would he be able to take her in his arms, caress her, kiss her coral lips?

Her hands settled in her lap, like two white birds in a red nest. "What is this building used for?" She cocked her head and smiled up at him.

"King Injo had it built for fishing. It is his favorite place."

She looked down, a blush creeping into her cheeks. "And now it is mine, too."

Blood roared in his ears. Had he heard right? He sank to his knees, close beside her. The warmth of her body called out to him.

Her fingers rubbed the red silk of her skirt. She cleared her throat and looked out over the frozen pond. "I had a letter from Youngsook today. Her son is born."

Suddenly she turned her face up, her jade-green eyes catching him, holding him. She smiled. "She says he is big and strong. His cries wake the whole house, and he suckles at her breast like a young piglet."

Coral glowed in her cheeks, but still she did not look away.

He longed to reach out, to touch her, pull her close, but he could not. "Im is a lucky man, to have such a woman, and such a son."

"Yes." Still she held his gaze. Her voice caressed him. "And you, Jongwhan, when will you have sons?"

His heart pounded in his chest. He shook his head. "I do not know. And you, Megan?"

Her green eyes flashed and her lips curved upward. "When the man I love tells me he loves me."

He crooked his forefinger under her chin. "Am I that man?"

She nodded.

"Megan." He breathed all his aching joy into the words. "I love you." He brushed his mouth against the softness of her lips.

Her arms circled his neck. She rose to her knees and pressed her body against his.

Without releasing her mouth, he slid his hands down her back and cupped her buttocks, pulling her closer still. He savored the softness of her breasts, her belly, her thighs.

She pulled her mouth away, her breath rasping against his ear, then stood and held out her hand. "Come, this is no place for the making of sons."

29

The scent of last night's lovemaking blended with the usual odors of her sleeping room—clean cotton bedding, burned oil from her lamp, the faint scent of jasmine from her clothes. Megan set the lid on the ceramic bowl with as little noise as possible and tiptoed back to the pile of bedding in the center of the room, the heated floor warming her feet in the chill morning air.

She slipped between the heavy quilt and the thick mattress. Now, with the pressure on her bladder gone, she could relax. She stretched and reveled in the total comfort of the moment, then curled on her side to watch Jongwhan sleep.

Dark lashes fringed his closed eyelids. Parted lips gave his face a boyish quality. The regularity of his breathing, the rise and fall of his broad chest, lulled her.

A rooster crowed somewhere outside, his strident call muffled by the snow covering the ground. Cold blue light leaked into the room through the paper-and-lath doors.

She nuzzled her face against Jongwhan's warm shoulder and rested her ear against his chest, listening to his heartbeat and reliving the night before—his lips, his hands, the murmured words of love.

She sighed. Even in his passion he had taken her with gentleness, slowing his caresses, bringing her to a fulfillment she'd never known before. Only then had he unleashed his own excitement, crying out in the frenzy of his own completion.

A damp warmth swirled through her loins and crept between her legs. She smiled and eased her bent leg over his hip.

"Mmm." His sleepy groan tickled the back of her head. An arm tightened around her waist. His finger traced a line from her thigh to her breast. His hand closed around it, tickling the nipple.

She drew a sharp breath and arched her back, grinding her pelvis against his strong thigh. Her hand slipped down his smooth chest to the flat of his belly.

"Wait!"

She jerked her head up.

Heavy-lidded gray eyes smiled at her. He touched her cheek with his free hand. "I must relieve myself."

Her cheeks warmed, but she pointed to the covered chamber pot and turned her head away. But she couldn't resist stealing a glance. He knelt facing into the corner, his naked back toward her. Not a very dignified position. She suppressed a giggle.

She drank in the lines of his torso, the smooth tight curves of his buttocks, and sighed. If he could excite such longing in her just by making water, she must really love him. A warm tenderness filled her chest.

The sound of liquid gurgling in the half-empty vessel echoed in the small room, then stopped. A sharp tang of urine scented the air and was gone.

He covered the earthenware pot and stood. Desire spread through her belly. He strode toward her, his desire shining from his gray eyes.

Jongwhan lifted the coverlet and stared down at her. Her breath caught in her throat. The dream! It must have really happened! She would ask him, but later.

Her pulse quickened. He knelt beside her, stroking her breasts, her belly, his fingers curling in the moist down between her legs. He bent and suckled her breast. She moaned and arched against his fingers.

When she spread her thighs, he lowered his body onto hers. She felt the hard heat of his desire pressing against her belly. She rocked her pelvis upward and hooked her calves over the small of his back.

Slowly he entered her, filling her. She slipped her arms around his back, pulling him down to her, pressing fierce kisses against his mouth, his face, his neck.

She rose to meet his thrusts, welcoming each one. Passion mastered her, melting her mind, her soul, her body into his, pulling her to a floating ecstasy. She cried out in an agony of joy, a cascading succession of thrills, ebbing to a warm pool of spent desire.

Now he drove into her, faster and faster, his breath ragged against her ear. At his pinnacle he tensed and moaned, thrust again, and collapsed atop her.

The tenderness welled up in her again, filling her chest so she could not breathe, forcing tears of joy from her eyes. At last he was hers, if only for now.

Megan held the gate open with one shoulder and emptied the washbasin into the open sewer. The warm water melted a hole in the icy surface. A whiff of frozen human waste wrinkled her nose. An eerie quiet filled the street.

She shrugged. She seldom awoke this early. Perhaps the bitter cold kept the usual travelers inside. She swung the wooden gate closed and latched it, then pulled her heavy padded silk coat closer and walked, shivering, toward the kitchen.

She'd fetched the washwater herself, not wanting the presence of a servant to intrude on their intimacy. They had sponged the sweat from each other's spent bodies. She smiled. When washing turned to caressing, he'd stopped her and pulled on his clothing.

The sleepy-eyed cook stared at her when she began dishing up rice and soup and setting it on a small table. She covered the food with a white cloth and hurried with it back to her room.

When she passed Pilsu's room, a shuddering groan stopped her. Was the woman ill? Then the sound of wheezing breath emerged, and a man's voice growled, "Hurry up, slut. Take it in your hand."

Her skin crawled. She recognized the voice of General Kim. Pilsu was in bed with that loathsome old man! The *kisaeng*'s high laugh screeched through the door. "Come, show me what kind of man you are."

Megan backed away, her stomach churning. Moans and the rhythmic sounds of flesh smacking against the floor followed her to her own door. Was that how she and Jongwhan sounded?

She took a deep breath and put the incident out of her thoughts. She'd not let those loathsome creatures spoil her joy today. She opened the door.

Jongwhan tightened the black horsehair string around his shiny topknot and smiled up at her. He slipped the sheer black skullcap over the top, then pulled the band tight across his forehead and tied it in place.

She knelt and placed the table in front of him, then turned to smooth the bedding. She started to roll and tie it, partly to get it out of the way, partly to give him privacy while he ate.

She'd come to accept the Korean custom of men eating

first. She'd eat later with the other *kisaeng* in the *chubang*. When he said her name, she let go of the *yo* and turned.

"Megan." She thrilled at the tenderness of his tone. "Come, sit with me."

She nodded and knelt beside him. He stroked her cheek with his forefinger, then lifted rice to her mouth with the silver chopsticks. "Eat."

She sank to her buttocks on the square floor pillow and chewed the gummy rice, the nutty-sweet flavor filling her mouth. She swallowed and smiled up at Jongwhan.

He returned her look, a gentle light shining from his gray eyes. Without speaking he handed her the shallow silver spoon and pushed the half-full bowl of soup toward her. She savored the steaming, garlicky beef broth and chewed the crisp greens.

With the chopsticks he picked a chunk of pickled cabbage from the *kimchee* bowl, powdered red pepper clinging to its wrinkled surface. He dropped it into his rice bowl, then scooped rice and *kimchee* into his mouth together and chewed.

They shared the meal in silence until he laid aside the silver utensils. She poured scorched-rice tea into tiny cups. He sipped and swished the bland, gold-colored liquid around his mouth before he swallowed.

She followed suit, suddenly not wanting her good-bye kiss to taste of garlic and *kimchee*.

He reached over and took her hand. "My love, I am concerned for your safety."

A thrill of fear tiptoed up her spine.

"I want to take you south, in case the Manchus make good their threat to invade." His eyes flashed like gray stone for a moment. "The King has sent an envoy to plead with General Mabuda, but it may be too late."

He stood and pulled her up beside him. "I must go to Pongnim now, but I shall be back to see that you get out of the city safely."

She nodded.

He pulled her into his arms. "If word gets out that the Manchus have crossed the Yalu River, the streets will not be safe."

He kissed her forehead. "You must promise me you will wait behind closed gates until I return." He bent his head and kissed her mouth.

Her lips clung to his. She pressed her body full against him, thrilling again at the hard muscles of his chest and thighs. She felt him swell and harden against her belly, stirring a sweet ache in her loins.

He released her lips and with a sigh, held her at arm's length. He chuckled and shook his head, but his soft words held love and hope. "I must go. But first you must answer. Will you wait?"

She drank in the lines and contours of his face. War! No, not now, when she had finally begun to live! She nodded, never taking her eyes from his. "I promise."

Messengers skittered to and fro, and knots of courtiers argued in loud voices outside the King's quarters. Jongwhan threaded his way through the chaos, searching for Pongnim. At last he reached the prince's private rooms, where he lived with his wife and small girls.

His feet echoed when he climbed the red lacquered wooden steps. He gave a polite cough, but silence pressed against him, broken only by the scratching of a pine branch against the blue tile roof.

He turned to go, then thought better of it. This was no time for etiquette. He swung the lath-and-paper shutter outward on squeaking hinges.

A white-gowned serving woman hurried toward him and bowed.

"I must see His Excellency the Prince."

She bobbed her head and skittered out of the room. Pongnim strode in a few moments later, a frown creasing his broad forehead. When he saw Jongwhan, a smile lit his handsome features.

"A gentleman in a blue coat was all she said. I thought it one of my father's advisers come to beg me for support in their idiotic schemes."

The frown returned for a moment, but he shook his head and smiled again. "And how is Megan?"

A warmth spred to Jongwhan's cheeks. He opened his mouth to speak, but nothing came out.

Pongnim laughed and clapped him on the shoulder. "So, luck has smiled upon you at last. No need to speak of it. Your face says it all."

Jongwhan chewed his lip, but returned his friend's smile.

The prince gestured him to a cushion and seated himself on another. "So, what brings the lovebird so far from his nest?"

Jongwhan took a deep breath. "I come to offer you my services, as your friend, and as your subject."

Pongnim shook his head. "A true friend, but not a subject, yet. My elder brother may not be bright, but his health remains excellent, as does my honored father's."

The square face sobered. "In truth, I do stand in need of your help."

Jongwhan nodded and waited for Pongnim to continue.

"Today I am to be sent to the fortress at Kanghwa with the Queen and the younger princes. The ancestral tablets will travel with us." He grimaced. "It is only a precaution. My father does not intend to go to war, no matter how many factions cry for it."

Jongwhan's belly chilled at the seriousness of his friend's words.

A ghost of a smile lit the prince's face. "It is difficult to ask a friend to leave the woman he loves."

Jongwhan's heart skipped a beat, but he nodded. He hadn't planned to leave Megan, but rather to take her with him to his family home in Kyŏng-ju Province. But how could he deny his friend's request?

"I shall not need your help for myself. Even if war comes, we shall be safe on Kanghwa Island." Pongnim shrugged. "The Manchus can hardly succeed in crossing the Han to attack us when the Mongols failed."

Jongwhan nodded. He'd heard the tales. But if Pongnim didn't want him as a personal escort, what help could he offer?

Pongnim stood and paced across the mulberry paper floor. "I need your help, not for myself, but for my father."

Jongwhan started. Help the King? How?

"My father is in need of cool heads, sound advice. He is surrounded by fools!" The prince's voice exploded with bitterness. He turned and smiled down at Jongwhan. "Besides, you're the best marksman I've ever seen with a bow!"

"But I'm an artist, not a soldier." He shook his head. "I've never even killed a rabbit. How can I protect a king?"

Pongnim shrugged. "I told you it was difficult to ask. Do not feel that you must agree. I will understand."

Jongwhan stood and bowed from the waist. "I accept your commission, My Friend."

The prince returned the bow. "My thanks, Cousin. Stay by him. Do not leave his side." He cocked his head. "But what of Megan?"

Jongwhan chewed his lip. He'd made her promise to wait until he came for her. There was no help for it. She must leave the city. "I'll send a messenger, someone I can trust, to take the message to her."

Pongnim nodded. "Be sure of the man you send. No woman will remain safe if the Manchus strike." He shook himself and looked up at Jongwhan. "I must leave now. Father received a message that the horde has already crossed Pungyan Province."

Jongwhan traced his steps back to the King's quarters and scanned the throng for a messenger. A voice at his shoulder cut through the babble of voices.

"Young Sir, what is it you seek?" The thick voice issued from the thin wet lips of General Kim.

Jongwhan bowed. "Uncle, I seek a trustworthy messenger. I must warn the King's ward to flee the capital."

The fat man pursed his lips and nodded. "Yes, indeed. May I offer you the services of my groom? A most trustworthy man, I assure you."

"Many thanks, Uncle."

Kim signaled to a sullen-looking man. The groom sauntered over and bowed, but kept his distance from his master. "Take this gentleman's message to the *kisaeng* house by the South Gate."

The groom gave an insolent leer, but dropped his eyes when Kim raised a hand as if to strike him. Jongwhan hesitated, but he could not insult the general by refusing after he'd accepted the offer.

He handed the folded paper into the man's filthy paw. He'd send another message later, to make sure it got through.

The boy turned to go, but Kim stopped him. "I have some messages to send as well." He patted Jongwhan's arm. "I'll see to it she gets the warning. I give you my word."

Jongwhan bowed and took a deep breath. He needn't worry. Kim was a gentleman—his word was good. Besides, wasn't the general a friend of his revered father? "Thanks again, Uncle. I must wait on the King."

Kim's eyes glistened. He bowed. "Your servant, Nephew."

Megan jiggled the metal latch. The pounding and shouting on the other side increased, the blows thudding against her shoulder through the heavy wooden boards of the gate.

The gatekeeper had been the first servant to disappear into the crowded streets. Damn the man! At last the metal sprang open.

A man thrust his head through the opening. His black eyes widened, then a leer twitched his lips.

She took a step backwards. "What do you want?" Her voice shook. She clenched her fists.

The dark eyes slid to one side, then the other, raking the courtyard. Finally he fixed his gaze on her until she dropped her eyes. She hadn't been looked at like that since the island. The odor of stale sweat choked her. She stepped back again. "What do you want?"

He chuckled. "Message for Miss Pilsu. Fetch her."

She hesitated a moment, wanting to slap the insolent smile off the servant's face. But she thought better of it and hurried toward the house. She ran the last few steps to the side door, but forced herself to a walk as she neared Pilsu's sleeping room.

She took a deep breath, then cleared her throat.

"Enter!" Pilsu's clear, high voice sang through the paper door.

Megan opened the shutterlike doors a crack. "Messenger for you at the front gate."

Pilsu scowled. "Well, show him in, you fool!"

Megan clenched her fists. "Show him yourself." She strode toward the servant's quarters near the front gate again. She'd been on her way to rouse the cook when she heard the man pounding.

Her mouth twisted. She'd never have opened it except she thought it might be word from Jongwhan. She smiled and hummed to herself. Jongwhan. Her lover!

She rounded the corner. The messenger still stood near the gate. His eyes followed her to the cook's door.

The sour stench of rice wine reached her even before she opened the door. The woman was drunk again. She pulled open the shutters. "Come, Ok's Mother, you worthless hulk. Time to get up!"

The fat cook snorted and heaved her body to one side, then rolled again to her back, mouth open and snoring.

Megan picked up a short stick and prodded the woman in the ribs.

Ok's Mother sat straight up, terror distorting her plump features. "Oh, Miss Megan. I thought you was the Manchus!" The woman's shoulders sagged, and she rubbed a hand over her eyes and nose. "Is the fire out again?"

"Yes!"

The cook clutched her head at Megan's loud answer. "I—I had trouble sleeping, you know—because of the soldiers. I just took a little wine to help me sleep."

Megan sighed and shook her head. They all had trouble sleeping since the news of the invasion. "Well, come on then, I'll help you cook breakfast."

"Oh, thank you, Miss." The woman struggled into a white jacket and skirt and followed her out the door.

By the gate Pilsu stood talking to the loathsome servant. He looked over and pointed toward Megan, but Pilsu slapped his arm down. The tall *kisaeng* scowled across the yard until Megan shrugged and followed Ok's Mother toward the cookhouse.

They were talking about her, that much was clear—but why? Oh, well, she had more important things to think about than Pilsu's hatred.

The fat cook stopped just outside the cookhouse. "I— I . . ." A sob shook the woman's portly frame.

Insung stood in the doorway. The mistress let out a heavy sigh. "Never mind, you old fool. Just get busy and build up the fire. The floors are cold!" She shook her handsome head. "And start some soup. We all need our strength."

Insung stopped Megan at the door. "My Friend, I have a favor to ask of you." She held out a carved wooden box. "Will you help me bury this near the *kimchee* jars?" She lowered her rich voice. "It contains my strings of cash and my jewels."

Behind Insung, the cook's fat face swung for a moment toward the door. Megan nodded a warning to Insung. Madame smiled. "Tell no one!"

"Now, Child." Madame caught her elbow. "Come with me and we'll find a shovel."

"She heard you, Madame!" Megan's whisper harmonized with the scraping of their satin slippers on the frost-rimed clay of the courtyard.

"I know. You needn't worry about her." Madame smiled up at Megan. "She is harmless."

Megan lifted the heavy square shovel and dug a small hole near the corner of the wall.

Insung laid the box inside and smoothed the earth over the top. "There. Thank you for your help." The dark eyes turned to her. "Megan, now that my valuables are safe, I have a question. Everyone else has fled to the south. Even the servants are leaving. Why have you stayed?"

She swallowed. "Why, Madame, hadn't you guessed? This is the only home I know. Where would I, a foreigner, take refuge?" The words tumbled unbidden from her mouth. "Besides, when Soonhee left, she asked me to stay by you, no matter what."

Tears welled up in the older woman's eyes, but she brushed them away and nodded. Insung cleared her throat. "Yes, Soonhee is a good daughter." With that, the *kisaeng* turned and walked away.

Why had she said that? Why had she lied to Madame? Her chest squeezed tight around her beating heart. She knew the answer. She had begun to doubt Jongwhan's word. She had lied to save her own pride if he didn't come back for her.

30

Jongwhan rested one hand on the pommel of the tall saddle and pressed the other thumb and forefinger against closed eyes for a moment. A painful glare came from the entire sky, glowing through the mottled clouds, but it shone brighter toward the zenith.

So, noon approached. Would they make it out of the city in time? He sighed, inhaling the stench of fear and unwashed bodies on the frigid air.

A gust of wind cut through his padded coat and leggings and sprinkled dry snow on the dark heads of the peasants crowding the avenue. The men and women cowered away from the party of horsemen, murmured to each other in curiously hushed tones as the King and his escort passed, then scurried forward again in their wake.

Poor creatures! Many of them carried all their household goods on A-frames on their backs. Weariness and terror etched the gray faces. Many stumbled beneath their burdens, but he knew their memories of past invasions would urge them ever onward, out of the city, away to whatever safety could be found to the south.

Ahead, the way joined the great palisade. His Excellency's grooms thrust their way into the stream of white-clothed peasants flowing down the thoroughfare. Jongwhan nosed his mount closer to the other horsemen as he made the turn. Already several servants had been separated from the escort by the masses flooding the streets.

At last the great South Gate came into view. His spirits

lifted, partly from relief that the King's party would escape before the Manchus invaded, and partly from habit. The *kisaeng* house stood in the shadow of the wall not a stone's throw from him.

He would rest easy when he saw for himself the deserted buildings. No smoke issued from the chimneys. No sign of servants in the part of the yard he could see over the wall. He took a deep breath.

Empty, just as Kim's groom had said. He should never have doubted the man. He shook his head. Still, the groom's surly leer made him nervous. Well, anyway, Megan had escaped to safety. He could forget about her for the moment and concentrate on the present predicament. Or could he?

He closed his eyes and conjured up her image in his mind. Curving coral lips, glowing green eyes, copper tresses cascading over smooth white breasts. An aching loneliness filled his belly and chest until he clenched his fists and pushed her from his thoughts. No telling how long before he would see her, hold her again. If he survived.

With one finger he traced the smooth surface of the bow slung across the saddle. The question echoed in his head. Would he survive? Would he be able to shoot another man, even one bent on killing him? Or would he disgrace his family beyond redemption forever and die a coward on the battlefield?

He shrugged. Maybe he would never know, never need to know. If the King and his escort could escape to Kanghwa, they might not need to fight.

Generations before, when Genghis Khan and his Mongol horde ravaged the land around Seoul, the King and his army remained safe in the island fortress. How could the Manchus hope to succeed where the Great Khan had failed?

He clenched his fists. If they could reach Kanghwa.

The shadow of the gate fell across his face. He rubbed his eyes, tired from squinting in the strange light.

A horseman, dressed in the red coat and flat black hat of a soldier, burst through the gate toward them, flailing a whip to clear the road before him. The man drew his horse to a halt before the King and leaped to the ground, bowing low before he panted out his message.

"Excellency, you must turn around. The enemy has reached the river at Yangwhajin. The way to Kanghwa is blocked!"

The man's clear voice carried to the crowd in the sudden hush. Then with loud cries, peasants bolted back through the gates, fighting the steady oncoming stream until the turmoil resembled water boiling angrily in a pot.

Jongwhan wiped sweaty palms against his trousers. He tasted the ashes of fear and disappointment. So, he wouldn't be spared his trial by fire. He wasn't safe, and more importantly, neither was the King!

The King's advisers murmured among themselves. At last General Choe spoke up. "Excellency, let us ascend the steps to the pavilion atop the gate. There we can consider the best course to follow."

The strain of the last few days showed on the ruler's thin face. King Injo nodded and swung one leg over the pommel. Grooms lifted the slight figure to the ground from the tall platform of the saddle. Guards hurried to surround the sovereign, and his advisers followed their pale leader up the broad stone steps.

Jongwhan hurried to accompany them, halfway expecting to be sent back to help watch the horses. No one seemed to notice him take a place on a window ledge in the wall. The bitter cold of the gray stones crept through the heavy padding of his *paji*. He shivered, but held his place.

Cold gray light seeped from the narrow windows into the damp interior of the pavilion. Because the gatekeepers only used the rooms above during the summer, the guards had to shake out the dusty cushions and spread them on the unheated floor before the royal party could sit.

The king and his advisers looked at one another with white faces. Their dry whispers reminded Jongwhan of frogs croaking in the country.

At last General Chi Yoha spoke. "Excellency, they have come down from the border in five days and must be very tired." The small man puffed his chest out. "I will take five hundred men and go out and hold them in check until you can reach Kanghwa."

A chaos of voices arose at this brave speech. Jongwhan knew the man must be a blowhard or a fool to make such a ridiculous proposal.

General Choe's calm voice broke through the babble. "We must decide immediately, for the enemy is at our very doors." He fixed General Chi with a steely glare. "We cannot fight them, but I will go out the gate and parley with them, and meantime His Excellency can escape to Namhan."

"Yes!" The King's reedy voice rang through the pavilion. "Yes, my good friend, go at once!"

Jongwhan trailed down the steps after the ministers, ignoring their bickering about the King's decision. He almost wished King Injo would send him with General Choe. If he must die a coward, it may as well be sooner than later. He could volunteer—but no, Pongnim asked him to stay with the King.

Soldiers pushed back the crowds still pouring through the gate. General Choe and a group of soldiers herded ten head of cattle and five packhorses ahead of them. Each sturdy pony bore on its back two tubs of wine. Meat and drink, gifts for the enemy.

The King's escort mounted again, all except the crown prince. Sohyon stood by his pony, blinking his round eyes. How could this simpleton be Pongnim's brother?

Jongwhan slid from his saddle. "Excellency, you should mount. Our party is leaving."

Sohyon fixed him with a blank look. "My groom has disappeared." His halting words mirrored the surprise on his round face.

Jongwhan took the bridle in one hand and cupped the other at the proper height. "Excellency, I shall help you mount, but you must hold the reins and guide the horse yourself."

The young man nodded and set his booted foot in Jongwhan's palm. Sohyon looked down from the saddle when he handed up the reins. A sudden, glorious smile lit the prince's face. "I know you—you're Jongwhan. Pongnim is my brother, you know!"

Jongwhan smiled back and nodded, then remounted

his own sturdy pony. If only the man were not a prince—then his dull wits wouldn't matter. Sohyon had a good heart, but he would never rule Korea in his own right.

The mounted escort forced its way back through the gate's great stone arch. The huge red wooden door swung closed behind them. Peasants screamed and beat on the heavy timbers, but to no avail. The King had ordered the south side of Seoul sealed.

Jongwhan couldn't meet the faces of the people swarming around him. Many of them fought their way back, following the King toward the East Gate. But without horses, they would be trapped within the city walls, to be killed or captured by the Manchus.

His belly twisted at the thought. He looked again at the *kisaeng* house as the horsemen pushed their way past it again. Still no signs of life.

At least Megan was safe, somewhere far to the south. If only he could have held her in his arms once more, told her good-bye and that he loved her. But no, his duty and her safety were more important. If he lived, he would never be separated from her again.

The lye smell of stale dishwater stung Megan's nostrils. Damn the servant girl! She'd sent her out into the street to see what had caused all the excitement, and the girl hadn't returned.

Well, she couldn't wait forever. Dishpans still needed emptying, rooms needed airing, and the floors felt as if the cook had let the kitchen fire die again.

She hated to drag the heavy basin and its soapy contents through the house, so she opened the outside door and carried her burden down the short steps.

Just then the back gate clattered shut and the white-coated servant ran toward her. "Hanyo, what's wrong?"

"Oh, Mistress! The Manchus!" The girl stood panting, her eyes wild with terror. "The signal fires! They say the horde rides from Changdan, only a hundred *li* from here!"

A dry sob racked the girl's thin shoulders. "I heard a man say the King has left the city by the South Gate. People are running for their lives!"

Megan tried to calm the frightened child with her voice. "It will be all right. The young gentleman will come for me soon, and I will take you with me to the south."

The girl just stared at her.

"Now, will you please take this and empty it at the front gate?" She held out the dishpan.

The maid shook her dark head and backed away, then whirled and ran to her quarters.

Megan grimaced. She couldn't blame the girl. The news terrified her, too. It had been two days since Jongwhan left, promising to return. A thought crept into her mind for the hundredth time. What if he didn't come back?

She'd been so sure of him, so sure he'd come back. No, he'd come, she just had to have faith. She sighed. She'd have to empty the pan herself.

Her hands ached from holding the heavy tub away from her. She could hear the contents slosh with each step she took. She tripped over a rock, barely keeping herself from falling, but the slimy gray liquid slopped over the edge and covered her hands, chilling them to the bone in the frosty air.

At last she reached the gate and set the bowl on the doorsill. With dripping hands she undid the latch and shouldered open the gate. Noise and movement beat at her through the portal.

White-colthed peasants hurried by on foot, carrying their possessions on towering *chiggis*. *Yangban* on horseback and in sedan chairs shouted at the people to make way, but no one seemed to listen to anyone.

She watched in horror as a blue-coated aristocrat laid his whip across a young mother's shoulders and shouted for her to get out of his way.

The woman screamed and clutched her baby to her breast. She tried to move to one side, but there was no place to go. The crowd pressed in around her.

Again the man struck her with his whip. She fell to her knees and the crowd parted around her. The *yangban* sidled his horse past and spat on the top of the woman's head. Megan's stomach turned at the sight of such inhumanity.

The young mother staggered to her feet and stumbled away. Only then did Megan lean out far enough to dump her burden. With shaking hands she relatched and barred the gate from within.

Jongwhan had better hurry, or they'd be trapped in that mass of humanity. Her heart sank. It might already be too late.

She hurried to the courtyard well and drew up a bucket and scrubbed her hands in the icy water, trying to get the greasy smell off.

She dried her hands on a rough cotton towel. The house echoed when she walked through the visitors' hall. Only she and Madame remained. All the others had headed south at the first sign of bad news. Pilsu had left with the mysterious messenger.

In the *chubang* she found just what she'd expected. The cook had stoked the fire the night before, set out cold food, and disappeared. Madame's jewels!

She stepped to the door. From there she could see the earth piled high, the handle of the shovel sticking up from the hole the cook had dug. Poor Madame! She should never have trusted that drunken baggage!

She turned back to the fire and piled kindling atop the glowing coals and blew until flames danced. When Jongwhan arrived, she'd have a hot meal waiting. It might be their last for a while.

The inns and roadhouses on the southern roads would be full. *Yangban* might presume on acquaintances or relatives, but she was unsure what reception a foreign *kisaeng* might receive. She hadn't forgotten the monks on Cheju Island.

She straightened and rubbed the small of her back, then stretched her arms high and closed her eyes. When she did, her mind filled with thoughts of Jongwhan, his face, his touch. She sighed.

Madame's voice cut through her reverie. "Megan, the Manchus will arrive soon, and I want to talk to you."

"Oh, Madame! The cook has gone, and she dug up your jewels. I'm sorry!"

She expected the woman's face to crumple, but instead Insung laughed. "Those were imitations. I knew Ok's Mother would look for something to steal when she left, so I made sure she'd take what I wanted her to."

The handsome face sobered. "I'm sorry I fooled you. My real treasure is buried under the roots of Grandfather Chang's cherry tree."

Megan breathed a sigh. "Oh, Madame, I am so relieved!"

Insung giggled, her face glowing with sudden youth. "It was a good joke!" She touched Megan's cheek. "But come, I have something more important to tell you."

She nodded.

The older woman's expression changed again. "I feel I owe you an explanation. I want to tell you why I have stayed here, risking both our lives, instead of fleeing with the others."

Megan's heart rose in her throat, but she followed the older *kisaeng* into the visitors' hall.

Insung's clear voice echoed in the empty room. "When I was a young girl in Pusan, we heard many stories of the yellow dwarves from the south. They occupied the port for seven years when my mother was a girl." The woman sat on a cushion and motioned her to another.

Megan nodded, arranging her skirts. "I have heard tales of their cruelty."

Madame smiled. "You are a good listener." The smile waned and the dark eyes clouded. "They leaped from their longboats, wearing demon masks and shooting muskets."

She folded her hands in her lap. What had this to do with her? If only Jongwhan would come!

Madame's voice shook. "It was the first time our people had seen firearms. Many died. My mother told me this when I misbehaved as a young girl, to frighten me, I think."

The woman twisted a fold of her silk skirt between her fingers. "They burned many homes, sometimes with the owners still inside. But they did not burn the houses of the *kisaeng*."

Megan leaned forward, suddenly interested. What did Insung mean?

"Megan." Insung stretched out a beautiful, slender hand to her. "This house is all I have. If it is destroyed, only the King can give me another." The dark eyes looked into hers. "You know why I can't go to him for anything."

She nodded. To save the house, Insung would sacrifice her own pride. She remembered Soonhee's story of the *kisaeng* who became the Japanese general's mistress, then leaped to her death and killed them both. Her pulse raced. She lay in a trap, waiting for the hunter to pounce.

Her only hope was Jongwhan. He would come for her. He had to. After that one night of love, he couldn't go off and leave her to the invaders.

The hinges on the back gate creaked, as if in answer to her thoughts. "Jongwhan!" Her voice rang through the empty house. She ran through the courtyard and reached the gate a step behind Madame.

Insung tugged open the small door and Kwangin spilled through the opening, eyes dark and wide, lips parted. "Megan, Madame, come quick! It's Grandfather. The Manchus have knocked down our gate and he's trying to fight them!"

31

The pain of the small boy's words sickened her like a physical blow. Megan's vision darkened and she clung to the gatepost for support.

Madame's voice pulled at her. "Come, we will face them. They may be savages, but they are men after all."

Tears blurred her eyes, but she swallowed them. The world took on an unreal quality—she, Madame, their words, their actions, all seemed strange and unimportant.

The Manchus, in Chang's garden! But they couldn't be. Jongwhan said he'd come back for her, said he loved her. He did love her—must love her! She knew it!

Kwangin's small, warm hand slipped into hers. "Don't be afraid, Megan. I'll protect you!"

Reality rushed back at her, a harsh, ugly reality. The Manchus had come, Jongwhan had not. He'd betrayed her, left her to the enemy. He didn't love her, didn't even care enough to send a message to save her. He'd only used her for his pleasure, only pretended to love her.

But why? Why had this happened to her? It was so unfair! She bit back a sob and shook herself, stiffened her back and tossed her head.

Feeling sorry for herself would do her no good. Anger welled up in her, anger at Jongwhan, at Devlin, even at Jemmie—anger at all men! They had done this to her. She would never forgive them, any of them, ever!

She pushed the hurt deep down in her being and held the anger, feeding it. She would survive, without any help from men, in spite of their betrayals!

She squeezed Kwangin's tiny hand. "We will protect each other."

Ahead of her Insung pushed Chang's back gate ajar. Through the open portal came guttural laughter. Chang whirled his long walking stick like a club about his head. Two men danced out of the way of his intended blows. A dozen more cheered them on.

One of the tormentors tripped over the root of a tree and Chang's stick caught him a glancing blow. The Manchu reeled backward and his head hit the hard clay of the courtyard with a sickening thud.

His companion roared and charged the blind man, wresting the stick from his grasp and advancing toward him with murder in his eye.

Kwangin's hand slipped from Megan's and he was away before she could stop him.

"Grandfather!" He ran at the surprised warrior and kicked him in the shins, then retreated to Chang's side.

The Manchu stood confused for a moment while his companions laughed. The tormentor's face darkened and he advanced again.

"Stop!" Authority resonated in Madame's voice. Insung took a step toward the Tartar. "Are these the great Manchu warriors of whom we have heard so much? Do they fight with blind men and children?"

At a signal from a tall man wearing a brass helmet and armor, the tormentor dropped the stick and dragged his fallen companion to the well, then pulled up the bucket and dashed water over the fellow's face.

Megan stepped closer to Madame, away from the barbarians. They stood a head shorter than most Korean men, with the darker skins and more slanted eyes of the Mandarins.

Their clothing consisted of quilted cotton overall breeches and sheepskin jerkins. Furred sleeves dangled from their elbows. Black pigtails hung down their backs and most wore fur helms, skin side out. Over their shoulders they carried quivers bristling with arrows and huge bows. Each sported a huge iron broadsword.

The leader stepped forward and bowed to Insung. "Madame, allow me to introduce myself. I am Yongolda, general to His Imperial Excellency, Emperor of the Ching Dynasty."

The man spoke perfect Korean, without any accent. Megan's mouth twisted. So, the rumors were true— Yongolda had been born Korean and had changed sides, a betrayer, like all men!

Madame bowed in return. "I am Madame Lee Insung." She tugged at Megan's sleeve. "And this is Megan." A murmur ran through the Manchus and Yongolda's eyes widened. "We are *kisaeng*. No doubt you have heard tales of our ability to entertain."

"Hmmph!" He turned to his lieutenant. "Bring them along. The older woman can cook."

Megan's heart sank. They were prisoners. What would become of them now?

The younger man answered in accented Korean. "What of the man and the boy?"

Megan edged closer to Kwangin and took his hand in hers. The man Chang had wounded coughed and sat up. He glared from beneath a huge purple welt on his forehead.

Yongolda surveyed them, then shrugged. "Perhaps they will amuse the men."

The younger man fixed cold black eyes on Megan. "And the creature of the red hair?"

The general laughed. "Save that one for Captain Obuto. He likes exotic creatures."

The men laughed and one called out a string of guttural syllables.

"What does he say?" Yongolda cocked his head.

The lieutenant cleared his throat and shuffled his feet. "He says Obuto will make love to anything, even his horse."

The general smiled and nodded. "Quite probably." He turned and made his way back through the ruined gate.

Until then, Megan hadn't noticed it hung askew, splintered on its hinges. They had done that without cannon or musket—these were not men, but beasts. She shuddered.

And what of this Obuto? She bit her lip. Perhaps his horse didn't fight, but he'd bear the marks of her nails and teeth before he had his way with her!

Her mouth twisted. Brave words! Then why did her belly quake so? She squeezed Kwangin's hand.

The Manchus circled around behind them, herding them through the broken gate.

Insung cupped her fingers around Grandfather Chang's elbow. The old man's voice rang hollow in the courtyard, as if it came from the bottom of a well. "Madame, you have undone us all!"

Megan shivered and drew Kwangin's warm little body closer.

"Nonsense!" Insung's voice held strength and hope. "We are all still alive, and what's more, the houses still stand!" She shook Megan's shoulder. "When this is over, we will have our homes to return to."

Chang raised his white head and stared straight ahead, as if he could see into the future. "At what price, Madame? At what price?"

Jongwhan hunched his shoulders against the rain and snow and leaned down from the tall saddle to pat his horse's neck. The wiry pony snorted and stamped, rearing a little when its feet slipped on the icy road. Clouds of breath froze on the short brown muzzle. With a gloved hand, Jongwhan removed chunks of snow knotted in the stringy mane.

Through the South Gate of Namhan Fortress the hills glistened white in the bright glare of first light. The road twisted and turned, following a small stream through a world of glass. Beautiful. He shivered. And treacherous.

He'd been against the idea of moving to Kanghwa. It made sense to flee to safety, but not in this weather. He sighed. The advisers had insisted so vehemently, and in spite of great fatigue, King Injo had finally agreed.

Jongwhan blew on his hands. He must resign himself to do what he could to help the King get there. But what if the advisers were wrong—what if the Manchus had blocked all the roads?

Terror swirled through him at the thought of fighting for his life. He had no desire to die, even less to shame himself and his family with cowardice. If only they could go, do it, get it over with! He was tired of waiting, tired of worrying about it.

He forced himself to think of other things. A trickle of icy water slid under his collar and down his back. He shivered and fingered the oiled paper cover of his *kat*.

If the starched black horsehair hat got wet, it would wilt around his head. He hadn't thought to bring an extra, couldn't carry one if he had. But to go without it in public would be like walking down the street without clothes— worse! With no pants he'd be naked, but still *yangban*. Only a peasant would go outside without a *kat*.

A door scraped open behind him and he turned his mount toward the royal sleeping quarters. The King and the crown prince emerged from the red-painted building, a smaller replica of the five palaces in Seoul. Padded silk coats encased the two men, and servants propped umbrellas over the royal heads.

Injo's gold eyes scanned the party of armed horsemen. Deep lines etched his grayed face, but he gave Jongwhan a tiny nod and a brief smile before mounting his horse.

Jongwhan bowed his head in reply, but his hands

clenched the pommel. The pleasure of being singled out mixed with fear for the health of his friend's father. Strain and fatigue had made the King ill, but the trip to Kanghwa, to the island fortress, could kill him. Impotence held him for a moment, but he fought for control. He could only stay close and make the trip as easy as possible.

Jongwhan pulled his horse into the formation surrounding the King's mount. The procession started slowly, the sturdy Korean ponies picking their way on the glassy surface of the road.

The King's horse, a great beautiful white stallion from the Mongolian steppes, snorted and pranced, then nipped at the flank of a nearby mare. Injo urged the guards to a faster pace to accommodate his mount's leggy gait.

The road clung to the white-covered hillside. It curved away, descending toward the valley floor. The royal mount screamed and reared as his great hooves skidded down the slope. When he found no purchase, he reared again and twisted his great body. His back hooves slid from under the long, thin legs. The great white body fell, the thud sending waves of nausea through Jongwhan.

Without thinking, Jongwhan slid from his tall saddle and skidded to the King's side. The horse screamed and reared its head, but Jongwhan clasped the fallen man under the arms and tugged him away.

His heart beat in his ears. Please let the fates be kind, let Pongnim's father be unharmed!

Terror gleamed for a moment from the King's eyes, then he drew himself erect and reached out to pat Jongwhan's arm. "Our thanks, Son." The royal stallion snorted and blinked huge gray eyes at them, then rolled to its feet and stood there, panting. Injo brushed snow from a blue silk sleeve. "Mount up! I believe I shall walk."

Jongwhan retrieved his own horse's bridle rope, but instead of mounting, he fell into step with the King.

The older man turned to him as if to speak, then shook his head. A blue tinge spread across the King's lips and two bright spots appeared on his cheekbones.

An icy blast whirled up the valley and right through Jongwhan's padded clothing. He could only guess what each careful step cost his royal companion. He had all he could do to keep his own footing.

Then it happened. One moment the King walked beside him, the next the man had crumpled to the ground. He held out his hand and Injo took it with surprising strength. But instead of pulling the King up, Jongwhan's own balance disappeared and he landed beside the monarch.

For an instant a memory flashed through his mind— toppling onto the frozen Han River with Megan, and Kwangin laughing down at them. An extremely inappropriate comparison, but it lightened his mood.

He sat up and tugged the King up beside him. "Excellency, will you go back now?"

Gold eyes bored into his, then closed. Injo's chin sank to his chest. "Yes." The colorless whisper hissed through the falling snow.

Jongwhan planted gloved hands in the snow and managed to stand. He called to the grooms to bring a straw floor covering. He unrolled the large mat and slid the King to the center, still sitting in the *yangban* position, knees bent and legs crossed.

Servants grasped the corners. Their straw sandals bit into the glassy roadway and they panted up the hill, back to the gate.

Jongwhan clambered into the tall saddle and turned his mount. Their choices had narrowed. This weather would not slow the Manchus. By the time the roads cleared, they would be cut off, unable to reach the sanctuary of the island.

The utter vulnerability of their position struck him. He clenched the bridle rope until it cut his hand. Now, no matter what, he would have to face the enemy. Somehow he had to learn to kill, or to die.

32

The bonfire threw a flickering reddish light over a hellish scene. Megan edged closer to the warmth until the crackling of the blaze almost drowned out the screams and groans of the dying and the guttural orders of the Manchu soldiers marching in and out of the palace buildings.

They reminded her of a line of ants, each entering empty-handed, then staggering out under a massive burden.

"The royal treasury," Madame had whispered.

Jade flashed in the eerie light, and gold, rolls of jewel-tinted silk, fine porcelains, barrels of wine, huge bags of rice, all loaded onto crude wagons.

Mixed snow and rain hissed into the fire at her back and crusted her hair and clothes. The wind changed, smothering her for a moment in acrid gray smoke. She coughed and wiped her streaming eyes.

The looting continued. She watched, unable to look away until something clamped around her ankle. She jumped and tried to pull away but couldn't free herself. Against the red light of the flames, a hand clutched at her skirts. One of the bodies at her feet still lived!

The man's black eyes pleaded with her. Although the whitened lips moved, no sound reached her ears. But the message could not be mistaken. "Help me!"

She wanted to say no, to run, to hide from the cruelty, the carnage, but she couldn't refuse the plea on the man's bloodied face. She glanced at the Manchu guarding them, but his eyes remained fixed on the warrior ants and their booty. Bending and unhooking the fingers, she hissed her reply. "Wait!" She stepped sideways.

Madame caught her arm. "What are you doing? Are you mad? They'll kill you!"

Megan wrenched her arm free. "They probably will anyway, or something worse. I have to try to help him."

Insung grabbed at her again. "He'd never do the same for you. Don't you know that?"

Megan glanced at the stricken man again. His mouth lay slack, his eyes closed. "Yes, I know. It doesn't matter." She slipped away and crouched behind a stack of corpses to shield her movements.

Face down among the dead she found the stiffening remains of a wealthy man still wrapped in a long, heavy coat. Sweat chilled on her brow as she struggled to turn the body over. At last the corpse flopped toward her, trapping her skirt for a moment. Poor fellow. His horsehair hat tilted across one temple, wrinkled and crusted with blood from the hole in his skull.

Shouts drew her attention to the bonfire. Ten Manchus heaved the King's wooden throne atop the blaze. As she turned back, flames leaped high behind her, lighting the handsome face.

Her heart thudded. Jongwhan! But no. Bitter anger swept the relief from her mind. He deserved to die after what he'd done to her! Still, through her rage, a fierce joy possessed her that some other poor soul, not Jongwhan, lay dead at her feet. She marveled that she could still love him, but she pushed the thought from her mind.

With trembling fingers she undid the stiff knotted sash. She bent and tugged, pushing the heavy limbs this way and that, working the coat free. Just as she finally freed it from the limp body, a broadsword glinted in the firelight before her face. Its point came to rest on the wadded silk coat in her hand.

Her mouth went dry. This time there would be no respite. Death had come to claim her. She looked up at her executioner.

Dark slanted eyes regarded her for a moment, then a gap-toothed smile split the broad, swarthy face. He nodded and gestured at the other bodies with the sword, then turned and walked away.

Air hissed from her open mouth. He'd thought she was taking the coat for herself. She shivered. Not a bad idea.

She poked through the bodies, looking for warm clothing for herself and the others.

Only once, as she undressed the body of a small girl, did the ghoulishness of her task hit her. The tiny body lay twisted and bloody, a look of terror still frozen on the innocent features.

Megan rocked back on her heels, bile burning her tongue. She turned away, then vomited suddenly on the frozen ground. Wiping her tears on the back of her chapped hands, she leaned forward and closed the staring gray eyes. Then she finished removing the heavy jacket and straightened the tiny limbs.

She rose and clasped the clothing to her chest. She clenched her jaw to keep from crying. Dead was dead, and Kwangin would need that coat. At least he was still alive, and she'd do whatever she could to keep him that way.

As she threaded her way back to the fire, she dropped a heavy coat over the face and body of the stricken man. She bent and fussed with a stocking. "Stay hidden until the fire dies down. Then you can crawl away. It's all I can do." She rose without waiting for an answer and stumbled toward Insung.

"Here!" She handed a warm covering to the *kisaeng* and helped Kwangin into the little girl's jacket.

Madame's mouth hung open, then snapped shut. Her brown eyes glittered. "You took these from the dead. It is forbidden!"

Megan wrapped a quilted coat around Mr. Chang. "They no longer need warm clothing. We do. I'm sure they won't mind." Madame stood, clutching the silk jacket, and glared at her.

Megan glared back. "Look! When that fire dies, we'll all freeze to death. It's either take from the dead or join them." She covered her head with a long green coat and let the sleeves hang down on each side like a merchant's wife.

Fatigue washed through her. She wanted very much to rest, to lie down and just give up. She turned to Insung. "Don't wear it, then."

Madame looked away, then slipped her arms into the garment. "You are right. We owe it to the dead to stay alive, to remember the wrongs and repay them."

Insung's desire for revenge sent nausea swirling through her belly again. Killing was killing, for whatever the reason, and it was wrong! Wasteful, stupid, WRONG! And somehow, she knew it had only begun.

The sound of hoofbeats roused Jongwhan from his daydream of Megan. From the gatehouse window atop the wall, brown grass once more showed in patches beneath the snow. The world of glass had vanished along with their chance of escape. The Manchus had blocked every road to Kanghwa. The King and his army lay trapped in Namhan Fortress, at the mercy of the barbarians riding toward them across the plain from Seoul.

The party of horsemen drew nearer. Surrounded by pigtailed Manchus on shaggy Siberian ponies, a Korean officer sat erect on his smaller domestic mount.

"Open the gates! It is General Choe!" Jongwhan's voice echoed back to him from the ground below. The gatekeeper nodded and grasped a huge metal bolt.

White-clad archers lounged in the open casements. Jongwhan pointed to the nearest officer. "You are in charge until I return. I must notify His Excellency the King." Without waiting for a reply, he took the stone stairs two at a time.

Slush seeped into the soles of his thin leather slippers. He'd have to trade a servant for some straw sandals and thick padded socks. He chewed his lip. What kind of reception would Choe receive? The words of the general's letter had run through his head a thousand times since the scribe read it aloud the day before.

"The Manchu general has come to make a treaty with us, but he says we are all afraid and that even the King has fled."

The King's advisers had grumbled at this insult, but Injo held up his hand for silence and nodded to the scribe to read on.

"He says if the King wants to make peace he must send his son and the prime minister together with the man who advised the King to break the treaty."

Prince Sohyon blanched. Jongwhan shuddered in

sympathy. He wouldn't trade places with the crown prince for anything just then. "They demand an immediate answer."

Injo's gold eyes blazed and his lips set in a firm line. When he rose, every man in the room scrambled to a standing position. "We shall send no reply until we are rested." The King turned and left the sitting room, his white-faced son, blinking like an owl, a few paces behind.

That was yesterday. The King had sent no messages, and now Choe approached the gate with a company of armed barbarians.

"We are all afraid . . ." The insult had been true, at least for himself. Jongwhan still hoped somehow his mettle would never be tested in battle, but his hope faded with each passing hour.

He took a ragged breath and slowed his steps. At least Megan had escaped, and Pongnim lay safe at Kanghwa. He stopped and gave a polite cough at the door to the royal quarters.

The door swung in a handspan. A serving woman squinted at him, then nodded and widened the opening. Leaving the damp shoes on the step, Jongwhan slipped inside, grateful for the warmth rising from the *ondol* floor.

With bowed head, the old woman gestured along the hallway, then preceded Jongwhan to the King's sleeping room.

The door stood ajar. Injo lay on a thick *yo*, a rich *ibul* drawn up around his chin. Jongwhan's chest tightened at the absolute stillness of the waxen features. Was he dead? The transparent eyelids flickered.

Jongwhan cleared his throat. It wouldn't do to let the King catch him staring.

Injo's eyes flew open and he sat upright. "Yes!" His bark brought the old woman skittering forward to settle a *chaddae* behind her monarch's back.

Jongwhan knelt and touched his forehead to the floor. Above his bowed head the ghost of the King's regal voice hissed, "Who is it?"

The servant's oddly musical voice contradicted her disheveled appearance. "Yi Jongwhan, Excellency."

"Ah!" The King's tone warmed. "Arise, arise!"

Instead of the tired old man of a moment before, a bright-eyed, vital ruler looked back at him. "What news, Our Son?"

"Excellency, General Choe approaches the West Gate. I ordered him admitted." He bowed again.

"Choe, here? We thought he would be dead by now. Hmmph!"

He peeked up through his lashes at King Injo in surprise. So he'd expected the Manchus to kill the messenger.

"Show him into our reception room and serve him tea, Son." The gold eyes twinkled. "We shall greet him after a suitable delay."

The thin-faced monarch twisted in his bedding. "And you, you old harridan, fetch our lackwit eldest son." The old woman bowed and smiled. The King's thin lips twitched. "And get us something to put on!"

Injo faced Jongwhan again and smiled. "We are pleased with you, Yi Jongwhan." The thin face grew somber again. "We do not forget friends or enemies." With a flap of a long-fingered hand, the King dismissed him.

He found the kitchen and ordered up tea. By the time he reached the reception room, the King's councilors were trickling in, haggling over possession of the floor cushions. He fought to restrain a smile. What a bunch of old maids!

He'd better find Choe and escort him to the chambers before someone shot the general for a traitor.

In the trampled clay inside the gate, a lone horseman struggled to alight from a tall leather saddle. Servants and soldiers ignored Choe's presence in the fortress. None would risk the King's displeasure by welcoming anyone arriving with the enemy.

"You there! Boy!" Jongwhan's voice held enough authority to inspire instant activity. "Help General Choe down from his mount!" A handful of men crowded around the officer's horse, steadying the bridle and stirrup while the man clambered down.

As long as they followed someone else's orders, their own initiative could not be punished. He snorted in disgust, then stopped. Wasn't he as much of a coward, but in a different way? He brushed the thought aside and stepped up to greet the general.

Choe's return bow seemed jerky. The man had aged in the three days since he had volunteered to act as intermediary for the King. What must he have gone through with the Manchus when his letter went unanswered?

"General, His Excellency asks that you accompany me to his quarters for tea." Jongwhan bowed again and gestured up the slushy path, then nodded at a nearby groom. "You, rub down that horse and feed him." The general walked a few steps ahead, his shoulders stooped and his step slow.

Jongwhan searched his brain for some words to say, some way to express his admiration for the man's courage. But something about the figure ahead stopped him. In spite of the dragging steps, the tautness of a coiled spring lurked in the man, like a powder keg ready to explode. What had brought the messenger back to the fortress?

Jongwhan sped his steps and opened the door for his guest. The raised voices of the King's advisers, still haggling over cushions and floor space, stilled in waves as Choe progressed through the crowd to the seat before the dais.

With trembling hands he poured tea for the general and placed cup and pot on the low table within reach, then retreated to stand against a side wall. Without a glance to right or left, Choe lifted the cup and sipped, then set it down and waited.

The moment stretched. Still the King did not appear. An all but inaudible whisper swelled like a chill breeze through the assemblage. Jongwhan squirmed in his heavy padded clothing. Would the King refuse to see Choe?

A casement rasped. A sigh ran through the company like one long-held breath suddenly released. The King.

A silken rustle stirred the warm air as fifty bodies stood. Scented oils barely camouflaged the rank smell of fear and sweat filling Jongwhan's nostrils. Would Choe offer help and hope? Would the King listen to reason from his diplomats, or pride and bloodlust from his generals?

The King ascended the shallow steps of the dais and sat cross-legged on the ornate wooden throne. Again sill whispered on silk as loyal subjects knelt. The floor warmed Jongwhan's hands through the bamboo mat.

"Our friend and loyal subject, General Choe, we are pleased to greet you. Are you come to save us?"

Jongwhan gasped. Such directness was not the way of the *Chosun*. From his vantage point against the wall, he looked from the King to the general.

Choe didn't even blink. "Excellency, the Manchu general was exceedingly angry because you did not answer my letter last night. He wanted to kill me." A note of bitterness crept into Choe's words. "Instead, they forced me to bring them here. He has brought a third of his whole force." He paused. "In order to pacify him, we cannot but comply with his three conditions."

The murmur burst forth afresh, but Jongwhan leaned forward to hear the King's reply. Surely Injo would see the sense in the general's words.

For a moment the King sat still as a stone Buddha. Then his words cut across the excited whispers of his courtiers. "You are deceived by him. Do you think he has come all this way to be so easily satisfied as that?"

33

Megan shifted Kwangin's weight a little higher on her back and slogged forward again through the slush and crusted snow. She avoided the roadway. Churned to mire by the passage of the Manchu horde, the way now consisted of deep pits and ruts frozen solid once more, ripe for turning ankles and barking shins.

Already they'd learned what happened to those who grew tired and lame, who wouldn't or couldn't go on. The first few the Manchus had used for sport, cutting off the heads and rolling them about the icy plain in a kind of polo game. Later they just slit the throats and left the bodies to freeze by the trail.

She risked a glance over her shoulder. Madame Insung clung to Grandfather Chang's arm, guiding him into the footprints Megan had just forged in the dirty white snow. Thank God none of them had tried to sit down to rest. Not that the thought wasn't tempting, just to give up and let the bastards kill them.

She reached up and loosened Kwangin's grip on her neck. She blew on the rough red skin of his tiny hands and wondered for the hundredth time if he would lose any fingers to frostbite. She rubbed them until he squirmed.

"Owww! Don't, Megan!" Sleep thickened his voice.

She stopped rubbing and kissed each little palm, then hooked her arms under his short legs again.

"Yuck!" He breathed a giggle in her ear.

"Go back to sleep."

He nuzzled his face in her neck like a kitten, and soon his breath came slow and regular again.

She sighed. He weighed more asleep, but the quieter she kept him, the less chance one of the guards would decide to leave him by the road with a hole in his throat and his blood spilling out.

An ache stirred deep in her belly and she pushed the gruesome thought from her mind. Not while she had breath in her body, by God!

Her feet weighed more with each step. Fatigue burned in her back and her legs. She cast about for something else to think about while her feet kept moving forward one step after another.

The thought of Jongwhan brought pain more intense than her physical discomfort. She flinched away from memories of their day and night of happiness before the invasion. Memories of Soonhee and Pongnim filled her with a weary sadness, and thoughts of Grandmother and the island seemed like a faraway dream, as far off as Scotland and Jemmie.

Only the thought of Youngsook and her son and the sweet heaviness of Kwangin gave her hope for the future. She clung to that hope as she'd once clung to a broken mast in a storm-blackened sea.

Mile after mile they walked, until the weak winter sun

threw her shadow straight and long in front of her. She frowned. The sun would set behind her, in the west, so the Manchus herded them east. But where, and why?

Her head buzzed. Was this the second or the third day since they'd left Seoul? If she forced herself to concentrate, she could remember sleeping beside a campfire, but last night or the night before? She shook her head. No matter. At least the Manchus had some use for them. Otherwise, she knew, they'd have been killed long since.

Soon, soon, soon—over and over the word repeated in her head. Let them stop, let them build a fire and cook some broth and sit near the blaze—but let it be soon!

The road rounded a rocky cliff. The man ahead of her stopped without warning and she walked into him.

"Look!" His voice came in a thready whisper. "Nam-han!"

The high rock wall ran up and down the slope, forming a crooked crown on the crest of the mountain, but no castle loomed beyond the stone fortification, no stony keep like a proper Scottish fortress. Just a wall with ornate gates, smaller versions of the city gates in the capital.

A prisoner in front of her snorted. "There stands our brave King, safe behind those walls, while we play servants to the filthy barbarians."

Her eye traveled down the slope, and the breath caught in her throat. There on the wide plain, black in the setting sun, the Manchu horde spread, too many to number, from horizon to horizon, like a noose around the neck of the mountain.

The sweet-sour smell of *makkŏlli* hung in the warm air. Jongwhan stifled a yawn and concentrated on pleating his trouser leg with his fingers.

After guard duty on the battlements until midnight, lack of sleep, a warm room, and a full belly conspired to lull him into a stupor. He concentrated on the argument raging around him.

"Surely, Excellency, 'Your Highness' is sufficient title for a barbarian." Kim On Yun's thick voice cut through the babble.

The crown prince blinked, then shook his head. "No, he is emperor. It must be 'Imperial Majesty' at the least."

On Yun smiled and bobbed his shiny head, fat cheeks jiggling. "As you say, Excellency. You know best."

Sohyon's simple face lit with the unaccustomed compliment. The plump shoulders pushed back and the narrow chest puffed out. "So, it is settled. We shall address the Manchu emperor as 'Your Imperial Majesty.'"

Jongwhan looked away to mask his disbelief. The faces of the King's advisers mirrored his own chagrin, except for Kim On Yun's blank face. Why had he backed the prince in such an obvious error? The general must realize the title conceded the Manchu's sovereignty.

He sighed. It did little good to argue with a prince, even one as slow-witted as Sohyon. Perhaps On Yun's loyalty bore closer scrutiny.

The crowd stirred and rose to their feet, even the crown prince. The King! Jongwhan clambered up, wincing at his aching calves. He must have walked a third of the wall last night. At least it kept the blood pumping. Better aches and pains than frostbite.

He winced again as he knelt and bowed. After the King settled himself beside his eldest son, Jongwhan slipped his right foot onto his bent left knee.

Injo had chided him for wanting to stand guard duty, but he'd begged the King's indulgence. When he walked the wall, he worried less about the fighting to come. He could concentrate on memories of those few blissful hours with Megan.

He blushed. Pongnim's father had taken it for patriotic zeal, and Jongwhan had been too ashamed to correct his king.

In private the man seemed almost like his own father, but now, on the throne, he grew in stature. The power and responsibility of his position altered his appearance, his expression. Even his voice rang crisp and strong in the reception hall.

"We have appointed General Nam Angap as conservator of our provisions. He informs us we have enough food to withstand the enemy for sixty days." The murmured approval of his councilors won a thin smile from Injo's pallid lips.

"Father, Your Excellency." Sohyon's reedy voice silenced the courtiers.

Injo frowned at the breach of manners, then nodded at his son.

The crown prince knelt before the King and gave a belated bow. "Please, may I present the message to the Manchu general myself?"

Injo's indulgent smile froze on his thin lips. "Who supports this rash petition?" Sohyon dropped his eyes. The King's icy gaze fixed each adviser in turn.

General Kim Nyu bowed. "Excellency, the sooner you meet the Khan's demands, the sooner peace will be achieved. I support His Excellency the Prince."

Sohyon looked up and beamed.

Jongwhan bit his lip. Injo was no fool. He knew his eldest son lacked all sense. Sending Sohyon would be a grave error. Would he agree with his commander in chief?

Choe Myongil bowed. "Excellency, I have been with the enemy. They outnumber us—their forces are a hundred times greater than ours. Their soldiers are more animal than human—they have no fear!" The general's lean body shuddered. "I beg you, Excellency, to make peace with them. Meet their demands, whatever they might be."

A voice rang out in the shocked silence. "Whoever talks of surrender so tamely is a traitor!" Another shout followed. "If the prince goes, I shall strangle myself with my own bridle!" A deeper voice chimed in. "Let us fight them. We are men, not straw mannequins!"

The King held up his hand for silence.

"Excellency, if I may."

Jongwhan recognized the voice of Kim On Yun again. He leaned forward to study the speaker.

The man's round face held no emotion. "Perhaps we could deceive the enemy—satisfy their demands without risking our courageous prince."

The fat man held the attention of all the courtiers now. The thick voice continued, "If we were to send a man who resembles His Excellency the Prince, and another who resembles the prime minister, might not the enemy accept them?"

Jongwhan held his breath. The thing smacked of dishonor, yet it might work, and thereby save them all from the battlefield.

"And if they are not deceived?" General Kim Nyu turned a strained face toward General Choe.

Choe's mouth turned down and his shoulders drooped. "There will be no escape. War will be inevitable."

"So be it." King Injo's quiet words rang in Jongwhan's ears. "I will die first before I surrender my son."

The mask of sovereignty dropped away, leaving only the prince's father. Injo placed a hand on Sohyon's shoulder. "We are proud of your courage, Son, but we must attempt to deceive these savages."

"Excellency, Cousin, I look like Your Excellency's brother." Jongwhan recognized Neung Pongsu, a distant relative of the King. "Let me pretend to be prime minister."

Sim Chip bowed beside the eager volunteer. "And I am said to resemble His Excellency the Crown Prince."

The man's face and build did look like Sohyon's, but instead of simplicity, Sim radiated intelligence. If only the volunteer could truly become the heir to the throne. Jongwhan clenched his fist and pushed the disloyal thought away.

Sim's voice continued, "I beseech you, let me assume his name and carry your message."

Injo closed his eyes for a moment. When they opened again, raw power flared in their gold depths.

Something warmed Jongwhan's blood and tingled in his fingertips. He forgot his fear.

The King spoke into the now silent hall. "It is settled. These men shall go today to the enemy." Power flowed from him in waves. "If they fail, we fight to the bitter end."

Injo rested his eyes first on Kim Nyu, then on Choe Myongil. The threat in his quiet voice sent a shiver up Jongwhan's spine. "Let no one expect or hope for peace."

* * *

Megan hugged her calves, her face pressed against her knees. The silk skirt she wore smelled of jasmine and snow, wood smoke, and the cold sweat of fear, odors clinging like memories from the past few days. She could blot out the sight of the nightmare around her, but not the sound.

Even now, with most of the soldiers sleeping, millions of tiny noises filled her ears. So many men and horses, even their breathing deafened her.

Far off, a sentry called out a guttural challenge. The trespasser answered. A pine branch sizzled and snapped in the campfire at her feet. She should turn and face the other way. Her arms and legs burned with the too intense heat, but cold crept from the ground into her buttocks and up her spine.

It wasn't so bad. Insung had ticked off the benefits of their present situation. Not only were they alive, but their captors kept them warm and well-fed.

Like cattle being led to slaughter. Megan spit a hollow chuckle from cracked lips. Cruelty, death, had become commonplace. Every day the Manchus killed prisoners, for punishment or just for sport—women, old men, children—especially children.

Without lifting her face, she reached out a hand and touched Kwangin. He rolled toward her in his sleep and nestled against her hip. Fear for him shivered through her, but she clamped her teeth against it.

Noise erupted from a nearby tent. Her head snapped up. A Manchu staggered out and vomited in the triangle of lamplight spreading across the snow. Guttural words followed, curses by their sound.

She dropped her face once more onto her knees. They all seemed to do that—drink themselves stupid, then vomit and go back for more. Scenes such as this punctuated the nights as the killing and maiming punctuated the days.

The cursing faded from a scream to a mutter. The footfalls continued for a while without any direction or rhythm. She took a deep breath and fell into the light doze that passed for sleep since her capture.

Screams filled her ears. She jerked upright again, twisting around to find the source of the terrible cries. The sound came again nearby, a sound of pain, but not human, thank God! An animal, a horse.

The fire leaped up and cast a reddish glow on the frantic churnings of the captive beast. A Manchu, staggering and cursing, held tight to the animal's bridle with one hand. With the other he swung a long whip, flailing it again and again at the rearing steed's back and legs.

Kwangin tensed against her body. Her warm breath hissed out in a white cloud. "Lie still."

Another cry split the night, a cry of rage, hatred, and bloodlust almost drowning the sound of the tortured animal. A stocky figure leaped from the darkness and picked the drunkard up by his neck, like a cat toying with a mouse, then slammed him to the frozen ground.

The drunk dropped both whip and bridle, then whirled and swung his fist at this new target. The horse reared and bolted. Firelight glinted on metal. A broadsword jutted from the hand of the second man, a Manchu officer by his dress.

The horse beater staggered back and fell to his knees, babbling. Every other word seemed to be *Obuto*. The word tickled her memory.

The kneeling man scrabbled backward, the swordsman following. Surely one savage wouldn't kill another over a horse! Even the Koreans seemed indifferent to their shaggy ponies, lacking any bond between horse and rider. And the Manchus meted out neglect and abuse to prisoners and mounts alike.

The drunk backed against a fallen log. He turned and looked at it, then burst into tears and buried his face in his hands.

The Manchu officer swung the broadsword, severing the weeping soldier's head and hands in one stroke. He sheathed the bloody weapon, then nickered in a surprising imitation of a horse. He waited a moment, then repeated the call.

The horse stepped into the circle of firelight. It whickered in response, then rolled its eyes and blew. The Manchu raised his hand. With slow steps the frightened animal advanced, finally nuzzling against the outstretched palm.

Gentle hands caressed the scored flanks and withers. Then, still making horse noises, the Manchu officer led the exhausted animal away.

The night seemed to hold its breath for long moments. The soldier's head and hands still lay beside his twitching body. Days before the sight would have sickened her. Now she didn't even look away. Death had lost all terror for her in its abundance.

Two servants skittered into the light. One grasped the dead man's feet. The other whispered in Korean as he picked up the severed members. "That Captain Obuto, he's crazy! Raised by horses, some say. Loves them more than people, even his own kind!"

The other tugged at the body and grunted. "Hush, you old fool! What if he comes back? Hurry!"

Megan tucked her red hair farther under the green headpiece. Captain Obuto. Now she remembered. The day the Manchus invaded Seoul. She shivered. The general had said Obuto would like her.

34

A terrible confusion of noise echoed up the twisted valley from the plain below, all the way to the North Gate. Explosions blended with the clanging of metal against metal and unearthly screams. Who would have thought a battle would be so loud?

Jongwhan stamped his feet to warm them. The straw sandals and padded socks helped, but it was damn cold! He paced the top of the high stone wall, his hands tucked into the ends of his sleeves against the bitter cold.

He should be down there, fighting with his countrymen, not waiting for word of the outcome so he could run and tell the King. Shame forced him to avoid the gatehouse where the regular guards warmed their hands over a tiny brass stove.

Men would die out on that plain, and he stood within the fortress, safe behind its solid stone walls and the invisible walls of friendship and birthright.

The King had forbidden him to join the raiding party, insisting he needed Jongwhan to act as messenger. It was a mark of favor, a well-meaning lie, an excuse to stay behind. And he had known the King would relent, would let him go with the soldiers, if only he asked.

But he had not asked. He'd accepted the King's offer, kept his life intact along with his honor. His relief had been a tangible thing—the dark secret of his cowardice would remain hidden a little longer.

It was only later that the guilt crept into his mind and drove him to walk the wall with streaming nose and stinging cheeks, straining eyes and ears for some sign of Korean soldiers returning, perhaps with Manchus close on their heels.

A faint, rhythmic pattering sound stopped him in mid-stride. He leaned over the parapet and held his breath. Hoofbeats! His heart pounded. Were they returning victorious, or retreating before an attack?

A lone horseman rounded the bend in the road, then another and another, until the whole company had made the turn. In the rear a half-dozen riderless horses signified the casualties. Jongwhan looked away, then back again. He released his breath in a loud sigh. No Manchus followed!

The lead horses pounded closer. In the cold morning air details stood out with sickening clarity. Blood smeared riders and horses alike. Some slumped across their saddles, while others held lumpy round objects in the air, like banners or prizes.

He moved down the wall for a closer look. The first horseman reached the gate and called to the guards to open the portal. The soldier held up a large black ball by some sort of handle. The thing turned on its tether.

Bile burned Jongwhan's throat. A twisted face stared up at him with lifeless eyes. A head! The soldier's hand clasped the base of the Manchu's long black pigtail. Red blood dripped from the severed neck.

Jongwhan turned away, then bent double and was sick on the flagstones. Flecks of vomit clung to his black trousers.

Never! He could never do that to another human being! Somehow he must find a way to keep from riding with the raiders, no matter how much shame and guilt he suffered.

The last vibrations of the huge gong faded into the afternoon air. The sudden silence buzzed in Jongwhan's ears. On his left, only an arm's length away, the King sat cross-legged on a wooden throne.

Sweat trickled down Jongwhan's back in spite of the frigid wind. Standing on the dais so close to Injo made him squirm. All around them the entire population of the fortress stood before the North Gate—twelve thousand people, their eyes turned toward him. He clenched his fists and told himself they didn't really see him, they watched the King, waiting for him to speak.

Injo gestured to the soldiers atop the parapet. At his sign, the six white-garbed men hoisted poles and set them in sockets along the wall. Atop each shaft sat a Manchu head, blood streaming down and freezing to the wood.

Jongwhan shuddered again, remembering the first sight of those gory trophies. The King had praised him, as if he had in some way been responsible for the victory instead of merely carrying the news.

The court welcomed good news after the failure of the fake prince and minister. The Manchus hadn't taken the trick kindly. They demanded the crown prince and swore they would deal with no other. The King had wept and refused to see anyone until Jongwhan brought news of the successful sortie.

Now the crowd cheered and shouted at the bloody spectacle on the wall. Finally the King held up his hands for silence. "Our soldiers have fought bravely, racing into the enemy's camp without fear, and returning with these prizes." He waited for the company to quiet again, then continued, "Shall we surrender or fight? It is for you to say."

A lone soldier stepped forward and bowed. The tall, thin man wiped his forehead. His voice shook, but each word echoed back from the stone wall. "Excellency, I am Sim Kwangsu. I speak for your loyal subjects." He paused. "Show us the head of the man who advised you to surrender!"

Deafening cries greeted this brave speech. Jongwhan glanced to his right at the still profile of Choe Myongil. The general's face shone white in the winter sunlight, but the thin mouth held in a firm line and the dark eyes didn't so much as blink.

What must the general be going through? Suddenly Jongwhan's private agony, his fear and shame, seemed small and unimportant. Choe had gone out and parleyed with the enemy, learned their strength. He knew his advice would not make him popular in the court, but still he gave the King his honest opinion.

Not like some men, Kim On Yun for one. How could he ever have trusted the man? His heart thudded. What if On Yun's groom had not delivered the message to Megan? But no, he'd seen the *kisaeng* house deserted with his own eyes. She was safe—she had to be!

A sudden silence brought him back to the present. The King lowered his hand. "Since it is the will of our loyal subjects, we shall fight!"

The crowd went wild again. A chill crept up the back of Jongwhan's neck. He turned. Far over to the King's left, General Kim On Yun's fat face turned toward him. No trace of the man's usual jolly smile touched the lumpy features. Why had he never noticed before the cold light in those small dark eyes?

Fat dripped from the carcass of the bullock and sizzled onto the flaming pine branches. Megan's arms ached from cranking the huge spit. The smell of roasting beef made her empty belly rumble and filled her mouth with saliva.

Insung bustled around the cooking area, stirring cauldrons of soup and rice and opening tall jars of stolen *kimchee*. Sometimes the *kisaeng* seemed almost to enjoy the role of head cook for the Tartar company camped near the West Gate. "Better a cook than something worse."

Megan shuddered. At first the women had screamed when the Manchus dragged them off to the hide tents for the night. Some had drunk lye and died in horrible pain.

But now the remaining women complied with the soldiers' gestured demands without a whimper. Afterwards they kept to themselves close by the soldiers' square-round yurts, as if they bore their shame more easily out of sight of the other Korean prisoners, the older women and the men.

It was almost as if they had all grown used to a new life, one in which death, mutilation, and rape no longer mattered. The only thing of importance was survival. A sick knot hardened in her belly at the thought of her own acceptance of their lot.

Thank God the Manchus thought her ugly and deformed. An image flashed through her head of Obuto's sword slicing off the drunkard's head and hands.

What would she do if he took a fancy to her? What could she do? If she resisted, he would kill her, and then who would look after Kwangin and old man Chang?

She looked over her shoulder and out across the plain. Finally she made out two figures coming toward her in the twilight, one tall but stooped, the other tiny. Both carried huge bundles of firewood in the A-frame packs on their backs.

She frowned. Kwangin's back would never grow straight after hauling loads twice his size. But her heart ached with love for his sacrifice. He carried more so that his grandfather carried less, and the old blind man never knew.

She let go the crank. The bullock swayed on the spit, then settled heavy-side-down. Megan rubbed her aching arms and dug her fists into the cramped muscles of her back.

Insung raked the glowing embers away from the carcass and cut huge slabs of smoking meat. "Better start serving the men. They get meaner when they're hungry. And tuck your hair out of sight."

Megan smiled at the older woman's back. Insung meant well. She sighed. Maybe the *kisaeng's* way was best, to accept her lot and make the most of it. Under that shell of practicality, she knew Insung suffered as much as any of the prisoners. It only made it worse to bemoan one's fate.

Still, she couldn't fool herself or hide from the misery around them. She gritted her teeth and pushed flaming tendrils under the collar of the green coat.

She'd come to loathe the neckline tied over her face. The stupid empty sleeves hung like floppy dog-ears from the side of her head. But it hid her difference from the eyes of Obuto.

Every day new stories circulated through the camp. Korean traitors passed on rumors about all the Manchus, but especially the crazy-eyed captain. Even the Manchus stayed clear of him, because he had no fear, and no compassion for humans, only for animals. Yet they respected his skills in battle and let him lead a company.

He spoke Korean, according to the turncoats, because his mother had been Korean. But he hated all Koreans, all people, most especially foreigners and women. His step-mother and sisters had mocked him for his impure ancestry and driven him out on the steppes to live with the horses.

Megan had searched her heart, but found no sympathy for this animal in a man's body. What did it matter how he came to be that way? He was a devil, and she longed to stay as far from him as possible.

She lifted the wooden platter, heavy with roast meat, and passed among the seated Manchus. They didn't notice her, just grabbed huge chunks of beef in their hands and sank their teeth into the juicy meat.

Funny, in Scotland most people ate just that way and she'd never thought anything about it. But after her time among the Koreans, the Manchus seemed like pigs, or wild dogs. Koreans cut all their meat into small pieces and ate everything with chopsticks, never touching the food with their hands.

She stopped in front of Obuto and held her breath. He didn't even look up, but pulled a smoking joint from the platter and began gnawing on it.

She let out a breath and moved away, but something tugged at her coat. The knot under her chin gave way and the green garment bunched around her feet. A smiling Tartar held one end in his filthy paw.

Loud laughter surrounded her. Her heart pounded. She bent and held the now near-empty tray with one hand. With the other she scooped up the garment and straightened. The back of her neck prickled. She turned and looked right into Obuto's black eyes.

Cold hatred burned there, and something much more frightening—lust, raw animal desire. This beast, this monster wanted her!

35

Obuto looked away, then turned and barked a few words in guttural Manchurian before bending to gnaw at the haunch again. Those nearby laughed.

Megan swayed on her feet for a moment. Had she only imagined his intention? She shivered. No, he wanted her, and he would take her. She could not run away—there was nowhere to hide.

She turned and hurried through the camp toward the cookfire. Something clamped around her wrist. She gasped and tried to pull away, but the brown-skinned hand held tight to her arm.

With a sob she turned to face her captor. A pigtailed soldier gave her a puzzled look. The man let go of her wrist and lifted the last slab of beef from the platter she still clenched in her hand. She'd forgotten it in her terror, forgotten her errand, forgotten everything except the menace in those cold black eyes.

Megan nodded to the soldier, but the Manchu just shrugged and turned back to his meal. She forced herself to walk at a normal pace to the cooking area.

Once there she threw the platter down and retied the hateful green coat over her hair. She avoided Insung and went to join Kwangin and Chang. They huddled with other Korean prisoners near a smaller fire, eating hot rice mixed with bits of beef.

When she settled between them, the old man said nothing, just patted her arm. Kwangin yawned and handed her a steaming bowl. The boy hadn't eaten much of his own dinner. Probably too tired to eat, poor little man. He yawned again, then buried his head in her lap.

She stroked the boy's silky black hair, the glow of his trust warming her in spite of her very real fear for his young life. She sighed. And now Obuto. It was just too much. Tears rolled down her cheeks and dropped onto her work-worn hands.

Frost rimed the gray stone wall of the burial mound. King Injo knelt on a bamboo mat. Between the prostrate ruler and the smooth round hill of the grave stood an offering tray filled with the finest foods.

Jongwhan's stomach growled. Rations had been cut again. His pitiful serving of morning rice wouldn't have satisfied even little Kwangin. He wondered again how the boy fared. Surely Chang had escaped the Manchus. After all, the old man had been wily enough to survive the Imjin War.

The savory smell of beef soup wafted to him on the chill morning air. He smiled at the irony. Guns and ammunition filled the storerooms of the fortress, but the Manchus had captured most of the rice stored by the river.

And now the King laid out a fine meal for the spirit of a man dead for sixteen hundred years. Did King Injo really believe the ancient ruler who built Namhan and made it his capital could aid them against a horde of barbarians?

Perhaps Injo ordered the ceremony to reassure the peasants. Probably another of Kim On Yun's ideas. The fat man's true character emerged more and more with each passing day.

When the King had asked his councilors for advice about the food shortage, On Yun had actually suggested that they stop feeding servants and others of no importance. Of course the fat man numbered himself among those to be fed.

Even if Injo seemed to sway from one faction to another, on some issues the ruler stood firm. "They came here trusting in me, and now shall I deprive them of food? No, we will all eat or go hungry together." Jongwhan's loyalty had soared.

Incense scented the frosty dawn. While Injo uncovered dishes and set out utensils, Jongwhan forced himself to stand still. His feet ached and the wind burned the raw skin on his cheeks.

The King's compassion had won again when it came to the cold. Injo had seen the guards returning from night duty on the wall with their frostbitten cheeks cracked and bleeding. After that, no old or feeble man stood picket duty, and no one stood guard at night.

A clatter of hoofbeats announced the arrival of a messenger, conquest loud in each shout. "Twenty heads! The West Gate! Twenty Manchu heads!"

Bile rose in Jongwhan's throat. Twenty more men dead.

Injo straightened, his face glowing from the news, as if his prayers to the dead King had been answered. A servant scurried off with the laden *chesa* tray. Someone would have a decent breakfast.

The lingering smell of the soup filled Jongwhan with nausea. He clenched his fists. Sooner or later, the food would run out, and then he would have the same choice as the rest—to fight or to starve.

Obuto's eyes followed her every move. She tried to tell herself it was only her imagination, but each time she looked up from her chores, his cold black eyes stared back at her, filled now with curiosity instead of dark hatred.

She shuddered. Thank God Kwangin and Chang had gone out to fetch firewood. She need only worry about her own safety for a while.

She set the water bucket down and stretched her tired back. She'd finally learned to sleep next to the campfire, with Kwangin's warmth curled beside her. That is, until last night.

Each time she'd closed her eyes, the Manchu's square

face haunted her exhausted mind. Now, in the sickly winter daylight, fatigue burned in every muscle, and her thoughts whirled round her head.

She lifted the bucket again and trudged, head down, toward Insung's cookfire. She stopped, sudden confusion breaking through her stupor. Heavy leather boots blocked her path.

"Megan!" Kwangin's voice pleaded for her help.

Her head snapped up. Obuto stared at her. In his hand he gripped the small boy's wrist.

Tears streamed down the tiny golden cheeks. "Make him let me go, please, Megan!"

Obuto barked an incomprehensible string of sounds, but she could only shake her head. She set down the bucket and held out her hands for Kwangin, but the Manchu pulled the boy's wrist out of her reach.

The rumor-mongers said the crazy one spoke Korean. She must try to make him understand. "Please, Sir, let the little one go." Her voice quavered, but she returned his level gaze.

He dropped the tiny wrist and exploded with laughter. "So, the foreign bitch speaks dog language."

Kwangin's soft hand tugged at her arm. "Megan, come away. I don't like him!"

She didn't dare look away from those cold eyes. Now she knew how a snake's prey must feel. She shook off the small boy's hand. "Go away, Kwangin, go back to your grandfather."

"Not without you! He might hurt you!" The sweet voice cracked, then became a sob.

"Go now!" She'd never used such a harsh tone with the boy before. It hurt to use it now, but it just might save his life. The little hand let go, and the sound of running feet reassured her. He was gone, safe, at least for the moment.

The Manchu's square hand came toward her face. She cringed away from the expected blow. He laughed again, then jerked the knot under her chin. The tie gave way and her silky green coat slipped from her head and onto the ground.

Obuto reached for her heavy copper braid, jerked it

once, then dropped it. "Hmmph!" His breath whistled from narrow nostrils. He pinched the white skin on the back of her hand, then let go. Red spread across the bruised surface. He chuckled.

She must try to get away. Scooping up the coat, she turned to leave, but a heavy hand clasped her elbow. She jerked away, but the fingers dug deeper into her flesh. Her heart pounded, and her breath came in short gasps.

He steered her toward one of the tents. No! Not this! Not now! She fought back harder, planting her feet on the crusty snow, but he only laughed and held tighter.

He stopped at the tent flap and turned his head, surveying the camp. Maybe he would change his mind! Maybe he wanted her to do some sort of work!

Then his thumb and forefinger grasped her chin and turned her face up. His breath reeked so of garlic and ginger she gagged. Hatred flowed from those black eyes again, just as it had in her dreams.

He let go of her chin and pulled her around the side of the tent toward a group of prisoners. The men squatted among heaps of Manchu bridles and saddles, chattering as they polished the dark leather. They quieted when Obuto dragged her into their midst.

He stopped beside a tall saddle standing propped against a stump. He jerked her around facing him, then took both of her wrists in one of his rough, square fists. With the other, he ripped away her silk jacket, then gathered one of her white breasts in his hand and squeezed.

She ground her teeth and closed her eyes against the pain, fighting for balance. When he loosened his grip, she raised her knee and plunged it between his bandy legs.

The heavy skirt bound her leg and weakened the blow. She searched his face for some response, some anger or pain, but he only laughed and cupped her other breast, squeezing it even harder.

Behind Obuto the Korean prisoners stared, mouths open.

"Help me!" Pain and fear sharpened her cry.

The Koreans shuffled their feet and looked at one another, then turned away.

Rage burned in her. She wrenched one hand loose and crashed it again and again into his body and his face, flailing her fist, striking without aim, without thought.

"So, you like this, you bitch-whore? Just so a mare fights a stallion!" The lust in the guttural voice chilled her. He yanked her around and pushed her face-down over the saddle. The leather stank of rancid oil. She gagged again, then tightened her muscles and twisted and kicked, but still he held her.

Cold air bit into the flesh of her legs and buttocks as he pushed up the heavy skirt and ripped off her pantaloons. No! She kicked out and up, but found only empty air.

Rough hands gripped her thighs, forcing them apart. Fingers pushed up between her legs. Then he mounted her, pressing against her buttocks. She screamed and thrashed around, but one hand pinned her shoulders to the saddle.

He entered her, scraping her dry passage raw. Her head whirled—pain and pressure burned between her legs and up into her groin. He pushed in and out, crushing her against the oily leather with each thrust.

Above her the barbarian snorted and moaned. Her agony stretched into forever before he cried out and collapsed atop her.

Hot breath whistled in her ear. His limp body crushed the air out of her lungs. She could not breathe. *Please, let me just die!*

Finally the noisy gasps slowed and the terrible weight lifted from her back. Air filled her bruised lungs. She lay still, not caring what happened to her, hoping he would take his broadsword and finish her as he had the drunkard.

A laugh crackled through the cold air, and a harsh slap stung her bare buttocks. After a moment she knew he'd gone.

She reached behind her and tugged the heavy skirt down to cover her exposed flesh, then slid to her knees and crouched beside the heavy saddle. The Koreans stared at her in silence, then one by one turned away. They bent to their polishing and started talking all at once.

Then the tears came. She sobbed until her throat ached and her lungs felt dry. She could cry forever. Perhaps she would never be able to stop.

"Megan?" She jerked. Kwangin's sweet voice reached out to her across a void, tethering her once again to a world of sanity and human kindness. "Don't cry. Did he hurt you?"

She shook her head and scrubbed the tears from her burning cheeks. "No, don't worry. He . . . he just . . ." How could she explain?

A frown creased the boy's round forehead. "Please don't be angry with me. I stayed away until he left." A warm hand patted her cheek.

She threw her arms around the small, wiry body, holding tight to him, to his love, to life.

"Owww! Not so hard!"

She loosened her grip. Kwangin's solemn little face peered into hers. "Why did he want to hurt you, Megan? Why do people do terrible things to other people?"

The words whirled around in her mind. She leaned back against the saddle and closed her eyes. "I don't know."

It was true. She had never understood such cruelty. A knot of anger tightened in her belly. She squeezed Kwangin's hand. She didn't want to understand, because then she might be able to forgive.

This she would never forgive, could never forgive. But maybe she could learn to hate as much as Obuto, maybe he could teach her that, enough to hurt as she had been hurt.

But the Manchu was only a bully, not really even human, hardly worthy of revenge. Much as she despised Obuto, she hated someone else more—the man who had put her here, at the mercy of these barbarians, who had stolen her love and then tossed it aside.

Somehow she would find a way to repay the man who had betrayed her—Yi Jongwhan!

36

Bright winter sunlight glared off the square of white rice paper. Jongwhan willed himself to stop shivering. The bitter cold crept through his padded trousers and numbed his buttocks. His red chafed fingers curled around a lump of charcoal.

The frosty air burned his nostrils, but it carried the scents of pine and snow. Jewels of light sparkled from branch tips, from the red tiles of the gatehouse roof, even from the crusty ridges of the churned-up road below.

His fingers danced across the page. For so long he'd wanted to capture the beauty of the mountain fortress, the splendor of the snowy mornings. And now, since the war would be over soon, he could return to his art.

A white rabbit scurried from its hole and reared up, the long-eared head turning from side to side. Even from the top of the wall, he could see the pink nose wiggle in the clear, sharp air. A snowbird twittered. Jongwhan smiled.

Word should arrive today. King Injo had summoned armies from every province. Couriers had crept out through every gate during the dark of night. Some would reach their destinations.

All they had to do now was wait. And he would never have to fight!

Hoofbeats echoed up the road. A messenger, so soon! He leaped to his feet, paper and charcoal falling forgotten to the parapet.

But no. The horseman bore a Manchu banner. He recognized the Korean renegade from the day before. His jaw clenched as he gathered his sketching materials.

He wouldn't stay to hear the man's treasonous talk again today. Yesterday he'd gone out the gate, tried to reason with the turncoat, borne the Manchu's message to the King.

Injo had listened with closed eyes. "The man is as slippery as an eel." The gold eyes narrowed. "Have no more to do with him." He had ordered the guards to speak with the traitor from the wall if he came again.

A white-clothed archer leaned from a turret. Jongwhan closed his ears to the exchange. Pinpoints of light poked at his eyes from everywhere. The pines twisted in the too-bright light, and the mountains disappeared into a smudge on the horizon. He longed to throw the lump of charcoal at the twittering bird.

He stared for a long moment at the sketch in his hand, then crumpled it into a tight ball.

Shafts of sunlight lanced through the black ceiling of cloud, making the edges glow like embers. In the gathering dusk a biting wind circled the camp, clattering the gongs and bells on the nearly completed pine branch wall and lifting the heavy leather tent flap.

Megan shivered but didn't move inside to the warm interior with the other concubines. She'd stay as long as she could in the cold, long enough to see Grandfather Chang and Kwangin settled by the prisoners' campfire.

She'd tried to join them the night before. Her hands clenched at the memory. All the other prisoners had left the campfire. They walked to the edge of the firelight and stood, staring at her, as if what had happened was her fault somehow.

She'd kissed Kwangin and Chang and hurried away. She wouldn't make that mistake again. She'd been mortified, but that wasn't the worst. What if the other Koreans ostracized her friends because of her?

She wriggled nearer the tent wall and clasped her arms across her aching breasts. Still, she had to know they were all right.

After her reception by the prisoners, she'd returned to the tent. It was the only way she could continue to watch over her two charges. After all, she'd promised Youngsook.

She tried to remember the loyalty she'd felt to the

young mother, the sense of duty. Now all that remained was her own love for these two vulnerable humans. Without them, she would have just given up.

Now caring for them was a habit that had grown up over the last week. Had it really been so short a time? It seemed a lifetime since they'd started across the snowy plain on foot.

She glanced around the tent. Lamplight flickered on the rough leather. She'd learned something else last night. She lay on her pallet, waiting for Obuto, knowing he would take her again, with as much viciousness and lack of privacy as the day before.

But this time she didn't care. He could do what he liked. She made up her mind not to fight, just to think of other things, to get it over with.

When he reeled in and dropped beside her and started fumbling with her clothes, she lay still. He squeezed and prodded her body, then fumbled with his trousers and fell on top of her.

She bit her lip to keep from crying out against the pain, but it never came. Then she realized he hadn't entered her. Something soft and small rubbed against her leg. He writhed some more, then muttered something about humping a corpse and rolled off, snorting in disgust.

In minutes he slept beside her. She'd lain there, wondering what had happened. She'd listened to the other girls complaining about their Manchu consorts all day. Finally she pieced together an explanation.

Obuto thought she enjoyed fighting him, being raped by him. When she fought, he wanted her; when she didn't fight, he lost interest. All she had to do was keep from fighting, and he'd leave her alone, maybe even let her go back with the other prisoners. She smiled.

There! She strained her eyes. A tiny shape and a tall, bent one stood silhouetted against the light of the cookfire. They'd made it back from the hillsides in safety. She pulled her knees under her and crept toward the circle of light in the center of the yurt, but a sudden wailing stopped her.

She rushed back to the opening. More cries joined the first. Women screamed, men shouted. In the last rays of the sun, the Manchus herded a group of children across the plain toward the new wall.

As she watched, Obuto's distinct figure strode through the prisoners' compound. He stopped beside Kwangin and Chang, still warming themselves by Insung's big cookfire.

The Manchu stood, bandy legs apart, square torso rigid. His short arm shot out and grabbed the small boy. When Chang swung at him, Obuto's hand felled him with one blow on the top of the head.

Megan's legs turned to jelly. Behind her a hollow voice murmured, "The children. They have no use for them. They eat, but they cannot work. So the order went out to kill them all."

Megan whirled on the girl, but the curse died on her lips. Tears streamed down the young beauty's cheeks. "My sister." The words turned to a sob. The girl buried her streaming face in her hands and turned back to the lamplight.

Anger and despair flowed through her. Without any conscious thought, she found herself racing across the snowy plain toward the new-built section of wall.

Obuto trailed behind the flock of children and guards. Her chest ached with the cold air, but still she ran. Kwangin's screams tore at her insides, pushed her until she barely skimmed the surface of the field.

At last she reached the Manchu. Without breaking stride, she leaped on his back and pummeled his head with her fists. The short body jerked beneath her. Then one iron hand clamped the back of her neck and he threw her to the ground.

He turned, Kwangin's wrist still clenched in his fist. "So. You are in heat again, so soon." Harsh laughter parted his wide mouth. "I will take care of you, soon." He turned and marched after the other Manchus.

Cold knives of air stabbed through her chest. She forced herself to stand, to chase after him, to attack him again, her strength fading. He fended off her blows as if they were insect bites, laughing in her face.

Finally he turned and swung the back of his hand. It crashed into her jaw. Black spots filled her vision, then cleared. She lay on her side, a few feet from the wall. She tried to move, but her feet, her hands wouldn't respond.

Obuto reached the cluster of Manchus and Korean children and barked an order. She couldn't move, couldn't turn away. Even her eyes wouldn't close.

One by one the soldiers plunged their knives into the defenseless children and tossed their bleeding bodies over the wall. Obuto turned and looked back at her, then took a long thin blade and sliced Kwangin's throat from ear to ear, heaving his lifeless body atop the others.

A tingling started in her fingers and toes. Her eyelids closed, but no tears came. Feet crunched in the snow beside her head. Hands grasped her shoulders, pulled her up.

She knew it was Obuto, and that her attack had inflamed his lust for her. But she didn't care. Nothing. She felt nothing, nothing but a hollow ache, a cold, numb void.

Kwangin was dead, and nothing else mattered. Jongwhan had betrayed her, and now Kwangin's body lay freezing on the plain. Nothing could ever hurt her again.

37

The acrid smell of burned lamp oil weighed the air in the reception hall. Dark clouds had blotted out the morning brightness, and now, at noon, only the glow from the red and blue lanterns pushed back the gloom.

Jongwhan's stomach twisted at the memory of the grisly sight of the East Gate. After the morning's sallies, it boasted ghastly trophies atop tall poles, like the gates of the north and the west.

With a groan, General Kim On Yun collapsed his great bulk onto the cushion next to him. He nodded, trying to keep the disgust from showing on his face.

Even if the general claimed to be his father's friend,

the man's lack of constancy revolted him. On Yun stayed true only to On Yun. A stirring on the dais saved him from having to speak.

A man he didn't recognize knelt before the King to present a memorial. An ancient scribe rose to read the long scroll of rice paper covered with black calligraphy.

"Excellency, your soldiers have fought and won many brave victories since our enemies the Manchus wrongly invaded our fair land." The scribe paused and cleared his throat. "I, Kim Singuk, as Your Excellency's humble servant, suggest we show our appreciation by offering prizes for every Manchu head taken."

The scholar smoothed the long white hairs on his narrow chin before reading the schedule of rates.

Jongwhan bit his lip. More dead, Korean and Manchu. He bent his head and stared at the whitened knuckles of his clenched hands.

"Too bad you are not more of a soldier." On Yun's plump hand weighed on his shoulder. Jongwhan nodded, but couldn't bring himself to look into that porcine face.

The thick voice continued its oily whisper. "A son's bravery would go a long way toward erasing a father's disgrace."

His head snapped up. The man was right. The thin lips curved into the folds of On Yun's heavy cheeks, but no smile lit the black piggy eyes. Just how much did the fat general know about the reasons for his father's banishment?

Jowls wobbled as the round head swung back and forth in mock sympathy. "Of course, I quite understand. Very clever of you to persuade the King to let you act as messenger."

Jongwhan started to protest, but On Yun held up a plump hand. "Now, now, no dissembling. We're friends, aren't we?" Again the insincere smile. "But if you want to prove your mettle, I can provide the King with a substitute. You remember my groom?"

Trapped! His heart sank. If he refused, he would lose all honor. On Yun would tell the story of his cowardice, and all his father's hopes would die. He forced a smile. "My thanks, General. I shall join a sortie tomorrow."

If he died at the hands of a Manchu, at least his honor would live after him, to aid his father and his younger brother.

Somehow, in the morning he must fight—or die. Only the thought of leaving Megan pained him. The hours they had shared were so brief. At least she was safe, away from the terror and bloodshed. If by some miracle he survived, he would seek her out and nothing would separate them again.

Hoofbeats and wild shouts deafened him. The horses on either side jostled his mount, vying for room on the narrow, winding road. The speed increased as the company rounded each curve. The tight formation forced his horse to match pace until the rocks and trees beside the mountain track blurred.

Jongwhan shivered. Fear, or the sharp morning wind? It made no difference. His teeth chattered. The quiver full of arrows bounced against his backbone with each jolt of his horse's stride, and the bowstring cut into his shoulder.

The track began to widen. Impossible as it seemed, the level of noise grew steadily greater as they rounded the last bend in the river gorge and spilled out onto the plain.

Jongwhan's breath caught in his throat. Fear paralyzed him. Men fought everywhere, spread out as far as he could see—Tartars and Koreans, horsemen, foot soldiers, archers—all doing their best to kill or maim one another.

His mind reeled. Horror after horror competed for his baffled attention. Manchu horsemen swarmed about them. A Korean general swung an iron club. It crushed the skull of one Manchu general and unhorsed another. Sickened, Jongwhan turned away.

Then his eye struck a vision that made the battle seem like a festival—a pile of bodies, heaped like firewood beside a wall, frozen in ghastly disarray. Bodies of children, babies, toddlers.

The noise and chaos crashed around him. The tide of the battle swept him past the barricade, but he knew the sight of those tiny maimed bodies would live in him until his mourners carried his dragon bier to his tomb.

Numbness gave way to rage. This enemy, these Manchus, could not be men. Only monsters could wantonly extinguish so many bright hopes. Those children, those babies—they were some men's sons, some mothers' daughters.

A fire spread through his veins, a grim lust, an eagerness to cut these monsters and watch them bleed. In a frenzy of death, he nocked each arrow and let it fly from his hand, then flung the empty quiver to the ground and unsheathed his sword.

The battle stretched to infinity. His sword slashed and darted like a serpent, striking again and again. His hand slipped on the hilt, slimy with other men's blood, and still he longed for more.

He leaned far down from his saddle and gripped a Manchu by his pigtail. With one stroke he severed the head and watched, fascinated, as a fountain of blood spewed from the neck and the leather-garbed body collapsed.

He slung the ghastly trophy across his saddle, wondering at its heaviness. How much should a man's head weigh? *Don't think, don't think about it!* He had to hold on to the anger, remember those tiny bodies.

Suddenly, above the din, the call to retreat penetrated his dazed mind. He turned his mount and spurred the frightened animal toward the mountain and away from the plain.

A path opened before him and he caught up with the company as they passed the wall. A horseman swung a torch and the pine branches flamed high. A symbolic gesture—the host of Manchus would rebuild it tomorrow.

The company broke free of the defenders and galloped up the steep mountain defile. When no one followed, he sheathed his sword. Blood caked and crackled on the back of his hand. He wiped the sticky palm against his trousers.

He wound the pigtail around his saddle horn, careful not to look at it, not to let its reality invade his consciousness. Yet the realization would not be avoided. He'd killed a man, more than one. The knowledge settled over him like a dark specter.

His pulse slowed. The heat of battle left him. He rode

up the steep track, shaking, sick, and more terrified than
when he'd ridden down it a few minutes before. A few
minutes—an eternity. The Yi Jongwhan he'd been was no
more. In his place rode a killer.

38

Moon of Melting Snow

Clumps of green needles and the raw ends of limbs
punctured the wall of fog covering the newly completed
pine branch wall. Gray mist swirled into the no-man's-land
between the Manchu barricade and the stone walls of the
fortress. The gathering dusk and a thin drizzle of rain
smudged the green and purple mountains in the distance.

Jongwhan shivered as he hurried down the stone steps
and across the compound, grateful to be done with his tour
of guard duty for the day. The King expected him for
dinner. His belly rumbled. Hunger sat even at the royal
table now, but this was New Year's Eve.

Seventeen days since he lay in Megan's bed, the
happiest man alive. A year since they'd sat in Chang's warm
house, listening to his dire predictions. He shivered again.
The old man had spoken the truth, at least about him.

He turned his thoughts to more recent days. Fighting
had become routine, an empty gesture. The few Manchus
he killed would no more push back the enemy than it would
raise those slaughtered children from the dead.

Soon even the fighting must stop. More horses and
cattle died each day, and the soldiers grew weaker from lack
of food. Supplies dwindled faster in the miserable weather
than anyone had predicted. Twenty days more at best, and
then the war would be over.

The only thing keeping him going was the love he felt
for Megan and the duty he owed his father and his family.

At least On Yun left him alone now, and the King continued to praise him and reward him.

His heart warmed to the selfless ruler. Injo and Sohyon had both given away their saddles, their fur robes, even their blankets, to help the soldiers endure the cold. And when the monks at the fortress monastery gave the King vegetables and honey, he had sent it out to feed the troops.

Jongwhan coughed at the door to the reception hall, then inspected the magpie nest in the tree nearby. No one had talked of anything else all day. The court had hailed it as a hopeful omen, but His Excellency maintained it would take more than one magpie to set things right.

The door opened and he slipped into the noisy hall. Warmth wrapped around him like a blanket and seeped through the soles of his stockinged feet. He collapsed onto a cushion.

Talk rose and fell around him, but to his relief no one greeted him. King Injo sat deep in talk with two of his advisers. The always-thin face now verged on gauntness. Deep lines etched the pale cheeks and dark blue half-circles lay beneath the golden eyes.

Jongwhan's sympathy deepened. The King had received so many crushing blows in the past few days. First, the Manchus had completely surrounded Namhan with a barricade of woven pine branches twice the height of a man, and in only seven days! Gongs and bells hung every ten paces to warn the enemy in case of an attack.

Then, only yesterday, a brave company of three hundred Koreans left by the South Gate to try to break through the enemy line. Only one hundred had returned. The fighting spirit of the Koreans had been broken.

Finally, this afternoon, Injo had sent the Manchu general a gift of a bullock and ten casks of wine, and now he waited for a reply.

A white-coated servant set a small table before him and Jongwhan turned his full attention to the food. In spite of the poor quality, he ate with gusto.

The oval slices of rice cake swam in a watery beef broth—a poor imitation of New Year's soup. Coarse brown hulls clung to some of the rice kernels, but he scarcely noticed. For the first time in many days his belly grew full. He scooped up the last few grains and settled back, trying not to think of the servants making do with a handful of barley for their one meal of the day.

A messenger scurried across the floor and prostrated himself at Injo's feet, then handed up a leather scroll. A hush fell over the assembly. The white-haired scribe stood and at the King's nod began to read.

"Heaven has given our Emperor dominion over all your eight provinces, cattle and wine as well. Take these paltry offerings back and give them to your starving soldiers."

A sob fell into the shocked silence. Tears streamed down Injo's lined cheeks. The King buried his face in his hands and wept.

Tears stung Jongwhan's eyelids. He knew the source of his sovereign's despair. The Manchus had made it plain. They had given the King ample opportunity to surrender. Now they could afford to wait.

A babble rose up again around him. Indignant at the insult and frightened by their ruler's weakness, the courtiers resumed the only activity in which they truly excelled—arguing and laying the blame on one another.

Jongwhan's heart quavered at their plight. The Koreans lay trapped in the middle of two concentric circles, the walls of Namhan and the Manchu barricade. The enemy intended to keep them there, to punish them, grind their will to dust.

Perhaps after they exhausted their supplies and hunger left them too weak to resist, the Emperor might accept their surrender, but not until he burned this defeat forever into the minds and memories of the Korean people.

A bitter wind pushed the nasty odor of pipe smoke into her face. Megan's stomach churned and she swallowed the bitter fluid that crept up her throat. With his supply of mild Korean tobacco exhausted, Grandfather Chang smoked bits of herbs and weeds he collected as he wandered among the Manchu camps.

He'd come to her the first day after Kwangin died,

"bumping into people and asking for a woman with flaming hair." He'd given a hollow chuckle, but it didn't fool her. Kwangin's death had hurt the old man even more than it had her.

"I'm practicing for the time to come when my soul will wander homeless and hungry forever, with no man to feed my spirit after I'm dead." He would say no more about it, just shook himself and tried to smile. His gnarled hand patted her hand. She'd started to speak, but the words died stillborn on her tongue. What could she say?

The same thing happened when she chided him about not working, fearing the Manchus might use that excuse to kill him. He'd only cleared his throat and rested his hands on his crossed legs. "They will kill me soon anyway. Other than that, they can do me no more harm. Besides, how can I gather wood with no eyes? Who will guide me, you?"

She sighed. If only she could. Every night for the past week Obuto lay beside her, sometimes pinching and prodding her, trying to get her to fight back. But she lay still, limp, until he lost interest.

And every day the old man came. They sat together in the snow outside the leather tent. Sometimes they talked, but sometimes they just sat in silence.

Today fog misted their faces and their clothes. They faced the fortress. The rough pine wall loomed in the middle distance, but the stone walls rose above, crowning the pine-covered hills. "From whence cometh my help." She smiled to herself at the thought.

Not likely. Any help she got would come from within herself. But she had grown so numb, so used to not caring, it seemed easier just to endure until the nightmare ended. She only regretted she had not already died.

"Do you know what today is, Little One?"

The old man's wheezing voice brought her out of herself again. She shook her head, then realized he couldn't see the gesture. "No, Grandfather. To me it is just another day." She fought to keep the bitterness from her words but lost the battle.

Chang seemed hardly to notice. "Today marks a new year." He lapsed again into silence, sucking on his pipe.

After a moment he spoke again, but this time his voice vibrated with excitement. "Tell me what you see."

Megan frowned but complied with the request, describing the cookfire, the prisoners' compound, the gully where the soldiers tethered their horses, the clearing where the Korean men cleaned and repaired the Manchus' bridles and saddles. She shuddered and turned her eyes away.

He still sucked on his pipe, his lined face intent. "Go on. What else?"

In the distance, more camps dotted the horizon. Soldiers marched along the barricade. And out across the plain, the brass cannon huddled, surrounded by stacks of powder kegs.

He grabbed her hand. "Where? Point to it!" The command silenced her questions. She pointed. He sighted along her outstretched arm, then sank back. "Thank you, my dear."

After a moment he stood, brushing the snow from his white pantaloons. Mist clung to the folds of his face and dripped from the tip of his nose. "I must go."

Megan rose beside him. On impulse she put her arm around his neck and kissed his withered cheek. He jumped and frowned. Koreans never embraced in public. Then he smiled. "I shall miss you, too."

With that, he strode off. She longed to call him back, make him explain, but she already knew what he planned. And she had no right to deny him this, to ask him to cling to a life that held nothing for him. In his heart he was already dead and had been for seven long days. It was only a matter of time anyway.

She ducked into the leather tent and crawled beneath the thick sheepskin coverlet. The wool stench filled her nostrils and turned her stomach again, but she closed her eyes and lay still until the nausea passed.

When the blast came, she started awake and sat bolt upright. She had dozed off, and it took her a minute to realize what the sound meant. Manchu voices blended with Korean shouts and the sound of running feet.

Another explosion split the air, followed by another

and another. Finally, out of the chaos, one Korean called to
another outside the tent wall. "What is it? What's happening?"

And another voice answered, "An old man, the blind
one, dropped a lit pipe into a powder keg, and the whole
armory is going up!"

The force of the words pushed her back down into the
sheepskin. Tears welled from the outer corners of her eyes
and trailed down her temples and into the edges of her hair.

She'd known all along. She twisted onto her belly and
pressed her hot cheeks into the vile-smelling sheepskin.
She couldn't have stopped him. A part of her was glad, glad
that he had gotten his revenge.

Sadness and self-pity washed through her. The old
man was gone, and with him went her last reason for
staying alive. Why? Why had he left her behind? Why
hadn't he taken her with her?

39

The great gong reverberated through the night air and
echoed back from the four stone walls. Jongwhan opened
his eyes and lay still. The warm darkness of the sleeping
room pressed around him. Had he dreamed it?

No. Faint cries reached him, and somewhere nearby
running feet crunched on the seashell path. He sat up,
fighting off weariness and gnawing hunger, trying to
understand the sounds outside.

He struggled into his heavy clothes. As he tied the
strings of his hat under his chin, the door flew open. A
servant panted out a message. "The Manchus. They're
scaling the south wall and the West Gate." The man turned
and disappeared into the night.

Jongwhan struggled to grasp the hurried words. The

enemy wouldn't attack now. The King had sent an apology and asked for a truce. His heart thudded in his chest.

But these were Manchus. Reason seemed not to enter into their actions. These butchers of children could and would do anything.

He slung bow and quiver over one shoulder and carried his sword unsheathed in his hand. He ducked out the low doorway and ran toward the gate. Torches cast grisly shadows over the ramparts.

Manchu soldiers spread along the parapet, like bees swarming to honey, then climbed or jumped to the flagstones below. Koreans fought in the courtyard before the gate, on the stairs, on the wall itself.

An inhuman roar filled his ears. It took a moment before he realized it had come from his own throat. He emptied his quiver, each arrow driving its point home into Tartar flesh. Then he ran toward the thickest point of the battle, swinging his heavy sword like a scythe before him, hacking at every foul-smelling, pigtailed barbarian he saw.

He reached the foot of the stairs after what seemed like hours and leaped up the steps two at a time. He slipped in a pool of blood and caught himself, scraping his hands raw against the rough gray wall. He jumped over a fallen body, not even stopping to wonder if it was friend or enemy, alive or dead.

Bodies littered the floor of the gatehouse. A lone Korean leaned from the casement, slashing at the invaders, pushing them down to die on the rocky ground below.

Jongwhan rushed to aid his countryman. Together they leaned far out the aperture and heaved the ladder up and out. Screams echoed up from the base of the wall. Jongwhan grinned. Not only those on the ladder, but those waiting below.

The guard nodded, too breathless to speak, and mopped his brow. Heavy footsteps sounded behind Jongwhan. He turned, sword extended.

The thin sliver of a new moon cast a bar of white light into the gloom. In it stood a stocky Manchu, dressed like an officer, feet apart, hands on hips. His shoulders filled the narrow doorway. Thin lips parted as he barked a harsh laugh. In guttural Korean he spat curses and insults. "So, two pig-dogs await their master." Again he laughed. "Well, I am here!"

He lunged toward them. Jongwhan backed toward the Korean soldier. Something bounced against the outside of the window. A ragged cheer echoed up from the base of the wall—the ladder.

He gestured to the soldier and positioned himself back-to-back with the man, each protecting the other. The Korean leaned out the embrasure, sword at the ready.

The Manchu advanced toward the window. His narrow blade whistled as he slashed the air.

Jongwhan clenched the hilt of his sword in both hands. His palms slipped on the sweat-soaked handle. He wished he could wipe them, get a better purchase. He wished for many things—most of all to be far from here and safe in Megan's arms. But the Manchu kept coming.

The tormentor stopped, tapped his blade against the tip of Jongwhan's, and threw his head back in a roar of laughter.

He knew he would never have another chance. With all his might Jongwhan raised the heavy broadsword and thrust it straight into the base of the Manchu's throat.

Blood gushed from the wound. The Manchu's sword clattered on the stone floor. Square hands grabbed at the weapon piercing his throat, squeezed the razor-sharp edges. Rage burned in the cold black eyes. He pulled the broadsword out of the wound. Blood gushed down his chest, flowing black in the cold moonlight.

Bleeding hands clawed at the jagged hole, but the burning eyes never left Jongwhan's face. The Manchu gagged. Blood bubbled from his lips and trickled from a corner of his mouth. Slowly the fire in those terrible eyes faded and died. The lifeless body crashed to the stone floor like a felled tree.

The noise of his own breathing filled Jongwhan's ears. He wrested his sword from beneath the still-warm body and turned back to the window.

At last the tide of enemies slowed to a trickle, then stopped altogether. With his ally's help, Jongwhan dragged the fallen Manchu to the parapet, tipped the dead weight over the edge, and heard it crash onto the ground below.

He stood panting on the wall's edge. Gray wisps of cloud veiled the narrow white-jade scythe of the moon. Perhaps, somewhere far to the south, Megan lay in warmth and safety, looking up at this selfsame moon, thinking of him.

A chill coursed through his veins. What would she say if she knew what he'd just done? How could he expect her to love a killer?

Cold seeped from the icy ground, through her heavy skirt and into her knees and shins. Three days since the old man killed himself, ten since Obuto murdered Kwangin. And now . . .

Two of Obuto's men emerged from the tent carrying his bedding and extra weapons. Their odor of sweat and wool and rancid oil nauseated her.

She'd watched Obuto grease his hair and braid the long queue from the crown of his head down his back. She'd never seen any of them wash their bodies or their quilted clothes. A slimy patina grayed everything they wore, even the edges of their fur caps. No wonder the Manchus stank.

She shivered. Soon the soldiers would return for her. She knew what happened to women when their Manchu masters died in battle. The men stacked all the dead man's possessions, including his concubine, around the bier and set a torch to it.

Her already queasy stomach rebelled at the memory of the screams and the smell of burning flesh. She searched her mind for sadness or regret, but she found only a fierce joy. The monster was dead, killed by a Korean atop the fortress wall! If she had to die, at least he'd gone before.

She bit her lip. She'd meet him in hell, if there was such a place. She surveyed the Manchu camp. How could even hell be worse than this?

She ignored the sound of running feet until they stopped beside her. Well, let it come. She bowed her head.

"Megan!"

She started. A woman's voice. Her head snapped up. "Insung!" The elegant *kisaeng* had changed. Disheveled gray hair hung in limp tendrils around the tired face. Smoke had yellowed the fine silk coat. Red welts covered the elegant slim hands, and small rips and snags dotted the heavy silk skirt.

But the brown eyes still glowed with life and determination. "Come quickly. We don't have much time."

Megan shook her head. "It's no use. The Manchus will come after me." She tugged at her greasy, sleep-fuzzed braid. "My hair will draw them like a beacon. You'll only endanger yourself. Go away." She bowed her head again, but hard knuckles rapped her crown.

"Don't argue. Just come, now!"

Megan shrugged. She'd had enough of protecting others, even from themselves. She was too tired to care if Insung wanted to kill herself, even if she was Soonhee's mother. She nodded and heaved herself up on unsteady feet.

Insung's strong grasp bit into her arm. The *kisaeng* pulled her across the plain, away from the cookfire, toward the draw where the horses snorted and reared on their lead ropes.

Megan jerked her arm away and turned. Vomit spewed from her mouth onto the snow. The bitter liquid stung her nostrils. She coughed and spat again, then wiped her hand across her wet mouth. She looked at the vile yellow stain at her feet and almost cried. It wasn't fair. After everything she'd been through, even her own stomach betrayed her.

The nausea and weakness ebbed a bit. She turned and trudged after her last remaining friend.

"What is it?" Megan's nose wrinkled and her stomach heaved again. The pot of black liquid stank of old urine, wood smoke, and rotted leaves. Green, spiny circles floated on the cloudy surface.

"Hair dye. My mother's recipe. The secret is the chestnut husks." The older woman frowned. "In the inner court the women used it to cover the gray in their hair, to try to look young and keep the men interested."

Megan nodded. Women would do anything to hold a man. Some women, anyway.

"Unbraid your hair." Insung's tone seemed brisk, even cheerful. She set to work, slathering the noxious stuff over every square inch of the coppery hair.

Megan's eyes streamed. She covered her nose with both hands and tried not to breathe. Finally Insung set the pot to one side and began rubbing off the excess with some heavy rags. Megan wiped her eyes and sat still while the other woman finger-combed the now-black tresses and redid the tight plait down her back.

"Now, take off those clothes and put on these rags."

Megan shook out the dirty white skirt and jacket. They reeked of grease and wood smoke and stale sweat. She shrugged and stripped off her once-fine silks. She'd had to discard the pantaloons after Obuto tore them. She stood naked in the clearing, shielded from the camp by the tethered horses.

She shivered. Goose bumps stood out on her arms. Her erect nipples ached in the frigid air. Funny, she couldn't keep a bite of food down, but her belly looked bloated. She tied the skirt across her ribs. The ghosts of fingermarks still smudged her breasts. Wincing, she tied the jacket over them.

Insung smiled at her and held out a small copper mirror. Then the elegant dancer bustled away, wadding up Megan's old silk clothing and stuffing it, along with the now-empty pot, into a hole in a hollow tree. "Look at yourself." She tossed the words over her shoulder.

Megan held the circle of polished copper in front of her. Her breath caught in her throat. Except for the round green eyes, the woman looking back at her was Korean.

Jongwhan sipped the watery broth. The sorry stuff only fueled his hunger, but it warmed his hands and soothed the gnawing in his guts for a little while at least. He ground his teeth. A man needed rice.

He leaned back against the parapet and closed his eyes. The King had even ordered his own food cut by a third, then ate but little and pushed his servants to eat what remained.

Weariness settled over Jongwhan. Even guard duty

drained him of strength, and hunger kept him awake most of the night. And the news didn't help.

Messengers came in daily with reports of battles raging outside the walls, with the garrison within too weak to join in. Defeat followed defeat, some of them in plain view of Namhan. The provincial armies tried to reach the stranded King, but the Manchus mowed them all down like stalks of ripe barley.

A shadow fell across his face. "Sleeping on duty, Yi Jongwhan?" On Yun stood over him, wheezing from the exertion of climbing the stairs. Even famine had not reduced the man's girth. The general must have his own private hoard of food to stay so sleek. An imitation of a smile curved the thin lips and creased the heavy jowls.

"No." Jongwhan bit back the reply burning in his brain. The fat general never stood watch, though all the other generals did. No need to insult the man. Rumors of On Yun's cowardice had finally reached the King. He had lost favor in court. Jongwhan smiled up at him.

Pudgy fingers smoothed the sparse mustache. "I am organizing a raiding party to bring back some more Manchu heads." Nonchalance filled the thick voice. "The morale of the troops needs a boost."

Jongwhan's mouth opened in disbelief. Such a venture spelled certain death. Few of the horses had strength to carry a rider, and no speed to speak of. The man must be insane. He closed his mouth. Or very, very clever.

Beady black eyes bored into him. "I knew you would welcome another chance to fight, so I came to ask you before I spoke to anyone else." The smile warmed into genuine, malicious glee. "You will join in, won't you?"

Jongwhan returned the man's evil leer with a level gaze. "No." He rose and brushed the back of his pants, turning his face outward toward the smoke spiraling up from the Manchu camps.

Behind him the fat voice wheezed, cold and insulting, "Of course not. I should have known. Just as your cowardly father betrayed the only woman I ever loved, so his cowardly son betrays his country."

Jongwhan whirled and faced the fat man. At last his

father's enemy revealed himself. This seeming friend, this ugly, simpering toad. Jongwhan's hand went to his sword, but On Yun backed away out of reach.

A thick chuckle bubbled from the twisted lips. "The King shall hear of this treachery. When I return victorious, your fine reputation will crumble into dust."

Jongwhan took a step toward the obese monster, but the gluttonous voice continued, "I shall destroy you as I did him. The dishonor shall follow your house through generation after generation."

With a laugh the villain turned and waddled away down the stone steps and was gone.

Jongwhan sank down onto the wall and balanced the tip of his broadsword against the stone floor at his feet. He rested both hands atop the hilt and leaned his forehead against them.

On Yun would do just what he said, ruin the Yi family honor forever, and he could do nothing to stop it.

40

Fog and darkness shrouded the quiet camp. Through the wall of mist came occasional muffled cries and footfalls. Ghostly figures emerged and disappeared. Only the warm circle of firelight pushed back the thick, clammy air.

Megan toyed with the last bite of *bulgogi*. She'd found the lean barbecued beef actually stayed down if she ate it slowly. Sighing, she brushed a tear from her eye.

Cry and puke, that's all she seemed able to do. She hated her physical weakness. She tore a chunk off the beef and forced herself to chew and swallow it.

She'd followed Insung's commands, at first because she didn't care what happened to her, then later because they made sense. "Don't look at anyone. Walk with your head down and say nothing."

With Madame's pampering, her nausea had diminished except in the morning. Insung insisted she lie flat on her back and chew and swallow a bowl of cold rice before she got up. Sometimes it stayed down, but even when it came up, it settled her stomach for the rest of the day.

The *kisaeng* sent her out with the old men to gather firewood—"to keep you away from the Manchus." The combination of food, exercise, and fresh air, coupled with complete exhaustion, meant she really slept for the first time since the invasion began.

Day by day she felt more human, and now after four days, she'd grown restless. She couldn't decide if she loved Insung or hated her. The woman had saved her life, but she'd done nothing to stop Obuto from raping her and killing Kwangin. And what about old man Chang? They had been friends for years.

Insung bustled over and settled herself beside Megan. She peered at the empty plate. "Ate it all? Good." She'd fashioned chopsticks from splinters of wood and used them to lift small mouthfuls of food. She ate quickly, but with delicate precision, never dropping so much as a grain of rice. No grease smudged the soft, smooth lips.

Megan shook her head at the mysterious combination of lady and courtesan. A question had haunted her for days. "Why did you do it, why did you save me?"

The chopsticks dropped with a clatter onto the plate. Insung's eyes flew open, then closed. "I thought you knew." When they opened again, tears glistened on the dark lashes.

"Megan, you are my friend, my daughter's friend. Don't you know you are almost like a daughter to me?"

Megan bit her lip. This was not the answer she'd expected. She'd thought Madame merely guarded her own interests, providing entertainers for wealthy clients. She took a deep breath. She had to know. "What about Chang, and Kwangin? Weren't they your friends?"

Insung nodded, her face turned toward the flames. Her voice, when it came, wrenched Megan's heart. Weariness and despair colored every word. "I helped you

because I could, because it was good, the right thing to do."
She paused.

The older woman wiped her eyes, then continued, "I
learned long ago not to torture myself with what could not
be." She turned a haggard face toward Megan. "I loved
them, but I could do nothing to help them. Don't you see?"
With that, the *kisaeng* buried her face in her hands and
sobbed.

A knot untied in Megan's chest. She touched Insung's
heaving shoulder. "Yes. Yes, I understand."

Fingers of fog curled around the trees and bushes
beside the seashell path and spread across the gray
flagstones of the courtyard. Jongwhan's feet tore gaping
rents in the gauzy stuff as he paced before the tall wooden
gate.

On Yun had finally ridden out on his campaign, alone
except for his groom. Fog hid the two horsemen even
before the gate closed after them, and only muffled sounds
echoed up the road from the plain.

Jongwhan had breathed a sigh of relief when no one
else agreed to accompany the fat general. The King had
praised On Yun's courage and chided his other officers. Still,
none of them changed their minds.

If the man returned . . . He clenched his fists. But
the man wouldn't return, couldn't! The Manchus would cut
them down.

Hoofbeats thudded far down the road outside the wall,
and a man's voice shouted something unintelligible. Almost
instantly a guard appeared in the gatehouse window. "They
return! It is General Kim On Yun! Open the gate!"

Jongwhan unclenched his fists and turned away, heart-
sick. Now his dream of reinstating his father at court had
truly ended. He trudged toward the dais in the center of
the square. Soon the King and all his advisers would arrive
to welcome On Yun as a hero.

He sighed. He'd done his best, but he wasn't a
courtier, nor a warrior. Not even a scholar! Once the
thought of returning to his old life had pleased him.

He looked down at his hands. They had once belonged

to an artist. Now they belonged to a killer. Could they still recreate the beauty he saw?

The tall gate swung open. The weak winter sun burned through the fog and bathed the two horsemen in pale yellow light. They trotted onto the flagstones.

A ragged cheer went up from the bedraggled soldiers surrounding Jongwhan. Two severed heads swung from On Yun's tall saddle.

He looked away. So the villain had kept his promise to return victorious. He willed himself to remain calm. He'd already accepted his fate. The play's end had been set. It only remained to walk through the action.

On Yun dismounted and knelt, laying the two heads before him. The King rose from the low wooden throne and walked down the steps of the dais to meet him. "Someone take these trophies that our friend has bravely won. Hoist them so that the barbarian enemy can see how true men fight."

A white-coated servant scooped up the grisly prizes and scurried off. A muscle twitched in Jongwhan's jaw. How could they have gotten through, just the two of them? Why hadn't the Manchus slaughtered them?

The white-coated groom stood holding both bridles in his hand. The man's clothes, for once, glowed immaculate white. Not a spot of blood, not a rip or a cut showed.

Jongwhan's heart pounded. Hooded gray eyes intercepted his gaze. A sneer twitched the corner of the surly mouth. He turned from servant to master.

On Yun's silk jacket and trousers gleamed in the morning light, as clean as when he'd ridden out. Jongwhan bit his lip. No one came back from a true battle unstained.

King Injo bent and touched the general's pudgy arm, signaling him to stand. "We knew all the time that you were a brave and loyal man. Arise and accept these gifts of silk." Another servant shuffled forward to present the bolts of jewel-bright fabric. "We only wish we had more to give."

The fat man smiled and bowed his head, then surveyed the rank of soldiers and councilors. The black eyes flashed triumph at Jongwhan.

A guard leaned down from the battlement. "We are ready!"

Injo faced the gate and lifted his arm. At this signal, guards hoisted the poles high on the battlements.

Cheers died to an echo. Whispers built to angry mutters. No blood ran down the poles.

Relief washed through Jongwhan. He shook his head in horrified admiration. This enemy's cleverness knew no bounds. He didn't know who had killed those two men, but it hadn't been On Yun or his groom.

Above the shocked murmur, a voice cried out, "Why is my brother killed twice?" A common soldier pushed his way through the crowd and knelt at the King's feet. "Sire, that is my brother's head." The man pointed a quivering arm. "He was killed two days ago and we couldn't bring his body inside the wall."

On Yun drew his sword and backed away toward the gate and his mount. The groom blanched and dropped the bridles.

Injo's face fell into furrows of sadness. "Take them." Weariness tinged his voice and weighed down his thin shoulders.

The soldiers rushed at the traitor, swarming like hungry tigers fighting over a lamb. Jongwhan grinned. More like angry lambs fighting over a tiger.

He turned to the King. Injo stood watching the soldiers carry out his orders. Hunger and fatigue had reduced the thin body, but not the spirit. A fierce light glowed in the gold eyes.

Shouts and curses echoed through the courtyard, then running footsteps and another ragged cheer. At last the sovereign nodded and turned to go.

Jongwhan looked behind him at the cheering crowd. His gaze traveled up the wall to the gatehouse and the two poles atop the battlements, now streaked with blood.

Features distorted in death, two lifeless faces surveyed the interior of the fortress. Jongwhan smiled up at the severed heads of Kim On Yun and his faithful groom. He'd never seen them look better.

* * *

Megan rubbed aching eyes against her rough, smelly cotton sleeve and pulled the tattered *ibul* tighter. The fog had finally left, and with clear skies came a bitter wind, blowing smoke from the campfire up her nose. She coughed and rolled over away from the blaze, but sleep wouldn't return.

A near-full moon lit the camp almost like midday. The night had looked just so a month before, when she and Jongwhan lay in her quiet room, desires quenched, enfolded in the warmth of each other's love. She rolled back toward the fire. She didn't want to think about the moon or Jongwhan or love.

Without the muffling fog, camp sounds traveled far across the plain. Each time she dozed off, a distant shout or a nearby drunken laugh would startle her awake again. With a white-knuckled fist, she pounded the hard ground.

Damn the Manchus and their noisy camp! Her body ached with fatigue. Each night she fell exhausted beside the campfire, and each morning she trudged off, still weary, to gather wood from the nearby hills. The days ground by in an agony of numb sameness. If she didn't get back to sleep, tomorrow would be even more miserable than usual.

She sank down once more into blissful unconsciousness, only to be startled awake by a name she knew. "Pongnim, he's our only hope of a successor." She rose up from her blankets enough to see the speaker's face. A group of turncoat Koreans sat huddled together across the fire.

The one who mentioned Pongnim sat facing her, his flat face smooth and blank in the red light. "Sohyon's feebleminded, and his son is too young to reign."

Another voice piped up. "What will the Manchus do with him when they capture him?" Megan held her breath.

The first speaker shrugged. "Who knows?"

A third voice, dry and cracked, came from the darkness. "Don't you mean *if* they capture him?"

A smile split the first speaker's blank mask. "Fool! They are sending seventy thousand men to take Kanghwa." He giggled, covering his mouth like a young girl.

The dry voice answered, louder this time. "Fool, yourself! No one has taken Kanghwa in the last four thousand years." A wheezing cough exploded out of the darkness, blotting out the first renegade's reply. Megan clenched her fists and strained to catch the next words.

From the other side of the fire, a woman's voice interrupted. "He speaks the truth. The Manchus tried to take the island ten years ago and failed, and the Mongols failed a hundred years ago."

The smile slipped from the first speaker's face. He rose. The flames lit his blank face from beneath, casting weird demonic shadows up his cheeks and temples. His lips spread wide, accentuating the skull-like quality. "I refuse to discuss politics with a woman."

The white-clothed man turned to go, then stopped and turned back again. "I still say the Manchus will take Kanghwa, and if they kill Pongnim, they kill the dynasty." The smooth face turned away from the light and was gone.

The other voices quieted to a murmur, but Megan did not drift back to sleep. Over and over she saw Soonhee's tearstained face, heard the sweet clear voice, thick with tears, asking her to help Pongnim. Again and again she heard her own words: "I promise."

She turned her back once more to the fire and watched the white moon set behind the distant hills. She'd only begun to realize that she wanted to live after all. Her heart swelled with gladness at the wonder of just being alive.

And now, death came to snatch at her again. Tears rolled down her cheeks. A part of her wanted to revoke her promise. Soonhee wouldn't want her to risk her life because of a vow. But if she let Soonhee down, broke her promise, her word meant no more than Jongwhan's.

No. She wiped at her cheeks with a clammy hand. She must do what she could, the right thing. Somehow she must get word to Pongnim, to warn him of the invasion to come.

She struggled to form a plan, but her numbed mind only chased itself around and around. At last she gave up. She would ask Insung for help tomorrow.

In the gray light of false dawn Megan closed her eyes and fell into a dreamless sleep.

41

Heat rose from the *ondol* floor, filling the air with the bitter scents of lamp oil and ink. Jongwhan laid the brush on its tiny ceramic holder and pressed clenched fists into weary eyes.

Black spots swam across his field of vision. Hunger did strange things to him. His moods ranged from restless to lethargic, and no matter how hard he concentrated, through it all the little voice of his belly whined and nagged in his ear.

He sighed and forced himself to reread the document before him once more. It described Kim On Yun's last acts in such a way as to cast doubt on the dead man's past. It then thanked the King for recent favors to Jongwhan and expressed gratitude for the opportunity to serve the kingdom against the Manchus.

He read it again, then nodded. It would do, as far as it went. Now it needed the finishing touches—the mention of his father's old friendship with the King and subsequent banishment and suffering, then a request for reinstatement.

He picked up the brush again and sat with it poised over the rice paper scroll. His mind grew empty, a desert where no words flowed. Finally he set the brush down again without writing one more character.

He would have to finish the memorial later, when he could think. He placed the cover over the wet inkstone and wiped the rabbit-fur brush on a soft cloth, then placed it in its lacquered case.

He climbed to his feet and swayed against the wall. More even than the gnawing in his belly, he hated the dizzy weakness. If only he could just give up, let go. Only the duty he owed his parents kept him fighting for his family's honor.

Honor seemed a costly luxury today, one even King Injo had all but forgone. Since the death of Kim On Yun, the King's letters to the enemy camp had grown more and more abject, begging the Manchus to allow a surrender.

But the enemy stalled each diplomatic attempt, sometimes with insults, asking why the Koreans didn't come out of the fortress and fight. Other times they sent no answer at all. Most of the King's advisers urged surrender now, even those who had demanded war.

Time and food. No one talked of anything else. How much longer would the food last, and when would the Manchus let Korea make peace?

He trudged to the door and stepped across the threshold. The clear, crisp air reminded him of the day more than a month ago when he walked in the Secret Garden with Megan.

He tried to picture her, but instead a jumbled string of blurred details filled his mind—hair the color of copper, arms and legs as white as *makkŏlli*, breasts, lips, thighs. A sweet longing ached in his chest.

The wind tingled his nose with the scent of smoke. Alarm crept into his sluggish brain. Fire! All the buildings within the stone wall were made of wood. If a fire started in this dry cold, all the buildings could go up in flames!

Distant shouts raced closer. The King might be in danger! He turned and walked as fast as his weakened legs could manage toward the royal dwelling. Wisps of smoke curled around him. Ahead, a layer of gray smudged the air in all directions. He pushed his quavering legs faster.

The smoke singed his nostrils and burned his throat. He held the edge of a sleeve over his face, but still the tears rolled from his eyes. The murky air parted occasionally to uncover a building, then closed over it again.

At last the blue tiles of the King's residence appeared. No flames licked the walls or ceiling. Relief made him giddy. He turned and peered through the haze. Something burned nearby, but what?

A guard came trotting toward him. Jongwhan held up a hand to stop the fellow. "What is it? What is burning?"

The man coughed and wiped his face on a once-white

cotton sleeve. "The royal tombs outside the walls. And across the plains, the ones near Seoul."

Sick horror gripped him. To desecrate the royal tombs! For four thousand years the tombs had been tended. Twice a year for at least that long, Korean kings had bowed to their ancestors and offered food to the spirits dwelling in the stone-walled grassy mounds.

Now, in one vindictive stroke, all that history lay smoldering. A weight descended on Jongwhan. He turned and paced back toward his sleeping room. His problems, his father's suffering, paled beside the enormity of these acts of vandalism.

He would set aside the plea for his father until this war came to some kind of end. No hope remained of an honorable peace. The Manchu emperor meant to crush the Yi dynasty beneath his barbaric heel.

The smoke thinned around him. He turned and wiped his wet cheeks. West across the plain, black smoke billowed into the clear blue winter sky. Behind him the wind tossed gray billows into a spiraling tower reaching up to heaven. Ashes sifted down around his feet, and fresh tears slid down his face.

A horse nickered and tossed its head. Megan froze, listening. No footsteps followed her, only normal night sounds of the camp. The horse turned toward her, then dropped its huge head and closed its eyes. She let out a noiseless sigh and sneaked forward again.

She worked her way through the herd of shaggy ponies to the farthest edge of the gully, keeping to the shadows thrown by the full moon. The wind freshened, blowing camp odors of smoke, roast meat, and human waste into the crisp starry night.

Heart pounding, she approached the horse she'd picked out earlier in the day. She reached into one of the wicker baskets of food dangling at her side.

Stroking between the dark eyes with one hand, she held a winter carrot under the tan muzzle. Velvet lips brushed her open palm. "Good boy." Loud crunching

blotted out her whispered words. She glanced behind her.
Still and quiet.

She smoothed the rough hair over the muscular
withers and tossed the quilted saddle pad across the swayed
back. Not likely anyone would miss this ancient nag. Still,
he had a calmer disposition than a younger horse, and she
had at least a day's start on the Manchu troops.

She tugged the lead rope and walked him toward a
boulder in the shadow of a grove of trees. She clambered
up onto the boulder and coaxed the pony close enough to
throw her leg across the broad back. Yes, he would do. She
settled the baskets across the withers so they wouldn't
bounce and turned the horse's nose toward the trees.

She glanced back at the camp. Insung had helped her
plan everything—the baskets had appeared, filled with
jerky, winter vegetables, and cold cooked rice. Then the
saddle pad and a heavy cotton coat. Finally, the *kisaeng* had
drawn a map in the dirt and explained how to ford the river
and follow it to Kanghwa Island.

"I don't know how you'll get across the water once you
get there." The *kisaeng* frowned, then her face cleared and
she patted Megan's back. "You'll find a way. I'll see no one
notices you're gone." She'd brushed away the map with a
pine branch and turned to the fire. "Wait until I'm asleep,
and then don't let me hear you leave."

She'd wanted to thank the older woman, to kiss her
good-bye. She might never see Insung again. But someone
might have noticed, so she just curled up by the fire and
pretended to sleep. It had seemed like forever until the
camp quieted enough for her to sneak away.

She strained her eyes to make out the pine-branch
wall. Somewhere on the other side lay Kwangin's body.
After the explosion, nothing had remained of Grandfather
Chang, and Obuto's corpse had burned to a pile of black
ash. Up above, moonlight glinted off the gray stone of
Namhan Fortress. Had the Manchus trapped Jongwhan
along with the other courtiers, or had the coward fled to the
south as he'd planned?

She ground her teeth and turned away, clucking to the
stallion. As she ducked under a low branch, darkness closed

around her. She fought back the fear crowding her brain.
The Manchus might catch her, and even if she reached the
island, what if they wouldn't let her see Pongnim?

She patted the horse's neck. She didn't know what lay
ahead, only what lay behind—pain, death, betrayal. If she
gave up now, it would all be for nothing. Her only hope of
turning the world right-side-up again lay in reaching
Pongnim before the Manchus did. She dug her knees into
the bony flanks. She had to try.

Tension hovered in the warm air of the reception hall.
Jongwhan squirmed on his cushion, trying to settle his legs
and arms into the least uncomfortable position. For the last
few hungry days, muscle cramps had plagued his waking
hours and robbed him of sleep.

Lack of food had taken its toll among the other
courtiers as well. Eyes sank into dark sockets. Skin hung
from hollow cheeks. Some who had started the siege with
black hair had begun to gray.

An eerie quiet hung in the hall. If the other courtiers
felt as he did, Jongwhan could understand how lethargy
and hunger could stop their usual clacking tongues.

Kim Shanghon sat to one side, hands clenched. A
week before he'd made an impassioned plea to fight "until
every soldier is dead, and all the common people as well."
Now the firebrand's eyes burned, but he kept still, for the
moment at least.

Jongwhan's head ached with arguments. The enemy
had sent seventy thousand men to take Kanghwa Island.
Some in the court still thought the island fortress impreg-
nable, while others realized the Manchus would cross the
Han River on a bridge of human bodies if need be.

If Kanghwa fell, not only would the barbarians capture
the royal family, they'd also get the ancestral tablets.
Jongwhan clenched his fist. After the royal tombs burned,
only the tablets remained as a dwelling place for the spirits
of the royal dead. And what of his friend, Pongnim?

The case for victory grew more hopeless each day.
Each time the King sent a message, the Manchu generals
replied with taunts to come out and surrender, or come out

and fight. At first, Injo had responded with bravery. "We will die and rot here in our fortress before we surrender thus. Then there will be no one to answer your insulting summons."

Then this morning a general had come to the South Gate, repeating the enemy's gibes. King Injo had called the advisers together to hear how he would answer their demands.

Injo slipped a scroll from his long sleeve and passed it to the scribe. The elderly scholar rose and read the message. Jongwhan's mind wandered as the ceremonial greetings dragged on. Then a sentence shocked him to attention. "We wish to come out and surrender, but we dare not while your soldiers prowl about the wall."

Indignant voices buzzed around Jongwhan as the dry voice of the scribe recited the ceremonial closing, but no one rose to challenge the King's decision.

At last the scholar presented the scroll for the King to stamp with his seal, then rolled the rice paper in red and blue silk and tied it with gold cord.

A messenger sidled by Jongwhan's cushion and bowed at the foot of the dais. The ancient scribe descended the stairs and extended the package, but before the messenger could reach for it, Kim Sanghon jerked off the cord and ripped the silk from the roll of paper. He unfurled the document and tore it into tiny bits, then scattered them over the yellow floor. He faced the advisers. "How can you bear to send such a letter?" The anguished tone wrenched at Jongwhan's heart.

The courtier turned and bowed, then tipped a pleading face up to the King. "Heaven will still favor us if we are patient, but if we send this, we are truly undone!"

Voices exploded from every side. Jongwhan's ears rang with the cries for and against the message. At last the King's commands for quiet resounded throughout the hall, and silence fell.

Kim Sanghon bowed to the King and turned away. His eyes flashed as he marched past Jongwhan and out the door. Others jumped up to follow him, some lending him support, others arguing the insanity of his position.

In moments, only a few remained in the throne room. The King sat with his hands folded and his chin resting on his chest. Lines creased the waxen cheeks, and the narrow chin trembled.

On the far side of the dais a man lumbered to his feet. Jongwhan recognized General Choe Myongil. He remembered the general's pleas for surrender after the Manchus took Seoul. Now the thwarted peacemaker climbed down the steps and bent to pick up the tattered fragments of rice paper.

Jongwhan closed his eyes and shook his head. He would never make much of a politician. He couldn't rally to either fight or surrender, because he agreed with both factions.

Not that it made much difference which side he chose. The honor of the Yi dynasty had suffered a mortal blow, and the Manchus had only to sit back and watch its death throes.

42

Moonlight filtered through the branches, spattering the layer of dead leaves beneath the horse's hooves. A few days past full, the moon looked far away and cold as her mount picked his way among the trees.

Megan had ridden until noon the first day, then curled up beneath a bush and slept until the cold winter sun went down. For the first time since the Manchus invaded Seoul, she'd been alone.

At first the danger of her situation had occupied all her energy, but after several hours of uneventful riding, her fear ebbed away. She still rode with caution, but it only took a small corner of her mind. Her thoughts wandered free over the landscape of her memory.

A month ago she and Jongwhan had watched the moon

rise and fall from her room at the *kisaeng* house, then lay awake all night in each other's arms, afraid to go to sleep and break the magic spell. A bitter taste filled her mouth. How could he have betrayed her?

So much had happened since the last full moon, the night the Manchus invaded Seoul. The horrors of death and pain crowded her mind, but she pushed them back and held to her anger. She'd need it to get through this night.

She leaned down to avoid a low branch. Whatever had possessed her to attempt such folly? She knew the answer, saw Soonhee's tearstained face. She must do what she could for Pongnim, warn him at least.

The moon followed her at every turn, nagging her memory. She knew she should remember something, but the thought eluded her. She'd tried so hard to forget these last horrible weeks. Well, she'd succeeded too well. She sighed. If it meant something, it would come to her eventually.

She rubbed her eyes and dozed in the saddle. Suddenly she started awake, chilled with fear. She reined in her mount.

The sound came again, almost like a woman's scream. The sturdy pony snorted and reared, turning away from the river, toward the clearing.

A tiger! She'd heard tales of the wild striped cats carrying off animals, even people. "For half the year the Koreans hunt tigers; the other half the tigers hunt Koreans." Who'd told her that? Still another scream, this time closer.

With shaking hands she dropped the reins and let the horse have his head. She shivered. Some choice! On one side a tiger, on the other seventy thousand Manchus. And no way of knowing what waited for her in the morning.

Wood scraped across rock; with a solid thud the East Gate shut. The clang of iron bolts shooting through cold metal brackets knelled behind him. He drew in the reins and clenched his knees around the horse's bony ribs. Gritting his teeth, he strived to control the dizzy weakness in his arms and legs. Only determination allowed him to keep his tenuous balance in the saddle. He wondered how the other two messengers sat so straight.

Broken pine-branch ladders and discarded weapons gave mute testimony to the Manchu raid of the previous night. Carrion birds picked at red stains in the snow, but no bodies remained. Trails of blood and churned-up snow showed where the fallen had been dragged away from the wall.

The Manchus always carried off their dead and wounded, making it impossible to estimate their losses. An admirable quality. He grimaced. One of the few. And frightening. The host of soldiers seemed to keep coming without end, no matter how many fell in battle.

For a moment the hellish scene of the moonlit battle swam before him. He'd helped drive away the barbarians scaling the walls once more, but he didn't know how much longer the starving Korean guards could hold off such a vicious and well-fed enemy.

Ahead of him, sunlight glinted off the general's round brass pagoda helmet and reflected off the brass and leather armor. The officer settled the butt of the pole in the socket of his high saddle and unfurled the diplomatic banner. Across the arched saddle horn lay the silk-wrapped letter from the King to the enemy commander.

Jongwhan sighed. If only the Emperor would accept the King's surrender. He shifted in the saddle. This morning they'd received an answer to the message Kim Sanghon tore and scattered in the reception hall. General Choe had pieced the scroll together and taken it himself to the Manchus.

The Emperor had called for the King to give up all those who advised him to fight and again insisted Injo come out in person to surrender. Jongwhan would never forget the Emperor's last scornful words: "One thing is certain—I will read no more of your letters."

Yet the King had written again and had honored Jongwhan by sending him to escort the messenger. General Yi Kiuchuk raised his hand in the signal to ride.

After weeks confined within the gray fortress walls, he should be elated to experience such freedom again, but every one of his pony's jouncing steps jolted through his aching body. He ignored the pain, and as always his thoughts turned of their own accord to Megan.

He pictured her, sitting quietly in a warm room, reading, embroidering. In his mind she leaped up and twirled about the room, dancing, her graceful body swaying. He longed to stop her, crush her in his arms, but there were others watching, watching her dance, wanting her too! He bit his lip and wrenched the hateful image from his mind.

What if she met another man, fell in love? No! She deserved more faith than that. It had taken her a year to declare her love for him. She'd not fall in love with someone else in one moon, or twenty. And if she did, he'd kill the man! In horror he examined the thought and realized its truth.

How much he had changed since he held her last. Perhaps her experiences had wrought differences in her, too. His heartbeat quickened. No, he couldn't bear the thought of any alteration. She must stay the same until he found her again. He had sent her away to keep her safe, to keep her for himself.

He swayed in the saddle and caught himself. Better pay more attention. He gripped the reins. It wouldn't do Megan any good if he fell from a galloping horse to his death. Or would it? He wasn't the man she'd fallen in love with. Maybe she'd stop loving him when she realized what he'd become.

He clenched his hands around the braided leather reins. If there was any chance his weeks inside the fortress could turn her away from him, then she must never know.

False dawn grayed the winter sky. A chill wind skimmed along the surface of the water, pushing small ice floes against the current and slapping tiny waves onto the riverbank. It carried with it the scent of pine and water plants. Across the channel, Kanghwa Island loomed black in the predawn light. Megan had arrived.

She'd passed the Manchu force at midnight, skirting the huge camp on foot with the swaybacked nag between her and the sleeping soldiers. They'd awaken soon, rested, fed, and able to march straight across open ground. Not much time.

She tugged the baskets from the horse's withers, emptying the last small carrots onto the frost-rimed mud. The pony bent and lipped the vegetables from the ground. She rubbed the stiff hair between the wideset dark eyes as the huge lower jaw circled, crunching the treat between massive molars.

After the long muzzle nudged at her shoulder, begging for more, she led the horse away from the water, slipped the lead rope from the heavy cheeks, and gave his flanks a resounding slap. He took off through the brush, tossing his head and snorting. Was it the indignity, or the sudden freedom?

The first rays of the sun glistened off the iron-gray water when she reached the riverbank again. She loosed the ugly white jacket and skirt, then wadded them into the basket. She pulled the locket and its heavy chain over her head and nestled it into the center of the clothing.

Gooseflesh covered her bare skin as she studied the current. There! An eddy, a backwash above a sandbar of some kind.

She took a deep breath and let the reality sink in. The river was wide, wider than she'd guessed. And colder. She smiled. But not colder than the sea off Cheju Do. Grandmother's words came back to her: "Let the water take you, be your lover."

Her jaw clenched. Better for her if the water had been her only lover. She shook her head to rid it of the memory and concentrated instead on the water. Yes, if she worked her way upstream, the current would carry her across to the island.

She knotted the rope between the baskets and settled them on her head. The tang of pitch filled her nostrils. Insung had covered the outsides with the sticky black resin. The containers would float and keep her clothes somewhat dryer than if she wore them. It would have to do.

She shivered. Better than facing the fortress guards without clothes. Obuto's face flashed through her mind. She took a breath and waded into the river, using the discomfort to exorcise the phantoms from her brain.

Cold bit into her feet, then her ankles and calves. She gritted her teeth as the cold climbed to the tops of her thighs. With a deep breath she bent her knees, lowering her torso beneath the rushing water.

Her chest ached, refused to expand. She forced air into her lungs, then pushed her feet into the slimy river bottom and paddled into the current. The crystalline water tasted sweet on her numbed tongue. She paced her strokes, letting the water carry her, not looking toward the far shore.

Finally, when her strength began to fade, she glanced around to take her bearings. Her heart pounded. Only halfway. She rested for a moment on her back. She'd never make it. The shore was too far, the water too cold. Despair rose up and smothered her. To come so far and then drown a few hundred feet from shore.

She saw Soonhee's face, her eyes glowing with life and hope, then watched as the happiness dissolved into pain and submission. She thought of Pongnim, his kindly face, his gentle humor. They had welcomed her, accepted her when the rest of the world saw her as a freak.

It wasn't fair. Her own agony, well, she couldn't do anything about that. But this time she might be able to help Pongnim and keep her vow to her dearest friend. Anger coursed through her veins—anger at fate for dealing them all such heavy blows, anger at herself for her weakness.

She *would* make it, or die trying. Better to die of exhaustion near the shore than give up in midstream. Her arms cut the water in powerful strokes. Pain lanced through her shoulders, and her thighs quivered with strain, but still she pushed herself on.

When she bobbed her head up, the island seemed closer, almost within reach. It must be her eyes playing tricks. She lowered her face into the river again and gave one more determined surge of energy.

An eternity passed. Her arms and legs slowed. The cold numbed first her body, then her mind. The current tossed her about. Darkness pressed into her eyes. She had to stop, even if it meant death.

Her hands scraped against a hard surface. Her mind reeled, unable to understand what had happened. She reached out, clung to the hardness. A rock. She closed her eyes and spat water from her mouth, then filled her lungs. Her pounding heartbeat subsided and her breathing slowed.

At last she opened her eyes. A fiery orange sun breasted the purple hills in the distance and glinted off the water. There, only a few strokes away, the rocky shore of Kanghwa Island awaited her.

Fires burned at intervals across the plain as far as he could see. Around them squatted Manchus. Among them sat others whose topknots and white clothing marked them Koreans, either prisoners or collaborators.

The air reeked of smoke, rotten food, and human dung. Even the whole bullocks roasting on spits gave off a greasy savor that turned Jongwhan's stomach.

Soldiers and prisoners alike looked up from their occupations to watch the mounted Koreans pass. Some worked, cleaning and repairing various articles. Others lazed near the fires, talking, drinking, cursing. Noisy groups shouted and cursed around games of skill and chance he didn't recognize. Far out on the snowy field a group of horsemen played a brutal game of polo with long sticks and a live animal for a ball.

Jongwhan clenched the bow of the saddle with both hands and kept his eyes straight ahead, in spite of the sneering faces and jeers and catcalls accompanying their passage toward the commander's tent. Theirs was a diplomatic mission. The general had ordered them not to engage in any fighting, or the whole mission, as well as their lives, would be forfeit.

General Yi drew rein before the largest yurt. Jongwhan halted his mount and clambered down beside his superior officer. A sneering guard ambled off to notify the Manchu general of their arrival.

After a long wait the commander ducked under the tent flap and stood glaring at them, narrow slanted eyes drawn down into slits in a mask of contempt. Jongwhan locked his knees to keep them from buckling and took a deep breath.

A rank odor of rancid oil and untanned hides came from the stocky Manchu. He planted fur-trimmed boots wide apart and drew his ermine-lined cape closer. Finally he spoke, a thick guttural Korean Jongwhan could hardly follow.

"Well? What do you want?" Garlic and putrid meat scented his words. "Why are you here bothering me again today? Did I not make it clear the Emperor will read no more letters?"

General Yi bowed. "I follow orders, just as you do, Mighty One." The Korean extended the silk-rolled scroll. "I bring further supplication from my king."

A sigh gusted from the sneering lips. The Manchu rocked back on his heels and stared up at the sky. "Very well, I will hear it. Read it."

Yi slipped off the gold cord and red silk cloth, then unrolled the snowy rice paper. He cleared his throat. "Korea to the worshipful, glorious, puissant, merciful Emperor, greeting."

The barbarian nodded and pursed his thin lips. He reached up a lined brown hand, and with a dirty, cracked fingernail, picked a string of meat from between his rotting front teeth. "Continue."

Jongwhan lost track of Yi's words in his fascination at the disgusting condition of the man's appearance and habits. The King's letter droned on. "We know that we must become subjects of the Manchu power."

The Manchu nodded again and smiled. "At last, some sense."

Yi bowed and cleared his throat before he went on. "But since the days of Shilla there has never been such a thing as a king going out from his fortress to surrender."

A roar issued from the Manchu's throat.

Jongwhan grasped the hilt of his sword and eased it up in the scabbard. Yi hurried on. "We cannot do it in that way. If you insist upon it, you will soon have a fortress full of dead."

Rage distorted the lined brown face, but still Yi read.

"I long ago banished the men who opposed making peace with the Manchus, so I cannot send them to you, but the Emperor must now be gracious and forgive our mistake."

Yi lowered the scroll and stood panting. The commander advanced toward him and seized the paper, shredding it and hurling the pieces to the ground. The wind picked up the thin white fragments and swirled them around the Manchu's feet, then carried them off across the camp.

Words exploded from the Manchu commander's thin lips. "How dare you waste my time with such mindless excuses? Be gone and bother me no more!" Dirty fingers clamped around a carved wooden hilt and he drew forth a wicked blade. The razor-sharp metal gleamed in the morning light. "Or do I need to silence you myself?"

Yi bowed and turned away without another word. Jongwhan hurried into his saddle and kneed the gaunt stallion into a gallop behind the general.

Once beyond the pine-branch barrier, he slowed the sweating steed to a walk. Pongnim's words echoed in his ears: "Help my father."

He had tried. Despair settled over him. But once again he had failed.

43

The dirty-faced guard looked down at her and laughed, then turned and called to his partner waiting nearby. "*Yobosayo!* Yun, this crazy woman says she just swam across the river from the other side."

Yun's eyes narrowed in his thin, sour face. "Why do you bother me with such nonsense, Hong? She's *michin*. Leave her alone!" He turned away again.

Megan caught Hong's arm. "Please! I have to speak with Prince Pongnim!"

The grinning face sobered. He signaled to his partner.

With a curse the thinner man strode toward them. "Well?"

Hong nodded to her. "Say it again."

She looked from one to the other and clenched her fists. Water from her drenched black braid soaked through the front of the ragged cotton jacket. Thank God Insung's dye hadn't washed out in the river. She was having enough trouble without looking like a freak. "I said I have to speak with Prince Pongnim."

Yun's thin face sneered. "What makes you think he'd speak to a commoner like you?" He elbowed his partner in the side. "One of his concubines, are you?"

Hong's face creased into a smile and laughter bubbled from the wet lips in thick dollops. "Ah, that's rich!"

She clenched her jaw and fought to keep her voice level. "No, just a friend. I have to warn him."

Hong sobered again. "*Aigo!* Maybe—"

Yun held up a slim hand. "Don't be stupid—look at the way she's dressed. She's crazy, I tell you." Eyes the color of dog dung peered at her from beneath thin eyebrows. "Warn him, eh? Of what?"

She bit her lip and shook her head. "I must tell him myself."

Yun threw up his hands and walked away, but Hong leaned closer. The odor of sweat permeated the air around him. "Tell you what. Give me the message, and I'll see he gets it, *nye?*"

She hesitated. Her arms and legs ached from the strenuous swim, and after the cold water of the river, the chill air sapped her small reserve of remaining strength. "All right."

He gripped dirty hands around the handle of his pike and stared at her, gray eyes fixed on her face. "So?"

"The Manchus." The words spilled from her lips. "Seventy thousand of them. They mean to take the island and capture the prince and the tablets of the royal ancestors."

His eyes widened and his lips parted just like a fish. A great roar of laughter echoed across the flagstones and through the gate. People inside the fortress turned and stared.

She stamped her bare foot. "I saw them, myself, at midnight last night!"

Yun sauntered over, a smile creasing his narrow face. He looked like a weasel, with that nose and those pointed yellow teeth. "What'd she say?"

She wanted to smash her fist into the sneering lips and punch a hole in the other man's belly.

Hong panted for breath, then words exploded in giggles from his slobbering lips. "Says the Manchus mean to take the island and the prince." He was off again into convulsions of hilarity.

"I told you she was crazy." Sewage eyes peered into her face. "This island can't be taken, *pabo*! Now go away!"

"Wait!" Hong's convulsions subsided into tremors. A meaty hand grabbed her arm. "Maybe you can be my concubine. I'm a prince, *nye*?"

His partner nodded. "Sure. You're a prince, all right!"

His laugh reminded her of the cawing of a carrion bird. She clenched her fist.

"I'm a prince, too. How 'bout a kiss for me?" The thin face leaned close to hers.

She swung. Her knuckles smashed with a satisfying crack against the yellowed teeth. She twisted and brought her bare foot up into the other man's belly. Then she was running, faster than she'd ever run before. She rounded a corner of the wall and slipped into a clump of bushes.

She covered her mouth to deaden her ragged sobs. Two pairs of feet crashed by, accompanied by groans of pain and muttered curses. She slid farther into the cover of a small grove of trees and sank down with her head on her knees.

She'd have to find another way to warn Pongnim. A grim smile touched her lips. At least she'd taken care of those two animals. She bit back a sob.

No man would ever again touch her against her wishes. She'd die first.

* * *

The air reeked of despair in the dim reception hall. It weighed Jongwhan's shoulders and paralyzed his soul. His mouth tasted of ashes. He rubbed his aching thighs and tried to make sense of the argument going on.

General Yi had relayed the Manchu commander's message, and the council had come to a decision. The King must send the Manchus some of the men who had urged him to war.

The crown prince stood and looked down at the noblemen. Hunger had aged and thinned Sohyon's simple face. For the first time, Jongwhan saw a hint of the royal presence in Pongnim's slow-witted brother. "I have a son and several brothers and there is no reason why I should not go myself." He nodded to his father and sat again.

Without giving the King time to reply, Chong On leaped to his feet. The rabble-rouser's eyes gleamed in his gaunt face. "I am the one who has most strenuously opposed the Manchu claims. Let me go!" The meaning of the words shocked Jongwhan less than the breach of protocol.

Not to be outdone, Kim Sanghon stood. Anger purpled his lined cheeks. His sneering lips showed sharp, crooked teeth. "Who opposes them more than I? I am surely the one to send!"

In the babble that followed, several more men shouted out their willingness to sacrifice themselves for the sake of peace. King Injo raised both hands high and cried out. "Silence!" Gold eyes flashed. One by one the standing men found their seats again. The King's voice rasped into the sudden quiet. "It is Our decision and We will make it Ourselves."

A coarse voice called out from the back of the hall, "Then why do you not send these men rather than let us come to skin and bones?"

All eyes turned to the doorway. Jongwhan recognized the man he'd fought beside in the gatehouse. A group of ragged soldiers crowded the opening.

Chong On jumped up and flailed his fist in the air. "How dare you speak thus to your betters?" The King's advisers mumbled agreement and encouragement. The firebrand took a step toward the door. "Be gone! Back to your duties and leave these decisions to those capable of making them."

The rebels shifted their feet but didn't retreat. Jong-whan held his breath. Then the King spoke from the dais, his voice filled with genuine sorrow. "We know what you have suffered, and We are grateful for your courage." The soldiers looked at one another as Injo continued. "Your plea has been heard. Please return to your duties and trust in your King."

The soldiers' spokesman hesitated, then bowed to the ruler and turned. In moments the doorway stood empty.

Surely the King must sue for peace now. Even the common soldiers cried out for it. Jongwhan clenched his hands on his knees and turned again toward the throne. He winced at the sight of that haggard face.

Not for the first time he found himself grateful that fate had made him an artist and not a prince. Poor Pongnim! Would his friend ever face a decision like this one?

At last Injo spoke. "We are fatigued and wish to retire. We will decide this at another time." The slender ruler pushed himself to his feet and left the room amid mutters from the councilors.

Jongwhan stood and headed toward the outside door. After all these arguments he longed for the cold silence of the wall.

Steam clouded the air, permeating everything in the huge room with savory smells of rice and soup. Megan mopped her wet forehead with a soot-smeared sleeve. She stirred sliced onion into the simmering beef broth, then lifted the spoon.

She blew until she judged it safe, then slipped the ornate metal spoon between her lips. She rolled the garlicky liquid around her tongue and swallowed, then set the spoon down and edged around the other women to the open door. A freezing blast gave her momentary respite from the dank heat of the royal kitchen.

She had stayed hidden until the two oafish guards

retraced their steps on their way to take up their posts at the gate again.

Then she had circled the wall until she reached another gate, then hid until a fracas inside distracted the guards. She slipped past the sentry post and wandered through the immense compound, afraid to ask directions to Pongnim's quarters.

Finally a petty official chased her into the kitchens to help fix breakfast. She hadn't minded. Kitchen help ate first, before they cooked the royal breakfast. And she could safely ask questions about Pongnim.

Her luck had changed. Pongnim's quarters lay nearby in another building. After they served up the morning meal, she would slip away and find him, then tell her story. Would he recognize her without her red hair?

She fingered the locket beneath the jacket. If her green eyes didn't convince him of her identity, the Clan Scott emblem would. He'd studied it many times, asking about the symbolism and the workmanship.

A hand clamped her shoulder. "Back to work! No time for dreaming!" The plump woman's smile softened the harsh words. The head cook had been kind to her.

Megan nodded and scurried back to the row of cookfires, each with its separate firebox and flue. She picked up the thin-bladed knife to cut some fresh greens, but a noise outside stopped her. It came again. A gong, like the huge brass bell that marked curfew and the closing of the city gates.

Frightened voices cried out in the distance. The Manchus! They had arrived. She'd come too late. The knife clattered to the floor. She bent to retrieve it, then on sudden impulse slipped it up her sleeve.

She might be too late to warn Pongnim, too late even to save herself from being captured again, but she'd kill any barbarian who tried to lay a hand on her, or die trying.

Moments later the Manchus herded white-garbed peasants out of the buildings and out the North Gate. Megan grimaced. Lambs to the slaughter. They even bleated like sheep. Bodies jostled her on every side. The smells of fear and sweat hung heavy in the air.

The kind-faced cook knocked against her but didn't bother to apologize. Terror gave the woman's face an unearthly glow. Another servant crushed Megan's toes beneath a heavy foot and mumbled something without even looking back.

She willed her heart to stop racing. The wooden handle of the knife rested in her palm and its cool, thin metal blade pressed against the inside of her forearm. Whatever came, she'd be ready.

With blows and gestures the Manchus bullied the servants into long rows facing the gate. Some of the peasants muttered questions at each other, then didn't listen to the replies. Others stood with eyes empty of expression, never speaking a word.

Atop the parapet a group of soldiers escorted some richly dressed Koreans. "The prince." The man beside her raised his hand to point. She squinted her eyes. Her heart beat faster. Pongnim stared out over the throng, then turned away.

"Pongnim!" Her heart thudded in her ears. He stopped and turned, searching the crowd. A Manchu guard moved down the line toward her, his head twisting right and left. She wiped sweaty palms against her skirt and stepped forward, away from the others.

She took in as much air as her lungs could hold. "Pongnim!" The guard moved toward her, increasing his speed when he saw her out of line. "It's me, Megan!" The man was almost to her now. "Help me!"

"Stop!" Pongnim's voice rang with authority. Megan had never heard him use any but the gentlest tones. The Tartar stopped and turned a bewildered face toward the wall. She smiled. It was going to be all right.

The prince gripped the edge of the parapet in both hands and leaned down. "Bring her to me. She is my consort."

Without waiting for confirmation from his fellow Manchus, the guard turned to Megan and bowed, then gestured for her to precede him. Murmurs followed in their wake. As she passed the front line, the kindly woman from the kitchen reached out and touched her shoulder, then gave a quick nod and smile.

The darkness of the gateway enclosed her. She emerged again in the sunlight and the guard bowed her toward the stairs. With shaking knees she climbed the stone steps. Beyond the gatehouse Pongnim waited. He touched her fingers with a gentle hand, then turned her away from the scene below.

For the first time since Jongwhan left her at the *kisaeng* house, Megan felt safe. She closed her eyes and breathed in the clear winter air, relief flowing like a warm river through her veins.

A scream sounded behind her, then another and another. She tried to turn back, to look, but the prince held her tight. Rage rose up in her, blinding her. As she struggled, he ceased to be Pongnim, her friend, and became just another man, holding her against her will.

Images of Obuto flashed through her mind. She slipped the knife from her sleeve and touched its point to Pongnim's thigh.

The prince stopped and looked down at the blade glinting in the sunlight. Surprise, then hurt, flitted across his broad face.

Megan bit her lip. "I'm sorry. I have to look."

He nodded and loosed her arm, then held out his hand for the knife. She lay it across his open palm and turned, then pushed her way past the Manchu escort to the edge of the parapet.

Below, the peasants waited in long rows. A Manchu carrying a red banner strode along the front. Behind him a pigtailed soldier carried a bare blade. As he went, he sliced the throat of each person he passed. While she watched, the cook looked up at the wall. The bannerman passed in front of her, and the soldier cut her down.

Megan clenched the cold gray stones. Horror and fear paralyzed her. A hand tugged at her elbow, but she shook it off.

"Megan." Pongnim's gentle face looked down at her. Tears glistened on his square cheeks. "Come."

She stared at the gold eyes for a moment, then nodded. She let go of the wall and turned to follow.

44

The explosion echoed up the hill, followed by a high whistle and a splintering crash. Pebbles spattered the courtyard. Jongwhan ducked behind a hastily erected barrier. The Manchus had been lobbing cannonballs at the gate since noon. Most of the shots thudded into the trees outside the wall, but enough hit their target.

The gate hung at a crazy angle. Only the iron fittings kept it together. Jagged holes gaped in the thick door. Brass cannonballs as big as a man's head glinted among piles of rubble and fingers of splintered wood.

Another shot resounded. The heavy gate shuddered and leaned in toward the interior of the fortress. After a pause, it described a slow arc and toppled to the flagstones.

A fierce yell arose outside the breached wall. Figures crowded the still-dusty opening.

Jongwhan unsheathed his sword. His countrymen pressed forward around him. Strength surged through his emaciated body. He ran into the fray, sword at the ready. Battle-crazed, he swung and stabbed. In moments the Koreans beat back the Manchu invaders.

A crowd of soldiers and white-coated peasants surrounded the fallen gate. Jongwhan walked over to the group and bent to grasp a jagged edge. With quavering legs and arms he strained with the others to right the twisted mess of iron and planking. While some braced their backs against the rickety structure, others carried over a log and braced it at an angle across the portal.

Jongwhan pushed his aching legs, following the gaunt Koreans, wedging fallen stone blocks and bags of sand into the opening. Serving women came running with pails of water to pour over the new barrier. He kicked at a soaked sandbag—frozen, hard as the stones of the wall. When they'd finished, he leaned against the wall and slid down to sit on the cold flagstones.

He turned to survey their masonry, and panic rose in him for a moment. Now they were even more trapped than before. The gate would remain closed. He sighed and rubbed his eyes. At least the blocked passage wouldn't admit any more Manchus.

He crossed his legs and rested his palms on his knees. Blood seeped from a slash across the back of one hand. At the sight of it, pain flashed through him.

He untied his heavy outer coat and reached inside to tear a strip from the lining. The silk ripped with a whining sound. He wrapped the soft, thin cloth around palm and back, using fingers and teeth to fashion a knot. He clenched his fist, testing his grip. The makeshift bandage stayed. He could hold the hilt of a sword. Odd, how much more important that seemed than a paintbrush now.

He closed his eyes and leaned his head back against the cold stones. Aching numbness stole through him. Even the images of Megan refused to come to him. No comfort anywhere—only pain, weariness, death.

Peace had better come soon. He searched for some spark of hope within him but found nothing. Tomorrow the Emperor would leave and they would lose their last chance to surrender. He opened his eyes and stared up at the pale blue sky. Even that didn't matter. Nothing mattered anymore—only death, and that was just a matter of time.

Smells of rice and soup filled the dark hallway. Megan's shoulder bumped Pongnim when he stopped beside a door. He glared at the escort. The Manchu guard shrugged, turned his back to the opening, and adopted a sentry's wide-footed stance, sword at the ready.

The prince beckoned her through the doorway, then turned and preceded her. A wail rose from within the room and running feet pattered across the warm *ondol* floor toward them. "Husband! I have been so worried! The Crown Princess couldn't escape so she sent Sohyon's son with Kim In—imagine! Poor little boy, not yet three years old!"

A sob interrupted the flow of words for a moment and two pale hands appeared on Pongnim's shoulders. Megan turned away, shaken by his intimacy with this woman whose face she couldn't see. Pongnim's wife! Poor Soonhee! She swallowed the lump in her throat.

The voice rattled on and on. "The crown princess tried to take her life with a knife but failed. She is resting. Oh, Husband! What will become of us!" The sobs returned.

With gentle hands Pongnim removed himself from the embrace and stepped to one side. "Wife, we have a guest."

The beauty of the delicate features surprised Megan. Soft brown doe eyes looked back at her. Grief, fear, and embarrassment warred in the slender face. With long, tapered fingers the woman wiped at her wet cheeks and nodded. "Forgive me."

Pongnim smiled and gestured at the tiny creature. "This is my wife." He turned and held out his hand to Megan. "*Yobo*, this is my friend. She is a *kisaeng*." The brown eyes narrowed a trifle, but Pongnim didn't seem to notice. "Please make her welcome." He wrinkled his nose. "And find her some decent clothes."

Megan's heart pounded. She tried to smile, but the images of the courtyard tumbled through her mind. Jongwhan's voice echoed in her ears, and Soonhee's gold eyes pleaded with her. "May I sit down?" Her whisper echoed inside her head.

"Of course." The diminutive woman led her to a cushion, then ran back to Pongnim's side. "Will you stay awhile, Husband?"

The square face moved from side to side. He sighed. "I'm sorry. I can't. The Manchus wish me to write to my father, telling him the fortress is taken." Pain flitted across his broad features. He crooked a forefinger under the quivering chin. "Take care of our guest."

Megan sank down onto the soft square pillow and rested her face in her hands. She wished the woman would go away, leave her with her confusion and terror. In her mind she saw the cook crumple again to the ground and the bloody sword flash red in the sunlight. Bile burned her tongue.

A polite cough startled her. Hard points of light glinted at her from the woman's brown eyes. She frowned. What now? Hatred, snobbishness? Whatever it was, she'd had enough. She glared back.

Color spread up onto the smooth cheeks. Long black lashes dropped, veiling the round eyes. Pain edged the woman's words. "I believe you are the one they call Soonhee."

So, that was it! His wife knew, and the knowledge hurt. "No!" Her voice came out in a croak. "No, I am Megan, Soonhee's friend."

Relief lit the dark eyes. A thin smile played over the soft lips. "Then perhaps you will be my friend, too?"

Warmth spread through Megan's chest. Why not? It couldn't hurt her friend to be kind to this woman. Soonhee could never be Pongnim's wife, but his wife could never have his heart. She smiled at the shy beauty and nodded. "Yes."

A great cry filled the audience hall. In the quiet that followed, despair whirled in Jongwhan's head. Kanghwa fallen! It couldn't be. Everyone knew the island was invulnerable.

Tears trickled from King Injo's closed eyes. For a moment he looked dead. Then sobs trembled through the seated body.

A voice echoed through the room. "Excellency, perhaps it is a trick of the Manchus to get you to surrender."

Anger burned in the King's eyes and hardened his voice. "No, this is my son's own hand." He crashed a fist against the throne. "Do you take me for a fool? I taught Pongnim his letters myself!" The man squirmed under Injo's wrathful glare. "Do you think I don't know my son's writing?"

Jongwhan held his breath. Would the King order the man killed?

The fire died out of the monarch's eyes. He slumped and tossed the letter to the floor. "As Kanghwa is taken, of course the ancestral tablets have been destroyed." The shoulders sagged and the ravaged face stared straight

ahead. "There is no longer any need to delay our surrender."

A sigh hissed from Jongwhan's lips. Around him the
advisers looked at the floor, at their hands, at their feet—
anywhere but at each other, or at their defeated king.

A soft cough brought his attention back to the messenger, still standing at the foot of the steps before the throne.
"Excellency, there is more." The man twisted the silk tie of
his jacket in his fingers. He coughed again. "They refuse to
see the Crown Prince. They say you must come out."

Injo closed his eyes again and nodded. The messenger
looked around at those seated nearby, but none met his
gaze. "They also said the Crown Prince and one of his
brothers must go to Manchuria as hostages."

Sohyon gasped. The simple face drained of color.

The King climbed to his feet, his face set in a mask of
despair. "So be it. I will send my son Sohyon, and with him
his brother Pongnim."

Waves slapped against the side of the ferry. Megan
turned back for one last look at Kanghwa Island and
shuddered. Smoke formed a black tower reaching high into
the wintry sky. The Manchus had burned all the government buildings on the island and killed all the people
except the royal family.

The wind freshened, blowing the stench of fire and
death across the river from the fortress. Megan clung to the
rail as the ferry jolted against the bank. Beside her,
Pongnim's wife swayed, clutching her baby daughter.
Megan nodded to her. The prince stood on the other side,
his face blank. She knew he ached for all the dead heaped
up behind the fortress wall.

Something wiggled against her palm. Pongnim's oldest
daughter looked up at her, the tiny hand clutching hers.
Megan smiled and gave the small fingers a gentle squeeze.
For a moment Kwangin's laugh filled her thoughts, but she
nudged the sadness away. Mourning couldn't bring him
back.

The ferry gate dropped and the silent Manchus
gestured with black looks for them to get off. Megan lost

her balance as her silk slippers wallowed through the mud.
The princess had given her heavy new clothes and shoes,
but by the time they reached their destination—she
pushed the thought away.

Loud voices erupted in front of them. A short Korean
man flailed his fists in the air and shrieked curses at a
Manchu soldier. The guard laughed and tossed a large sack
to another guard. The man ran after it, shouting something
about ancestors and tablets and blasphemy. The second
Manchu held the cloth bag out of reach and tossed it back to
the first.

The Korean panted back, but the Manchu leered at
him and heaved the sack into a ditch, then ordered the
prisoner to move on. The man sank down in the muddy
road and begged the soldier to kill him. The Manchu spat
on the man's shiny top hat and walked away.

Pongnim's eyes blazed. He sidled toward the crouch-
ing man. "Yun Pang, do not give up!" The Korean looked
up, despair etched in every line of his face. "Remember
your duty!" The man nodded and lumbered to his feet. He
disappeared into the ditch.

Prisoners eddied around them, pushing them out
toward the plain, but Pongnim held fast. A moment later
Yun Pang panted up out of the ditch, dragging the dripping
sack behind him.

Pongnim bowed to him. The man bowed in response,
then straightened his back and strode off with the water-
logged package clutched to his chest.

They followed the other prisoners out of the woods.
Ahead of them on the plain, a row of sedan chairs waited.
How many days since she stole a horse and galloped across
the plain to reach Pongnim and warn him?

Her mouth twisted. A lot of good it had done. The
Manchus had come anyway, taken the fortress, captured
Pongnim. And now, worst of all, she was headed right back
where she had come from. The Manchus meant to take
them all to Namhan Fortress.

Jongwhan shifted his feet. Weak sunlight glowed
behind the paper door, casting a dim light into the King's

private chambers. In the center of the room King Injo sat before a low table. On the inlaid top, three cups of *makkŏlli* waited, their sweet, rice-wine scent tingeing the air.

In his imagination he tasted the milky white liquid, but instead of sweet, it rolled bitter around his tongue. He shuddered, glad he wasn't to drink with His Excellency today.

A puff of wind chilled him. Two men ducked through the low doorway. Oh Talche and Yun Chip nodded to him, then advanced to kneel before the King. They wore fine ceremonial coats of bright silk with high black boots and new black scholar's hats.

But it was their faces he vowed to never forget. Serene pride smoothed their emaciated cheeks and lit their deep-set eyes. He didn't agree with their politics, but he had to admire their courage.

Injo lifted a fine blue-green celadon bowl. He leaned across the low table and placed it in Yun's hands, then bowed his head.

With the deliberate movements of ceremony, he lifted another cup, placed it on Oh's cupped palms, and bowed again. Then, lifting a bowl to his own lips, he nodded. All three sipped the fragrant rice wine.

Jongwhan swallowed his own spittle. He knew King Injo offered them the greatest honor, but how could they sit there, so calm, so sedate, knowing what would come next?

The King set his empty cup onto the ornate table and burst into tears. "Is is possible we have come to this?" He covered his eyes with his hands. "I am ashamed to look you in the face."

Yun smiled, his voice calm and gentle. "There is no cause for mourning on our account."

Oh nodded and placed his empty cup beside the King's. "It is our own fault."

Injo dropped his waxen hands into his lap. "I will see to it that your families are well cared for."

The men thanked the sobbing monarch, then bowed low and turned to leave. Jongwhan followed them from the room. Shame gave way to sadness, then relief—at least he was only to be their escort.

He looked over his shoulder at King Injo. He could never be a ruler, bearing the responsibility for an entire kingdom. What must it be like to send two close friends to the enemy to face certain death?

45

Moon of Gray Mists

Fog swirled through the open tent flap. Megan shivered and pulled the fur robe closer. Even with gray mist enveloping everything, the stench of the Manchu encampment brought back phantoms to fill her nightmares. She clenched her jaw. Better not to sleep.

She turned away from the gray dawn and dropped the leather tent flap. By the dim lantern light she could make out the shapes of Pongnim's wife and daughters, asleep on the yurt's wooden floor. Thank God Pongnim had given her his protection.

The image of the bannerman and the flashing sword swam before her aching eyes. She stepped over the sleeping family and crouched beside the flickering lantern, warming her hands. The trip back across the plain had been hard on the princesses. She shook her head. Not half so hard as her nightmare journey there on horseback.

All for nothing. She shrugged the thought away, but memories lingered of the tiger's scream and the baleful eye of the moon following her at every turn. She never had figured out what it reminded her of.

A movement caught the corner of her eye. She tensed, ready to fight.

"Megan?" Pongnim's wife stared at her. "Can't sleep?"

She shook her head.

The brown eyes studied her. "Was it awful when you were here before?"

Megan closed her eyes and nodded. "Yes." She hugged her knees to her chest and rested her face against them.

Silence filled her ears until she could hear the children breathing, feet tramping outside the tent wall, her own heart beating in her chest.

"Will you tell me about it?" The soft voice pleaded with her.

She lifted her eyes to the delicate face. How could she ever tell this fragile blossom the horrors of those weeks? This woman had seldom been beyond the women's quarters until three days ago. Would a princess ever be able to understand? The somber face offered only friendship and kindness.

She nodded. "Someday." She buried her face against her knees once more, hoping the princess would go back to sleep. She didn't know how much longer she could stand the madness swirling in her brain. She had to get out of this camp, away from the Manchus soon.

A hand rubbed her shoulder. The princess looked down at her. "It won't be long now." Tiny teeth bit into the soft lower lip. "Today the King will surrender." The tiny figure floated down to sit on a cushion. "After that, we shall return to Seoul."

Hope blossomed in Megan's chest, but she'd learned not to trust the future. She crushed the warm bud and pushed it deep into the well of despair. Her eyelids closed and her head sank once more. She pulled the robe so tight it hurt and pressed her eyes into her knees. But still the thought echoed in her mind. *Please, let it be true.*

Dull hoofbeats echoed up from the hard-packed mud of the road. Only the riders nearest Jongwhan showed through the thick fog. Although he knew a thousand men pressed around him, not even faint shapes pierced the wall of mist.

He slumped against the tall wooden saddle. Trotting through this gray tunnel, he could almost believe they rode alone, coming from nowhere, going nowhere. He sighed. Too bad it wasn't true.

He glanced at the man on his left. General Choe had

seen this end coming the day the Manchus encircled the fortress. Did he feel vindicated? He studied the fine-boned profile. Only sadness showed in the drooping mouth and hollow cheeks. Choe was not a man to rejoice at his country's shame, no matter how he'd suffered personally.

Jongwhan turned his eyes to the front and concentrated on the blue coats of the King and crown prince directly ahead. His jaw clenched. The Emperor had insisted the Korean princes forgo their royal robes to wear the color symbolizing the east. China stood at the center of the world—all other countries took their positions from her, making Korea the East Country.

He gripped the braided reins. Instead of leaving by the more auspicious South Gate, the Manchu had insisted Injo leave by the West Gate as an admission of wrongdoing.

The list of conditions for surrender had been long and humiliating for the courtiers. How much worse had it been for Injo to endure? Yet the King sat straight in the saddle, his head, with its crisp black hat, held high.

A gust of wind lipped Jongwhan's cheek. The fog swirled and thinned. Figures emerged from the mist. With a start he recognized Manchu horsemen lining the roadway, swords unsheathed, bows strung, and arrows nocked. His heart hammered in his chest. Would the barbarians cut them down as they surrendered?

Ahead, King Injo reined in his tall white stallion. The swirling mist muffled his words. "What is the meaning of this? Why do these men stand ready to attack us?" His voice rose to a wail. "Is it not enough that We break thousands of years' tradition by coming out of Our fortress to surrender? Do you mean to kill Us, too!"

A Manchu lieutenant stepped into the roadway and bowed, the sideflaps of his brass helm swinging forward. "Excellency, they stand in honor of your coming, to guide your passage."

Relief rushed through Jongwhan, leaving him dizzy. He'd taunted death too many times on the battlefield to be led like a bullock to slaughter.

The King turned once more to the front. The narrow, blue-clad shoulders trembled for a moment, then he kneed the stallion to a trot.

The breeze freshened again and sickly yellow light filtered through. They rode for several minutes in silence, the only sounds the rushing of the river in its bed, the jingling of harness, and the thud of hooves on the road.

Once again the procession slowed, then stopped. Prince Sohyon turned a stricken face back to Jongwhan. "What is it?"

He shrugged. "Excellency, I do not know." His hands tensed on the bridle.

"Greetings!" A hoarse voice echoed out of the mists.

Choe Myongil leaned forward and whispered to the frightened prince, "It is the Manchu generals, Yongolda and Mabuda. They will salute your father."

Jongwhan loosed the reins and let out a deep breath. Not a threat, but another honor. Perhaps the Manchus had satisfied their desire to shame Korea. He shook his head. No, he wouldn't let himself hope for mercy from these barbarians.

A groom hurried to hold King Injo's bridle and help him to dismount. The three men exchanged bows. Distance and fog muffled their words, but he knew they mouthed the proper salutations and civilities.

His mind wandered forward, past the humiliations of the day. With the war over and his father's enemy dead and rotting, he would have no trouble persuading the King to recall the elder Yi to court. With the familial obligation satisfied, he would again be free to return to his art, and to the woman he loved.

Megan! He rolled the whispered word around his tongue, savoring its sweet flavor. Warmth stole into his loins and glowed throughout his body. He saw her again, bending over Kwangin. His heart swelled in his chest, making it difficult to breathe. Yes! She would give him a son!

The horse he sat atop sidled to the left. He caught the curved pommel of the saddle, barely avoiding a fall. The taste of ashes filled his mouth, as gray as the bank of fog smothering him. He grimaced. From paradise to hell.

The King had regained his saddle and the procession

started again. The fog pushed back enough to reveal the two enemy generals leading the way. The armed Manchu soldiers closed around the column, marching on either side.

His sword hand twitched. The rank odor of grease and unwashed men suffocated him. He pictured again the pile of tiny bodies tossed aside and left to freeze. Rage flashed through him. He gripped the hilt of his broadsword, longing to pull it from its sheath and slice through the wall of Tartars pressing in on him.

The bloodlust seeped out of him, leaving weakness in its place. His heart pounded in his ears, willing him to fight, but his body lacked the strength, and his mind spoke of duty, honor, and peace. The war was over, but he would carry its mark always.

The column of horsemen and foot soldiers slowed, then stopped. The wind blew in earnest now, clearing the last hazy wisps of gray. The sky brightened, and in the lull between icy gusts warmth caressed Jongwhan's cheek.

Sunlight sparkled on a bright yellow silk awning. Beneath, on a high platform, a man sat enthroned—the Manchu emperor. At the foot of the dais a host of trumpeters stood, yellow brass horns glinting at their lips. They gave a mighty blast, a sound as wild and savage as the Manchu horde.

The hair stood on the back of Jongwhan's neck. These animals, these not-quite-men had vanquished their nation. And now a Korean sovereign must submit forever to their barbaric leader's right to rule over the kingdom.

The signal came to dismount. One of the brass-helmeted Manchus led King Injo toward the platform. Jongwhan followed, shame dogging each step.

In the distance a row of palanquins glittered in the sun, each lacquered a bright color. The ladies of the Queen's court must be inside the curtained sedan chairs. He pictured Pongnim's sweet wife and his flowerlike daughters. What terrors ravaged their innocent imaginations? He ground his teeth and looked away. Thank God Megan had escaped!

At the eastern entrance to the dais Injo and the enemy

general stopped and bowed low. Both men raised their hands and hit the back of their own heads.

Jongwhan cringed at this final humiliation. To see his King reduced to bowing before a bloodthirsty Tartar who called himself emperor—it was almost more shame than he could bear. The King repeated the *kowtow* twice more, then knelt on a mat at the foot of the stairs.

The man on the throne called out a string of garbled words. The Manchu general turned to Injo. "You may rise and ascend the platform." As the King climbed the polished stairs, an interpreter signaled the royal entourage to sit at the foot of the platform. Jongwhan squinted his eyes against the winter glare.

On the platform a row of men sat cross-legged facing the throne, three of them Manchus, probably the Emperor's sons. Beside them—his heart raced. Pongnim! The square face turned toward him. The gold eyes glowed, but no muscle so much as twitched in his face, except for the ghost of a nod.

He longed to cry out to him, to tell him all he'd been through, to ask how his friend had fared under the Tartar yoke. A thought chilled his veins. Did the prince know his father had chosen him to go as a captive with his brother to Manchuria? If only he could go with them. But no— Pongnim had asked him to stay by the King. For the sake of their friendship, that's what he must do.

He bit his lip and turned back to the ceremony. Yellow gold covered the Emperor's ornate throne. Over this perched a yellow umbrella. A plume banner snapped in the breeze. Amid this splendor sat an ugly toad of a man, twirling an arrow between stubby fingers. Jongwhan's stomach churned at the sight of this savage usurping the power of the Mandarin Empire.

King Injo's shrunken figure dwindled beside this monster. With shaking fingers the King sipped from a steaming cup. The flowerlike fragrance of tea drifted from the platform to the Korean advisers seated below. Saliva filled Jongwhan's mouth. He swallowed.

The Emperor spoke to a servant. The man stepped forward and bowed to Injo. "The Emperor says, 'Now we

are inmates of one house. Let us try our skill at archery.' If
you tell me your reply, I will translate." The silk-robed
Manchu bowed again.

King Injo set the cup on the small table at his side. His
thin lips curved into a smile. He nodded at the Emperor,
then turned to the interpreter. "Tell him I said we know
letters, but we are not skilled in archery."

The Emperor frowned when the servant translated
this. Jongwhan held his breath. Everyone knew Korean
archers were among the best in the known world. The lines
smoothed from the barbarian ruler's face. He barked a
laugh, then gestured to the serving men.

The pigtailed servants scurried forward with food and
drink for both rulers—the same exact food filled Injo's tray
as did the Emperor's. The symbolic gesture of equality
eased the knots in Jongwhan's chest, but the smell of meat
cooked with ginger and garlic brought such intense hunger
he feared he'd faint.

The Emperor lifted a shiny gold winecup and drank
deeply, then gestured for the servant to refill it. Injo lifted
his cup, following the host as custom demanded. The
Manchu drank, then nodded to the banner man once more.

After downing the third cup, and without eating a bite,
the Emperor ordered the food removed. As the Tartars
carried away the still-steaming dishes, a soft groan came
from somewhere to Jongwhan's right. He swallowed a
mouthful of spittle and looked down at his clenched hands.
To his left, a man sobbed.

The Emperor smiled down at the Koreans, then
barked out an order. Another servant scurried in, holding a
pair of jeweled leashes. The Emperor's mastiff dogs danced
about the man's feet. Another servant appeared with a
platter of raw meat, and His Imperial Majesty cut gobbets
of flesh and tossed them in the air for the imperial curs to
catch.

Renewed anger surged through Jongwhan. How dare
this savage feed pets in front of starving men? He closed his
eyes, willing the ordeal to end. The barking stopped and
heavy steps sounded on the stairs. Injo descended from the
platform, his glazed eyes focused in the distance.

Bright colors blurred past the corner of Jongwhan's eye. A woman sobbed at King Injo's feet, her hair and clothes in disarray. The gaunt ruler bent and lifted her to her feet. Jongwhan's jaw dropped open. The crown princess! He strained to make out her words. "Please, Excellency! Your grandson lies at Tangin. I must go to him!" Sobs wracked the slender woman. "A boy of two needs his mother!"

Injo touched her wet cheek. "My Daughter, there is no more I can do about it. You must go with your husband. It is as the Emperor wills."

The young woman's head fell forward onto her chest. Her shoulders drooped and her whole body trembled with sobs. She covered her face and turned away. Tears dewed Prince Sohyon's eyes.

Jongwhan tried to imagine how he would feel if it were Megan, begging to stay with his son rather than go with him. Would he love his child enough to part with its mother? He'd been away from her less than two moons and it felt like years. Jongwhan sighed. Much as he wanted her with him, he'd choose his son's needs over his own. A warm glow began deep within him. *His son.* Someday. His heart pounded. Unless—was it too much to hope she already carried his child?

46

Megan had never seen Pongnim so angry. His square face flushed red and he stomped back and forth across the floor of the tent. He stopped and fixed her with a flinty gaze. "Why? Why didn't you go to him?"

She bit her lip and shook her head. She couldn't tell him about Jongwhan's betrayal, about Obuto, and Kwangin.

Pongnim threw his hands up in the air and stared up at the yurt's rough hide ceiling. He took a noisy breath and lowered his arms. Kneeling beside her, he took her hand in his own and spoke in his gentlest tone. "I thought we were friends, you and I." He cleared his throat. "I care about you, and about Jongwhan."

She looked into the sweet, honest face. Sobs rose in her throat, but she pushed them down. She gritted her teeth and shook her head again.

He sighed. "Megan, I want you to be safe, away from these barbarians. All you had to do was get out of the palanquin and walk over to him!" His voice hardened. "Don't you think I'd get my own wife away from here if I could?" He shook his head. "And you let a chance like this slip by, a chance to be free, to be with the man you love."

She looked down at the square fist in her lap. He couldn't understand. Even if she told him, he'd never understand why her love for Jongwhan had turned to hatred.

Pongnim dropped her hand and leaped up, giving a cry of rage.

Her head snapped back. Anguish distorted the man's smooth features. "So, you are like *her*! You tire of a man and don't even bother to tell him. You just leave!" He turned away, his shoulders heaving.

She opened her mouth to speak, to deny his words, then closed it without a word. What had happened between her and Jongwhan had hurt her deeply, so much she still wondered sometimes if she'd ever recover. But she had no right to use it to reopen the prince's wounds. Soonhee left him out of love, but Megan could never tell him that.

Pongnim turned back to her, all the angry red drained from his face and an ashen pallor in its stead. His voice rang hollow in the stuffy interior. "Well, if you want to get away from him, you'll have your chance. I am ordered to Manchuria. As my consort, you must accompany me." His eyes glittered with an obvious desire to strike back, to hurt her. "Maybe we'll be gone long enough to forget our lost loves." He leaned his face close to hers. "We can't come back until my father dies!"

* * *

Manchus poured in a steady stream from the East Gate of Seoul, carrying booty and leading hundreds of captive Koreans. Their rancid body odor mixed with the cloying smell of decay coming from inside the wall. With one hand Jongwhan clutched tight to the reins. The other clenched the pommel of his sword. He fought the tide of men buffeting him on both sides and pressed forward to stay near the King.

Their retinue had dwindled. When the column reached the river at Songpa, the ferries could not hold all the men at once. The Koreans forgot their little remaining dignity, pushing and shoving to be taken aboard first. Jongwhan had to draw his sword to get his own countrymen to make way for their King. He shook his head. What had they been reduced to?

Then, as darkness fell, they'd met the enemy leaving the capital in droves. The Emperor had ordered his men from the city to make way for the King. Some of the soldiers and servants from Namhan got caught up in the confusion and were carried away as prisoners. Weakened by a moon or more of hunger, the captives could hardly resist. Even a few nobles had drifted away, unable to fight their way through the throngs.

Now Jongwhan made out the King's blue jacket in the dim lantern light and nudged his mount still closer. At last the stream of evil-smelling bannermen slowed to a trickle. A thin new moon peeped over the mountains as the King urged his white stallion through the great gate. After almost two moons of starvation and fear, they were home.

Time swelled and shrank in Jongwhan's mind. The days since the invasion seemed one moment eternal, and the next, compressed into one hour. So much had happened, yet an air of unreality colored his memories of patrols and battles. Only his time with Megan remained true. His arms ached for her sweet body. As soon as he could, he must find her—she was his life.

Grim reminders of the war lay on every side as he trotted through the streets of Seoul after the King. Ashes blew in the wind. Where houses had once stood, only rubble and burned timbers lay in heaps.

Jongwhan covered his mouth and nose with his sleeve to keep the stench of rotting flesh and burned wood from his nose. Dead men lay in heaps along the gutters. Snarling dogs fought among the bodies and gorged themselves on the remains of the fallen. His stomach heaved. He turned away, bile stinging his throat and tongue.

General Choe headed toward Changyong Palace, since it lay closest to the entrance to the city. The company passed street after street, only destruction and waste showing in the circles of yellow light cast by the lanterns. Several times the general stopped and cast about for landmarks amid the rubble.

At last the palace gates loomed into view. The company drew to a halt in the wide cobbled street. The remains of a huge bonfire lay strewn about the avenue. In the stillness of the deserted city, small scratching noises whispered across the cobblestones.

Jongwhan's flesh crawled. He raised his lantern higher. Tiny red eyes peered at him from behind a pile of rotting corpses. Rats! His horse shied and he patted the arched neck. He unsheathed his sword and clambered down out of the tall saddle. All the royal grooms had been lost along the way. As he held the lowest rank of any present, it fell to him to open the palace gate.

He strode across the littered pavement, cinders squeaking beneath the heavy soles of his high boots. With relief he noted the gate's soundness. He set the lantern in a niche in the wall and stood his bared sword against the stones, then lifted the cold brass handle. Bracing his shoulder against the thick wood, he gritted his teeth and pushed. The portal swung inward with a groan.

He held the lantern inside the opening. Destruction and chaos showed here as well, but no bodies rotted on the seashell path and nothing moved. He turned and beckoned the others, then walked back to fetch his mount.

He stroked the animal's muzzle while the King and his nobles limped through the gate. A sad parade indeed. He gazed up at the new moon, so lovely and white, like Megan's skin. The noises of the retinue diminished. He realized he stood alone outside the palace wall. Something skittered across the stones and stopped beside his boot.

With slow, careful movements he raised his sword. In one flashing stroke, he skewered the fat-bodied rodent and hurled it up into the air. It described a perfect arc and landed with a thump. Lumpy bodies converged from all directions, drawn, he supposed, by the smell of fresh, hot blood. He grimaced, then turned and led his horse through the gateway.

Once inside the opening, he dropped the reins and turned to close the high, round-topped door. The brass fittings pressed into his shoulder as he heaved against the stout timbers. The stone arch resounded with a satisfying thud, and he shot the iron bolts across.

In the distance an explosion split the darkness. An orange glow lit the sky beyond the tiled roof of the gatehouse. Guttural shouts echoed through the still, moon-lit night. The Manchus, ignoring their Emperor's orders, worked their terrible will on the city of Seoul for the last time. He clenched his shaking fists. He prayed to God it would be the last time.

Jongwhan sighed and leaned back against the *chaddae*, rubbing his aching legs. With enough to eat, his returned bit by bit, more each day. At first he'd eaten his fill, but his stomach rebelled and sent everything back up. In the three days since the surrender he'd eaten light meals of soup and rice, adding meat and greens a little at a time. The pains subsided, and he focused again on the conference taking place.

The King had bid the Manchu emperor good-bye the day before outside the East Gate. Now the two turncoat generals had come to meet with the King. The fact that they'd been born Korean and defected to the enemy made them doubly odious. Their sneering condescension insulted Jongwhan far more than the barbarians had. At least the Manchus had been born and raised savages and didn't know any better.

Injo must have shared the sentiment. He sat to one side, playing with his grandson, pretending to ignore the traitors, but by the tiny muscle twitching in the royal cheek, Jongwhan could tell the King followed every word.

The toddler pulled on his grandfather's finger and smiled. Poor little tyke! Most of the time he cried for his mama. The round face turned toward him, brown eyes blinking like a baby owl's. The boy's slow movements and simple expression recalled Sohyon's dim wits. Jongwhan sighed. The crown prince's son would be no more able to rule the kingdom after Injo's death than his father.

The prime minister's obsequious manner toward Yongolda and Mabuda grated on Jongwhan's nerves. Kim Nyu always managed to serve his own interests first, no matter what the cost to others.

Jongwhan had never trusted the King's minister. His faith had lessened even more since Yun Pang's return. The old gentleman had managed to escape from Kanghwa with the King's grandson. Only the day before, he'd brought the child to Seoul. And with him he'd also carried stories of Kim Nyu's son, Kim Kyung-jeung.

Just as the father had been in charge at Namhan, the younger Kim had been in charge of the fortress at Kanghwa. According to Yun, Kim had sent his own household across the ferry to the island first, leaving the crown princess waiting for two days on the mainland side. When she demanded to be taken across, Kim finally acceded. The royal family made it to the island only moments before a band of Manchus attacked and killed the thousands still waiting to cross.

Jongwhan grimaced. Such loyalty! Kyung-jeung had also appropriated stores of government rice and set no guards, but instead feasted and played chess all day. When Pongnim had questioned the man, General Kim scoffed and did nothing. Even as the Manchus had crossed the channel on rafts, the general had refused to issue arms from the arsenal. Then, as the bullets began to fly around him, Kim Kyung-jeung ran. The cowardly general escaped to the coast in a small boat, leaving his men to defend the island, alone and without weapons.

Jongwhan studied the elder Kim, wondering how the man could ignore the dishonor of his son's cowardice. He knew Kim Nyu intended to serve his own ends in the meeting today.

The ceremonious greetings ended. The minister bowed to the generals and asked to be allowed to speak for the King, pleading Injo's ill health. Jongwhan noted the color in King Injo's cheeks, the sparkle in his gold eyes as he tossed a small persimmon to his delighted grandson. The sweet smell of the ripe fruit cloyed the air. The King had been very ill, but he'd regained much of his health in the last few days.

Yongolda and Mabuda made solicitous inquiries, but by their facial expressions, Jongwhan knew they recognized the lie.

Kim Nyu bowed low. His oily voice flowed out into the royal chamber. "The relation between us now is that of son and father." The generals looked at one another and nodded as the King's minister continued. "We stand ready to fulfill our obligations on that basis, even though you ask for soldiers to help in the invasion of China and the seizure of Nanking."

Jongwhan caught his breath. The King raised his eyes and gave a slight nod. So, now the army must fight against their unsuspecting allies. The Mandarins had always come to Korea's aid, even against the yellow dwarves from Nippon. And now they must repay that loyalty with betrayal. He fingered the silk tie at the bottom of his trouser leg. If the King asked him to fight, he would, no matter how his conscience plagued him. Loyalty to his father and his King must come before loyalty to another sovereign nation. He sighed. And that probably lay at the heart of most wars.

Another courtier bowed and asked for leave to speak. General Yongolda nodded. The man explained the scarcity of gold in Korea and asked that part of the tribute be remitted. Mabuda snickered. Yongolda covered his mouth, then with trembling solemnity told the man the Emperor's order must stand.

Kim Nyu bowed again. "I wish to put before you a personal matter."

King Injo raised his eyes, surprise written in his still-

deep-set eyes. Jongwhan's heart raced. Now Kim Nyu
would strike for his own benefit.

The minister's face filled with sadness. "My daughter is
now your prisoner. I have begged you to let her come back
to me. Now I wish to offer you all my wealth for her
return."

Jongwhan found his astonishment and concern mirrored on the faces around him. Mabuda leaned forward,
greed lighting his black eyes. "How much?"

Kim Nyu bowed low. "Twenty thousand ounces of
silver." He raised his eyes. "All I have."

Mabuda leaned back. His smile revealed a row of
sharp white teeth. "Done!"

Jongwhan's heart sank. Men whose wives and daughters had also been captured looked at one another in
despair. Twenty thousand ounces. It was too much! No one
else could raise so large an amount. And now with the
ransom set, the Manchus would accept nothing less.

Kim Nyu turned a triumphant face toward the King,
but Injo refused to meet his eye. How could the man have
done such a thing! Jongwhan set his teeth. What if it were
Megan? He didn't have twenty thousand ounces of silver.
Sympathy gave way to relief. Thank God his mother and his
wife were safe at the family's estate, and Megan had
escaped—none of the women he loved had been captured
by the Manchu horde.

47

The palanquin swayed with the rhythm of the bearers'
feet. Megan leaned against the padded cushion at her back
and shifted the baby girl into a more comfortable position in
her arms. The round head nestled in the crook of her
elbow. Black hair formed a halo around the square face,
clinging in damp tendrils to cheeks and forehead and

spreading across the bright green silk of Megan's sleeve. Dark lashes fringed the closed eyelids and lay like birds' wings on the golden cheeks. The tiny open mouth reminded her of a pink lotus blossom.

Facing her on the opposite seat, Pongnim's wife slept. Their other daughter curled up, her small dark head resting on her mother's lap, thumb firmly planted in her mouth.

Without disturbing the sleeping passengers, Megan pushed aside the curtain. Bright sunlight burst through the gloom. Chill air brushed her face, carrying the odor of damp earth and early flowers. Winter still held the land, but it would soon give way to spring.

Outside, a village sped by. Megan recognized a burned-out cottage. Beside it stood a gnarled "spirit tree" with a pile of stones at its base and paper prayers fluttering from its branches. A pair of painted wooden demon posts leered at her in passing, their frightful carved faces meant to scare away evil spirits.

She dropped the curtain and sighed. From the time the Manchus took Kanghwa she'd been retracing her steps, dragged back along the same route. Soon they would reach Seoul. Back where she started. Still a captive, still a pawn in someone else's game of chess.

A chill crept up her spine. In a few days she would face the unknown again. She tried to visualize Mukden, the Manchurian capital, but only savage images came to her. All she'd known at Manchu hands was pain. How could she hope for anything else?

She had feared Seoul when Jongwhan—she pushed him from her mind—when she had left Cheju Island, and at first the city had seemed strange to her. But people had shown her kindness there, and now she longed for it almost as much as the Highlands. Fate seemed to be carrying her farther and farther from home. Tears stung her eyelids.

The little one stirred in her sleep. A tiny arm stretched, the soft fist bumping against Megan's breast. She winced. Must be the new jacket. She'd loosen the ties next time. With gentle fingers she pressed the arm down and turned the compact body across her lap, out of reach of her tender bosom. She crooned a tuneless lullaby until the baby relaxed and slept again.

"You're very good with her." Pongnim's wife smiled, her brown eyes puffy with sleep. When any other woman would look her least attractive, the princess startled Megan with her delicate beauty. "Do you have children of your own?"

Megan shook her head. "No." And not likely to have any. A part of her still burned with fury when she thought of Jongwhan, but another part acknowledged her continuing love for him. Perhaps the love made the hatred even stronger. She sighed. She would never love any other man enough to want his child, of that she felt sure. She leaned back and closed her eyes, too tired and confused to talk.

A stillness startled her. She realized she'd dozed. The sun's light pushed through the curtains in horizontal rays. It must be near evening. The palanquin stood still.

Pongnim's wife leaned forward to take the sleeping infant, but Megan shook her head. With a grateful nod the young mother handed her the babe's warm outerwear and began bundling the toddler beside her.

Megan wrestled the tiny girl into the complicated outfit, wondering why anyone would bind a child in grown-up's clothes. In Scotland a bairn, lad or lass, wore a smock for the first three years. When a woman carried a young child out of doors, she simply wrapped it in her wool tartan. A sniff drew her eyes from the task.

Tears trickled down the smooth golden cheek of the princess. She wiped at them with the palm of her flawless hand, then tried to smile but failed. "We have arrived." The yearning in the soft voice made Megan ache. "So close to home, yet we cannot go in. It is like sitting next to your husband, knowing you dare not touch his hand."

Sympathy flowed through Megan. She longed to offer some comfort, but knew the taboos against touching a hand or embracing another. No words of comfort came to her, though she searched her mind.

Finally she bent to the job of dressing the babe in her lap, surprised to see the child still sleeping in spite of all the tugging and turning. She finished, then pulled on her own padded silk coat. Looking down, she traced the round cheek with a finger. Perhaps helping to tend this child would keep her sane.

The memory of a knife slicing Kwangin's throat flashed through her mind. She pulled back the finger as if she'd been burned. No, she wouldn't allow herself to care that much about this child. Someday they would be parted, and she must save herself from that pain. But until then, she couldn't help loving the tiny princess.

"Ready?" Pongnim's wife smiled at her, composed and more beautiful than ever. At her nod, the princess pushed open the curtained door and stepped out, then reached back and lifted the toddler after her.

Megan balanced the still-sleeping baby against her shoulder and ducked out the low door. Reaching from horizon to horizon, the tall gray city wall dwarfed the Manchu camp spread around its base.

The sight of Seoul struck a deep longing in Megan. If only she could go back to the *kisaeng* house, back to those happy months before Soonhee left. Back to a time when she'd had three friends and life had tasted sweet on the tongue. It seemed like a dream now.

Pongnim stepped up and gestured them toward a tent. He turned a grim face toward Megan, then looked away. He'd hardly spoken to her since their argument. Anger flashed through her again. She could blame Jongwhan for that, too!

She glanced back over her shoulder at the East Gate, set deep in the stone wall. If only she could pass through it. Did Jongwhan wait on the other side?

If he came looking for her, he'd find nothing at the *kisaeng* house to help him, unless—no, Insung would've managed to survive, probably even escape. And Madame had promised before Megan left for Kanghwa not to tell him anything about her.

Megan bit her lip. Why had he betrayed her? Tears welled up in her eyes, but she stiffened her spine and turned away from the wall. If she ever saw Yi Jongwhan again, he would pay for what he'd done to her. She didn't know how, but she'd find a way.

* * *

Jongwhan cringed with shame at the spectacle spread across the broad plain at Changneung. In all, according to the enemy general Yongolda, the Manchu army numbered one hundred twenty thousand, including Mongols and Chinese. More than half that number had been sent on ahead, but sixty thousand soldiers lined up to march north to Mukden. In the clear spring air they stretched back to the horizon. And with them went two royal households and thousands of other captive Koreans.

At the head of the column a row of palanquins waited to convey the women of the household. The two princes bowed to their father and mounted their horses for the long ride. Injo's arms dangled loose at his sides, tears wetting his lined cheeks. The man had endured much, but giving up his sons to the enemy must be the hardest of all to bear. Jongwhan turned his head, unable to watch the pitiful sight.

His heart gave a sudden skip, then raced. A woman opened the door of one of the palanquins and climbed inside, disappearing from view. Megan! His mind reeled. He hadn't gotten a clear view of her face, but only one woman stood and walked like that. So close! He could run across the field and take her in his arms!

Stop! It couldn't be Megan—she had escaped to the south, to safety. He had to believe that! Besides, this woman had dark hair and she carried a baby in her arms. The bitter taste of disappointment burned his tongue.

As if in sympathy, small drops of water fell from the gray clouds overhead, spattering the grassy field. Within moments the rain fell in earnest, drenching everyone in sight. Not an auspicious beginning for this shameful procession. He shivered. How many would die of the wet and cold before they reached the Manchu capital?

He turned and followed the King and the other courtiers to their horses. Two new grooms held the stirrup for him while he clambered onto his mount's broad back. With head bowed against the rain, he fell in behind the King's advisers as they fought their way south, toward Seoul.

Groups of prisoners crowded the way. Some of the

women wept and held up their arms to the King, begging him to save them. Others laughed and flirted with the Manchus, obviously delighted at the prospect of going north. He alternated between sorrow and disgust.

The King's party veered from the road. Coming toward them, an open sedan chair swayed above eight bearers, pushing up the center of the roadway. Servants held brightly colored silk umbrellas over the occupants' heads.

At a command, the chair stopped alongside the King. The man leaned out into the rain to bow to Injo. Jongwhan recognized the rebel general, Yongolda. The King bowed and waved. Yongolda turned to the woman beside him and said something Jongwhan couldn't make out.

A laughing face peeked from under the silken parasol and bobbed in Injo's direction. Dark eyes surveyed the royal horsemen and stopped at Jongwhan. Pilsu! A dark sickness radiated through him. The beautiful *kisaeng* sneered and tossed her head, then disappeared from view again. Beneath the fringe of the umbrella, only her hand moved, caressing Yongolda's chest and squeezing the turncoat's arm.

The general barked out an order and the chair swayed past them. The royal party pressed into the opening in the crowd made by the general's passing. Soon the mass of bodies closed in on them again, but Jongwhan gave their progress only the most cursory attention.

Emotions roiled within him as he tried to sort them out. Disgust became sadness, then pity, and finally guilt. How could she give herself to that man? Worse than an enemy—a traitor! Could she not have found someone honest to love? Someone besides himself? He writhed in his saddle. He couldn't help it that he loved Megan instead. But had his brief affair with Pilsu somehow turned the woman into a whore, selling herself to the highest bidder?

The image of the dancer and her traitor-lover receded. In its place he saw a graceful creature with white skin and red hair. He knew Megan wouldn't give herself to a man she didn't love. For all her fragile beauty, she had more strength and determination than many men, and a stronger sense of right and wrong. He pulled his hat down to shield his eyes from the rain. Too bad Pilsu didn't share some of that strength.

Warmth softened the breeze as it blew through the open air of the pavilion. A faint perfume of lotus and water lily whispered of spring. Jongwhan smiled and tapped his hand on his foot in time with the court musicians. A fine day for a feast honoring the loyal and the brave.

He sobered. Not so pleasant for the unfaithful. The King had ordered some killed and some banished, among them Kim Nyu's cowardly son. He glanced at the Prime Minister. The man gave no sign of shame or grief at his son's disgrace. Pity touched Jongwhan for father and son, not because of their disgrace, but because each cared only for himself—a lonely existence.

His smile returned, this time even broader. He didn't plan to be lonely ever again. After the feast, he'd be free to ask the King to reinstate his father. Then he'd find Megan.

He opened and closed his hands, studying the long fingers. And he'd be able to put down his sword and pick up his brushes again. He clenched his jaw. If he still could record the beauty of life instead of destroying it.

Delightful odors of cooking food danced upon the wind. He frowned at the sudden reminder of the Manchu feast. The barbarians had set out a fine feast for the starved court. A few of the Koreans ate with gusto. He'd been afraid to overload his temperamental belly after the long and hungry siege. Some who'd been well-fed at Kanghwa also refused to eat out of nobility, or stubbornness.

Then, at last, the Manchus had gone, and today he could eat without regret. He lifted a fine cup to his lips. The smooth sweet-sour *makkŏlli* cooled his tongue. He savored the rich flavor, then sampled the fine food set before him.

Usually only those who sat at the royal table received such delicate fare. A cheer rang out from the far end of the pavilion. The King honored all his brave soldiers today, even the commoners. He smiled at their honesty. He knew many would cherish this day above all others in their lives and talk about the sumptuous fare for years to come. He lifted a slice of ginseng and dipped it in honey, smiling at the balance between the sweetness and the earth-tang of the precious root.

Jongwhan sampled every dish. Servants brought course after course, each more delicious than the one before. Rare mushrooms, rich seafoods, and fine meats at last gave way to delicate green bowls of hot persimmon punch and plates of honey-coated rice cakes. Leaning back against the *chaddae,* he gave a satisfying belch and closed his eyes.

Food, drink, and music lulled him into a harmony he thought he'd lost. He looked deep in his soul and found peace.

Silence descended after the final notes of the *kayagum,* then riotous applause. The King rose from his throne on the dais. At his command four grooms each led out a flawless stallion. With much ceremony the King bestowed one on each of his bravest generals. Jongwhan's breath caught in his throat at the beauty of the animals. What he wouldn't give for such a magnificent gift! But no, he wanted only to restore his family and return to his former life—with Megan!

After accepting the thanks of the generals, Injo cleared his throat. "We wish to reward all who remained loyal at Namhan." A smile lit the pinched face. "Every man who stood with Us against the invaders, We now elevate by one rank."

In the chaos that followed, jubilant men congratulated one another. Jongwhan sat still, his mind racing. Higher rank meant more money and more power. It mattered little that all those around him had moved up as well. Rising status would make many things simpler. He downed another cup of milky rice wine. Surely his luck had changed.

King Injo cleared his throat. All those in the pavilion quieted. A somber look fell on the ruler's face. "As you know, We have agreed to send troops to aid Our new allies in routing the Mandarins from our land." The rumble of discontent in the pavilion mirrored Jongwhan's own. To turn on one's old friends—they must obey the Manchus to survive, but the price was very high.

The King raised his hand for quiet. "We wish to honor those who fought bravely during Our long siege by commissioning them to ride forth to victory at Kado Island." Blackness seeped through Jongwhan's veins, souring his joy in the honors bestowed on him. He hardly noticed his name when the scribe read the list aloud. He'd known it would be there, hadn't even hoped Injo might have omitted him.

The wind puffed in his face, blowing the cloying fragrance of lotus with it. How much of the spring would be gone before he held his beloved Megan again? He clenched his fists. Precious moments, hours slipped away, never to return, while he rode off to harry innocent men from their ancient homeland.

He shoved the low table away from his knees, upsetting the near-empty cup. White *makkŏlli* spread in milk-white rivulets across the inlaid top. Visions of white limbs taunted him. Megan!

48

Moon of Earth's Awakening

A rare moment of peace descended on Megan. She sat cross-legged on a cushion near an opening in the yurt she shared with the prince and his family. Both of Pongnim's daughters slept, exhausted after the jouncing restrictions of the palanquin. Pongnim's wife had gone on an errand, leaving Megan to safeguard the tiny princesses.

The last rays of daylight glowed in the darkening sky. A night wind pushed at the hide flap like a newborn nuzzling its mother's breast. The cool air spoke of melting snow and promise.

For fifteen days the Manchus had pushed their captives toward Mukden, the capital of Manchuria. They camped each night in landscapes bleaker, colder, and rockier than before. Yet spring followed them northward. She smiled. Even the barbarian host couldn't stop the advance of the seasons and their enduring renewal.

A tranquil sigh escaped her lips. After so much hating and pain, she'd come to accept captivity with the royal family. The princess had shown her nothing but kindness and asked few questions. The daughters delighted her with their wiles and gave her a focus, a purpose other than fighting and revenge.

Even Pongnim had relented, joining the women in the tent at night, laughing at the antics of the little ones and listening to the prattling of their mother. Finally, with the children asleep, he'd taken to discussing the future with Megan, considering her ideas, while his wife embroidered in a corner.

She'd feared the princess might resent this attention, might grow jealous. But as the days wore on and the pattern established itself, nothing occurred to obstruct their friendship. She marveled at the resiliency of human nature, that under these circumstances they had found a form of happiness.

She pulled her knees up and hugged them to her. It so easily might have been different. She traced her memories backward, through the King's surrender, her journey on horseback, Obuto, back to the beginning, looking for some way things might have been changed. At last she shook her head. The way she'd come was all she knew. Speculating about things that could never be would profit nothing.

A brief thought of Jongwhan flitted through her mind and was gone. She'd tried to find excuses for his actions, tried to forgive his betrayal, but to no avail. Although blunted, her hatred remained as strong as the love she wanted so much to deny.

A shrill laugh resounded from a nearby tent. She grimaced, then stuck her tongue out in the direction of the grating sound. She'd seen Pilsu often enough in the van moving northward. General Yongolda's favorite let everyone feel the importance of her position.

Megan sobered. Thank God the dark-eyed dancer hadn't known her. Their mutual dislike stood unresolved, and Megan knew Pilsu would begin to plague her again if the disguise failed.

She smoothed the black hair back from her forehead. Insung had applied the dye more than a moon ago. The copper roots had begun to show. What if Pilsu recognized her? She turned the thought aside, but her moments of fragile peace had fled, broken by the intrusion of the old hatred.

Darkness fell and lanterns flared across the plain. Smells of roasting meats wafted from bright cookfires. Her appetite had returned and the nausea abated. She must be getting used to the spicy Manchu fare. She yawned and lay on her side across an empty pallet. Now she wanted to sleep all the time, no doubt from riding all day in the covered sedan chair.

The baby stirred and whimpered in her sleep. Without getting up, Megan reached a hand across and patted the wiggling back until the sweet bairn sighed and fell back into a deep slumber.

Megan closed her eyes, listening to the sounds of the camp. She'd eat later. A sweet floating sensation enveloped her. Time spun out, minutes into eternities.

A sniff awakened her. The unmistakable sound of flint scraping metal disturbed the darkness. A lantern flared, illuminating the strained face of Pongnim's wife.

Alarm bolted through her. She sat up. "Princess, what's wrong?"

Tears glittered on the smooth cheeks. A sob erupted from the slender throat. "Only one question I ask. Is the child you carry my husband's?"

Megan's mind reeled. Child? What child?

The willowy creature knelt beside her, holding the light close to Megan's face. Harsh words grated from the young mother's throat. "Today, when the moon reached its last quarter, I opened a trunk to find rags for my time. I thought back to the day Kanghwa fell, when my husband brought you to me." The soft brown eyes narrowed. "The moon was then also in its last quarter." She shook the lantern, its blue-and-red-silk shade throwing flickering shadows on the tent wall. "When did you bleed last, woman?"

Darkness crashed in on her. She pressed her hands against her temples, feeling the jagged scar on one side. The moon! That's what she should have remembered. A child! The word echoed through her mind.

A hand clamped her shoulder and shook her. The princess stared down at her. "Answer me!" The harsh voice cracked and the soft mouth trembled.

At last Megan found her voice. "No, I have never been with your husband."

The princess sat back on her heels and set the lantern aside. Her head drooped and she wiped at her eyes. "I am sorry."

Megan sat still, the reality of the woman's words sinking in. Pregnant! Jongwhan would be so happy! The hatred she'd held since the invasion seeped away, and the love she felt for him blossomed again. All that had happened since they last parted seemed like a dream, a horrible nightmare. For a moment Obuto's face floated before her eyes.

And then she knew. Fate had not finished its great joke on her. Pain descended, filling every corner of her mind. She carried the child she and Jongwhan had wanted, but she didn't know, couldn't ever know, if its father was a lover who betrayed her or a barbarian who raped her.

A high, horrible laugh filled the tent. In a daze she realized it came from her own throat. Then she buried her face in her hands and wept.

Jongwhan shaded his eyes. The pale new moon dimmed as the rising sun glowered over the mountains, illuminating the channel and the forty boats moored below. General Im had ordered the vessels left unguarded, saying he needed all his men to fight. Jongwhan clenched his fists. If only some of the Mandarins would use the boats to escape.

Regret tasted bitter on his tongue. It was one thing to kill Manchus who murdered babies, but quite another to attack unsuspecting allies. He knew the turncoat general named Mabuda had landed on the western bank of Kado Island with plans to attack at dawn from a hill above the Chinese camp. Perhaps the barbarian forces would succeed without the aid of the Koreans.

Distant shouts grew louder. Thousands of Mandarins converged on the waterfront, more than the boats could hold. Men pushed and shoved in their panic to get aboard. The crowded boats put to sea, wallowing low in the water, crammed full of human bodies.

Others dove into the waves and swam to the sides of the vessels. Some clung to the gunwales or clambered aboard. Jongwhan's heart raced. Too many! Didn't they see they were overloading the boats? The lead boat foundered. Waves crashed over the sides, swamping the overload junk. Horror crept up Jongwhan's spine as water crashed over the screaming passengers and the boat sank beneath the waves.

Men leaped from the other vessels and tried to return to shore, but the crashing waves swallowed them. One by one the remaining boats capsized. He turned away, sickened by the sight.

General Im barked the order to advance toward the mountains. Cries of fright and clanking blades sounded ahead. Jongwhan nocked an arrow. The company picked up speed, trotting through the mountainous interior.

Suddenly the path widened. In the clearing men struggled and died. Jongwhan stood, immobilized by the carnage. Before, he'd relied on the battle fever to burn in his veins, to cry out for revenge. But now he felt only pity, both for those who killed and those who died. An alliance of thousands of years had ended in moments.

The sick-sweet smell of blood cloyed the air. It reminded him of the butcher on Cheju Island, the oaf who'd attacked Megan.

A body jostled against him. "Let fly!"

He blinked at his countryman, then raised the bow and aimed. The arrow found its target. A Mandarin fell, clutching at his bleeding throat. With a heavy heart Jongwhan reached over his shoulder and slid another shaft from his quiver.

A man ran toward him, waving his arms and shouting. "What cause for enmity is there between Korea and China?" He jerked to a halt an arm's-reach from Jongwhan. His back arched and his eyes rolled up in his head. Without another sound he fell forward. An arrow quivered in the fallen soldier's back.

The fighting raged on and on without anything to cushion the sights and sounds of death. Even Jongwhan's own danger meant nothing to him. Sickness grew in him with every arrow he loosed. Each detail stood out—each sight, each smell, each sound engraved itself on his senses.

After an eternity, the last Mandarin fell. Dead and wounded littered the clearing. General Im rallied the men under his banner. With a haggard face the commander surveyed the battlefield, then ordered the company onward.

Jongwhan trudged after the leader. He shrank from the thought of the day to come. Fifty thousand Mandarin Chinese lived on Kado Island, and Mabuda intended to kill them all.

After the first few sorties, Jongwhan managed a sort of numb detachment. The day dragged on, long periods of toiling up mountain draws interrupted by short bursts of intense fighting. The surprised defenders ran until cornered, then stood and fought, their actions clumsy and their faces bereft of hope. More a slaughter than a battle— the attackers took few prisoners and gave no quarter.

By sunset General Im's company met another Korean party under General Yu. Soon a company of Tartars joined them. The three armies had swept the Mandarins from the hills. Intense pity filled Jongwhan for the few hundred captives shivering in the clearing. These Manchus had much to answer for—killing children, sacking palaces, and worst of all, turning Koreans into heartless killers.

A Manchu officer stepped forward and greeted the two Korean generals. "I am General Kong Yuduk, commander of the Emperor Chung Te's own guard." The last angry red fingers of light from the dying sun stained the man's brass helmet with fire. "You have fought well and honorably today against the enemies of the empire." A smile split the bronzed face.

At least this man had been born a Manchu. In another situation Jongwhan might have liked him, or at least given him grudging respect.

General Im bowed to the barbarian. "You do us great honor to say so." The cold gray eyes narrowed as they beheld General Kong.

The Manchu swept his arm toward the captive Mandarins. "As a reward, I offer you two hundred fifty captives." Again he smiled.

Had the man no sense of decency? To foist off these captured Chinese, to leave them in Korea as reminders of the kingdom's greatest betrayal! Jongwhan ground his teeth. General Im stared out over the heads of the prisoners. His mouth set in a thin line. When he turned back to the Manchu, his eyes blazed with hatred. In barely civil tones he addressed the savage leader. "I do not care for these men. Exchange them for a like number of captives who are going into Manchuria as slaves."

General Kong stiffened, then gave a curt nod. "As you wish. I will have the document drawn." He gestured to a scribe, then turned and surveyed the pitiful crowd of Mandarins. His eyes glinted once at the Korean general, then he motioned to one of his officers. "Kill them."

The Manchus advanced toward the helpless captives. One by one the Chinese fell, the animal stench of fresh blood filling the dusky air. Disgust twisted through Jongwhan's belly.

A scribe hurried toward General Kong and handed him a rolled document. With pursed lips the Manchu opened the scroll and scanned the contents, then nodded and passed it back to the scholar. The man scurried to where Im stood. Bobbing his pigtailed head, he presented the roll of parchment and withdrew.

Kong faced the Koreans and made an elaborate bow, then turned and walked off the field. The cries of the dying Mandarins disturbed the silence. Bile rose in Jongwhan's throat. The Manchus finished their grisly chore, put away their weapons, and followed their commander.

Im stood looking at the scroll in his hand. Would the Korean general follow the barbarians, revenge the helpless men who lay slain in the gathering dusk? Jongwhan waited, willing himself to indifference and obedience. Whatever the general decided, he would lend his support.

As twilight dimmed to black, Im gave a sudden low growl and crushed the parchment tube in his fist. "Light the lanterns!" He shoved the scroll at a lieutenant and strode toward his horse. The foot soldiers straggled after their leader.

Jongwhan stood for a moment in the silent glade. The distant moon breasted the dark trees, touching the bodies of the fallen with silver light. He studied his double-arched bow as if seeing it for the first time. He started to sling it over his shoulder, then stopped and dropped it. It landed with a soft thud in the grass, the string humming for a brief moment. He loosed the scabbard at his side, caressed the pommel, then dropped it as well.

Looking up again at the purity of the moon, he made a silent vow. No matter what price he must pay, what dishonor befell him or his family, he would never kill again.

49

Moon of Swelling Buds

The wind blew off the snowy steppes, buffeting the wall of the yurt. Although the sun glared down outside the triangular opening, spring came late to Mukden. Chill air seeped into the room. Megan shivered and pulled the fur robe closer. She closed her eyes and composed herself for sleep, but instead the debate inside her raged on.

Jongwhan's or Obuto's? Life stirred in her belly, like tiny butterfly wings, reminding her over and over of the child she carried. She pressed her hands against her swelling middle. The quickening of the child within her should bring her nothing but joy. Instead, the tiny movements tugged her back and forth from delight to despair.

Some days she knew the child to be Jongwhan's. She pushed all rational thought from her mind and concentrated on the love flowing through her, love for the child she carried and for its father.

Other days, such as today, her mind insisted on reliving the weeks before and after the invasion. She'd bled every month at the new moon since she was little more than a child. The twelfth moon of last year had been no different. And then, two days before the full moon, she and Jongwhan had shared one glorious night of love. She ached at the memory. A longing for her tender lover engulfed her for a moment. With a dry sob she forced herself to continue. The Manchus had invaded, and before the dark of the moon Obuto had raped her, not once but many times.

Four months had passed since then. At first she'd hoped the princess erred in her conclusions. Megan fashioned every possible excuse, but deep inside she knew the truth, had known it since the words fell from the woman's lips. She kicked off the covers and lay panting. She didn't want Obuto's child!

She pushed hard against her belly, hating the man who had forced his way into her, maybe left his seed there. Tiny hands and feet drummed against her palms. With a sigh she eased her hands away and rolled onto her belly. What was she doing? It might be Jongwhan's child. A voice inside her answered: *Or Obuto's*. She kneaded her aching eyes. If only this child had never been conceived. Better for it to be stillborn, and for her to die in childbirth.

She bit her lip. No! She didn't want to die. Her hands found her round belly again. What was wrong with her—how could she hate this innocent child? Poor tiny wee bairn.

A footfall startled her. She sat up, pulling the fur over her thin white dress.

"Megan?" Pongnim's calm voice washed over her.

She smiled up into the gentle square face, welcoming any interruption in the war raging inside her.

Pongnim settled on a cushion beside her. "My wife tells me you don't eat."

She grimaced and dropped her gaze. This argument again. "I eat enough." She pulled the fur away to reveal the shallow dome beneath her gown. "See?"

"Megan, be serious." Two grooves appeared between his wide-set eyebrows. "We are concerned for your health, and that of the child. You must eat!"

She bit her lip and shook her head. "I can't."

The gold eyes glittered, and his voice grew harsh. "Do you hate him so much you wish to destroy his only child, and with him the woman he loves?"

Her mouth dropped open for a moment. She pressed her lips together and shook her head again. "No." She swallowed. "I don't hate him." Her voice quivered and tears stung her eyelids.

So many times she'd longed to tell him the truth, that it might not be Jongwhan's child. But what if he didn't believe her? What if he thought she'd enticed Obuto? She took a deep breath. What if he told Jongwhan? She couldn't bear it.

She looked into the face of her friend, grown gentle once more. "All right, I will try to eat."

The genuine delight in his smile rewarded her. "I will tell my wife. She will be pleased." He stood and walked to the tent flap. "You rest now."

She lay back on the narrow pallet and threw one arm across her face. Her mouth quirked into a painful smile. Yes, more rest. That was just what she needed!

Color and noise swirled around him, but Jongwhan gave little notice to those around him in the throne room. He smoothed the front of his blue silk jacket and checked the knots at the side of the embroidered square emblem. He wore the two-crane symbol for the first time since the King elevated him to a higher status two months before.

It pleased him to see how well he filled out the new clothing. He looked around the hall at some of the nobles who'd survived Namhan with him. A few still bore hollow cheeks and dark circles under their eyes, but most had returned to their previous good health. He nodded at the chief members of the *Soron*, his father's party. He'd called upon each one, asking for their support of his father's return.

Many remembered the elder Yi, and those who stood beside Jongwhan in battle praised his courage and offered their influence in his behalf. He shifted his weight from one foot to the other. He'd done all he could to prepare for this day, and now he must wait.

The three days since he'd sent the memorial letter to the King had dragged by in an agony of uncertainty. At last, this morning, word had arrived commanding him to appear at noon. He glanced past the open shutters to the palace grounds outside.

His distance from the doorway made it impossible to see the sun's position in the sky. Instead he watched the shadow cast by a small tree. It had shortened until it lay in a black pool around the roots, and now its shade lengthened in the other direction. Noon had come and gone and still he waited.

With slow movements he slipped his hands under the lower edge of his jacket. He shifted his eyes to one side, then the other, to be sure no one watched him, then wiped sweat from his palms on the back of his black *paji*. He took a deep breath.

Smells from the royal kitchen reminded him he hadn't eaten since early morning. He swallowed the moisture that filled his mouth. When his stomach clenched in a tight knot, he decided food wouldn't be a good idea right then anyway.

He caught his lower lip between his teeth. What if the King rejected his pleas? He ran through the words of the letter, wondering if by accident he'd made some error in judgment or etiquette. After agonizing over the document for two months, he could call up every phrase from memory. He gave his head a tiny shake. No, the wording followed custom in every detail. He sighed and clasped his hands behind his back. It took every bit of control he owned not to pace back and forth, but he stood his ground. It wouldn't do to let others see his nervousness.

A dark thought crossed his mind. What if he hadn't been summoned in reponse to the letter? What if the King assigned him a new duty? His heart thudded. What if Injo asked him to fight again? He squared his shoulders and in silence reaffirmed his vow. Not even for his father would he ever kill another man.

"Yi Jongwhan!"

He jumped at the sound of his name.

"Yi Jongwhan!"

He turned and hurried toward the ancient scribe. He gave a hurried bow and panted out his name. Hooded brown eyes squinted up at him for a moment. "Well, proceed." The rusty voice snapped at him. "His Excellency will see you now."

Jongwhan bowed again and turned toward the audience chamber. He forced himself to a slow stride, though his heart pounded in his throat, making it difficult to breathe. If he didn't win a reinstatement for his father, he must spend more weary years as a member of the court and try again and again until he succeeded. He would never make a politician. He'd tried, but his mind didn't work like other men's. Deceit was as alien to him as suspicion.

No, he must not fail. He couldn't stand to wait any longer to get on with his life, to take up his paintbrushes again. A glowing image of Megan filled his mind. He sucked all the calm comfort from the vision he could before it faded.

He stood before his King and bowed.

"You may rise."

The strength in the rusty voice surprised him. He hadn't seen Injo since the great feast after the Manchus left. He glanced up through his lashes. Vigor moved in every line of the King's being. If not for his own discomfort, Jongwhan would have rejoiced in the King's renewed health.

"We are pleased you attend Us, Yi Jongwhan." A broad smile creased the narrow face and the gold eyes sparkled. With a wave of his hands the King dismissed all of his attendants.

Jongwhan stood alone in the audience chamber with King Injo.

"Please sit, son of my old friend."

With knees shaking from relief, Jongwhan lowered himself to a cushion facing the throne and waited. The greeting promised a favorable interview, but much could still go awry.

The King reached a bejeweled hand to one side and held up a roll of fine white rice paper. The letter he'd sent! So, King Injo had chosen to respond to his memorial.

The slender monarch unrolled the paper and scanned the writing.

Jongwhan waited, his pulse racing.

Injo lowered the scroll, letting it curl up again in his hand. His gold eyes studied Jongwhan.

He held his position under the stern gaze, clenching his fists to keep from squirming on the cushion.

The old man cleared his throat. "Some years ago, grave charges were brought against your house. Certain proof was offered of your father's treachery to the crown."

Jongwhan's bright hopes collapsed. It was over. His father had been proven a traitor. He could almost hear Kim On Yun's laughter from the grave. Even in death he'd triumphed over the house of Yi.

Injo placed his hands on his knees and leaned forward. "The one who bore witness against Yi Dong Chul was dear to Us and above reproach." The hooded eyes closed. "It was a great sorrow to discover his cowardice and send him to his death." The rusty voice quavered for a moment, its strength lost.

Jongwhan teetered between relief and despair. He still couldn't be sure in which direction the sovereign headed.

The gold eyes opened. Misery cleared from their depths, and a smile touched the thin lips. "We are not fond of admitting Our errors, or having them pointed out by Our son's playmates."

Jongwhan gripped his bent knees.

A low chuckle echoed through the room. "You need not fear, Our Nephew. We are not displeased with you."

Tension drained from him, to be replaced by quiet joy. His long quest had ended.

Injo lifted the rolled paper from his lap and returned it to the lacquered tray at his side. "We thank you for teaching

Us the true meaning of loyalty. We sent word this morning to your honorable father, asking him to return to Us without delay."

Jongwhan bowed, then swallowed. Words failed him. At last he croaked out his gratitude.

The King laughed and held up his hand. "Please, no long speeches." The slender hands steepled. Injo cocked his head. "And now, how about a game of chess?"

50

Megan sneezed, then frowned at her reflection in the copper mirror. The wide stripe of red-orange on either side of her center part made her think of a skunk, or a fox marked in reverse. Jade-green eyes stared back at her, blue half-moons smudged beneath them. Her narrow cheeks had swelled to puffy roundness. Some women blossomed in pregnancy. She let the metal circle drop to her lap. She wasn't one of them, even if her hair hadn't been two colors.

"Are you ready?" Pongnim's wife bent over her, an evil-smelling pot in her hand. Black liquid, the texture of tar, swirled inside.

For a moment the odor reminded her of pitch and the black swirling waters of the shipwreck. She hadn't thought of that for months. She wrinkled her nose. "It smells different. What's in it?"

The princess smiled. "It is a secret—my mother's recipe."

Megan frowned. "What if it doesn't work?"

The delicate Korean put one hand on her hip. "It always worked in my mother's kitchen." She smoothed her own dark tresses. "We all had black hair, but it gave our braids an extra sheen."

Megan dipped a forefinger in the black goo and rubbed

a drop around the ball of her thumb. It darkened the white skin of her fingers to a reddish brown.

Pongnim's wife dipped a brush into the pot and held it dripping in the air. "Besides, if it doesn't work, you're no worse off."

She shrugged. "All right." She closed her eyes. If it didn't work she'd have no choice but to hide her odd coloring from prying eyes beneath a hateful green merchant's-wife coat.

Megan smiled as the princess daubed the hair dye onto her head. The woman's kindness touched her. She didn't inspire the same fierce loyalty as Megan would always hold for Soonhee, or the protectiveness she'd always felt toward Youngsook. For a moment loneliness for her two friends overwhelmed her. She sighed. But Pongnim's wife had proved to be a true friend in spite of the circumstances that had brought them together and kept them trapped in each other's company.

Some of the cold liquid trickled down the back of Megan's hair and onto her neck. She shuddered at the sudden chill.

"Does it tickle?" The princess started to giggle, then choked. Megan's eyes flew open.

Pilsu stood in the doorway of the yurt, a sneer lighting her fine features. "So, it *was* you I saw wallowing about like a sow ready to litter."

Megan clenched her teeth at the grating sound of the *kisaeng's* voice. Pilsu would make her life miserable from now on. All this suffering was for nothing.

The dancer swept into the room and bent to sniff the pot of dye in the princess's hand. "Whew!" The delicate nose wrinkled. "What a stench. Trying to make yourself beautiful? Or just hiding from your brat's father?" Her high laugh raised the hair on Megan's neck.

"How dare you!" Pongnim's wife pulled herself to her full height. Red spots appeared in her cheeks and her brown eyes flashed. Megan had never seen this side of her friend. This regal and commanding girl would make a fine queen someday. The princess brought her arm up and pointed toward the doorway. "Get out of my quarters!"

Pilsu frowned, then shrugged. "Your quarters? Only at my husband's orders." She turned to survey the hide tent.

Megan knew Pongnim's wife had gathered the bright silk cushions, pottery, and other items, buying them outright or trading her own clothes to give her family what comforts she could provide.

Pilsu turned back to the princess, one eyebrow lifted and a smile curving her sensuous lips. "Very nice, but of course not as nice as mine."

Anger swept through Megan. How dare this witch attack a woman of the royal household? She took a deep breath. "'Husband' is it?" She poured months of frustration and anger into her words. "'Pimp' is more like it from what I hear!"

The *kisaeng* whirled to face her. Thin nostrils flared. Megan knew the woman would gladly kill her if she had a weapon at hand.

The dancer's hand clamped her shoulder. The once beautiful face hovered inches away from Megan's, rage distorting it into a snarling mask. "And what of you, foreign bitch? Is this Jongwhan's whelp you carry, or Pongnim's?"

The cloying musk of the woman's perfume turned Megan's stomach. "Or maybe you fancied some greasy foot soldier of the Emperor's guard!" She pressed closer still, her breath hot against Megan's cheeks. "Well, answer me, freak! Who sired the bastard you carry?"

Black and red spots blinded her for a moment. She stared up into Pilsu's flashing eyes. ENEMY! The word echoed through her. Her mouth filled with warm saliva, and she opened her lips and spat.

Pilsu reared back, spittle dripping from her face. She brought up her arm to strike, but a square hand closed around her delicate wrist.

Pongnim jerked the dancer away. His lips smiled, but murder filled his eyes and his fingers dup deep into Pilsu's wrist. She squirmed in his grasp, the color draining from her smooth cheeks. His calm voice mocked her. "So kind of you to pay a call on my family."

He turned and nodded to Megan and his wife. "But as you can see, they are fatigued and wish to retire."

Pilsu's breath rattled in her throat. She clawed at his fingers, but he only dug them deeper into her soft flesh.

"Let me escort you to the general's tent." He laughed, a soft sound that made Megan's flesh crawl. "After all, these Manchus are but barbarians, and I would hate for you to come to any harm at their hands."

Pongnim moved to stand between Pilsu and Megan, then dropped the woman's wrist. She clamped her other hand around the bruised limb and sucked in a hissing breath. Over Pongnim's shoulder she glared at Megan. The delicate lips opened, but fear must have overcome her desire to speak. She whirled and ran toward the door, with Pongnim close at her heels.

Megan's hands went to her belly. Poor fatherless babe. And now they must face Pilsu's anger—the dancer would never let the day's indignities rest unavenged.

Tears rolled down her face, staining the bright silk stretched over her bulging middle. A gentle touch caressed her hair, then lit on her shoulder. Megan tipped her head and rested her hot cheek against the princess's cool hand.

Happiness buoyed Jongwhan's steps as he walked through the city streets. Here and there, new houses arose like phoenixes from the rubble and ashes of the past.

Fresh mud-and-stone walls surmounted the clay flues of intact *ondol* floors, and bundles of bright straw rose through the morning air, hoisted on long ropes to thatch raw-timbered rooftrees. The cries of the laborers competed with the babble of the shopkeepers lining the gutters with their temporary plank-floored tents. Everywhere people bustled about the business of rebuilding their lives.

Jongwhan smiled, breathing in the odors of city life. Dust and wet-clay smells blended with the perfume of blossoming trees and the hint of waste from the open sewers. Decay gave way to new growth. Today he would begin to rebuild his life as well.

He paused at a flower-vendor's shop to buy a spray of jasmine, Megan's favorite flowers. Their sweet fragrance brought images of white limbs and copper hair dancing through his mind. He redoubled his pace.

At last he'd discharged his duty to his family. His father would arrive in a few weeks with the entire household. The King had even restored his father's house, the walled mansion of his youth. His steps slowed. In addition to his parents and his brother, his wife would also return. Munja's narrow, unsmiling face pushed its way into his mind. He clenched his teeth. He must decide what to do about his wife—later!

Now he hurried to the *kisaeng* house. He'd waited long enough to give Megan time to return from the safety of the southern provinces. Perhaps fate would smile on him and she'd already arrived. If not, he would at least learn when Insung expected her, so he could be at hand to welcome her home.

He turned into the broad avenue leading to the South Gate and stopped. *Namdaemun* stood unscathed, its roof tiles gleaming, its wooden gates open wide. Above, the silent bulk of South Mountain rose, its sides covered in spring greenery. Most of the buildings inside the walls stood erect, but here and there piles of blackened timbers and rubble interrupted the row of homes lining the way. Some citizens had resisted the invaders, and they'd paid a high price. Still, many buildings survived. The street smiled at him in gap-toothed welcome.

He strode forward and soon found himself in sight of the *kisaeng* house. Next to it, the remains of Grandfather Chang's home glistened black in the noonday sun. Only the cherry tree still stood, it pink-lined green buds showing its readiness for another spring. Soon Koreans would again celebrate *Tano* day. He offered a silent prayer to his ancestors that the old man had survived and would celebrate with him.

A moment of doubt beat black wings behind his eyes. What would he find within the *kisaeng* house gates? He forced his leaden feet to cross the threshold of the open portal. Smoke spiraled up from the chimneys. A weight lifted from him. Someone had returned.

He climbed the steps and coughed at the paper-and-lath door. A sleepy-faced serving girl peeked out and bobbed her head. Her eyes widened at the insignia on his chest and a smile transformed the homely features. *"Nye?"*

"I wish to see—to see Madame Insung. Tell her Yi Jongwhan greets her." He smiled in spite of his pounding heart.

The girl stared up at him a moment more, then blushed and nodded. The door swung wide and she gestured him inside. "Please, Noble Sir, follow me. I know my mistress will see you." She scurried off down the dim hallway.

Jongwhan trailed after her, breathing in the balmy warmth and the familiar sights and smells of the *kisaeng* house. Peace crept through him. Here he had met and loved his exotic beauty. Any moment now he might hold her in his arms again. He peered through the gloom, hoping to catch sight of her milky skin, her fiery hair. His arms ached for her, his eyes hungered for the sight of her green eyes laughing up at him.

The girl stopped before a door and coughed. The paper-and-wood shutters swung inward. Madame Insung stared up at him. The color drained from her smooth cheeks and her mouth set in a grim line. "So, you are come." She stepped back and motioned him inside, then turned to dismiss the gawking servant.

Jongwhan bowed and seated himself on a bright silk cushion. Doubts circled in his mind. He waited.

Insung settled herself on a cushion and turned soft brown eyes on him.

He squirmed under her gaze, then willed himself to calm. His hopes sank after her brusque greeting.

At last the head *kisaeng* spoke. "Gentle Sir, to what do I owe the great honor of this visit?"

He sat back, stung by her formality. What had he done to engender such distance? He bit his lip. "I come to ask after your health and those of your friends and neighbors." Something in her manner kept him from asking about Megan directly.

The beautiful mouth smiled, but the dark eyes remained cold. "As you may see for yourself, I fare well." A cloud passed over her face. "As for friends and neighbors, some do well, others poorly. Of whom do we speak?"

He swallowed, his throat suddenly dry. Again he

stopped himself from asking what he really wanted to know. "The old fortune-teller and his grandson—how are they?"

The beautiful lips turned downward and a sigh escaped them. "Both dead at the Manchus' hands." Her husky voice cracked.

Tears prickled beneath his eyelids. A hollowness grew within him, a dark void of pain and fear. He leaned forward, unable to withhold the question any longer. "And Megan?"

The dark eyes narrowed. "Alive, the last I knew."

His panic eased. Words bubbled from his mouth. "How is she? Where is she? When will she return?"

Insung pursed her mouth. "I cannot say."

Anger welled up in him. He clenched his fists and fought to control his voice. "What do you mean, woman? I must know!"

The *kisaeng* looked down at her lap. With both hands she smoothed the silken fabric of her skirt before she lifted her eyes to his. "It is her wish. She made me vow to tell you no more than this."

He recoiled as if he'd been struck. Why? Why would Megan do such a thing? Perhaps the woman lied. He studied the serene beauty of the *kisaeng*'s face. Truth glowed from her eyes and lips. It must be so, but why? Why, why, why!

He took a ragged breath. "At least do me this kindness, I beseech you. When Megan returns, will you send me word?"

Madame Insung passed a slender hand across her eyes and sighed. "She did not forbid it." The woman nodded. "I will."

51

"You have served His Imperial Majesty well, General Kong." Yongolda smiled at the Manchu officer.

Megan leaned on one stiff arm, trying to find a comfortable position. Sitting on the floor made pregnancy even more miserable than otherwise. She gave up and gritted her teeth, then took a deep breath and concentrated on following the conversation between the men.

She and Pongnim had been ordered to welcome the Tartar general, newly arrived from Korea. Besides the two Manchus, only Pilsu joined them. The dark beauty knelt beside Yongolda, occasionally reaching out to caress him. Each time the woman touched the turncoat Korean, her venomous eyes turned toward Pongnim.

Megan hadn't understood all of General Kong's report—something about cleaning out a nest of Ming rebels on Kado Island. But judging from Pongnim's white face, it meant more disgrace for his father and himself. She sighed and stopped listening, watching instead the interactions of the dancer and the two generals.

She grimaced as Pilsu placed a shapely hand on Yongolda's thigh. Irritation crossed the man's face. He covered the slender fingers with one hand and squeezed for a moment. A brief look of pain spasmed across Pilsu's lovely features. Yongolda frowned down at the *kisaeng* and brushed the offending hand away with the same indifference of one swatting a fly.

Megan winced. In spite of what she'd suffered at the woman's hands, watching Yongolda inflict his evil temper on his consort brought Megan nothing but sorrow.

The dancer bit her lip and rubbed at the reddened fingers with her other hand. She scowled up at the Manchu for a moment, then dropped her gaze to the floor.

General Kong watched the delicate dancer, his face alight with interest. When she tossed her head back and glanced around the room, he nodded and smiled, licking his already wet lips.

Megan shuddered at the obvious lust on the Manchu's face. Thank God she'd grown fat and ugly. She leaned closer to Pongnim, grateful for his protection. If their captors ever learned the truth, that she and Pongnim were friends instead of lovers—she pushed the thought from her mind.

Pilsu's eyes widened at the blatant desire on Kong's face. The dancer turned away, horror written across her delicate features. She laid her head on Yongolda's knee. The general frowned down at the woman, then jerked his knee away.

Pilsu threw both hands out to catch herself. Anger flashed in the dark eyes. The delicate lips twisted as she turned to face her lord, but something in the man's bland face kept her silent. She drew her arms about her knees and sat still, her gaze fixed on the rich rug beneath her feet.

Yongolda cleared his throat. "General, it has come to my attention that you have no woman to share your yurt." Pilsu stiffened. Megan drew a deep breath, sickened by what she knew would come next.

The smile on Kong's face broadened. "I regret to admit you have heard the truth."

Contempt twisted Yongolda's lips. "I find I have one I no longer desire." The color drained from Pilsu's cheeks. "Allow me to make a gift of her to you." The dancer's mouth flew open. She looked from one man to the other. She moaned, then bit her lips again.

Pity welled up in Megan. Poor Pilsu!

Lines crinkled at the corners of Kong's eyes. "With pleasure." His laugh boomed through the huge tent.

Yongolda held up one hand. "See to it you discipline her well." The general nodded at Pongnim. "She has caused much trouble to our royal guest and his household."

Megan turned to Pongnim, but he stared straight ahead, his face a mask of calm. She hadn't known he had complained to Yongolda.

General Kong threw his head back and laughed again,

a cruel, harsh bark. "Again, with pleasure." He caressed the riding crop in his hand.

Yongolda turned to Pilsu. In a voice reserved for servants he ordered her from the room. "And take all your clothing to your new master's tent." A faint light of hope dawned in Pilsu's eyes. "But leave all the jewelry and silks. You can make do with plainer surroundings, and I may wish to give them to my new consort." He smiled at Pongnim. "Your cousin, I believe, the Emperor's former wife."

Only the whitening of his knuckles betrayed Pongnim's anger. He bobbed his head and pressed his lips together.

Yongolda raised an eyebrow, then pointed a finger at Pilsu. "You, worthless baggage. Leave, and thank your gods I let you live." His voice cracked like a whip. "Trouble me no more!"

The dancer swayed to her feet and ran toward the door. She tripped and caught herself at Megan's feet. Her voice hissed like a angry cat. "Don't bother pitying me! Look to yourself, foreign bitch!" Then she was up again and gone.

Megan swallowed, her mouth suddenly dry, from fear or pity—she hardly knew which!

General Kong turned from the empty doorway to his countryman. "Many thanks, my brother!" A broad grin creased his leathery face. "I shall enjoy taming that one. Perhaps you will excuse me in a few moments, but one more item I must report."

Yongolda nodded for the man to continue.

"I offered two hundred fifty Mandarin captives to the Korean generals who performed well at Kado." He frowned and toyed with his dark mustache. "They asked for the release of a like number of their countrymen instead." He bowed toward Yongolda. "I hope I performed your will when I granted my consent."

The other general's face twitched once, then he smiled. "Well done again!" His expressionless face turned again toward the Korean prince. "But we must not forget our honored guests."

Megan's heart pounded. Would he send Pongnim home? No, she forced herself not to hope.

Yongolda steepled his hands and tilted his head. "You may choose one of your household to return home. Which shall it be?"

Pongnim faced Megan, a gentle light glowing in his gold eyes.

Whom would he choose? One of the princesses, or a favored servant?

His hand came up. Blood rushed in her ears as he pointed toward her. "I choose this woman, my consort, to return to Seoul."

The sound of children playing in the street brought him awake. Sunlight stabbed his eyes. Throwing his arm over his face, Jongwhan rolled away from the door. A dozen brass gongs resounded in his head whenever he moved it, and his tongue felt as if he'd swallowed his padded socks.

Never again would he drink so much *makkŏlli*! With great care he opened his eyes a slit and surveyed the room. He barely remembered the innkeeper ushering him there after the great bell sounded at midnight. He'd stumbled to the *yo* and fallen into a dreamless sleep at once.

Now in the daylight the room appeared to be clean but plain. He'd never spent the night in a *yokwhan* before. Aristocrats generally stayed with others of the *yangban* class when away from home overnight. He rolled onto his back. At least he didn't itch from lice bites, though he'd heard vermin awaited travelers in inns of this type. He closed his eyes again. Travelers. Was Megan traveling back to Seoul right now?

A groan escaped his lips when he sat up. His head spun and his stomach heaved. How could something as pleasant as drinking rice wine have such dire consequences? He rubbed his open palms across his face. But then, how could loving Megan bring such heartache?

He crawled to the latticed door and pulled it open. Silence filled the inner courtyard of the *yokwhan*. By the foreshortened shadows cast by the trees, Jongwhan guessed the sun had climbed to midmorning. Most of the inn's customers had already left on their journeys.

He pushed the twin doors shut again and looked for a

place to relieve himself. As he crawled to the chamber pot and fumbled with the strings of his *paji*, he cursed Insung under his breath. If she'd told him more about Megan, he'd have gone about his business instead of winding up hung over in a flea-bitten inn.

With his bladder empty he stood and splashed water from a washbasin onto the tender skin of his face. His stomach heaved, but nothing came up. He wondered if vomiting could make him feel any worse. He rinsed cool water around his mouth and spat. Although stale, the water looked clear and seemed a vast improvement over the foulness that had covered his tongue.

Memories of the night before nagged at him, clouded by drink. He saw himself bent over, remembered spewing rice wine from his mouth and nose. He glanced in the dark corners of the small chamber. Must have been before they dragged him here. That might explain why, as well.

He stared at his reflection in the round copper mirror hanging above the washbowl. His face reminded him of a Buddhist painting of sufferers in hell. He sighed. No help for it—he couldn't stay here. He winced at the thought of going outside, but set his jaw and gathered his possessions.

Jongwhan picked up the stiff black *kat* from the table and settled it on his head. With trembling fingers he knotted the strings under his chin. He knelt and hefted the eared purse before sliding its string over his belt. Although Korean innkeepers earned a reputation for honesty, some might lighten a guest's purse on occasion. He loosened the drawstring and dumped the contents onto his cupped palm.

Most of the silver pieces of *cash* remained, except for a small amount probably spent on wine. But in among the coins a small square of folded rice paper nestled. A dark foreboding filled him as he strove to remember its importance. A servant had delivered it last night, after he'd sat drinking alone for hours.

He fished the paper out of the mess of coins and set it aside while he refilled the purse and slung it on his belt. He took a deep breath and leaned back against a threadbare *chaddae* to unfold the small white square. His heart raced at what he read. The note, in his father's crisp hand, informed him of the household's expected arrival this same morning and ordered him to await them at the family's mansion.

He dropped the slip of paper and leaped to his feet. Ignoring the explosions in his head, he hurried through the door and out of the inn without even paying the innkeeper's fee.

After sending a street urchin to fetch a sedan chair, he stood gritting his teeth at the noise and light of the street. He wiped his forehead on a long sleeve. Already the sun burned hot and the air hung damp and heavy. He'd acted like a crazy man the night before, and now he'd pay for his folly.

Four runners lumbered up and set the open chair at his feet. They wore black bands around their heads and sweat glistened on their faces. Their threadbare white clothes and worn straw sandals matched the peeling lacquer of the carrying poles. He shrugged. In this neighborhood, only good fortune had brought him a chair at all.

He clambered into the seat and ordered the runners to Myongdong, near the palace. Jingling the coins in his purse, he offered a rich fee if they ran all the way. Without a word the men bent and heaved the wooden poles to their shoulders. Jongwhan's stomach churned and he closed his eyes. One of the men called out a cadence as they moved forward and picked up their pace.

The streets passed in a blur of white-clothed men in black hats hurrying about their business. Naked children played in gutters and shopkeepers hawked their wares from roadside stands.

At last the chair lurched around a corner and into a street of wealthy homes. Bleak, ill-kempt walls faced the roadway, but red-tiled roofs rose behind, giving evidence of riches and royal favor.

At his father's gate Jongwhan called the runners to a halt and loosened his purse strings. He retrieved a string of pierced silver coins, run through with a copper wire. With a glance at the sweating men in their ragged attire, he tossed the entire string to the spokesman. He'd paid too much, but at least he didn't have to count the noisy things.

The man's eyes glowed as he bowed his thanks. "Shall we await your convenience, Sir?"

Jongwhan started to shake his head but thought better of it and motioned the runners away. The peasants broke into an excited babble as they trotted away beneath the empty chair.

He turned toward the gate and groaned. The thick plank door stood open, its iron fittings glinting in the sunlight. His parents had already arrived, and by the look of the courtyard, some time before. Inside, a servant unloaded a packhorse. The man turned and grinned, then bobbed his head as Jongwhan stepped across the threshold.

"Park, is that you?"

His boyhood friend, the son of the old gatekeeper, nodded and strode around Jongwhan, eyeing his apparel. "You, My Friend, have grown tall. War and court life agrees with you."

Jongwhan grimaced. "I'd rather be at the estate, away from the intrigue and all these people." He closed his eyes for a moment. "Sometimes I feel them pressing around me, stealing the air from my lungs."

Park cocked his head, then nodded.

A warm glow started in Jongwhan's chest, dispelling the hangover a little. Park had always shown more depth than most servants. They'd managed to talk a great deal about life, in between their more roguish exploits. "And you—what brings you to the city?"

"Your father." His friend's face sobered. "And it might be wise for you to seek out that gentleman now and question your servant later." A hint of a smile returned. "You're late." He made a show of sniffing the air. "And the reek of a wineshop hangs about you." Park bowed again and turned toward the horse, muffling a chuckle against the animal's side.

Jongwhan sighed and hurried toward his father's quarters, the rooms at the front of the house kept for entertaining male visitors. He mounted the steps and tugged the black suede boots from his feet, then gave a polite cough.

"Enter!" Although the sound of his father's voice

gladdened him after so long a time, it also sent a ripple of fear through his bowels. Or maybe that misery came from the night before.

He took a deep breath and opened the door. No heat rose from the *ondol* floor. As eldest son, it was his duty to see the house prepared for his parents' arrival. He should have ordered the fires lit and the rooms aired. He cringed at the dust outlining the pattern of cranes woven in the bamboo mat. With a sinking in his middle, Jongwhan knelt and placed his forehead at his father's feet.

"My Son, you disappoint me."

Jongwhan sat back on his heels. The years of exile had etched themselves in his father's face. Smoke from a long-stemmed pipe circled the proud head, matching the sprinkling of gray in the black topknot. The reality of his father's mortality had never hit Jongwhan before. The man before him had grown old!

Then a sudden smile creased the corners of the thin mouth, returning a glow of youth to the narrow features. "But because of your success in reinstating the family's honor, I will forgive you."

Jongwhan tried to speak, but his father held up a hand. "No, I don't want any explanation. We will speak no more about it." Tears sparkled in the gray eyes, twins to his own. "Thank you."

Words failed him. He'd never witnessed a display of emotion from this always-strict parent. Not knowing what else to do, he nodded and bowed again.

His father cleared his throat. The old stern tone returned. "Your mother awaits you in the inner court. You are excused."

Jongwhan drew himself up and trudged down the hallway, phantoms of childhood punishments trailing his passage. He coughed in front of the intricate latticework doors. They sprang open and his mother's round face peered out. "You're late!" She stepped aside and gestured him within. As he passed her, she reached out a still-beautiful hand and cuffed his ear.

He gritted his teeth and forced down the excuses trying to bubble from his lips. Sinking onto a cushion, he marveled again how his parents could make him feel like a child instead of a grown man. What would his mother think if she knew he'd killed not one man in the war but many? He hoped she'd never find out.

His mother's voice rang through his aching head. "So, where were you this morning? Never mind—I don't want to know." She sat across the room and scowled up at him. "You smell of rice wine!"

He flushed with anger. In the Confucian world a man must honor his parents, but a woman must also show respect for a man.

The tiny woman who had borne him sat back against a *chaddae*, smoothing her gown, then folding her hands in her lap. He stared at her until she dropped her gaze. Her lower lip protruded.

He laughed, warmed in spite of himself at her little girl wiles. "Mama, what is it you're really upset about?"

The dark eyes came up and the round face moved closer. "Your wife." A delicate hand touched his knee. "She reads all the time, books about Buddha, books of old poems." The generous mouth puckered. "No wonder she doesn't conceive! Of all the nonsense!"

Jongwhan frowned. He'd had this conversation with his parents many times in the last seven or eight years. He braced himself for a string of complaints.

His mother leaned back. Her voice softened almost to a whisper. "You know what you must do. Divorce her!"

He clenched his fists, striving to keep his voice calm. "Mama, please don't ask me to do that." He took a deep breath. "It's not all her fault."

The tiny woman shook a finger in his face. "It is the vengeance of the gods for a hidden sin. She deserves to suffer for her evil."

He reached out and patted the soft arm. "No earth can yield crops if seeds are not planted."

His mother's eyes widened. She opened her mouth, then snapped it closed.

He rubbed his aching eyes. "You see, Mama, there is no honor in divorcing a woman simply because I don't like her."

His mother's eyes traveled past him to the door.

He turned, following her gaze. "Munja!" His wife's pinched face radiated anger for a moment, then the doors swung shut. The clap of lath and paper against the doorframe echoed in his head like thunder. Light footfalls echoed away down the hall. He lowered his heavy head into his hands and sighed. "Oh, Munja!"

52

Moon of Dry Wind

Dust devils picked up bits of yellow grass as they danced over the dry steppes. Megan turned from the open tent flap to add another cake of dried horsedung to the fire, sneezing at the harsh smoke spiraling up through the smokehole in the rawhide roof. She straightened, arching her spine and rubbing at the weary muscles in the small of her back. Beneath her hand, ropes of sinew knotted, balancing the new weight of her belly.

She picked up a paper-wrapped bundle from a corner of the floor. Somehow Pongnim's wife had procured dried meat and fruit for the journey. The princess touched Megan on the arm, then glanced around the tent.

Pongnim had been ordered to Yongolda's yurt and the two tiny girls played on the earthen floor in a shaft of sunlight. The princess took Megan's wrist and pressed a cold metal object into her hand. A small, ornate silver knife glittered on her palm. The delicate mouth came close to her ear. "In case you are attacked—to preserve your honor."

Megan unsheathed the finger-length dagger. "Not much of a weapon to fight off bandits."

The princess shook her head. "Not to fight them. To end your life before they soil your reputation."

Megan nodded. If she'd had this when Obuto raped

her—she shuddered. "*Kamsa hamnida*. Many thanks." She slid the ornamental knotted cord over the tie of her rough white *chima*, letting the weapon dangle as she'd seen other women wear similar knives. Now she understood their more-than-decorative purpose.

As she stepped into the bright sunlight to join the other captives, she fingered the jeweled knife sheath and wondered again at the lack of pockets in Korean clothing. She shrugged. No buttons or hooks, either, but they managed.

The sun warmed her shoulders through the rough weave of her white jacket. She'd put off bright silks for peasant white again. She sighed as the princess tied the hated green *changok* over her hair. The empty sleeves of the coat dangled on either side of her head like donkey ears. She grimaced. Better ugly and poor and unmolested than attacked by roving bands of thieves.

The two little princesses came at their mother's call, the baby toddling after her older sister. Megan bent to hug the fragile bodies and kiss the silky cheeks. They'd grown so much since Kanghwa. The baby reached up and batted a tiny paw against Megan's rounded belly. She smiled—so had she!

She turned to Pongnim's wife, blinking back tears. She stood for a moment, longing to embrace this dear friend but uncertain of the custom. Finally she reached out a hand to touch the princess's shoulder. "Good-bye, My Sister."

Pongnim's wife smiled and gave a slight bow. "May fortune attend your journey." Wiping at her large brown eyes, the princess turned away and hurried her daughters into the tent.

Megan moved into the stream of prisoners wending their way to the southern edge of the Manchu city. After many twists and curves of the dusty road, she turned at the sound of her name.

Pongnim strode toward her, his forehead furrowed and the corners of his mouth turned down. With him he half-dragged a sullen Korean man. "You shall have to walk. These barbarians refused to let me send a sedan chair." He gave her cheek a gentle tap with a square forefinger and shook his head. "I'm sorry."

She smiled up at him. "Don't worry. It'll do me good. I'm growing much too fat anyway."

The prince blushed and cleared his throat.

Megan giggled, then grew serious as Pongnim's frown returned.

"The Manchus will escort you as far as the Yalu River. Once across, you will be in Korea, but stay with the others and watch out for bandits." He pulled the unhappy peasant forward. "I've promised this fellow money for protecting you, but don't pay him until you reach Seoul." Pongnim turned his blackest look on the fellow. "I don't trust him!"

The man stammered out a defense, but Pongnim silenced him with a look, then took a folded piece of parchment from the eared purse hanging on his belt. "When you return to Seoul, if you need anything, take this to my father."

Megan slipped the paper-thin sheepskin inside her bodice and touched the square hand. She smiled. "I'll manage. Don't worry." If only she believed her own words. She pushed down her fear and sadness at leaving. Pongnim had given her the gift of freedom and she couldn't disappoint him. "Good-bye, my dear friend."

The prince nodded again, then hurried away.

With a sigh Megan rejoined the ragged procession. Manchu children flocked to the roadside, staring and laughing at the white-coated Koreans. Huge mastiff dogs threaded their way through the crowd, barking and growling. To Megan they seemed as large as the small Korean ponies. The travelers leaped to one side as the curs passed, avoiding the long iron spikes on the dogs' leather collars.

Behind the crowds of children, Manchu women stopped their tasks and peered from tent flaps. With a start Megan recognized one of the women as Pilsu. She hadn't seen the Korean beauty since the day Yongolda had given his mistress to General Kong. The woman's long black hair hung in a disheveled mass and a red welt striped one cheek. Hatred distorted the beautiful features into an ugly mask. At a sound from inside the yurt, the *kisaeng* jumped and dropped the rawhide tent flap.

Pity touched Megan for a moment before a grim smile curved her lips. It seemed Pilsu had finally met her match.

Megan glanced behind her at the guardian Pongnim had provided. From the dirt under his long fingernails to the arrogant look on his pointed face, the man's appearance shouted rogue. With a sigh she turned her face toward the south and Seoul. She knew her life would change again when she arrived, either for the better or the worse. But first she had to get there.

Jongwhan gritted his teeth and pressed his face into the *pyogae,* hiding his eyes against the hard bolster with its scent of clean cotton and dried rice husks. The sound of Munja's quiet sobs provided a fitting background to his own shame. Never before had he been unable to perform in bed with any woman, least of all his own wife.

He calmed himself by holding onto that small comfort. It had never happened before, would never happen again. Still, a small doubt lingered.

He'd waited many moons without touching a woman, all through the war dreaming of Megan's earthy enthusiasm. When Munja blew out the lantern, he'd felt himself harden. But instead of Megan's soft, warm, yielding flesh, he touched his wife's cool skin, her body tense and still. His ardor had died, and he rolled away, disgusted as much by his own reactions as her lack of warmth.

He roused himself and reached out for the sobbing woman beside him. "Hush, *Yobo.* You will wake my parents."

The sobs stopped, but she drew away again. The sounds of flint striking metal filled the darkness. The hot scent of friction tingled in his nostrils, then orange sparks leaped into flame. Munja dropped the red-and-blue-silk shade back into place over the lantern and turned to glare at him. "As you say, Husband. Your parents have cause enough to hate me without disturbing their rest."

The bitterness in her voice shocked him. What must she have gone through the last three years while he saved the family honor? He had never thought of Munja as having feelings before. It surprised him almost as much as his failure to make love to her.

The plain, narrow face turned away. Tears muffled her voice, suddenly grown soft again. "Please, I beg you, just kill me. I am no good to you."

The horror of her words rocked him. "No!"

Her face came up, eyes wide with surprise.

He realized he'd shouted and lowered his voice. "Munja, this is not your fault. Do not blame yourself."

Her eyes widened more, then she shook her head. "I alone must take the blame, Husband. I have failed to please you and this is my punishment." A loud sigh escaped her lips.

He reached a hand toward her, but she flinched away from his touch. He frowned. "Wife, I do not wish to harm you. It is only that I—" How could he tell her about Megan?

"You want another!" White teeth bit into her narrow bottom lip. "And your parents urge you to divorce me." Sudden anger flashed through her dark eyes. "Why don't you do it and be done with me!"

"And what happens to you if I divorce you?" He kept his voice soft and gentle.

Shock registered again on her narrow features. Her mouth twisted and she strangled a sob. "I will return to my parents, if they will take me." Her hollow voice echoed in the stillness of the night. "I will live to a lonely old age, unless I take my own life." She fixed her eyes on him. "These things you know. Why do you ask me?"

He took a deep breath. Could he make her see? "And what happens to me if I divorce you?"

A frown creased her high forehead. "Your parents will choose a wife for you, a lady of quality." Her voice cracked. "One who can give you sons."

He nodded. "And I would have no choice."

A glint of hope shone in Munja's dark eyes. "You do want another, but she is not *yangban!*" Understanding dawned on the woman's intelligent face. She nodded once. "You wish to borrow other earth in which to plant your seed, but if you put me away from you, you must take another wife, not a mistress."

Jongwhan smiled in relief. "Yes."

A frown creased Munja's face. "But what of me?"

Jongwhan tried to imagine the hell of Munja's life with his mother and sister-in-law. Without him there to temper their sharp tongues—he loved his mother, but he'd no doubt her insults had tormented his quiet wife. And his sister-in-law! Even his father avoided that saucy baggage, and since her son's birth, she must have lorded it over Munja daily. No wonder divorce and suicide looked attractive to her.

He leaned forward and rested one hand on her knee. "What life would you desire for yourself?"

The woman's mouth flew open and she stared up at him. He realized he'd never asked her before what she wanted. Perhaps no one ever had. And a year before, he wouldn't have considered her wants and needs. As it was, if his family or friends knew he even thought about her feelings, they'd brand him a fool. He smiled. His love for Megan had changed him, perhaps more than the war.

In a convulsion of movement Munja knelt and placed her forehead on the bedding at his feet. She raised brimming eyes to his. "Kind Husband, I desire only two things." Her voice shook. "First, to be returned to your family's estate in the provinces." She clasped her hands. "I wish to read and study, to use my mind." Her mouth twisted. "Since my body is of little use." Bony fingers wiped at her wet cheeks. "Second, to be a loving aunt to your children when they are born."

Jongwhan placed his hands on either side of his wife's plain face, then bent and placed his lips against her thin mouth.

For the first time her lips softened and she kissed him in return.

He leaned back and smiled at her. "With pleasure I grant my wife's two requests."

Tears wet Munja's thin cheeks again.

He patted her narrow shoulder. "Wife, blow out the lantern."

She lifted the silken shade and plunged the room once more into warm darkness.

He rolled onto his back and closed his eyes, letting the

images of Megan lull him. A hand closed over his for a
moment and squeezed. Then he heard the woman beside
him turn over. In moments her breathing grew regular. He
let out a contented sigh. In eight years of marriage, this
night marked the first time he and his wife could count
themselves friends.

53

Moon of Heavy Heat

Megan turned onto her back and stared up into the
early morning gloom. Pearl-gray light filtered in through
the paper door, illuminating strings of dried garlic, onions,
and strips of some kind of green squash hanging from the
rafters. She breathed in the rich blend of odors and smiled.
The inn might be rough and ill-kempt, but it smelled of
Korea—a heavenly perfume compared to the animal smells
of Manchuria.

She pushed back the threadbare *ibul*. The warmth
radiating from the floor teetered between cozy and suffocating. As if the nausea and heavy belly didn't plague her
sufficiently, now she sweltered in temperatures others
found pleasant.

She stretched aching arms and legs. For more than a
month she'd walked southward. At first the rains turned the
dirt roads to a quagmire. Then overnight they dried to a
fine dust, blowing into eyes and nostrils. Every day she
walked from sunup to sundown. Some nights she'd slept in
barns or peasant cottages, other times in fields or groves of
trees, whatever Choi found for them. She grimaced. This
yokwhan represented luxury by comparison.

The child inside her stretched and rolled. She sighed.
Somehow she knew what it felt like to be possessed by a
demon. Her body no longer belonged to her but answered

to this small intruder. Fatigue swept through her. God, she was tired! Tired of this pregnancy, tired of this endless road, moving one foot in front of the other.

She'd gotten vague answers from everyone about how many more *li* to the capital, but the owner of the *yokwhan* had pursed his lips and said one hundred and twenty. She thought a *li* about a third of an English mile. Her mind whirled as she tried to figure how many more days she had to walk. Finally she gave up and closed her eyes, willing herself to sleep.

Instead, the pressure on her bladder turned to a dull ache. Damn! She rolled to one side and used both arms to lever her body up, then tiptoed to the chamber pot and relieved herself. Yawning, she cleaned herself with thin paper and made her way back to the soft *yo*.

She stopped at the edge of the thin mattress and frowned, sensing something out of place. A corner of the pallet stood up, as if someone had turned it back and not smoothed it down again.

Her heart thudded. She knelt and threw back the *yo*, but she knew what had happened before she saw it. Her purse, all that money, gone! Choi must have taken it. Some protector! If she ever saw him again—not much chance of that. He'd be long gone into the rocky hills nearby by now. Damn the rascal!

She felt inside her bodice, then sighed. Pongnim's message to his father still nestled between her breasts. She sat and ran her hands over the lower edge of her *chima*. At least he hadn't found the strings of *cash* Pongnim's wife had sewn into the hem. She picked the thread loose and retrieved one string, enough to pay for the room and some food. If she took great care and slept outside, she might have enough to last another week.

She offered up a silent prayer that the innkeeper knew his distances. If so, she'd arrive in Seoul in the next seven days. If not—well, she wouldn't think about that.

She flipped the thin mattress back onto the floor. The sun hadn't risen high enough for her to buy breakfast. She settled herself on the thin mattress and pulled the quilt up to her chin, her skin chilled by the morning air. She closed her eyes and willed all thoughts of the future from her mind.

White-coated men eddied around her, some moving past her through the gate, others coming toward her on the way out of the city. After several long moments she realized she stood before the North Gate of Seoul. Her sluggish thoughts quickened. Home!

She forced her feet to move, focusing all her energy on each step. One need whirled through her numbed brain— to find the *kisaeng* house. After thousands of steps, she raised her head. Everything looked alien. New buildings rose on all sides, shimmering in the afternoon heat.

An old man passed close beside her. She reached out a hand and tapped his arm. He whirled and glared at her, then his eyes widened and he took a step back.

She must look a sight. Her hands went to her belly. She was so tired. At least the baby had stopped moving the day before, or was it two days since? Fear stabbed at her. Should the child be still so long? No, he was all right—must be all right—just tired, as she was. Still, she wished she could ask someone. Insung—she'd know. She must find Insung!

Her eyes focused again on the white-clad gentleman. "South Gate?" Her voice cracked.

The man stroked his thin, straight beard and glanced around, then pointed to the left and hurried away.

She turned into the side street and forced herself to go on, losing her thoughts in the rhythm of the movement, her aching legs swinging forward on their own.

Hours passed, or maybe minutes. At last a shadow fell across her path. Her head came up and she blinked in the waning daylight. The South Gate stood before her. She took a deep breath and stumbled forward, past the pile of charred rubble where Grandfather Chang's house had stood, past his cherry tree, laden with ripe red fruit.

She leaned against the lintel of the gatehouse and took a deep breath. Smells of smoke mixed with the heavy perfume of rhododendrons in the courtyard. Home! The word echoed inside her head.

She trudged to the doorway and pulled her leaden feet up the three steps, then scratched at the door. She noticed her dirty, cracked fingernails, stained from digging in the mud for roots. Scratches covered the backs of both hands, and purple stains remained from the berries she'd picked. Past her belly, her bare feet peeked from beneath her muddy hem. Her mind reeled. What had she become?

The door opened and Insung appeared. The handsome face frowned up at her. "Yes?"

The rich voice brought tears to Megan's eyes. "Madame?"

The woman's mouth opened and her eyes widened. "Megan?"

She tried to answer, but the muscles in her throat refused to move. The stairway rose up toward her, then fell away. Finally she nodded.

Hands reached out toward her. She felt herself slumping forward as darkness crowded her vision. She knew she was fainting, but it didn't matter. Nothing mattered anymore. She was home!

Jongwhan sipped milky-white rice wine, rolling the smooth, sweet-sour liquid over his tongue. He set the black cup down on the sticky tabletop and frowned at his hands. He'd once thought them the best part of his body, when they imitated life instead of taking it. He turned the palms up and flexed the long, tapered fingers. He'd used them to paint, to show love—the slender hands curled into tight fists.

Where was she? Why hadn't she returned? Weeks passed, and hope fluttered in his chest less and less often. The tension drained from him, leaving a sick void in its place. He lifted the cup and sipped again. Maybe this time he would forget.

A cough demanded his attention. He followed white trousers up past a clean white jacket. The homely face of his boyhood friend smiled down at him.

"Park! Come, sit with me, have a drink!" He struck the table with his palm. "More wine!" His voice blended with the noise of the crowd. The serving man either didn't hear or chose not to hear. Jongwhan pushed himself to his knees, but a hand pressed him down again to his seat.

"Please, Master Jongwhan. I have an urgent message." Park handed him a folded square of rice paper.

Jongwhan lifted the message and sniffed. Lotus perfume tinged the air. Insung had written at last. He sighed. He'd hoped for Megan's own jasmine. With trembling fingers he unfolded the fine white paper. Three words stared up at him: "She has returned."

His heart pounded. All the fear and frustration of the last months melted away. He had to bite his lip to keep from screaming, laughing, and crying all at once.

He leaped to his feet and grabbed Park by both shoulders. The man's eyebrows shot up, but Jongwhan only laughed.

"*Kamsa hamnida*, thank you, thank you, My Friend!" Joy trembled in every part of him.

He bolted through the open door and motioned to a waiting palanquin. He climbed aboard and clutched the armrests as the city sped by. "Hurry! The sun is falling. The curfew bell will ring soon!" Swaying high above the crowds, he willed the runners to a faster pace. Images of copper hair and green eyes swam through his mind. The tinkling sound of laughter filled his ears. At last she had come back to him!

As the last rays of the setting sun sent orange arrows of light across the darkened streets, the palanquin lurched around a corner and stopped in front of the *kisaeng* house. Jongwhan clambered out and tossed two strings of copper coins at one of the men and dashed through the open gate.

He stopped in front of the steps and surveyed the courtyard, drinking in the perfume of the warm night air. He would remember this moment for the rest of his days.

A sudden chill crept up his spine. What of Insung's silence, the promise Megan had wrung from the mistress of the *kisaeng*? Where had she gone and why had she stayed away so many moons? He took a deep breath and pushed the clamoring question from his mind. She waited inside. Nothing else mattered. He slipped off his light summer shoes and coughed at the top of the stairs.

The wood-and-paper doors opened. A pretty young

girl smiled up at him, one he'd never seen before—a new *kisaeng* by her dress.

"I come to see Megan." His voice trembled.

Disappointment shadowed the girl's delicate features. "I am new—I don't know everyone."

He smiled. "She just returned from a journey."

The girl's eyes widened and her mouth twisted. "You wish to see that one?"

He frowned. What did she mean? Before he could ask, she shrugged her slender shoulders and turned away, beckoning for him to follow. She led him past a crowded chamber where a woman played a *kayagum* and sang a love song, then down a long hallway. She stopped two doors before the end and pointed her beautiful hand. "In here." Without another word she floated back toward the visitors' hall.

He stood for a moment studying the pattern of the latticework doors. A certainty grew in him. Behind these same doors he'd held Megan in his arms. And now, just beyond this thin barrier, she lay, waiting for him.

He took a deep breath and clasped his hands behind him to keep from bursting into the room. He coughed, then waited. Silence. He cleared his throat. Still no response. Finally he reached out a hand and scratched at the casement.

"*Yobosayo*—come in." The faint voice startled him. Could this be the robust woman he'd known? He pressed shaking hands against the doors and they swung inward.

One lantern dimly lit the figure of a woman lying on a *yo* in the center of the floor. He took a step inside, then stopped in confusion at the sight of the face resting against the *pyogae*. Green eyes looked up at him from a puffy, mottled face. Strings of hair hung limp and greasy on either side, from the crown to her cheekbones a dull copper color, but below that black.

His heart rose in his throat. He took another step. "Megan?"

Something flashed through those green eyes—anger, or madness? "So, you come at last." Bitterness and fatigue couldn't disguise that voice.

He knelt beside the pallet and took her hand. "My Love, you are ill."

A ghost of a smile flitted over cracked lips. "No, only tired." She withdrew her hand and rolled away, then pushed herself upright. With heavy steps she turned to face him.

Her belly loomed in front of his face. Fierce joy shot through him. It all made sense—her strange appearance, Insung's silence, the long weeks of waiting. He smiled and reached out a hand. "You carry my son!"

The strange light flickered across her jade-green eyes again. "Perhaps." Her voice sounded hollow.

The chill crept up his spine again. "Or daughter—I do not mind."

The odd-colored hair brushed back and forth against her swollen breasts as she shook her head. "No, I mean perhaps it is yours."

He sat for a moment, paralyzed, then leaped to his feet. A dark and bitter rage, one forged of love and pain, propelled him from the door. The cornerstone of his life crumbled to dust as he raced to the exit. The dark smells of the *kisaeng* house pressed against him, taking the air from his lungs.

He clambered down the stairs and thrust his feet into his shoes, then bolted for the gate. Once in the street he pushed his way past groups of startled women. In his haste he'd forgotten the curfew.

He turned down an alley, trying to escape, but he knew there was no place to hide from the terror pursuing him. Above the noise of the crowded streets, one word roared in his ears. Betrayal!

54

Megan closed the doors and sank down onto the *yo*. Pictures of Jongwhan's face revolved through her weary mind—expressions of disgust, pity, hope, pain, and hatred. Why had she lashed out, used the truth to lie to him, to hurt him?

The images tumbled, slowed, then stopped. In her memory disgust and pity settled over his handsome features. She bit her lip. He had deserted her, left her to the mercy of the Manchus, then had the nerve to be disgusted by her appearance. All her pain and hatred had welled up and she had told him the truth, or just enough of it to drive him away. Once said, the words could not be recalled. Instead they grew dark wings and blotted out all light and joy. She must be crazy, to turn away the man she loved, to make him hate her. Their love was dead, and she had killed it.

She lay back on the *pyogae*, pulled the heavy quilt over her, and closed her eyes. Faces and words spun through her mind, faster and faster, until she sank beneath them. Confusion receded and she fell into a well of darkness. She floated there, numbed by grief and exhaustion.

Then, suddenly, Obuto stood over her, leering down at her. He fell atop her bulging belly, crushing her. Pain flowed through her body, rings spreading ever outward from her womb.

She tried to scream, but no sound came out. She beat on his back, pushing him away—he was killing her child—their child! When she tried to tell him, to make him understand, he just smiled and lifted her skirt, then thrust himself inside her, tearing her flesh.

He grew and grew, plunging into her belly. Agony

crashed over her like waves, like the black ocean, sucking her down, drowning her. She reached up a hand and battered it against the Manchu's face. His mouth fell open and his eyes rolled back in his head. A wound gaped at the base of his throat and blood gushed out, covering her breasts, trickling down her belly and between her legs.

With both hands she pushed at the bleeding corpse, wrestling it away. Then the face changed, became Jong-whan's. Pain and rage glittered in her lover's gray eyes. She sobbed aloud and reached up to caress his handsome face, but his hand crushed her wrist, pinning it to her side. He laughed, a bitter, hollow sound, then disappeared.

She sat up, trembling in spite of the warm night. Clammy sweat covered her face. She wiped at it with a sticky palm, then drew up her knees and clasped her arms around them. In horror she stared at the dark liquid soaking her skirt, making it cling to her shivering body. Something warm gushed out between her legs. Her mind reeled. Blood! She was bleeding!

She forced herself to her knees and crawled toward the door. As she reached a hand to the casement, white-hot pain girded her belly. She writhed on the floor, her face pressed against the smooth oiled paper until the pain passed. With one hand supporting her heavy stomach, she pulled the latticework door ajar, then wriggled forward, trailing her long wet skirt behind.

She inched across the hall and banged a hand against the door opposite her own. "Help me!" She shouted, but only a croaking sound emerged. She cleared her throat and took a deep breath. "Help me!"

An iron band of pain cut through her middle and she sank down onto the floor. Dark waves crashed over her again, but this time she let them take her down, down into oblivion.

Hands took hold of her, lifted her. Voices babbled in her ears. The darkness receded. Lanterns lit the gloom and cast flickering shadows on the ceiling. She lay on her back on the *yo* in her room. Someone had removed her stained skirt. Her belly loomed like a ruddy harvest moon between her raised knees. A hand with a white cloth dribbled cool water over her, leaving white streaks across the red.

Pain took her, carried her into the blackness again. This time when she emerged into the light, Insung knelt between her legs, and beside her crouched another woman. The wrinkled round face turned toward her. Auntie Soh! Why was she here at this hour? Then she remembered—Grandfather Chang's housekeeper also served as a midwife. But it wasn't time yet—the child couldn't come for three more months.

"She's awake." Auntie Soh pushed her face closer to Megan's. "*Yobosayo!* Listen to me!"

Megan forced herself to nod. Maybe if she answered, the woman would leave her alone, let her rest.

"Megan, has the child moved at all today?"

Fear stabbed through her. She'd forgotten to ask Insung what it meant. She shook her head.

The midwife frowned. "What about yesterday?"

Panic rose in her throat. She shook her head again.

The face turned away. "It is too late. We may be able to save her, but the child is dead."

No, that couldn't be true—she hadn't wanted the baby at first, but now she loved it—they couldn't take it away! She started to sit up, to tell them they were wrong, but the pain pushed her back. She gritted her teeth and let the blackness wash over her.

The torment came and went, but she kept her eyes closed. It was just a dream, a horrible nightmare. It would be morning soon, and then it would end. Even nightmares couldn't last forever.

For hours agony and respite played tug-of-war with her body. After an eternity, a giant hand reached inside her belly and pushed again and again, pushing the pain out and down. Then, at last, it ended.

She opened her eyes. Sunlight glowed through the translucent outer doors. She longed to throw them open and drink in the warm summer air, instead of the stink of blood and burned lamp-oil filling the room.

Something cool wiped at her aching thighs, then hands unbent her knees and rested her legs on the mattress. She turned her head and watched the *ibul* fall across her flat belly.

The *kisaeng* talked in a hushed voice with Auntie Soh. The old midwife looked tired and sad. Red rimmed her watery eyes and deep lines cut into her round cheeks. Insung bent and wrapped a white cloth around something.

"Let me see him."

Insung turned a haggard face toward Megan at the sound of her voice. "It is best you do not see."

"Let me see my son!" Megan's voice quavered, but it grew louder.

Insung glanced at the midwife. "Megan, trust me. Don't insist." The *kisaeng*'s voice took on a pleading note.

Megan raised herself on her elbows. "Very well, if you won't bring him to me, I shall come to him." She sat up. Warmth gushed between her legs and the room spun. Hands pressed her down again.

Insung brought the white bundle over and nestled it into the crook of Megan's arm. "Go ahead, tear your heart out." The woman strangled a sob. "Just don't kill yourself trying to stand up."

Megan reached for the corner of the white blanket, but Insung caught her hand. "Wait! Promise me you will lie still. You are not well, you might even die!"

Megan smiled up at her. "I have no wish to die. I promise." She pulled her hand free and lifted the blanket. Red streaks of blood covered the tiny head. She rubbed it off with her fingertips, marveling at the transparent skin.

She unwrapped the tiny body, counting the ten fingers and toes, smiling at the tiny genitalia. "A son. Jongwhan will be so happy." She stroked the smooth skin of the tiny boy's chest, running a finger over the small, still ribs. "He must be tired—see how quiet he is? What a good baby; to sleep so sound."

She brushed her lips across the wide forehead. "But you're cold!" She wrapped the blanket around the still form and smiled up at Insung. "You can take him now, but keep him warm." She held up the tiny wrapped bundle. He seemed so small—why, he hardly weighed as much as a pound of flour!

As Insung took the child, pain flashed across the *kisaeng*'s face. A look passed between the two older women, and the ancient midwife shook her head. Insung nodded and left the room, holding the small body against her.

Auntie Soh bent and smoothed up the quilt. "You rest now."

Megan turned her face toward the bright square of paper and lath. "Would you please open the doors?"

Auntie Soh lumbered to the casement and tugged the latticework shutters inward.

Megan breathed in the fragrant morning air. A son! Wouldn't Jongwhan be pleased? It was going to be a beautiful day.

Jongwhan shifted his weight from one foot to another. Even in the shade of the stunted pine, the heat of the sun sent rivulets of sweat down his back and chest. He breathed deep, the dry scent of pine needles and dust filling him with unease. Sunlight sparkled on the yellow grassy mounds. He'd seldom ventured among the tombs in summer.

Why had he come today, to see the bastard of a *kisaeng* laid to rest? The child born of a woman who'd betrayed him with another man—maybe several others! Why torture himself?

He locked his jaw. He knew the answer, in one word— "Perhaps." Had the child been his? He'd never know, any more than he could guess the reason for Insung's second cryptic message. "Megan's son died at birth last night." He'd received the note two days before, but still the reason eluded him. The *kisaeng* mistress must think him the father, or why send him word? He knew Insung would never tell him who the other man—or men—might be.

He sighed and turned to study the patterns of the pine tree's bark. He traced the grooves in the twisted trunk with a forefinger. He'd had no trouble learning the location of the burial. Park had visited the *pansu* nearest the South Gate and had learned the auspicious location the man had cast for Insung. In this heat, the man had been prudent to choose a burial date so soon after the boy's death.

A boy! Megan's son, perhaps his son, dead. Grief welled up in him and he blinked back tears.

A hot summer wind carried the sound of pipers and the wailing of mourners. He stepped behind the tree, out of sight. Only Park knew of his presence here today. He could not tell his parents, or even his wife, could not trust himself to control his anger or his tears.

His heart clenched in his chest as the tiny bier came into sight around the curve of a burial mound. The small carved dragon's head glittered in red and blue. Streamers danced a bizarre rhythm in the sultry wind. He leaned both hands against the trunk of the tree. Four men carried the red lacquered posts on their shoulders, and a string of hemp-clothed mourners straggled behind.

The music stopped and the wailing quieted. Insung motioned for the bearers to lower the bier beside a small dark hole in the hillside. She'd spared no expense, hiring mourners. Who else would wail over a fatherless infant? Then there was the cost of the musicians and the price of a prime burial plot. He flushed with shame. He'd send her a purse filled with coins. Perhaps that explained the note—she'd hoped for him to share the expense.

As he watched, she moved forward and lifted the tiny corpse from the bier, then laid it in the shallow grave. When she rose, she turned toward him, and he could see tears glistening on her cheeks in the bright sunlight. Whatever Insung's reasons for writing him, she grieved in earnest for this little bit of humanity.

She motioned for the gravedigger to fill in the depression. Later they would built a wall of stone and carry earth to form a mound. She turned and looked around the peaceful hillside, then sighed and waved the mourning party to precede her down the hill.

But where was Megan? Why wasn't the child's loving mother there to bid the boy farewell in his final rest? An image of her mottled, swollen face floated before him. Perhaps she was too ill. His heart pounded. What if she lay in danger, near death? He shook his head. No, Insung would have written that in the note. His mouth twisted. Perhaps the boy's mother simply didn't care, any more than she cared about him—maybe Megan was incapable of loving anyone, even her own child.

When Insung disappeared past the crest of the hill, he made up his mind and hurried down to where the gravedigger sweated in the hot sun. He took a deep breath. "I want to look at the body."

The peasant turned, his eyebrows shooting up. He leaned on his shovel and looked Jongwhan up and down. "Why?" The man turned and spat into the dust of the path, then regarded him with a curious expression.

Jongwhan fished in his purse and tossed the man a coin.

The gravedigger caught it, then shrugged and moved away to sit in the shade of one of the mounds.

Jongwhan knelt and reached into the square depression, then lifted out the white wrapped bundle. He brushed the dirt from the cloth and lifted one corner. He memorized the pale, still features, the reddish fuzz on the round head, the tiny flowerbud mouth. He touched the tiny fingers.

Tears stung his eyelids. With gentle hands he wrapped the fragile body again and laid it back in the womb of the earth, then turned and walked down the hill. He'd never know if that baby boy was his son, but he knew a part of his heart would always stay atop the hillside in that tiny grave.

55

Moon of Waning Heat

The baby laughed up at her, a sound so infectious Megan couldn't help joining in. Little Im sat next to her on the bright *ibul*, slapping his chubby palms against the silk squares of the quilt top. His round cheeks jiggled as he opened his mouth and crowed with delight.

Megan smiled at Youngsook. "He is a fine boy, so healthy and strong."

The young mother beamed and nodded. "I think so too! My husband is so proud!" The sweet face clouded. "My Friend, I am so sorry about your baby. Madame Insung told me."

Megan turned away for a moment, then turned back, a smile pasted across her face. "Yes, my son is small and weak, but he is very good, very quiet—he never cries." She swallowed a sob. "And someday he will be a big man."

Shock and confusion colored Youngsook's face.

Megan rattled on, anything to fill the void. "But tell me about your life. How is your husband, and your mother-in-law? What does she think of your son?"

Youngsook cocked her head, then shrugged. Her smile brightened as she launched into a description of her dragonlike mother-in-law and her new status as the mother of a son. She blushed when she described her husband's recent growth spurt, and amid giggles she extolled his new virtues in bed.

Megan listened with half her mind, nodding and smiling, but part of her cast about for a way to be rid of her guest. Almost a month had passed since her return to Seoul, and still she hadn't the strength to get out of her bed.

Insung came and pestered her, tried to tell her things she refused to believe. She managed to sidestep all but the woman's most blatant lies.

At last Youngsook quieted and fixed Megan with a worried expression. "Are you all right?"

Megan nodded. "I am very tired, that's all." She made a show of yawning. "I think you should leave now, so I can rest."

Chang's granddaughter stared at her for a moment. "But Madame said—" The girl stopped, shook her head, then said good-bye and lifted her son from Megan's bed. At the door she turned, puzzlement still showing in the furrows of her brow and the set of her mouth. The young mother hugged her baby to her and left without another word.

Megan closed her eyes and let the quiet wash through

her. After a moment she smiled to herself and turned to look out the open door. A pair of magpies made their home in the low branches of Chang's cherry tree. She had counted five nestlings. The mother bird scolded the chicks as she pushed them to the lip of the nest. *"Chak-chak-chak!"* With a gentle poke of her beak in their backs she launched them into the air.

One after another fell, then flapped delicate wings and soared across the yard. The last and smallest teetered on the edge of the mud-and-grass nest. The mother bird nudged it into the air. It fell, flapped its wings, then plummeted to the earth. The mother bird cocked her head, then bounced along the branch, calling her other four babes back to the nest.

Bile rose in Megan's throat. She squeezed her eyes shut and fought back tears. She wouldn't think about it anymore. She rolled away from the door and called up Jongwhan's face in her mind. He'd be back to see her soon—he'd forget about the last time. She brought herself up short, then turned her thoughts away, to her son. He didn't seem to be growing, but then he never ate. He was so tiny, like the smallest baby bird. No! She opened her eyes. Even her own mind betrayed her—no refuge existed anywhere.

The door opened. Her heart swelled with gratitude. Insung had come to rescue her from her thoughts. She smiled up at the aging *kisaeng*.

Madame's face wore a frown, as it had since she returned from Mukden. Perhaps the woman was unhappy or worried, maybe about Soonhee. Megan bit her lip, sadness and pity welling up in her. Poor Insung, poor Soonhee, poor Pongnim! Too bad they couldn't share her good fortune, her happiness.

Insung knelt beside the *yo*. "My Daughter."

Megan smiled at the gentleness in the woman's rich voice.

"You told Youngsook your baby lived and would someday grow to be a man."

Oh, no! Not this again. Megan closed her eyes and turned away. She just wouldn't listen. Hands clamped her shoulders and shook her until she opened her eyes.

The gentleness left Madame's voice. "Listen to me! Your baby is dead! Dead! Do you understand?"

The world blurred, then came again into sharp focus—too sharp. Her eyes watered at the sight of her room, of Insung's face. Reality shattered into brittle shards. The words sank into her mind, cutting into her heart until she longed to scream. The ache swelled in her chest until it burst forth in a sob. "Yes! Yes, I understand."

She rolled over and hid her eyes against the hard bolster. She knew, had always known. Her son lay dead in a dark hole in the ground, and the man she loved hated her. Sobs racked her body, washing away all the joy she'd constructed over the last weeks. At last her belly stopped convulsing and the tears slowed. She turned back to a gray world, a grim place of loss and pain.

Insung stood over her. Tears wet the *kisaeng*'s handsome face. "It is better to face life's blows. If you hide from them, they will cripple you." The handsome mouth set in a straight line, and conviction rang in her next words. "And now you must get up and begin to live again."

Megan clenched her jaw and shook her head.

Insung's face fell. "If you lie there, you will wither and die. You must get up!"

Megan bit her lip and turned once more toward the door. The baby bird lay unmoving at the base of the tree. Madame didn't understand. She'd lost her son and her lover—she had nothing else to live for.

Jongwhan sighed and set the brush in its holder. He'd almost finished the painting before him, yet he felt no satisfaction in the accomplishment. He'd spent weeks sketching the scene—two wrestlers in a *surrim* match, each struggling to throw the other off balance and win the match. Around the combatants, peasants in white cheered and wagered on the outcome.

He frowned, then sighed. The techniques, the theme, the composition all pleased him, yet somehow the painting lacked spirit. As he did since Megan's return. In spite of her betrayal, he longed for her. Only his pride kept him away.

He lifted a tiny detail brush and dipped it in black ink.

Only flesh tones and black detail lines etched the whiteness of the scene. As his fingers traced delicate lines, his mind turned back to worry at the source of his misery, like a tongue probing an aching tooth.

As if he hadn't troubles enough, his mother nagged at him daily about his life. She had disapproved of sending Munja back to the estate, but he held firm. Munja was his wife, to do with as he pleased.

He smiled at the memory of their parting. She had reached up a hand to his cheek and pressed her lips against his. "*Kamsa hamnida*, my husband. Thank you." Then she'd stepped into the palanquin and dropped the curtain. He sighed. At least he could count one good thing to come from the last half year—their new relationship.

He placed the brush against the edge of the inkstone and flexed his fingers. He must take care. One misstroke would ruin the work.

He grimaced. He'd already ruined everything else in his life, at least according to his mother. Now, with his wife gone, his mother needed someone else to complain about. He shook his head. Sometimes he thought she wanted to avenge the pain she'd suffered at her own mother-in-law's hands. He still remembered his grandmother shrieking at his mother. The old beldame had always had a soft word for everyone else, but she made her daughter-in-law miserable. Perhaps the old woman's mother-in-law had ill-used her as well, and so on, back to Tangun and the founding of the kingdom.

She wanted him to agree to a mistress of her choosing, to "borrow the earth" in which to plant his seed. He closed his eyes. No, he wouldn't bring another woman into this house, no matter how his mother berated him. He'd never opposed his mother's will before, and he hated to do it now, but he'd live celibate before he'd take any woman but Megan to his bed. And how could he trust her now?

A footfall brought him from his reverie. Park stood over him. The servant gave a half-bow. "Master Yi, your honorable mother wishes your company."

Jongwhan groaned. "Thank you, Park. Did she say what she wanted?"

Park's face remained neutral. "I believe it's something about your new mistress."

"Damn!" Jongwhan leaped to his feet. The two brushes resting against the inkstone flopped onto the painting, smearing trails of black across the delicate figures. He winced at the sight of weeks of work destroyed in a moment by a display of temper.

Sympathy flitted across Park's face. "I am sorry, Old Friend. I'm at fault for telling you so abruptly, and I apologize." The servant had spoken in the most formal tones and phrases.

Jongwhan nodded. "It doesn't matter. It wasn't very good anyway." He looked away from the ruined picture.

He could tell from the look on his friend's face that Park recognized and appreciated the lie. Jongwhan bent and wiped his hands on a cloth, then wadded it and tossed it atop the ruined painting.

He stood for a moment, undecided. He couldn't bear an hour of the old woman's harangue. Much as he loved her, honored her, he couldn't withstand her barrage of words. Nor could he agree to her demands to take another woman.

Oh, Megan! Why did she betray him? If only she'd been true to him, he could have pleased his mother and himself at the same time. In spite of the pain she'd caused, he still loved her.

Anger and frustration flared in him. He made a decision. "Tell my mother you couldn't find me, that I'd gone out." He stepped into his shoes and turned toward the gate.

Park called after him. "Where shall I say you have gone?"

Jongwhan pursed his lips for a moment, then frowned. "To get drunk!" He strode through the gate, his heart heavy and thoughts of a beautiful red-haired *kisaeng* twirling in his head.

Insung squeezed Megan's hand. "This is the Birth Grandmother. She will give you another child to replace the son you lost."

Megan frowned. What heathen nonsense was this?

When she'd refused to leave her bed, Insung had insisted on hiring a sorcerer to rid the house of the evil spirits.

Madame didn't understand—the only evil spirits lived in her own mind! She didn't care if she ever got well. She didn't deserve another child. She blamed herself for the loss of her son. Maybe if she'd wanted him, truly wanted him, he wouldn't have died. Unshed tears tightened their grip on her chest. He might have been Jongwhan's son. And even if he wasn't, he was her baby, part of her. And he had died, poor wee bairn!

She bit back the tears and closed her eyes for a moment. She'd grown tired—tired of this never-ending party for the spirits, tired of the noise and the motion of the dancer in one costume after another. Insung had explained why the shaman changed clothing. Each outfit represented a different powerful spirit, possessing the woman and allowing her to intercede with the dead on behalf of the living.

She sighed with fatigue, marveling at the dancer's endurance. And the trick of standing barefoot on the sharp swords, that had looked real enough. But how could this slender dancer help her get another child? She'd have to make Jongwhan fall in love with her again, and that could never happen. Megan had hurt him beyond the possibility of forgiveness.

The sorceress danced wildly for a moment, kicking up the hem of the white Buddhist monk's robe, then tossed a handful of nuts and sweets onto Megan's quilt.

"Put this in her begging bag. Go on." Insung's voice both coerced and commanded.

Megan allowed her hand to be guided to the dancer's pouch, then dropped the money inside.

The *mudang* squatted beside the bed, blowing stale fishy breath into Megan's face, and pointed a dirty fingernail at her. The woman's raw voice cracked, and she gave an evil smile. "You worry that your son hates you, hates you for not wanting him." The shaman's smile showed blackened stumps of teeth. She patted Megan's arm. "He doesn't hate you. He understands and wants you to be happy. You will have more children, and soon!"

Ice chilled Megan's belly. How had the woman known? Maybe she did have the power to speak to the dead—maybe she spoke the truth about the baby. If only she could believe!

The dancer leaped up, arching her back, then drew her hands above her head and bowed to the floor. The drums and cymbals increased their rhythm. The woman leaped and kicked again and again, as she had done since the sun went down.

Megan brought her hands together. Hope welled up in her for the first time since she acknowledged her son's death. Please let the *mudang's* words prove true!

56

Moon of Autumn Cool

The paper-and-lath doors swung open. Megan resisted the impulse to turn toward them. Instead, she kept her eyes fastened on the birds skimming the grass of the courtyard.

"Megan, when will you get up?"

She sighed and bit her lip. Madame Insung had asked her the same question every morning since the *kut* a week before. Someday she'd get up—her mind shied away from the thought—but not yet. She knit her brows, concentrating on the dun-colored magpie fledglings.

Insung's voice continued. "Without Soonhee or Pilsu, you are the only one left to dance the *salpuri* for the King."

Part of Megan's mind noted the sadness and frustration in the woman's tone, but she kept herself focused on the open door. Now the young magpies strutted across the yard, bobbing their heads into the ground and pulling out long earthworms.

Without warning, hands gripped her shoulders and turned her away from the morning sunlight. Megan gasped at the anger contorting Insung's face.

The dark eyes glittered and red crept up the *kisaeng's* cheeks. "Today you will listen to me!"

Megan had never seen Madame so angry before. She cringed away from the woman's gaze.

Insung's shoulders drooped and her mouth twisted. "Do you think you are the only one to suffer?" Lines deepened between the woman's brows. "We have all lost—I have lost my daughter, Youngsook has lost a brother and a grandfather."

Megan closed her eyes, but the hands still gripping her shoulders shook her until she opened them again.

"Look at me! You have suffered, you have lost much, but life must continue." The rich voice quavered, then cracked. "I need you. The new girls try, but they are too young to understand."

A tiny glow began in Megan's chest, but she ignored it. She bit her lip and shook her head. "I can't." Her words came out in a hoarse whisper.

Insung's hands loosened and the woman rocked backward as if Megan had struck her. The color left the handsome face, and her voice hardened. "If you will not work, you cannot stay." Madame rose to stand over the pallet where Megan lay. "We are *kisaeng*, not *yangban*—we do not lie about in idleness while others wait on our whims."

Serenity once more smoothed the lines from Insung's handsome face. Ice edged the calm voice. "Either get up and begin to learn the dance today, or I will have you carried into the street." The woman turned and sailed out the doorway, closing the paper-and-lath shutters behind her.

Megan lay on the soft *yo*, paralyzed with shock. It wasn't fair, after all she'd been through. How could Madame be so cruel? She was ill, not lazy—hadn't she always worked hard before? Anger washed through her. She would show Insung!

Megan rolled to one side, braced her hands against the

mattress, and pushed herself upright. She swayed for a moment, struggling with dizziness, then stood on shaking legs. Her weak knees tried to buckle under her, but she clenched her teeth and forced herself to walk to the lacquered chest and open it.

Stacks of silken skirts and jackets glowed in jewel colors in the morning light. She reached out a quivering hand and stroked the soft, smooth cloth, then loosened the tie of her cotton robe and let it fall to the floor.

She donned embroidered white *paji* and padded socks, then slipped the straps of a powder-blue *chima* over her shoulders and tied the skirt under her armpits. She shrugged on a peach-colored *chogori* and pulled its embroidered tie into a smooth loop over one breast.

Megan lifted a carved wooden comb and ran it through her long red curls, then set to work braiding one long plait. She looped the resulting copper rope with one hand, and with the other grasped the carved dragon head of a long jade hairpin, weaving the smooth shaft through her hair to hold the knot in place.

She stared at her reflection in the round copper mirror. Dark circles smudged the skin beneath her green eyes, and the hollows of her cheeks made her cheekbones stand out. Her coral lips were set in a thin line. Insung had cut the dyed ends from her hair, and copper curls fanned out in a halo around her head, making her skin ever paler. She nodded once, then turned away.

No one could get away with calling her an idler. If Madame wanted a dancer, a dancer she'd get.

Jongwhan glared down into the cup of *makkŏlli*, then ran a fuzzy tongue over dry lips. He blinked in the dim light of the *kisaeng* house. Why did he come here alone night after night? Megan might not even live here anymore. He clenched the cup. Insung wouldn't even tell him that when he'd cornered her.

He smothered a twinge of guilt with another gulp of rice wine. The woman deserved the tongue-lashing he'd given her, but she just glared at him and walked away. The *kisaeng* treated him as if he'd done something to hurt Megan.

His mouth twisted—he hoped he had hurt her by leaving. After what she did—but he was weak and couldn't stay away. Black anger welled up in his chest, frustrated anger at himself. Pride should prevent him from ever seeing Megan again, but his need for her pulled him to this dark room again and again.

He stared into his empty cup, then reached for the *makkŏlli* pot, slopping the white liquor onto the tabletop. He glanced around at those seated nearby. Two *yangban* men glared at him for a moment before turning back to their conversation with the young *kisaeng* serving them.

He passed a hand over his face. What was he doing here? He knew it broke every Korean tradition to drink alone—he should have at least asked for a woman to serve him. But he wanted to sit alone, to think, to try to sort out this confusion in his mind.

He managed to pour wine into the cup again and filled his mouth with the sweet, smooth liquid. Cradling the cup in his hands, he closed his eyes and dropped his chin forward onto his chest. A profound self-pity filled him. What could he do? He loved her, wanted her, but she'd done the unforgivable. He stared at the white *makkŏlli*, then took another drink. He didn't even know where she was.

A hush settled over the room, but Jongwhan didn't bother to look up. Every evening an entertainer would mount the raised dais in the center of the room to sing or dance or recite poetry. He'd given up hope of seeing Megan there.

The soft strains of the *kayagum* floated across the room as the unseen musician bowed the strings. The first notes of a popular folksong eddied around him, then a clear, sweet voice began. "*Arirang, Arirang, Arariyo, Arirang Kogero, Nomoganda.*"

The voice seemed familiar to him, but changed, sadder, older. His head came up. Megan! He stared, enraptured as she sang verse after verse. He drank in the sight of her form, her face, her hair. He saw the thin cheeks and the tired eyes, but they only made her more beautiful to him.

The last note of the last verse fell into a well of silence, then hung quivering in the air. After a long moment the room exploded with applause. Megan bowed her acknowledgment, then rose and glided from the chamber. Tears welled in Jongwhan's eyes.

A voice from nearby brought him out of his reverie. "So, Pak Sonsaeng, what do you think of this mystery?"

Jongwhan turned toward the two men who'd glared at him earlier. The older of the two men shook his head in response to his young companion's question. "It goes against nature, Chun—so beautiful a sound from such an ugly creature."

Jongwhan's heart pounded and his fists clenched.

The younger man smiled and nodded. "But what manner of creature is it, Sonsaeng?"

Pak pursed his withered lips. "A woman, I would wager."

Chun's eyes glittered. "With respect, Pak Sonsaeng, I wager it is not a woman at all, but an animal."

Pak slapped a gnarled hand on the low table. "Done! But how shall we settle this bet?"

Chun bowed. "I shall take it upon myself to examine the creature quite closely, Sonsaeng." The young man blinked and giggled.

Red anger flared in Jongwhan. He leaped up and jerked Chun to his feet, then slammed his fist into the young man's jaw with a satisfying crack. Surprise registered on the downed man's face.

Voices babbled around Jongwhan as he bent over Chun. "Stay away from the woman with red hair." Hands pulled at his arms, but he shook them off and flung himself out the door into the sultry darkness. He stopped and leaned against a wall and covered his eyes with his hands. To brawl in a *kisaeng* house like a peasant in a tavern. What had become of him?

His breathing slowed and his pulse dropped to normal. Shame gave way to a bittersweet joy. He had seen Megan, and now he knew what he must do.

* * *

The notes of the *kayagum* swelled through the room. Megan visualized each step and turn of the dance. She'd learned the motions, but Insung just shook her head and told her to do it again.

She frowned. Madame had explained the significance of the white gown and the trailing scarf. "You must strive to free your spirit of trouble and anguish." Insung's words echoed in her mind.

Megan sighed, then took the frist slow steps, swaying and turning. The sad notes of the *kayagum* strings turned her thoughts toward the son she'd lost. Since she'd returned to work, the pain of his death eased little by little. She had changed, she knew—she'd never again be the young woman shipwrecked in a strange land. A part of her had died with her child, but the rest of her lived on.

She flowed through the movements of the dance, now slow, now fast, letting the music and her thoughts move through her. She relived her time with Grandmother, the fear and fascination of her first days in Seoul, the bitter-sweet counterpoint of Pilsu's hatred and Soonhee's friendship. She raged again at Obuto, walked the long miles home from Mukden, and as the last strains of the *kayagum* quivered, she sank down to the floor, the image of Jongwhan's disgust and pity filling her mind.

At the sound of clapping, she turned toward the doorway. She hadn't known anyone was watching but the musician. She blinked her eyes, then opened her mouth and closed it.

"Mother was right. You dance the *salpuri* better than I ever could."

The sound of that sweet voice released her and she ran to the young woman. One word echoed over and over in her mind. "Soonhee!"

Megan clenched her jaw. Pacing the confines of her tiny bedchamber, she forced herself to rehearse the steps of the *salpuri* in her mind. Since Soonhee's return, Megan's desire to do her best had grown to an obsession.

The doors swung open. Megan stopped and turned.

Soonhee smiled up at her. "Relax! You'll do it perfectly. The King will be enthralled."

Megan took a deep breath. The little *kisaeng* was right—nervousness would destroy the mood of the dance. She sank down on the *yo* and tried to quiet the butterflies churning in her stomach. She had to do well—for Madame, for herself.

She chewed her lip. Would Jongwhan be there? A longing filled her, to lie in his arms, taste his kisses. Would the memories of their love never stop haunting her? She had to believe he hated her, he'd never want her again. It was easier to bear than empty hope.

Forcing a smile to her lips, Megan turned to Soonhee. Thank God Insung's daughter had returned. She said little about her time in Pusan, only confiding her relief when she'd found herself not pregnant after all.

Nothing could erase the sadness from Soonhee's life, but at least she'd been spared that—to have a child by your own brother, to love it and raise it, to be reminded every day of its tragic conception. And hadn't she heard such children often turned out to be idiots or horribly deformed? She pressed her lips tight. Better never to conceive such a child.

An image of her tiny son flashed through her mind. She let the love soothe her aching emptiness. She would never forget, but she'd savor the life ahead of her. Soonhee had taught her that.

The young *kisaeng* had changed in her months away. Tiny lines etched the corners of her eyes and mouth. She looked older, calmer, not so ready to laugh and play.

Megan smiled. Judging by the young men courting Soonhee, sorrow only increased the woman's appeal. Soonhee still rebuffed the men's advances, but now with gentleness and sympathy. She'd told Megan she never intended to marry or have children.

Maybe she'd change her mind someday. Megan considered. Could she forget Jongwhan and love another? She shook her head.

Soonhee's quiet voice calmed her. "If you're ready, the runners have arrived with your sedan chair."

Megan clasped her friend's slender hand. "Ride with me?"

The young *kisaeng's* smile blossomed. "Of course."

Megan picked up her long white scarf and surveyed the room. She took a deep breath. In a few hours the ordeal would be over. Would she be able to do it? Confidence crept through her body. Yes! She'd do credit to her loyal friends.

57

The last glow of sunlight haloed the rows of brightly clothed *yangban* and their *kisaeng* companions. Jongwhan squinted into the horizontal rays at the soldiers lining the walls and the musicians seated opposite the pavilion where the King sat on his carved and lacquered throne.

Faint sounds of the city drifted from beyond the distant palace walls, but only the murmuring of the crowd behind their painted fans interrupted the quiet within the courtyard. A cool breeze carried the summer scents of pine and dust, dry grass, and night-blooming flowers.

Jongwhan sighed, his heart heavy in his chest. He'd decided what to do to win Megan back, but each time he set out, his courage failed him. If only he could forget his emptiness, raise his spirits to join in the air of celebration.

The King had made a special request for a *kisaeng* to dance the *salpuri*, the dance of spiritual cleansing, to rid the court of the sorrow and shame of the Manchu invasion. Much of the talk around Jongwhan centered on the question of who the solo dancer would be.

In his mind he ticked off the possibilities—Soonhee and Pilsu, both gone. He shied away from the image of a red-haired woman, clothed in white, whirling across the yard. Perhaps another dancer had survived the war, or Madame had been able to train a new girl in the last six moons.

As the sun dipped below the western horizon, light glowed from dozens of silk-shaded lanterns. A drummer tapped out a rhythm and the crowd fell silent. Soon a brass horn picked up a thin melody, then the brass gong and strings joined in. A lone figure in white emerged from the shadows.

Jongwhan's mouth dried and he stared at the apparition gliding across the yard. A slender figure, robed in spotless white, a long white scarf trailing from her narrow hand, and a blaze of copper hair framing her white features. The faces of the courtiers seated nearby mirrored his own shock. What had possessed Insung to choose a foreigner to dance the most spiritual, the most Korean, of all dances? At the same time, his spirit soared at the sight of her grace and beauty.

As she danced, his anxiety melted away. Not only did she execute the floating steps of the dance with precision, but every movement radiated intense emotion, the epitome of *mŏt*. Never had he seen the *salpuri* danced so well. His heart swelled, rejoiced, then plummeted with her. As she sank into a graceful pool of white and the music sighed to a close, tears closed Jongwhan's throat. Those around him wiped wet cheeks with their silken sleeves amid cheers and applause.

In the tumult following the dance, Jongwhan slipped through the crowd and down the winding path to the palace gates. Once he was in the streets his feet hurried him down narrow alleyways toward the *kisaeng* house, harried at each step by questions he couldn't answer. What would he say to her? How would she greet him? Would she order him to leave?

At last he stood before the gate. He ducked into the shadows until six runners carried a palanquin through the portal and settled it to the clay of the lamplit courtyard. A white-clothed figure stepped from the curtained sedan chair and handed some coins to one of the men. All six bowed, then retreated at a trot, carrying the empty conveyance into the streets.

The figure stood a moment, then turned and mounted the steps, disappearing within the yawning dark mouth of the visitors' hall.

Jongwhan's heart tripped and indecision tore at him. In the end it was the image of her face, alight with joy, serene in sorrow, that tugged him toward the building. He clenched his jaw. No matter what pain it cost him, he must see her, tell her how much he loved her.

He pulled his stockinged feet from his silken shoes and padded through the dim hallway, drinking in the flower scents of the women who lived there. He hesitated at her room, its white paper door aglow with lamplight from within. He reached out a hand to scratch at the casement, but instead gave it a gentle push.

The shutter swung inward. The woman within turned, surprise and fear flitting across her delicate white face. Something kindled and burned in the jade-green eyes staring up at him, burning into his soul. He longed to quench that hatred, to smother that fire.

"What do you want?" The slight accent of her words tugged at his heart, in spite of the coldness of her gaze.

"Megan, I—" He cursed his inability to say the right words, to conquer her hatred. The weight of the last months descended on him, threatened to smother him. He rebelled against the sadness, the hopelessness suffocating his words. "You." His voice rumbled with frustration. He bit his lip. Had his anger frightened her? He drew a breath, took one step forward. The green eyes never wavered from his face. "You, I've never wanted anything but you."

Something flickered behind the delicate porcelain of her features. Doubt, hope? Or had he imagined it? Her lips thinned. The hard, shiny glaze returned. "Why? So you can use me, then discard me again?"

His mind reeled. Discard her again? What did she mean?

A snarl lifted one corner of her beautiful mouth. She

mimicked his deep voice. "Promise me you'll wait for me here until I return."

He frowned. He'd said those words, but—horror crept up his spine. "But I sent a messenger to tell you to flee." The words tumbled over themselves in their hurry to leave his lips. "Pongnim asked me to stay with his father. Honor prevented me from refusing."

The smooth white features sagged. God, she thought he left her behind, at the mercy of the invaders. Damn Kim On Yun! He heard the fat man's laughter, reaching out from the grave. At least she'd gotten away. A new chill, darker still, advanced on him. "But you were gone. The house was empty, the fires were out when I passed by." Desperation colored his words.

The green eyes widened. A ragged whisper came from Megan's trembling lips. "The cook let the fire die—she was old and drunk and frightened—we were all frightened."

"So that's why you took another lover." His mouth twisted in a bitter smile. "You thought I deserted you. I—I understand. I forgive you." He realized the truth of the words as he said them. He did forgive her—he'd forgive her anything if only he could have her love again. Nothing else mattered. His heart lifted. Now everything would change between them, be as it was before. He smiled into her eyes.

She stared back at him, then her coral lips opened and laughter came pouring out.

He frowned. What was so funny?

She threw her head back and shrieked until the hysterical laughter turned to sobs and she crumpled to the floor. Tears rolled down her cheeks, and she wailed as though her heart would break.

Jongwhan stood and watched her, his feet rooted to the floor.

The tears left her exhausted, hollow, dead, like ashes in the wind. With quivering hands she wiped at her wet cheeks and looked up at Jongwhan. Pain and confusion etched themselves across his handsome features. Another lover? He *forgave* her? Her mouth twisted in a grim smile and she shook her head.

She rose and planted her feet wide to keep her knees from shaking. "Thank you for your forgiveness." She fought to keep the irony from her voice. "But I took no other lover."

Jongwhan's frown deepened. "Then you lied to me, and that child was mine?" Pain edged his words.

Megan shook her head. "It wasn't a lie. I—I don't know if he was your son or not." Her voice caught on a sob. She swallowed, then poured all the gentleness she possessed into her next words. "I wanted to believe—I hoped he was your son. I—I loved him as though he were."

Pain and pleasure flickered across his face like firelight on a hearth. "Then how . . . ?"

Megan passed a hand across her eyes. Her voice sounded old to her ear, older than Grandmother or Chang, older than South Mountain. "The Manchus captured us. One of them—" She knew most Korean men would consider a woman tainted after she'd been raped. Taking a deep breath, she looked directly into Jongwhan's eyes. Everything depended on what she would read there when the last of the truth slipped from her mouth. "One of them took a fancy to me." A ragged sob clenched her throat. "I never knew if the child I carried was yours, or his."

Pain screamed from the dark gray eyes, and love. "Against your will?" Anger darkened his golden complexion.

Megan nodded, her eyes never leaving his face, watching for signs of shame, disgust, pity—signs that would forever end the love and hope bubbling near the surface of her being.

Jongwhan clenched his jaw and his fists. "I'll kill the bastard!" His words exploded into her small bedchamber.

Relief washed through her, loosening muscles she hadn't realized were clenched. "No need. Some Korean soldier killed him at Namhan." For a moment she saw Obuto's lifeless body again. A deep satisfaction filled her at the memory—the animal had deserved to die.

Jongwhan's fine white teeth chewed his full lower lip. A shadow passed over his face, and lines furrowed his fine dark brows. "But when you first returned, why didn't you explain?"

Megan's lips quirked up into a grimace. "Pride." She shrugged. "I couldn't bear the pity on your face, or the disgust." She clenched her teeth and swallowed fresh tears.

Jongwhan's lower jaw dropped. "Pity? Disgust?" He shook his head as if to clear it. "I was in awe of you. I thought you carried my child." He clenched his fists. "I knew you were ill and sad, but to me you were the most beautiful sight I'd ever seen." He stepped forward and rested one hand on her arm. "My God, woman! I loved you." He shook his head. "Megan"—his voice caressed her ear—"I love you now!"

He pulled her into his arms, pressing his lips against her mouth. For a moment she tensed against him, then her arms went round his neck and she opened her mouth to receive his tongue.

Megan's mind melted and swirled inside her head. Jongwhan! His name echoed over and over in her mind. He'd come back to her. All the long months of pain and sorrow welled up and became a fierce joy.

She clung to him, her hands memorizing the curves and planes of his shoulders, his back, his buttocks, holding him close in a possessive embrace. She longed to hold him, be held by him like this forever.

The faint scent of sweat and wine perfumed his skin. A heady languor filled her, swirling through her body and her mind. He lowered her onto the soft bedding in the center of her floor.

He raised up, his gray eyes never leaving her face, and with gentle fingers loosened the white tie at her breast. Bending, he covered her throat with a rain of kisses as soft as butterfly wings. She moaned as his mouth found first one nipple then the other, teasing, licking, sucking. Passion flamed through her. She arched her body against him, a yearning emptiness aching in her groin.

Then his hand slipped beneath the hem of her *chima*,

traveling from ankle to knee to thigh. A thrill ran through her as his fingers twined in the moist hair between her legs.

She reached for the waist of his *paji*, startled at the rigid warmth beneath her hands, and loosened the knotted tie. She slipped her hand inside, her palm sliding over the skin of his groin, her fingers stroking the smooth, hard shaft.

She whimpered, then pressed her palms against the small of his back and guided him into her. Waves of passion crashed over her as he entered, then drew back, his tempo increasing with each thrust.

She closed her eyes and lifted her hips to meet him again and again. Then, just as she knew she must faint or go crazy from pleasure, her body exploded in a haze of delicious agony. She heard a voice crying out and recognized it as her own. Then another voice joined hers. Jongwhan tensed, grew larger, filling her utterly, then burst in a rush of warmth inside her and lay still.

Megan held her breath, afraid to move and break the spell. Contentment stole through her. Jongwhan had returned. Nothing else mattered.

58

Soonhee's smile held no trace of envy, just genuine pleasure at her friend's happiness. Megan had hesitated at first to share the news of Jongwhan's visit with the young *kisaeng*, but she couldn't keep her joy bottled up for long. He'd gone out in the morning with promises to return at nightfall.

Relief flooded through Megan as Soonhee squeezed her hand. Insung's daughter had listened with sympathy throughout the past weeks to the story of Jongwhan's betrayal and Megan's captivity, but the young dancer had offered little of her own life in Pusan. She only said she'd decided to remain *kisaeng* and leave marriage and children to others.

Whenever Megan spoke of her time with Pongnim and his wife and daughters, Soonhee's eyelashes would lower and her smile would waver. Megan knew the girl's passion for her half-brother hadn't waned. She sighed. Perhaps it never would.

Soonhee cocked her head and smiled, her dark hair shining in a shaft of morning sunlight. "What will you do?" She leaned forward. "Will you live with him and have his children?"

Megan considered. They had talked until dawn, piecing together the love shattered by war and misunderstanding. He'd explained the pact with his wife, but then he bit his lip and stopped.

She shook her head. A cool morning breeze blew through the doorway, carrying a hint of harvesttime from the courtyard. "He didn't ask me, and I don't know how I'd have answered."

Soonhee turned away and nodded. "Some decisions are difficult to make." Sadness colored her soft words.

A cough came from the other side of the closed hall doors. Megan rose and opened the latticework shutters.

A breathless young serving girl stammered out an incomprehensible string of words.

Megan held up her hand. "Slow down, Little Friend. Say it again."

The girl's eyes widened and she took a deep breath. "Miss Megan, a man brought this letter for you." She thrust a folded square of rice paper into Megan's hand. "He said it's a message from His Excellency the King!"

Megan steadied herself on the doorpost. What could King Injo want with her? She forced herself to remain calm. "Thank you." With trembling fingers she took the letter and closed the doors.

Excitement sparkled in Soonhee's gold eyes. "Well, what does it say?"

Megan turned the packet over in her hand, then

seated herself on a cushion and smoothed the paper onto
the yellow floor. The square red seal stamped in one corner
reminded her of the letter Pongnim had sent with her.
She'd never used it, but if this meant some kind of trouble,
she might need his help.

The sweeping brush strokes blurred before her eyes.
She handed the paper to Soonhee.

Her friend studied the paper, then looked up, a tiny
line between her eyebrows. "He asks for you to attend him
in private audience, today."

As Megan dressed in her best skirt and jacket,
possibilities whirled through her mind. Perhaps he simply
wanted to thank her for her dance, or maybe he'd been
attracted to her. She shuddered. Perhaps he knew of her
relationship with Jongwhan and disapproved. She clenched
her jaw. After the last months, she'd lost all faith in the
rightness of things. This could only mean more heartache.

She had begged Soonhee to accompany her, but the
girl shook her head. "I can't—you know that. Please don't
ask." The hollow voice wrenched Megan's heart.

While she rode through the streets, her thoughts
returned to Soonhee's plight. What would it be to know
your father, but never tell him you were his child?

She thought of her own father, of the strength his love
had given her. Was he well? Did he ever think of her? She
pushed aside the questions. They lived a lifetime away from
her, and now she must concentrate on today.

She clenched her fists, ignoring the sweet-decayed
smell of the city and the noise and bustle of the crowds.
What did the King want with her? The question revolved
through her aching brain until she thought she'd go mad.

At last the palanquin stopped. She stepped out into a
small courtyard and the runners scurried off. A long, low
red building stretched around three sides of the rectangle
of grass. Trees and bushes dotted the grounds, and white
seashell paths ran around all four sides.

The roof of the building caught her eye. Blue tiles!
She'd only seen red tile roofs before. And the center wing

had no roof ridge. Instead the tiles formed a smooth curve at the top.

"We call the roofpeak the dragon ridge, because it looks like a sleeping dragon."

Megan whirled at the sound of a voice, her heart pounding.

King Injo smiled at her, his gold eyes twinkling. "The builders of my quarters thought it unwise to place one sleeping dragon above another." He leaned closer. "But do not fear—I never blow smoke in the daylight."

Megan bowed, trying to hide her smile. Pongnim's father was not very scary after all.

The King waved his hand. "Please, let us forgo the formalities." He waved his hand. "Will you do me the honor to walk with me?"

Megan nodded, took a deep breath, and followed.

Injo strode ahead on a winding path, his hands clasped behind him. "My son has written me of your courage against the Manchus." He turned and fixed her with a steady gaze. "Your bravery shames many of my soldiers."

She gulped and bobbed her head. "Thank you, Excellency."

Injo resumed his meandering path through the palace garden. "My son also asks me to grant you a reward."

Megan's heart leaped. Of all the possibilities, this was the one she hadn't foreseen.

Injo stopped and pointed at a small cloth pavilion. Inside two cushions waited. "Let us rest."

Megan nodded and waited until the King had seated himself with his legs crossed. She knelt on the other cushion and chewed her lip while he lighted a long, white clay pipe. The sweet odor of tobacco smoke scented the autumn air.

The King pointed his pipe at her. "I didn't know where to find you until last night. I sent several anonymous messages to Madame Insung, but she refused to give any information about you." He chuckled. "I take it this was your request?"

Megan nodded and looked down at her hands. Her cheeks flushed. If he asked her why, what could she say?

"When you danced for me last night, I remembered the first time I saw you."

Megan's head came up. She saw herself, in her tartan dress, standing defiant before him, risking her life for all she knew.

The gold eyes still twinkled at her. "As I recall, you wanted to leave my kingdom although you had only just arrived."

She opened her mouth to speak, then closed it again. He spoke the truth—there was no sense trying to deny it.

He leaned forward. "Now, Young Woman, I offer you a choice. If you still wish to leave, I will grant you safe conduct to Nagasaki and enough silver to buy your passage to wherever you were born." She should be pleased. Why then did the day seem suddenly bleak? She gulped and tried to remember she was in the presence of a king.

He cocked his head, and for a moment he looked just like Pongnim. "Someday I should like to hear about your distant land."

His eyes looked past her, as if he saw a world far-removed from his palace walls. For the first time she sensed the heavy responsibilities that went hand in hand with power. The King cleared his throat and sucked at his pipe a moment.

His eyes pierced her again. "I would prefer to have you stay in my kingdom and breed strong, brave sons instead, but if you choose to go, I will permit it."

Megan swallowed. A numbness gripped her mind. "Excellency, I don't know what to say."

The King chuckled and tapped the upended bowl of his pipe on the edge of a small dish. "Take your time. You needn't decide now." He reached into a silk purse tied to his gold belt. "If you stay, you may ask any other reward you wish." He handed her a circle of smooth white jade with the image of a dragon carved into its face. "Send me a letter in your own hand and include this. I will know it comes from you." He stood and ducked under the silk awning.

Megan scrambled to her feet and followed.

The King tucked his pipe into a pouch and pointed a

finger. "And now it is time for you to go. Follow this path to the gate. A chair waits there to take you home."

Megan bowed low, then hurried down the seashell path, her thoughts in a jumble. At the first turn she looked back. King Injo waved, then turned away.

Choices whirled through her brain as she left the palace gate and swayed through the crowded streets in the closed sedan chair. Indecision gripped her, pulling her in two. Before she knew it, the chair stopped at the *kisaeng* house. For long moments she stared at the clay walls and red-tiled roof, then at Grandfather Chang's cherry tree.

She took a deep breath and made her way to her room. Kneeling in front of the lacquered chest, she spilled bright silks around her onto the paper floor. At the very bottom lay a package. With shaking hands she lifted the paper-wrapped bundle and set it before her on a low table.

Megan tugged the edges of the rice paper apart and pulled out the red tartan dress. She buried her face in the rough wool. The scents of smoke and seawater clung to the fabric. She set it aside and toyed with the black leather strings of her gillie shoes. Finally she lifted the thick gold chain from around her neck and cradled the heavy Clan Scott emblem in her hand.

She reached for the secret catch to open the locket, then stopped, trying to remember the portrait inside, trying to picture Jemmie smiling up at her, just as he'd looked the day he asked her to marry him. Instead, she saw high cheekbones and gray, slanted eyes.

Megan set the locket on the creased white square and bundled the gown and the shoes on top. She folded the paper again and set the package once more in the bottom of the chest, then covered it with bright silk *chima*s and *chogori*s. She closed the lid with a soft thud and turned to her writing table.

She was no longer Jemmie's wife, or her father's daughter. That girl had ceased to exist. In her place stood a woman, a *kisaeng*, a *haenyo*, but most of all, a mistress of her own fate. She dropped the white stone onto the table. The King had given her the freedom to decide, and she knew now how she must choose.

* * *

At the sound of the cough outside the door, Megan closed her fingers around the object in her hand. "Enter."

Jongwhan burst through the doors, then turned and swung them shut behind him.

Megan ran to him and stood on tiptoe to place a gentle kiss on his lips.

Light danced in his gray eyes. "Megan, I have wonderful news."

She slipped her fingers into his large, warm hand and tugged him toward a cushion. "Sit and tell me."

She knelt beside him and rested one hand on his knee, enjoying the warmth radiating through the soft silk of his *paji*. She smiled up into his excited face.

"The King has given me an honorary post." Two coral spots appeared on Jongwhan's cheekbones. "I am to study painting anywhere I wish."

"I am very happy for you." Megan dropped her gaze to the closed fist at her side, waiting for his next words. What if he didn't say them? She held her breath—it must be his own idea. She raised her eyes to his face once more.

His expression grew serious. He swallowed and wiped his palms on his pants, then cleared his throat. "I—I've decided to return to Taejong Village on Cheju Do." Something flashed through his eyes. Hope, fear? "Will you go with me, live with me, give me sons?"

Megan knelt before him and touched her fingers to his cheek. Her whispered answer echoed back from the smooth clay walls. "Yes."

She leaned forward and slipped her arms around his neck, then slowly opened the fingers of her right hand. In her palm lay a circle of white jade engraved with the likeness of a dragon. A thin piece of rice paper bore the King's red seal and three words. "It is done."

Megan strode along the sandy road toward the sea. She fingered the soft, white cotton jacket, strange after her silks, yet so familiar. Trees lined the roadway, their branches ablaze with color. Fallen leaves skittered across the sand and clung to rocky hollows, perfuming the air with the tang of decay.

The noonday sun warmed her in spite of the chill autumn wind. A smile crept across her mouth. *Home.* The word kept time with her every step, taking her closer and closer to the waves crashing against the golden-brown rocks.

A woman appeared around a bend in the road ahead. Megan held up her hand for silence as Tai's Mother stopped, eyes wide and mouth ajar. Tai now walked beside her, his baby plumpness giving way to lanky arms and legs, but his velvet eyes and silken hair remained unchanged. The small boy looked up at her, then stepped closer to his mother. The young *haenyo* placed a loving hand on his head, then smiled and nodded a greeting.

Megan smiled and gestured the other wives and children to silence as they clustered around her. She pointed down the trail and they nodded and giggled.

Straw sandals rasped across the sandy roadbed, closer and closer until a gruff voice called from behind the wall of bodies. "What is this nonsense? Why are you all stopped here? Have you lost your senses?" The voice still sounded strong, but it held a new note Megan hadn't heard before, one of loss and sadness.

Her heart swelled with love for the crusty old lady. She pushed her way through the standing divers. Grandmother stood, her bright yellow gourd buoy slung over one bent shoulder, her huge basket of seaweed over the other. She took a step back, her eyes wide. The color came and went from her lined face. Her pinched lips moved, but no sound came out. The hand holding the float suddenly let go, then the one holding the basket. They landed with two soft thuds in the sand at the old woman's feet. "May-khan? Little Fish?" Disbelief and hope clung to the whispered words.

Megan stepped forward and sank to her knees in front of the aged *haenyo.* She prostrated herself, placing her palms on the rough sand of the road, then touching her forehead to her hands. She sat back and smiled, memorizing the beloved face, the lines made by age, sorrow, sun, and wind—like soft tanned leather. "Ŏmŏni, My Mother, I have returned to you as you asked."

Tears followed the grooves in the old woman's face, glistening in the autumn sunlight. A knotted hand cupped Megan's elbow, lifting her to her feet with surprising strength. A glow as bright as the sunlight shone from the snapping dark eyes. "So, My Daughter, you have come back."

Megan nodded, her own tears of joy closing her throat. "Home, Ŏmŏni. I've come home."

ABOUT THE AUTHOR

In addition to an admitted passion for the fine and performing arts, STEPHANIE BARTLETT's first novel also expresses a lifelong interest in other ways of life. Although initially skeptical when a fellow writer suggested Korea as a setting, she soon became fascinated by the four-thousand-year-old culture. A research trip there in 1986 reaffirmed her belief in "universal human emotions."

Born and raised in Oregon's fertile Willamette Valley, she has spent the last five years writing and teaching in the southern part of the state, where she currently lives with her daughter, Ariel.

THE LATEST BOOKS
IN THE BANTAM
BESTSELLING TRADITION

DON'T MISS
THESE CURRENT
Bantam Bestsellers

☐ 26807	**THE BEET QUEEN** Louise Edrich	$4.50
☐ 26808	**LOVE MEDICINE** Louise Edrich	$4.50
☐ 25800	**THE CIDER HOUSE RULES** John Irving	$4.95
☐ 26554	**HOLD THE DREAM**	$4.95
	Barbara Taylor Bradford	
☐ 26253	**VOICE OF THE HEART**	$4.95
	Barbara Taylor Bradford	
☐ 23667	**NURSE'S STORY** Carol Gino	$3.95
☐ 26322	**THE BOURNE SUPREMACY**	$4.95
	Robert Ludlum	
☐ 26056	**THE CLEANUP**	$3.95
	John SKipp & Craig Spector	
☐ 26134	**THE EMBASSY HOUSE** Nicholas Proffit	$4.50
☐ 25625	**A CROWD OF LOVERS** Laddie Marshak	$3.95
☐ 26659	**DREAMS & SHADOWS**	$4.50
	Rosemary Simpson	
☐ 26850	**GOLDEN FIRE** Jonathan Fast	$4.50
☐ 26888	**THE PRINCE OF TIDES** Pat Conroy	$4.95
☐ 26892	**THE GREAT SANTINI** Pat Conroy	$4.95
☐ 26574	**SACRED SINS** Nora Roberts	$3.95
☐ 26798	**THE SCREAM**	$3.95
	Jonathan Skipp & Craig Spector	

Prices and availability subject to change without notice.

Buy them at your local bookstore or use this page to order.

Bantam Books, Dept. FB, 414 East Golf Road, Des Plaines, IL 60016

Please send me the books I have checked above. I am enclosing $_____
(please add $2.00 to cover postage and handling). Send check or money order
—no cash or C.O.D.s please.

Mr/Ms _____

Address _____

City/State _____ Zip _____

FB—6/88
Please allow four to six weeks for delivery. This offer expires 12/88.

NORA ROBERTS

BRAZEN VIRTUE
Some virtues are negotiable . . .

☐ 27283 **BRAZEN VIRTUE**   **$3.95**

HOT ICE
Shimmering with diamond-like heat. HOT ICE sizzles with romance and suspense!

☐ 26461 **HOT ICE**   **$3.95**

SACRED SINS
Some sins are unforgivable . . .
There's no escaping the sizzling heat of the Washington summer . . . or the twisted ministry of "The Priest".

☐ 26574 **SACRED SINS**   **$3.95**

Buy them at your local bookstore or use this page to order:

- -

Bantam Books, Dept. NR, 414 East Golf Road,
Des Plaines, IL 60016

Please send me the books I have checked above. I am enclosing $_____ (please add $2.00 to cover postage and handling). Send check or money order—no cash or C.O.D.s please.

Mr/Ms _____

Address _____

City/State _____ Zip _____
                                              NR—8/88
Please allow four to six weeks for delivery. This offer expires 2/89. Prices and availability subject to change without notice.